About the Author

Tracy Corbett lives with her partner Simon in Surrey and works part-time for a local charity. Tracy has been writing for a number of years and has had a few short stories published in *My Weekly* magazine. As well as belonging to a local writing group, she enjoys amateur dramatics and can regularly be found dressing up in strange costumes and prancing about the stage pretending to be all manner of odd characters. *Secret Things and Highland Flings* is Tracy's fourth novel.

Also by Tracy Corbett:

The Forget-Me-Not Flower Shop
The Summer Theatre by the Sea
Starlight on the Palace Pier

Tracy Corbett

SECRET THINGS AND HIGHLAND FLINGS

A division of HarperCollins*Publishers*
www.harpercollins.co.uk

Published by AVON
A division of HarperCollins*Publishers* Ltd
1 London Bridge Street
London SE1 9GF

www.harpercollins.co.uk

A Paperback Original 2019

First published in Great Britain by HarperCollins*Publishers* 2019

Copyright © Tracy Corbett 2019

Tracy Corbett asserts the moral right to be identified
as the author of this work.

A catalogue copy of this book is available from the British Library.

ISBN: 978-0-00-829950-7

Typeset in Birka by
Palimpsest Book Production Limited, Falkirk, Stirlingshire

Printed and bound in UK by
CPI Group (UK) Ltd, Croydon CR0 4YY

MIX
Paper from
responsible sources
FSC™ C007454

This book is produced from independently certified FSC™ paper
to ensure responsible forest management.

For more information visit: www.harpercollins.co.uk/green

For Simon, thank you for helping
me find my smile again. x

Chapter 1

Lexi Ryan wasn't having the best of mornings. She'd managed to slice open her finger while chopping apricots for the muffins she'd baked first thing, and then she'd torn a contact lens and spent the next thirty minutes trying to locate the broken pieces in her eye. By the time she'd recovered and rushed down from the flat to open up her art gallery below, her finger was throbbing and her eye was bloodshot. Not exactly the composed and professional look she was aiming for.

She'd hoped wearing her favourite emerald-green fifties wrap-around dress might cheer her flagging spirits, but not even her love of vintage clothing was working today.

It was now lunchtime and things hadn't improved. She had a pile of bills that needed paying and insufficient funds in her account to cover them. She'd phoned a few long-standing clients, hoping to encourage them into settling their accounts, but it had proved a fruitless exercise. Exceeding her overdraft limit this month was looking highly likely.

Concealing her agitation, she returned her attentions to her waiting clients. After all, she had a business to run. Stressing over her finances wouldn't save her precious gallery from foreclosure, or prevent her from inflicting GBH on the annoying businessmen who couldn't make up their mind between Livemont's *Scent of a Rose* and Munch's *The Scream*. Professionalism was called for.

'Original?' the older of the two said, pointing to the post-Impressionist masterpiece.

She joined them by the glass cabinet. *Of course* it's an original, she was tempted to say. The Munch Museum grew tired of generating millions from displaying the Norwegian's best-known expressionist work and decided to loan it to a small independent gallery in Windsor.

Except she didn't say it, of course. She fought the urge for sarcasm, kept her smile in place and pointed to the index card. 'All of the paintings displayed along this wall are copies,' she said, refusing to catch the eye of the *Woman at the Window* in case she gave the game away.

'Very good.' He nodded manically, gesturing to the painting again. 'Very good.'

'I agree. They might not be originals, but they're all exquisite works of art in their own right, painted by some of the country's leading artists.' She tried to dazzle them with a winning smile and brushed her blonde hair away from her face … except the plaster on her finger got stuck in her fringe, ruining the effect.

As she attempted to disentangle herself, the gallery door opened.

She glanced over, momentarily distracted by the sight of a huge bouquet of pink roses being carried through the doorway. And then she realised who was carrying the flowers and her day went from 'mildly irritating' to 'catastrophic' in an instant. It was her ex-husband.

The throbbing in her finger increased … until she realised she was gripping her hair.

She tried to regain her composure, but the sight of Marcus made that impossible. He was wearing a fitted shirt with black tailored trousers, looking tanned and relaxed, his beguiling smile enhanced by straight white teeth and deep brown eyes. He made quite an impact standing there, grinning, holding the flowers aloft like he was God's gift. It didn't stop her wanting to scream and throw a sharp object at his head, though.

She didn't, of course. She hid her ensuing panic, smiled at her customers and said, 'Excuse me a moment,' then darted over to the doorway, her four-inch heels clicking on the tiled floor in time with her accelerated heart rate.

She hadn't seen Marcus for over a year and although his sudden appearance in her gallery should be a complete shock, in truth she'd been expecting him.

It was hard to compute the range of emotions racing through her. He was as handsome as ever and looked younger than his thirty-four years. He smelt delicious too, a mixture of lemon and pine. Her heart ached a little at the reminder of what she'd lost.

Thankfully her head came to the rescue, absorbing the sight of his enticing smile but refusing to be taken in by it.

There'd been a time when he'd charmed her with his persuasive persona, showered her with gifts, and promised her a life filled with love, laughter and adventure. But that was before she'd discovered he wasn't a decent, hardworking man but a prized rat who rarely told the truth. He'd played her one too many times for her to be fooled by his 'charming-rogue' routine. She was older and wiser now. A tougher nut to crack.

His opening gambit of, 'Baby, it's good to see you,' was accompanied by him reaching for her like she was the answer to his prayers.

3

She lifted her hand, stopping him from hugging her. Breathing in his scent might tip the balance in favour of her hormones, derailing her motivation to draw blood.

It helped that his smile faded as he took in her attire. He'd never liked her in green. Tough. Unlike him, she couldn't afford fancy new clothes and had to make do with items from her existing wardrobe.

'Your hair's shorter,' he said, his eyes grazing over her appearance. 'And what have you done to your eye?'

His disapproval helped to relax her. She'd almost forgotten how picky he could be. 'What do you want, Marcus?'

A grin appeared. The glint in his eye was a reminder of all the times he'd tried to swindle her. 'I wanted to see you. I've missed you.' He offered her the flowers.

She refused to take them. 'How's Cindy?'

Mentioning his twenty-two-year-old PA had the desired effect. His smile instantly faded.

'She's still in Spain.'

'Staying at the Finca, I presume?'

It still annoyed her that under Spanish law, their villa was excluded from UK insolvency laws. As such, his dodgy solicitor had managed to secure him ownership in the divorce. They'd purchased the place shortly after they'd married and spent two summers holidaying there – before his shady business dealings came to light and he ran off with his PA.

'Lucky Cindy. Andalucía's lovely in the spring.'

'I didn't come here to talk about Cindy.'

'I'm sure you didn't.' But Lexi needed to feel more in control and reminding him of his girlfriend helped to do that. If she showed any weakness, he'd only take advantage. 'Now, what is it you want? I have customers.'

He lowered the flowers. 'I think you know why I'm here.' He held her gaze. 'You have something that belongs to me.'

'And what would that be, Marcus?' God, she hoped her left eye wouldn't start twitching. She was a terrible liar. 'Are you referring to your belongings following the house repossession? The bailiffs took most of it. As for the rest, I donated it to charity. I didn't have room to store anything upstairs in the flat. Sorry.'

She wasn't sorry at all. The bastard had buggered off and left her to deal with his mess. He should be grateful she hadn't burnt his stuff.

'What about my clothes?'

'They're boxed up in the storage basement below. Give me a forwarding address and I'll send them to you. If you want them shipped to Spain you'll have to pay yourself. My funds are somewhat depleted since the bankruptcy.'

'I don't believe that for a second.' His gaze settled on the *Woman at the Window*. The sultry Italian temptress was hanging on the far wall, her astute dark eyes watching their exchange with interest. 'You can still afford to buy valuable paintings.'

Trust him to notice. 'Marcus, as you well know, I specialise in replicas, not originals. It's a copy.' Her eye immediately started twitching.

'It doesn't look like a copy.'

'None of my paintings do, that's why my business is so successful. A business that was severely jeopardised by your shady dealings.' Attack was the best form of defence, she'd learnt.

He placed the flowers on the counter and went over to the painting. She watched him study the signature, which she'd carefully concealed behind a display card.

'I remember you buying a preliminary sketch of this painting. We'd gone to London for the weekend and I'd got us tickets to see the Arsenal game, but you insisted we attend some fancy auction. It was always your ambition to own the original painting.'

She remembered the weekend well. It was supposed to be a romantic getaway ... until she'd realised his idea of 'romance' was to take her to the blessed football. Stopping off at the auction had seemed only fair.

She followed him over. 'You're right, which is why I took the opportunity to display this copy when it was offered to me by an aspiring local artist.' She'd rehearsed her answer many times, using a mirror to perfect her performance. She suspected Marcus didn't believe her. He was too shady to be outwitted, but she wasn't going down without a fight.

He resumed looking at the painting. 'I assume you found the holdall?'

And there it was. The bombshell she'd been waiting for.

She cleared her throat. 'What holdall?'

His gaze remained fixated on the painting, so he didn't see her left eye twitching like a malfunctioning washing machine.

He turned slowly to face her. 'I think you know exactly what holdall.'

'Like I said, I gave your belongings to charity.' She walked off.

He caught her arm. 'Let's go down to the basement and check.'

She yanked her arm free. 'I have customers. I can't leave the gallery unattended.'

'I'll go then.'

No way was she letting him loose downstairs. Not that he'd find anything, but that wasn't the point. 'It's locked.'

'I have keys.' He had the audacity to dangle them in front of her.

She tried to swipe them, but he moved his hand. 'Keys that my solicitor has repeatedly asked you to return.'

He shrugged. 'Change the locks if you're that worried.'

'I can't afford to do that. The security system is highly sophisticated. It would cost a fortune to replace it.'

He took a step closer, a calculating glint in his eye. 'Tell you what, I'll hand over my keys once I have *all* of my belongings back.' His expression turned menacing. 'And that includes the holdall containing my money.'

Her cheeks became instantly warm. 'Wh ... what money?'

He laughed. 'Oh, I think you know what money. I must say, I was surprised. Little Miss Perfect finally did something wicked.' He tapped one of her large hoop earrings, making it sway. 'You actually stole from me.'

One of the businessmen glanced over. Lexi waved and assured him everything was okay before refocusing on Marcus. His cruel taunting had dissolved any guilt she might have felt at scamming him. 'What a shameful accusation, Marcus. I mean, who would steal from their loved one, right?'

He had the good grace to look uncomfortable. 'I never stole—'

'Yes, you did. You didn't bank the sale proceeds for my Franz Gerste collection. Instead, you ran off to Spain with your PA and left me to deal with your mess.'

'I never meant for that to happen. You don't know the pressure I was under. The garage was going bust. People were chasing me for money. HMRC were on my back. Everything I tried made it worse.'

'That doesn't justify you running off with *Cindy*, of all

7

people. A woman who thinks Liverpool is a country.' Lexi didn't normally slate other women; she liked to think of herself as an advocate for women, empowering each other. But that was before she'd been dumped unceremoniously for a women ten years her junior. It stung.

Marcus sighed. 'She's certainly not you.' He looked almost wistful.

Lexi resisted the urge to yell, *then why did you run off with her?* Instead, she opted for, 'You're damned right she's not,' trying to salvage something of her bruised self-esteem.

He took her hand before she could move it. 'I miss you.'

Ignoring the familiar warmth of his touch, she met his gaze. 'Well, I don't miss you, Marcus. I don't miss being lied to, stolen from or cheated on.'

Far from being deterred, he saw this as a challenge. He'd always been seduced by things he couldn't have. She'd suddenly become unattainable. Nothing turned Marcus on more than the temptation of a woman saying no to him.

He stroked the back of her hand. 'You forget all the good times we had.'

'You're right, Marcus, I do. I've made a conscious effort to forget every single one of them.'

'I don't believe you.'

'Frankly, I don't care what you believe. Now, please leave and don't come back. I don't want you in my life anymore. I've moved on.'

He was staring at her mouth like he used to when he was about to bedazzle her with his charms. 'Christ, you're sexy when you're angry.' He reached forwards to kiss her.

She pulled away. Jesus, his flattery skills had taken a dive.

'I still love you, Lexi. You know that. We could be together again. Think of the fun we'd have.' A glimmer of the old Marcus was back. A scheme forming in his mind as his eyes roamed over her body, no attempt to hide where his thoughts were headed. 'We'd make a great team. You and me, hustling the world. I'm not angry you took my money. Actually, I admire you for it. I never thought you'd have the balls. Think what we could do with it? You've been a goodie two-shoes for too long. It's time to unleash your inner bad girl.'

Words every woman *longs* to hear ... not.

What an idiot Marcus was. What an idiot *she* was for marrying him.

She was about to tell him as much, when someone banged on the gallery door.

A tall man with thinning beige hair and matching raincoat was peering through the glass. He drew out an identity badge and held it up.

Oh, Christ, what now?

'Who the hell is that?' she said, praying it wasn't the police. Not that she'd done anything wrong. Well, not much.

'No idea, but I'm not hanging around to find out.' Marcus shot over to the steps leading down to the basement before she could stop him.

She was about to go after him, when she realised she needed to deal with the official-looking man first. Not to mention her customers. Marcus wouldn't find what he was looking for downstairs. He was a problem for later.

Unfortunately, she realised the businessmen had left. They'd obviously grown tired of being kept waiting. She'd missed out on a sale. Bloody Marcus!

The man in the raincoat stepped inside. 'I'm looking for

Mrs Alexia Aldridge,' he said, tucking his glasses inside his worn coat.

She turned to him. 'Well, you've found her. Although Aldridge was my married name. I've reverted to my maiden name of Ryan.'

He held out his name badge for her to read. 'Brian Falk, investigating officer with the insolvency headquarters. I have a few questions.'

Jesus, hadn't they quizzed her enough fifteen months ago? 'Now isn't a convenient time. My assistant isn't in. Can you come back another day?'

'This won't take long.' He obviously wasn't going to leave.

With a sigh, she locked the door and flipped the closed sign. The sooner she answered his questions, the sooner he'd be gone. She needed to get Marcus out of her basement.

'Follow me,' she said, showing him into the back office. 'Tea, coffee?'

He placed his briefcase on the floor and sat down. 'Just water. Thank you.'

She went over to the kitchenette, trying to stem the rising feeling of panic. Why was he here? Did he know what she'd done?

Water slurped over the edge of the glass as she carried it over to him, her nerves betraying her. 'So, how can I help you, Mr Falk?'

He put his glasses back on and laid his briefcase across his lap. 'As you know, we've been looking into the matter of undeclared assets for you and your husband—'

'Ex-husband.'

He peered over the top of his glasses.

'We're no longer married.'

'My mistake.' He removed a document from his briefcase. 'Further evidence has come to light with regard to a life insurance policy taken out for you and your husband.' He handed her a document. 'Are you familiar with the policy I'm referring to, Mrs Aldridge?'

'It's Ms Ryan.' She took the document from his outstretched hand. 'And no, I'm not.' She carried the document over to the table and sat down.

'If you would care to look at the policy details and the withdrawal section on the back, you'll see both documents bear your signature.'

She gazed down at the document in her hand, a document she'd never seen before. The Royal Sun Alliance policy appeared to have been taken out in August 2014, shortly after they were married. Both of their names were listed. Why the hell didn't she know about this?

The investigator cleared his throat. 'I note from your interview with Mr Dickens, the official receiver, on 9 February 2017, that this policy wasn't mentioned as part of your marital assets. I wonder why that was?'

She stared at the document. 'Because I never knew it existed.'

'I find that a little hard to believe. After all, that is your signature on the policy, is it not? How do you account for that?'

'I ... I can't. What I mean is, I've never seen this document before in my life.'

It was clear he didn't believe her. He removed a pad from his briefcase and scribbled something down. 'Are you quite sure? Forgetting about its existence would seem a little strange. Especially as you and your husband surrendered the policy shortly before the bankruptcy hearing.'

She felt something hard hit her in the chest. There was no way she'd have forgotten that. She lifted the document closer, studying the handwriting. 'I ... I don't understand. How can a life insurance policy be cashed in if both parties are still alive?'

'As I said, the policy was surrendered. The terms and conditions allowed for the refund of premiums paid into the account up until its cancellation. Surrendering the policy would have incurred hefty fees, but there would still have been a substantial payout.'

She stared at the document, trying to make sense of it. Had she really forgotten about it? Surely not. The print was tiny, the list of terms and conditions hard to distinguish, but true enough, there at the bottom of the page appeared to be her signature. She peered closer, trying to fathom why she couldn't remember signing it. 'And when did you say it was cashed in?'

He checked his notebook. 'Third of November 2016.'

The text on the page blurred before her as tears filled her eyes. That was two weeks before Marcus had run off with Cindy. The familiar pain of betrayal settled over her. The realisation that Marcus had been defrauding her since the day they were married was a feeling like no other she'd experienced. She'd been convinced his illegal antics were solely linked to the financial problems of his used-car business. But this was premeditated. A deliberate action designed to scam his own wife. Jesus. Marcus really had been a cheat. In more ways than one.

Trying to contain her anger, she looked at the investigating officer. 'This is not my signature.'

'I beg your pardon, Mrs Aldridge?'

'My name is *Ms Ryan* ... and I said, that's not my signature.' She flipped over the page, looking for the withdrawal section. There it was again, her signature ... but not. 'The reason I don't remember taking out this policy, or cashing it in, is because I never knew it existed.' She got up and handed him the papers.

He raised his eyebrows. 'Are you saying that your husband forged your signature?'

'I ... I suppose I am.' She shrugged. 'All I really know is that I didn't sign it.'

He scribbled something down in his notebook. A few seconds ticked by before he looked up.

'Have you been in contact with your husband recently, Mrs Ald ... err ... Ms Ryan?'

Her left eye began twitching again. She moved away and tore off a wodge of kitchen roll, wrapping it around her finger, which had started to bleed again. 'Marcus and I are divorced, Mr Falk. He's with someone else now and currently residing in Spain. Thanks to his incompetent finances and illegal business ventures, I lost my home and suffered substantial financial hardship.' She glanced around the office. 'My business is all that I have left.'

'That's not what I asked.' He watched her carefully. 'I asked whether you'd been in contact with him recently.'

Her cheeks started to burn. She had two options. Deny all knowledge and be rid of him or admit that her ex-husband was currently rummaging around in her storage basement looking for a holdall containing twenty-seven thousand pounds.

A more pressing thought struck her. 'How much was the insurance pay-out?'

He paused before answering. 'Twenty-seven thousand pounds.'

Oh, cripes!

Time slowed ... and then sped up, causing her stomach to dip.

So that's where the money had come from ... She'd assumed it had come from the sale of her Franz Gerste collection. Only it hadn't.

A mixture of anger and dread filled her gut. Once again, Marcus had shafted her. But she was equally annoyed with herself. That single momentary lapse of judgement nine months ago was coming back to haunt her. And now she was paying the price.

But she'd been in such a desperate place. She was still reeling from discovering that Marcus was sleeping with his PA and had a gambling addiction. And then the court bailiffs had turned up at her home to seize goods. She'd had to endure a humiliating court hearing, employ an expensive solicitor to argue the gallery's exclusion from the bankruptcy and borrow money from her sister Tasha to pay for it.

She'd won her case, but every other asset had been sold to pay off Marcus's business debts, leaving her with a frozen bank account, a poor credit rating and no home. All because Marcus's business hadn't been a limited company, leaving them personally and jointly liable.

And she'd accepted her fate. Through it all she'd been stoic and honest – she'd even assisted the official receiver in complying fully with the insolvency regulations. But the discovery that Marcus had failed to bank the money from the sale of her Franz Gerste collection had sent her over the edge.

When she'd gone to the house to collect the last of her

belongings before the enforced repossession, she'd stumbled across a black holdall containing twenty-seven thousand pounds. All the promises she'd made to be trustworthy and law-abiding evaporated. She took the money and didn't declare it.

Despite her overwhelming guilt, she'd reasoned that the money had come from *her* paintings. Paintings that belonged to the gallery so weren't a joint asset and therefore shouldn't have been included in the bankruptcy. But getting the official receiver to agree to that would have involved another expensive court hearing, which she couldn't afford.

She'd considered using the money to pay off her debts, especially the money she owed to her sister, which she'd now cleared. But she'd decided against it. Mainly because she was still within the twelve-month bankruptcy period and the official receiver was monitoring her personal finances. He would have wanted to know where the money had come from and she hadn't wanted to drag Tasha into her mess.

So, instead of declaring what she'd found, she'd kept quiet and used it to purchase the *Woman at the Window* painting. It was supposed to be an investment, compensation for her suffering. But however much she tried to justify her actions, she'd still broken the law. Not to mention using her art dealer credentials to cover her tracks and avoid any suspicion of money laundering.

And now an investigator was threatening to expose the one tiny chink in her otherwise flawless existence.

She needed time to think. She also needed to throttle her scumbag, cheating liar of an ex-husband, who was currently in her basement.

'In answer to your question, Mr Falk, I've not been in

contact with my ex-husband.' The twitch in her left eye increased.

'Hmmm.' He removed a business card from his pocket and stood up. 'We'll investigate your claims further, Ms Ryan. But perhaps you'd be good enough to contact me should you hear from him. We have several questions we'd like to ask Mr Aldridge.'

He wasn't the only one.

He handed her the card. 'Thank you for your time. Good day to you.' He collected his briefcase. 'We'll be in touch.'

She followed him over to the door, trying to keep a neutral expression. 'Good luck with your investigations.'

'Luck has nothing to do with it, Ms Ryan. The truth will always out in the end.'

And that was what worried her.

She let him out, locking the door behind him. As fast as her heels would allow, she ran across the gallery showroom and charged downstairs. 'Marcus? MARCUS! Did you forge my bloody signature?'

He was nowhere in sight.

He'd obviously been searching for the holdall, because his belongings were scattered on the floor, a trail of discarded clothes leading to the rear doors ... which were left open. Bastard! She had a stack of valuable paintings stored down here, including a recent shipment from the Wentworth estate in Scotland, and Marcus had left the place unsecured. Arsehole!

And then she spotted his note next to the empty black holdall:

I WANT MY MONEY.

16

Chapter 2

Oliver Wentworth took the opportunity of his sister's phone ringing to take a breather from playing the dutiful carer. The distress at witnessing his pregnant sister being trampled on by an irate Shetland pony had sapped all of his energy. Thankfully, apart from a fractured fibula, she and the baby had escaped relatively intact.

As his sister answered her phone, he listened to her attempting to calm her distraught husband, reassuring him she was okay and relaying the story of how she'd toppled over the feeding trough when the aptly named Goliath had upended her. Having spent several years trying for a baby, he couldn't imagine Harry taking the news of his wife's injury too well. Poor bloke.

When the conversation switched from Louisa's health to declarations of love, Olly tuned out. He adored his sister, but he didn't need to hear about the intimate details of her marriage.

Instead, he gazed out of the taxi window and admired the scenery outside.

Medical services were few and far between in the Highlands, so they'd ended up at the Broadford Hospital on the Isle of Skye. The treatment had been first-rate, but it was a slow drive back to Shieldaig, the lanes winding and narrow. At least it allowed him time to recover from the trauma of Louisa's accident and absorb the sight of his heritage passing by bathed in the May sunshine.

Shieldaig was sixty-eight miles west of Inverness in the Wester Ross region of Scotland, a quaint village with a miniscule population but with a huge influx of visitors during the summer months. It was both beautiful and brutal. Mountainous landscape dominated the view, framing the expanse of lochs and villages nestled between. It was the stuff of postcards, picturesque and enticing. But it was also challenging – as many an inexperienced walker had discovered when attempting to conquer Beinn Eighe ill-equipped. Even more so as the area had a poor phone signal.

As an adult, he could appreciate the appeal of the rugged terrain, where land merged seamlessly into sky. But as a kid, he'd hated the place. It had been a prison. A punishment. A place from which he'd been desperate to escape. And although he still harboured painful memories from those early years, he was hopeful of finally shedding his dislike of the place and reconnecting with his siblings.

As the taxi driver negotiated the narrow lanes, Rubha Castle came into view. The grey stone construction sat ominously against its tranquil surroundings. It was strange to think this was his home. There'd been a castle on the site for over eight hundred years, but the Wentworth family had only been resident for four hundred. His grandfather had briefly opened the castle to the public during the Sixties, hoping it would generate an influx of cash, but closed it again when the venture failed to prove cost-effective. They still hired out the venue for weddings and special occasions, but it wasn't enough to maintain its continuing upkeep – a current bone of contention between his two sisters.

As the current Earl of Horsley, Olly was expected to take over running the family estate, socialise with blueblood aristocracy and sit in the House of Lords – something he had absolutely no interest in doing. Thankfully, recent reforms had abolished automatic hereditary rights, so he was off the hook in terms of his peer duties. And Louisa was more than happy running Rubha Castle, so he was superfluous to requirements.

Okay, so he was the Edward VIII of the family. The wayward black sheep who'd shirked his ancestral duties in favour of chasing pipedreams. It had been his parents' favourite accusation, thrown at him many times during his adolescence. And they'd been right, of course. Even as a kid he'd craved freedom, a desire to see what the world had to offer. But his departure from their lives at barely eighteen was entirely down to their doing, not his.

Louisa had just ended her call when the taxi bumped onto the bridge joining the castle with the mainland. The driver pulled up in front of the open portcullis but left the engine running, an indication that he wasn't offering any assistance. Olly couldn't blame him. Trying to manoeuvre an eight-months-pregnant woman with her leg in an orthopaedic boot out of a car wasn't going to be easy.

With a sigh, Olly got out the taxi and went around to open the door.

Louisa smiled up at him, her green eyes rimmed with dark circles. 'Are you feeling strong?'

He grinned. 'Positively herculean.'

She laughed and took his hands but winced when he tried unsuccessfully to pull her from the vehicle. He could tell she was in pain, however much she tried to hide it. Louisa's outward fragility concealed an inner strength that enabled her to cope with adversity. Which was just as well, considering the upbringing they'd had.

Assistance appeared in the form of Gilly Jennings scurrying across the courtyard, red-faced and panting. Technically, she was the hired help, a cook-cum-housekeeper, but she'd always been more of a 'parental figure', bossy but warm-hearted, filling the gap caused by their own parents' coldness.

'Och, you poor love,' she said, reaching the taxi. 'Here, let me help you.'

Olly was bumped out of the way. He was about to object, when he realised his seventy-year-old housekeeper had already eased Louisa out of the car, usurping him as primary carer.

He tried not to feel disgruntled. But then he remembered they'd survived without him for eleven years. They didn't need him. It stung, but it was the price he had to pay.

He paid the driver and unloaded the wheelchair from the boot.

As they made their way across the inner courtyard, Gilly issued instructions, sending him ahead to open doors, clear the stairway and put the kettle on.

Suppressing his frustration at being ordered around, he did as he was told, knowing he was still 'in the dog house' and it would be a long time before anyone felt he'd made amends. Gilly only allowed him to push the wheelchair when they reached the steps leading into the west guard tower.

Shortly after Louisa and Harry had married, they'd moved into the private area of the main keep, near the grand banqueting hall and billeting room, which were used for events. In contrast, upon his return, Olly had been given a small room in the south-west wing, an area previously used to stable horses. That said it all, really.

Having deposited his sister in her bedroom, he went to make drinks.

He returned armed with sugary tea and shortbread biscuits, grateful for Gilly's baking skills. He'd always had a sweet tooth.

On entering the bedroom, he heard Louisa yelp.

Gilly was trying to roll her onto her side. 'Her back's hurting,' she said, continuing to push.

'I'm not surprised,' he said, placing the tray on the Jacobean sidetable. 'Move over, will you.' He pulled up short when he saw the hurt look on Gilly's face. He tried for an apologetic smile. 'Sorry, Gilly. What I meant to say was, as my sister is currently the size of a small elephant, it might be better if I do it.'

Louisa threw a pillow at him.

Gilly laughed and stood back to allow him access. Disaster averted. He winked at Louisa, who normally didn't carry an ounce of fat on her and would therefore forgive him for likening her to a large land mammal.

He eased her onto her side.

'Look at you, being all tender and caring,' Gilly teased. 'Perhaps you should follow your sister's example and get married yourself.'

He suppressed a shudder. 'Not going to happen.'

'Why ever not? A good-looking man like yourself shouldn't have any trouble finding a lass.'

Finding one? No problem. Holding on to them? Another matter entirely. Of course, it didn't help that he rarely stayed in one place long. But all that was about to change.

'I'm sure the right girl's out there,' Gilly said, tucking in the bedsheet. 'Although she mightn't be too impressed by a man pushing thirty and yet to secure a proper job.'

And there it was, the scolding he'd been waiting for.

He didn't need Gilly to tell him he was a waste of space. He was painfully aware of his shortcomings.

Emotionally, he still felt like an eighteen-year-old kid backpacking the world while scraping a living. Only he was twenty-nine now and still searching. For what, he wasn't sure, but something was missing from his life, he knew that much. It was a sobering thought – one that depressed him – so he pushed the notion from his mind.

'Still, you're here now.' Gilly handed Louisa a mug of tea. 'It's just a shame Lady Eleanor isn't around to see it.'

Actually, it was a blessing. His mother had been the main reason he'd left home aged eighteen. He couldn't stand the hypocrisy. All his life his parents had banged on about 'protocol' and 'tradition' and the need for 'honesty'. They'd beaten him down with draconian rules and restraints, expecting him to behave in a suitable way for someone in his 'elevated' position. And yet the whole time they'd been two-faced liars.

He'd discovered this one night in 2007, when he'd stumbled across their illicit plan to falsify the provenance of a valuable painting. The painting was several hundred years old, but there was significant doubt surrounding its authenticity. So they'd created a set of false documents to make it look like it was an original work by renowned Renaissance artist Albrico Spinelli.

Overhearing their conversation had been shocking and unbelievable. But the tipping point had come when he'd realised they'd managed to pass off one of his replica sketches as an original Albrico Spinelli, too. The sketch had sold ahead of the auction for several thousand pounds, creating a 'buzz' around the main painting and increasing its value.

He hadn't known which had angered him most: the fact that his mother's art tutelage and insistence on using genuine sixteenth-century materials hadn't been about showing an interest in developing her son's talent but a way of making money, or because they'd gone behind his back and made him complicit in their crime. Suddenly, it all made sense. The reason his mother had made him paint replicas wasn't for his own benefit but so his parents could flog them and improve the family's finances.

A huge argument had followed. His parents' excuse? That it was a necessary evil to save Rubha Castle from financial ruin. They'd refused to apologise or admit any wrongdoing. Instead, they'd accused him of being selfish for not wanting to help the family. But how could he continue to paint when he knew his works were being created deliberately to defraud people? It wasn't moral or right, not to mention a contradiction of their holier-than-thou principles. So any loyalty or admiration he might have felt for his parents' so-called traditional family values had evaporated in that moment.

He took a swig of tea and dunked a biscuit, something his mother would never have permitted. He no longer cared.

He was by no means a saint. But even as a teenager he hadn't been able to reconcile the knowledge that his parents were crooked. So he'd left home the moment he could, not returning for eleven years, even to attend their respective funerals.

He ate another biscuit.

The irony was that having fought so hard to lead his own life, ending up alone and abroad at eighteen had scuppered his dreams to become a renowned artist. Instead, he'd drifted from one country to another, fruit picking and bartending, ending up as the 'drop-out' his parents had predicted.

But after years of being estranged, he'd decided it was time to stop punishing his siblings for something that wasn't their fault. They didn't know about their parents' shameful secret, only their charitable work in the community. So they'd never understood why he'd left, or what had kept him away so long. And he still couldn't tell them. He never would. He'd just have to hope that in time they'd forgive him.

Louisa yelped, reminding him he was supposed to be playing nurse.

'We need to elevate your foot,' Gilly said, lifting Louisa's booted leg with all the tenderness of a caber tosser.

'I can manage, Gilly.' The pain of a broken leg was clearly testing the bounds of his sister's normal chirpy demeanour. 'If you could pass me that pillow.'

He intervened. It was the brotherly thing to do. He might fall short in all other areas as far as family duty were concerned, but protecting his sister from a well-meaning Gilly was at least within his capabilities. He grabbed the pillow before Gilly could inflict further damage and eased it under Louisa's foot. She mouthed him a 'thank you'.

He touched her cheek, wondering how she'd managed to blossom into such a tender human being when their upbringing had been devoid of any real affection. Neither parent had been the warmest of people, but his mother's cruel streak had been magnified by the untimely death of their father and the bitterness she held towards her only son. His siblings had taken the brunt of his mother's meltdown, the knowledge of which only added to his guilt.

Despite not being close to his parents, he still felt a loss. Loss for not having had an adult relationship with either of them. Loss at being separated from his siblings for so long and loss for carrying a grudge around for eleven years that had slowly eaten away at his belief in the 'happy ever after'.

He tucked his hands under Louisa's arms and eased her upright.

She kissed him on the cheek. 'I'm so glad you're here,' she whispered, tears pooling in her eyes.

'Are you in pain?'

She shook her head. 'You still don't get it, do you?'

He frowned. 'Get what?'

He never did find out. His phone rang.

He left Louisa in Gilly's care, nicked another biscuit and ducked into the corridor to answer his phone. But when his older sister yelled, 'Louisa's had an accident?' he knew his day wasn't getting better any time soon.

He leant against the stone wall and braced himself for a bollocking.

'Why didn't you call me?'

Sophie sounded pissed off, which was par for the course. If Louisa were a margarita, bursting with colour and flavour, her life garnished with a paper umbrella and bright red cherry, Sophie was the ice in the glass. An antidote to joy.

'How come I got to hear about it from Gilly?'

'Sorry, Soph. There was no phone signal at the hospital.'

'And you couldn't have gone outside?' Her voice rose another notch.

'I didn't want to leave her alone. She was upset.'

'But you don't mind upsetting me? Cheers, Olly. Some brother you are.'

25

He let her rant; he deserved her wrath. And it wasn't her fault she was bitter – it was the upshot of growing up in a loveless household.

When he'd returned to the UK, Louisa had welcomed him with an open smile and unadulterated joy at having him home. In contrast, Sophie's reaction had been to slap his face, call him a bastard and refuse to talk to him for two weeks. He supposed her yelling at him was progress. It was painful, but at least she was talking to him.

'Selfish ... arrogant ...'

'You're right, Sophie. I should've called you. No excuses.'

'Too bloody right! I've been there for her, you haven't. All through IVF, all through the miscarriages—'

He dropped his head against the cool stone wall. 'I know and I'm sorry, but I want to make amends for that.'

'Too effing late!' This was followed by a series of more expletives.

Hearing Sophie swearing was like witnessing a Disney princess in a bar fight. She was tall and curvy, with long blonde hair and stunningly beautiful. She looked 'expensive', a real upper-class society girl. She was a freelance columnist for various fashion magazines and attended events with the who's who of London society, where she smiled, charmed and spoke with a plummy accent. It was only behind closed doors that the façade slipped.

He took another bite of biscuit, waiting until she'd finished ranting.

It took a while.

Finally, she said, 'Is she okay? Do I need to come up there?'

He swallowed. 'I don't think so. Gilly's here and Harry's planning to cut short his business trip. He should be back later tonight. And I'm here—'

'*Ha*! For how long? You're not exactly Mr Reliable.'

He smothered a sigh. 'How many times, Soph? I'm not going anywhere.'

'I'll believe that when I see it.' She mumbled another expletive. 'And if you are staying, make yourself useful and help us sort out the estate.'

'Can't we leave it to the solicitors?'

'Which part of we're running out of money don't you understand? If we leave it to the solicitors we'll have nothing left.'

He pushed away from the wall. 'But I know nothing about probate. I wouldn't have a clue what to do.'

'I'm not talking about probate. You need to persuade Louisa to sell Rubha Castle.'

Oh, no. This was one argument he wasn't getting involved in. 'You know I can't do that. Rubha Castle's Louisa's home, it's her livelihood. It's where she wants to raise a family—'

'We can't afford to keep both properties. The terms of the will state we're only allowed to sell one. If we get rid of the Windsor townhouse, it won't solve our financial problems. Plus, I'll be out on the streets. At least Louisa has an alternative. Harry's family own half of Scotland, but I don't have anywhere else to go. Or don't you care?'

'Of course I do. I just wish there was a way of keeping both.' He rubbed his forehead, feeling as exasperated as Sophie sounded.

'Well, there isn't. Rubha Castle costs a fortune to upkeep. It no longer attracts many visitors and Louisa's insistence on rescuing random animals is adding to the expense. If we sell it now we'll get a decent return, but if we wait until it crumbles to the ground it'll be worthless. It doesn't make good business sense.'

'But Louisa loves it here. She'd be heartbroken to sell. And you know how much she adores those animals.'

There was a weighted pause. 'I know.'

Despite his sister's determination to sell the castle, he knew she was worried about Louisa and didn't want to cause her any distress. His youngest sister worked part-time for an animal charity, she'd built a life for herself in Scotland, she'd even married a local laird. She was a sensitive soul who was trying to rid herself of her own childhood demons by making Rubha Castle a 'happy home'. Olly could understand that.

And so did Sophie, despite what she claimed.

'I wish there was something we could do.'

Sophie sighed. 'Did Louisa tell you her great plan?'

'What plan?'

'To sell Mother's paintings. She's sent them to an independent art gallery in Windsor for valuation.'

He wasn't sure how he felt about that. The subject of art was a sensitive one.

'I think she's hoping they'll sell for a shedload of dosh and solve our problems. I've no idea what their value is. The gallery owner asked for any preliminary drawings of the works to be sent over, but neither of us has any idea what those are. Do you?'

'They're the preparatory drawings an artist sketches before painting the main work.' He frowned. 'Why do they need preliminary drawings?'

'Apparently, it helps to evaluate the paintings. Mother never sold anything during her lifetime, so it's difficult to put a value on the work.'

Technically, that statement wasn't true. His mother had sold a painting in 2007 for a whopping 1.7 million quid. But as the world at large, and in particular the French buyer of the painting, believed it to be painted by Italian Renaissance artist Albrico Spinelli, Olly wasn't about to correct that assumption. Especially as he was complicit in the crime – albeit unwittingly. If the truth ever got out about the painting's real origins, the fallout would be immense. The family's reputation was shaky enough. There was no way they could withstand the scandal of forged masterpieces, a lawsuit and a criminal investigation.

He shuddered at the thought.

Part of him worried that selling his mother's paintings posthumously might be exposing them to overintense scrutiny. But they didn't have a choice. And it's not like she'd forged the Spinelli herself, was it? He had no idea who the real artist was, or how his parents had come into possession of the painting. But the point was, they needed cash, and he wasn't about to stand back and let four hundred years of family history flush down the loo without a fight ... no matter how averse he was to his relatives. His mother had been a bloody good painter. If he was right, her work was valuable. And, more importantly, finite in number. Nothing like a dead painter to inflate the asking price.

He rubbed his forehead, his mind returning to the present. 'I think they're boxed up in the billeting room somewhere. Leave it with me and I'll see what I can find.'

'By the way, Louisa found another painting hidden among Mother's collection. It was boxed separately and covered in a dustsheet. It was a painting of a religious bloke reading from a scroll. It wasn't like her other paintings, but Louisa thought the gallery might as well have it.'

Olly's world skidded to an abrupt halt. His heart followed

suit, banging into his ribcage, sucking all the oxygen from his brain.

He must have made a noise, because Sophie said, 'Olly, what's wrong? Is it a bad painting?'

A bad painting?

On the contrary, it was a bloody phenomenal painting.

It was the second forged Spinelli.

Shit!

Chapter 3

Later that day ...

Lexi peered through the glass-fronted oven door to check on the development of her cupcakes. Unlike the problems associated with trying to run an art business and avoiding her ex-husband, baking never gave her headaches, inflated her overdraft or cheated on her with a younger woman. Plus, whipping up a batch of naughty treats gave her something to nibble on with her caramel latte. And boy, was she in need of a sugar rush tonight.

She removed her oven gloves and reset the timer.

Her sister appeared in the kitchen having selected The Five Satins 'In the Still of the Night' on their recently acquired jukebox, complete with crackling speakers and flashing disco lights.

'So, what's eating you?' Tasha fixed Lexi with a frown. She was wearing her black mesh bodice dress with buckled sky-high stiletto boots, rendering her a good inch taller than her twin – even with Lexi in four-inch heels.

'Who says there's anything wrong? Maybe I'm fine. Maybe I'm so relaxed I'm—'

'Baking.' Tasha nicked one of the chocolate orange truffles cooling on the wire cake rack.

'I bake all the time.'

'Yeah, but you only bake large quantities of coronary-

31

inducing confectionery when your stress levels are through the roof. You're very predictable.'

'Predictable?' Lexi slumped against the sink. 'That's highly depressing.'

Tasha licked the chocolate-coated truffle. 'Do you want to talk about it?'

Lexi sighed. 'What's there to say? I'm a thirty-two-year-old predictable woman who put her trust in a cheating gambler. I'm beyond help.'

'This is true.'

Lexi glared at her twin. 'Thanks.'

Tasha gave a nonchalant shrug. 'Trusting someone isn't a flaw. You had a bad experience and got burnt. Shit happens. But you'll get over it. Time heals and all that crap.'

Lexi rolled her eyes. 'You should be a marriage guidance counsellor.'

'It's a gift, I know.'

'Right at this moment it doesn't feel like I'll get over it. I no longer trust myself, let alone anyone else. My judgement is clearly abysmal.'

'Only when it comes to men. In everything else you have impeccable taste.' Tasha pointed to their latest acquisition. 'Like that coffee table.'

'Liar. You said it was a piece of crap.'

'The mosaic tiling converted me. I couldn't see how a fifteen-quid reject from eBay would complement your other eclectic pieces. I was wrong.'

'Eclectic? Careful, Tasha, that almost sounded like a compliment.'

Tasha folded her arms. 'I say it as I see it. This place needed a makeover, I was just too lazy to do anything about it.'

Which wasn't true. Her sister's desire for change had nothing to do with needing a makeover.

They'd inherited the three-storey townhouse when their grandmother had died ten years ago. It was situated within a stone's throw of Windsor Castle, nestled in the cobbled side streets along with the other quaint shops and eateries. Their grandmother had run Elsie's Teas & Treats for nearly forty years and she'd been a key figure in their lives growing up. She'd encouraged their individuality, wanting them to be independent, self-sufficient and resourceful women.

When she'd died, she'd gifted them the building in the hope they'd fulfil their desire of running their own businesses, which they had. They'd divided the space into two areas, with two flats above: one for sharing, the other for renting out. Below, they'd opened Tainted Love Tattoos and Ryan Fine Arts: two contrasting businesses, linked by a shared love of art.

The set-up had worked perfectly. As twins, they'd always been close, despite their differing personalities. In fact, most people didn't even register they were identical. It was amazing how changing your hair colour and throwing in a few tattoos could mask the obvious. Lexi's preference for lightening her hair and wearing colourful retro clothing contrasted with Tasha's ebony hair and penchant for body art and metal piercings. But underneath the camouflage, they shared the same DNA. More than that, they were best friends. There was no one on the planet Lexi felt closer to than Tasha.

When she'd married Marcus and moved out of their shared flat, it had been a wrench leaving Tasha, but at least working next door had ensured their close bond remained. And when her marriage had broken down, it was Tasha who'd been there for her, insisting she move back into the flat. It was just like old times, the pair of them living together and being the emotional support they both needed.

Lexi watched her sister wipe chocolate from her black nail-polished fingers. 'Thanks again for letting me move back in, Tash. I don't know what I'd do without you.'

'Luckily, you'll never have to find out. Besides, you were having a meltdown. It was my duty as your loving sister to rescue you.'

'And I appreciate it, really I do. But you didn't have to let me loose with a paintbrush.'

'Actually, I did. Even I could see this pad needed your style input.'

Another white lie. The flat had looked fine. The real reason Tasha wanted a change of décor was because of Harriette.

Tasha had only had one serious relationship before Harriette, a woman called Sara, whom she'd dated for two years. But the relationship had soured when Sara became clingy and jealous of Tasha and Lexi's close bond. In the end, Sara left, claiming Tasha never put her first. Tasha was heart-broken.

Tasha had steered away from relationships for a few years, but then she'd met Harriette, who seemed like the real deal. She was funny, kind and brought a lightness to the relationship that balanced out Tasha's tendency for melancholy. They made a great couple and Tasha adored her. So much so, Harriette moved into the flat and they spent months doing up the place and making a home together.

But then Harriette fell pregnant and returned to her ex-boyfriend, whom Tasha had no idea she was still seeing. Tasha was devastated. More than that, she felt betrayed, which manifested into rage, resulting in her smashing up the flat, destroying furniture and ripping up curtains and soft furnishings. Hence the need for a makeover.

Tasha had recovered, but there was a hardness to her now, as Marcus had discovered when Tasha had slashed his tyres. Not that she felt sorry for Marcus. But Tasha wasn't someone you wanted to get on the wrong side of.

Tasha leant against the worktop. 'Besides, this place is a damned sight better than that monstrosity of a mansion in Notting Hill. You never looked right there. This place is more you. Retro-chic.' She inspected a chipped nail. 'Marcus would hate it.'

Lexi grinned. 'That's part of the appeal.'

Tasha laughed, something she rarely did. 'Talking of Dickwit, have you heard from him lately?' She reached over for the bottle of orange liqueur Lexi had used for baking. 'Christ, paint stripper's more palatable than this stuff. We need something decent to drink.'

'I meant to restock, but I ran out of cash. I'll pop to the wholesalers on Friday. I'm planning a big shop.' She untied her blue chequered apron.

Tasha looked appalled. 'What have you got planned for Saturday, sorting through your sock drawer?'

Lexi threw the apron at her. 'Make yourself useful, there's a sink full of washing-up.'

Tasha grunted something unintelligible. 'Fine, but then I'm heading to the off-licence.'

Lexi checked the progress of her cupcakes. 'In answer to your question, my beloved ex is—'

'Hang on.' Tasha held up her hand. 'If we're going to discuss Scumbag, we need suitable background music.' She went over to the jukebox. A few seconds later The Platters started up with 'The Great Pretender'.

Lexi glared at her sister. 'Are you trying to be funny?'

'Hell, no.' Tasha came back into the kitchen. 'If I'd wanted to be funny, I'd have chosen 'I Could Have Told You'. Ole blue-eyes says it much better than I ever could.'

'And with slightly less sarcasm.'

Tasha picked up the pink rubber gloves draped over the sink. With her kohl-black eyes and asymmetric bob, she looked the most unlikely of domestic staff. But then, she'd always been a contradiction, a cocktail of sweet and sour ... only these days it was more sour than sweet. Heartbreak tended to do that to a person.

'So, news on Scumbag? Please tell me he's been kidnapped by guerrilla terrorists and is being held at gunpoint somewhere deep in the Amazonian jungle.'

The timer on the oven pinged. Lexi opened the oven door and removed her cakes. 'You have a warped mind.'

'Naturally.'

Lexi rested the baking tray on top of the oven. 'Until today, I'd assumed Marcus was still in Spain with Cindy.'

'And he's not?'

'He showed up at the gallery this morning.'

Tasha spun away from the sink, dripping foamy suds over the kitchen floor. 'You're kidding me? What did he want?'

Lexi refused to meet her sister's inquisitive gaze. 'Usual stuff. He's sorry, he didn't mean to hurt me ... where's his money. You know the pattern.' She spoke quickly, hoping her sister wouldn't catch on.

'Where's his money? What money?'

There was no point hiding anything from Tasha, she was too astute ... which was why not telling her about taking the twenty-seven grand from the house was so stressful. 'It turns out he surrendered a life insurance policy, which I knew nothing about. He forged my signature so he could cash it in. The official receiver's got wind of it and wants the money returned. Twenty-seven thousand pounds.'

'The little shit!' Tasha threw the saucepan in the sink. 'And Marcus thinks you have it? After everything he did, the guy's lucky I don't put a contract out on him.'

Lexi wondered if her sister was being serious. Some of Tasha's customers at the tattoo parlour certainly looked capable of inflicting a knee-capping.

'And even if you did have his filthy ill-gained money, as if you'd give it back after what he did. He virtually bankrupted you, jeopardised your business and hooked up with a woman who could've auditioned for the starring role in *Barbie Does Dagenham*!'

Lexi sighed. Tasha losing her rag wasn't a surprise, but it was slightly puzzling as to why her sister was still so angry after all this time. Lexi had moved past wanting to dismember Marcus a long time ago. Well, mostly anyway. She still loathed what he'd done, the way he'd done it, but there were no active emotions left, just an overwhelming sense of sadness that settled over her when she dwelt on things too much.

Like the day they'd first met.

It was Valentine's Day 2014 and she'd gone to London for an exhibition. She'd stopped off for a coffee on the South Bank and became aware of a man staring at her. The next thing she knew, he was sitting next to her, making her laugh and persuading her to join him for dinner. By the end of the evening, she was smitten. When he'd kissed her goodnight and told her she was the woman he'd been waiting for all of his life, her fate was sealed. A six-month whirlwind romance followed, filled with love, laughter and excitement. He lavished her with expensive gifts and took every opportunity to 'flash the cash', keen to demonstrate his wealth and back up his promises of a financially secure life. She never doubted his honesty or sincerity and ignored her sister's concerns that he was 'too good to be true'. They married in a registry office and for the first year everything was fine. But then he started disappearing for days on end, stressing over his used-car business and behaving strangely. He became secretive, moody and defensive when questioned. But it wasn't until he cleaned out their savings account and ran off to Spain with his PA that she'd discovered the depth of his deception.

Seeing him today had been hard, a test of her resolve, but it had confirmed one thing: she no longer loved Marcus. Cindy was welcome to him.

But Tasha hadn't finished ranting. 'Money-laundering, scum-sucking wanker! Why the hell does he think you have his rotten money? Anyone with an ounce of sanity knows you'd never touch anything illegal.'

Lexi decided it was time to change topic. If her left eye started twitching it would be game over.

Although, why she hadn't told Tasha about taking the money, she wasn't sure. She hadn't said anything at the time, because she'd genuinely believed the money was from the sale of her paintings. But now it looked like the money was from the insurance payout, what was her justification for continuing to keep quiet? Perhaps it was because she didn't want to fuel her sister's hatred of her ex-husband. Or, more likely, she didn't want to risk Tasha's disappointment in her. Because however she tried to justify it, she'd broken the law. She was a thief.

No better than Marcus ... Well, marginally better than Marcus, but equally guilty. Would her sister forgive her if she came clean? Based on her reaction to Harriette's betrayal, she wasn't sure.

'Tasha, calm down. I told Marcus to take a hike and I explained to the investigator that I had no knowledge of the insurance policy. I'm sure once he looks into it he'll realise I'm telling the truth, and they'll go after Marcus and not me.'

'They bloody better had. If I ever get my hands on Marcus—'

'Tash, let it go.'

'But—'

'Seriously, I've had enough. What with dealing with money problems, being investigated and then seeing Marcus again, I'm shattered. And I still haven't sorted through the shipment from the Wentworth estate. I know you mean well, but can we please discuss this another time?'

Tasha sighed. 'Fine.' She didn't look happy. 'What do you need?'

'Help me sort through the shipment, and then we'll be free to eat cake, drink liqueur and make voodoo dolls of Marcus to stick pins into. Okay?'

'My kind of evening. Lead the way.'

It was still light outside. The May sunshine was reluctant to call it a night, but Lexi flicked on the lights as they descended the stairs leading to the thermostatically controlled storage basement below the gallery. The chill tickled her skin. It was welcome after baking in a hot kitchen.

She caught the eye of the *Woman at the Window* propped on an easel and smiled. She'd relocated the painting after

Marcus had visited. It was a shame not to display such a beautiful piece of art, but Lexi wasn't taking any chances. The Italian temptress was staying out of harm's way.

'Remind me again whose paintings these are?' Tasha tore off the protective wrapping from the crates.

'Eleanor Wentworth.'

'Never heard of her.'

'You wouldn't have. She never sold anything during her lifetime. But she's dead now and her daughter has asked me to evaluate her work. She's also asked me to catalogue and value the art collection at Rubha Castle in Scotland.'

Tasha binned the discarded sheeting. 'Are you going to accept?'

'I wish I could. The castle is centuries old. I can only imagine the art they must've collected over the years. But how can I with everything that's going on at the gallery? The business won't repair itself. Especially not now Marcus is back on the scene.'

'Even more reason to accept.' Tasha used a Stanley knife to cut through the plastic safety strips. 'Marcus is only back to cause trouble. My advice? Get as far away from his sorry arse as possible.'

'What about the gallery?'

'You have an assistant, don't you? Ask Mel to cover while you're away. She's more than capable.'

It was true – Mel was proving to be a good investment. She was studying for an art degree and working part-time around her lectures. The university year had concluded, so maybe she'd be available to cover for a few weeks.

Tasha binned the plastic strapping. 'The break'll do you good. Whereabouts in Scotland is it?'

'Somewhere deep in the Highlands.'

Tasha looked incredulous. 'You've been offered an art gig in a castle in the Highlands and you're not sure you want to go? Are you batshit crazy?'

Lexi laughed. 'Maybe.'

'There's a fee involved, right?'

'Yes.'

'And the possibility of further commission if they decide to sell any of the collection?'

'I guess.'

'Then it's a no-brainer. Take the job and go up to Scotland. Mel and I can run the gallery. And you can focus on forgetting about Scumbag and the investigators hounding you for money.'

'You'd do that for me?'

Tasha jimmied off a crate lid. 'Like you even have to ask.'

Could she accept? It certainly sounded like the dream commission. And she'd never been to Scotland. Marcus had insisted they holiday at the villa in Spain.

'So you think I should go?'

'As long as you promise not to run off with a Gerard Butler lookalike because you've been enticed by what's under his kilt.'

Lexi laughed. 'That I can promise. I'm off men for good.'

Tasha grimaced. 'God, me too.'

'Idiot.' She kissed her sister's cheek. 'I'll give it some serious consideration.'

'Good.' Tasha removed the bubble wrap from the crate. 'Right, what have we got?'

Lexi lifted a canvas and held it up.

It was a portrait of a middle-aged man leaning against a large ornate desk. He looked relaxed, his pale eyes smiling over the top of a pair of wire-rimmed glasses with such tenderness it spoke volumes about the relationship between artist and subject. All the paintings were reputedly of similar style, portraits of the Earl of Horsley's family at various stages of their lives. The paintings had struck a chord with Lexi, which is why she'd agreed to exhibit the work when she'd seen the photos.

As well as specialising in replicas, she occasionally freelanced for a few museums and private collectors helping to value and catalogue their work. She'd also started mentoring new up-and-coming artists, wanting to diversify her collection. The combination of collecting copies of the masters along with discovering new talent was proving an exciting development.

She angled the painting so her sister could see it. 'What do you think?'

Tasha tilted her head. 'Fine, if you like family portraits. Too elitist for my liking.'

'Maybe, but I like the contrast between conventionality and intimacy.'

Tasha shrugged. 'Still looks like some posh git with too much money to me.'

Lexi replaced the painting. 'Philistine.'

'Excuse me? I have a degree in fine art.'

'I know, I was there, remember?'

'Just because I choose skin as my canvas, doesn't mean it's not art.'

'I agree.'

Tasha was by far the more talented sister. With a shared love of art and an unwillingness to be separated, they'd both won places at Oxford Brookes to study fine art. But whereas Lexi had gone on to study for an MA at The Courtauld

Institute in London so she could focus on evaluating and selling art, Tasha had attended the Tattoo Training Academy in Essex. The result was two slightly unconventional outcomes but two highly successful businesses ... Well, one successful business and Lexi desperately trying to hang on to the other, thanks to her cheating ex-husband.

Tasha frowned. 'Hang on. There are twenty paintings here, but only nineteen listed.'

Lexi checked the list. 'That's strange. If I go through them, can you check for the corresponding listing on the inventory?'

'Sure.' Tasha picked up a pen. 'Fire away.'

'Okay. So we know the first painting is the middle-aged man.' Lexi placed it to one side. 'The second painting is a child's portrait.' She viewed the reverse of the canvas. 'Thomas Elliott-Wentworth, aged nine, garden scene, fifteen-inch dark wood frame.'

Tasha made a note.

Lexi systematically went through each painting, casting her eye over the quality of the work. The more she saw, the more she warmed to the artist. The intimacy of the poses, the awkwardness of the human form had been captured perfectly.

Tasha ticked off each painting as she went through the collection. 'That's everything on the list.'

Only one remained.

Lexi picked up the last painting. 'This must be our stow-away.'

After removing the protective sheet, she placed the nineteen-inch frame on an easel and stood back to look.

When Tasha swore, she knew she wasn't the only one startled by what had been uncovered. For a moment, neither of them moved.

Finally, Tasha came over. 'Is that Renaissance?'

'Looks like it.'

Tasha let out a slow whistle. 'It has to be a fake, right?'

Logically, Lexi would have to agree. The chances of it being genuine were almost non-existent and yet every artistic instinct she possessed screamed that it wasn't.

'Can you tell if it's real?'

'Perhaps, but I'd have to carry out a series of tests. I'd need the owner's permission.'

'What's your gut telling you?'

'I suppose it wouldn't do any harm to make a quick assessment.' Lexi tried to switch off the art fanatic in her and view the painting through critical eyes. 'The frame clearly isn't as old as the canvas, so it's been replaced,' she said, pointing to the main body of the painting. 'In contrast, the canvas has evidence of multiple repairs and restoration, which is hard to fake.'

She searched out her magnifying glass and ultraviolet fluorescent wand. After switching off the lights, she waved the purple light over the painting, her skin prickling with nervous excitement. 'There's an intricate pattern of spiderweb cracks covering the surface.'

'So we know it's old.'

Lexi's pulse quickened. 'Really old. Look at the long, confident brushstrokes. Most fakes are revealed by a sense of hesitation, an effort to replicate rather than create.' She studied the canvas through the magnifying glass.

Tasha peered closer. 'What do you see?'

'Shiny pigments, indicating the use of lead whites, and possible traces of azurite and smalt infused in the paint during the 1600s.' She pointed to the detailing on the cloth around the old man's neck. 'Can you see the way the minerals dance on the surface, like the sun sparkling off the ocean?'

'Very poetic.'

Lexi switched the lights back on. 'Judging by the thickness of paint and swirling brushstrokes, the paint has been applied with a palette knife instead of a brush.' She handed Tasha the magnifying glass. 'The style is very distinctive.'

Tasha studied the canvas through the magnifying glass. 'So if this is a fake, then whoever painted it really knew their stuff.'

'A master in his or her own right. Without further lab tests on the paint I couldn't be sure, but they don't appear to have made a single obvious mistake.'

They both descended into silence. It was Tasha who broke it.

'So, this is either a really good forgery ...'

'Or it's an original Albrico Spinelli.'

Tasha let out a low whistle. 'Fuck me!'

'My thoughts exactly.'

Chapter 4

Wednesday 30th May

Less than two hours after receiving the news that the forged Spinelli had already been packed up and sent to a gallery in Windsor, Olly had boarded the overnight sleeper and was now heading out of London, bound for Berkshire. If he'd had more time he could have formulated a better plan, one that didn't involve him running out on his injured sister. But he'd been forced into a knee-jerk response.

Having grabbed an overnight bag, he'd given Louisa the lame excuse of 'needing to see Sophie urgently' as explanation for leaving her and bolted from the castle. Her tearful concerns that he wouldn't return had nearly been his undoing. Thankfully, Harry had arrived back from his business trip and the distraction of being reunited with her husband had diverted Louisa's attentions, allowing Olly to escape.

Although how he planned to deal with the problem in hand, he didn't know. But he had bigger things to worry about. Like where he was going to sleep tonight.

He hadn't realised Sophie was staying with friends in Central London. So not only was his lie already unravelling, but he also had no place to stay. Why hadn't he thought to bring a key?

He could have called Sophie and begged her to return. But then he'd have to explain why he was in Windsor, and Sophie was a lot more astute than Louisa and harder to fob off. It was better she didn't know.

Besides, she wouldn't thank him for ruining her social life. She was probably partying at some swanky venue with one of the numerous men she dated but that no one ever met. Sophie kept her family and friends separate. Having done the same, he could hardly complain.

It was late afternoon by the time he walked up the hill to where Windsor Castle sat proudly overlooking the town centre. It was a far cry from the rustic and remote Rubha Castle – the epitome of a royal residence, with its manicured lawns and troops of guards wearing impressive red coats and busby hats, proudly protecting the crown. Hordes of tourists mingled outside, snapping photos and trying to get the unresponsive guards to smile.

He checked his directions and walked past the statue of Queen Victoria. He found himself in the old medieval area of the town, the lanes narrow and cobbled. The crooked houses either side dated back to the 1600s, but they'd all been converted into souvenir shops, cafés and taverns. But it was the dwellings ahead that drew his attention.

Tainted Love Tattoos looked classy and discerning, with a neon sign that glowed in the window advertising 'Room to Let'. Handy.

Of course, the place of real interest was next door: Ryan Fine Arts.

Now he was here, he wasn't quite sure what to do. If it were any other painting he'd simply walk in there, introduce himself, explain that there'd been a mix-up and ask for the painting to be returned. But it wasn't any old painting.

According to the website, the owner of Ryan Fine Arts had

a degree in the history of art. There was no way she wouldn't recognise a Spinelli. *The Cursed Man* had been missing for nearly three hundred years, so if it suddenly turned up now it would be a huge deal. News that the family who'd sold *The Sacrificial Woman* were found to be in possession of its sister painting would hit the headlines. Especially if that painting turned out to be fake. The French buyer of the first painting would probably sue, the Wentworth family would lose both properties, his parents would be labelled crooks, his siblings shamed and four hundred years of family history would be wiped out.

The secret he'd spent the last decade running away from would be exposed.

There was no way he could let that happen. He had to get that painting back without raising suspicion. How the hell he was going to do that, he didn't know.

He decided a little reconnaissance was required before formulating a plan. He needed time to think.

The front of the gallery was mostly glass, displaying a few works in the window. Good-quality pieces, mounted against a soft white background, indicating the owner knew their stuff. Of course, it was a classy joint. When Louisa had searched for a gallery to take their mother's collection, she'd done her research. She wouldn't have proceeded unless she was confident the curator was professional and a genuine art-lover. Which was great as far as selling their mother's legitimate paintings was concerned, but bad news when trying to outsmart an expert.

Had the owner discovered the painting yet? And if she had, would she be fooled into thinking it was real, or would she simply assume it was a copy? Any decent curator would carry out a series of checks before making an assumption. It would take a while to scrutinise the materials used in the work, especially a sixteenth-century piece. They'd need to analyse the canvas and formulate a paper trail back to the artist. His mother had been thorough and had managed to fool the experts back in 2007, but whether her efforts would dupe current testing methods remained to be seen.

He noticed a side alley next to the art gallery. It led to a service area at the rear of the property. It was empty apart from a row of refuse and recycling bins. The large industrial doors leading to what looked like the gallery's storage facility were ajar. The lights were on, indicating someone was working inside.

His heart rate increased. The painting might still be in its crate. Undiscovered. Supposing he could sneak inside and remove the painting without anyone ever knowing he'd been there? There'd be no need for elaborate explanations or lying.

So why did he feel so nervous? He normally enjoyed bending the rules. He'd spent his entire life fighting conformity, deliberately pushing boundaries, mostly to annoy his parents. Not exactly original behaviour. He didn't need Freud to analyse his reasoning. But contemplating stealing a painting was hardly the same as boyish mischief.

But then he reminded himself the painting was already his. His family's, at least. He was merely retrieving lost property. He wasn't trying to con anyone, or cause anyone suffering. This was a mop-up job. A necessity to keep his family scandal-free, solvent and out of jail. All valid reasons intended to make the task easier, justify his actions and ease the guilt of deception. It wasn't working.

He decided to take a closer look.

Dumping his rucksack behind one of the bins, he crept up to the doors. It was quiet inside. The rational voice in his head told him he was crazy for even contemplating entering, but the desire to retrieve the painting overrode logic. With a pounding heart, he checked the coast was clear and went inside.

The space was painted white. It was also chilly. He couldn't see any unopened crates, but the walls contained rows of racking, so he went over. He discovered numerous quality copies of the classics. At least, he assumed they were copies. Botticelli, Raphael, Rubens, even Shouping and Cézanne. He liked the mix. It was unpredictable, random. But there were no signs of his mother's paintings.

He spotted a smaller painting displayed on an easel. He read the card pinned to the wooden frame: *Woman at the Window*, circa 1510–1530, Italian, North. He peered closer. It was bloody good, the brushwork exquisite ...

'Stay where you are.' The sound of a woman's voice made him jerk forwards, knocking the painting off the easel. 'Don't you dare move another muscle.'

Shit. He'd been sprung.

He turned slowly, opening his arms in a suitably submissive gesture.

He wasn't sure what he'd been expecting to see, but it wasn't the gallery owner brandishing a Stanley knife. He recognised her from the website. In her photo she'd looked serious and businesslike. She certainly hadn't been wearing a Fifties-style circle skirt with a cherry-patterned blouse and bright red lips. Far from looking old-fashioned, she looked like something out of one of Sophie's style magazines.

She walked towards him, shaking her mass of pale blonde hair away from her face. 'Wh ... what do you want with that painting?'

'What painting?' He hadn't found it yet. And then he realised she was talking about the *Woman at the Window*.

Her eyes darted nervously between him and the canvas on the floor. 'Don't play dumb. Who sent you?' She edged closer, her hand visibly trembling. 'My ex-husband?'

Ex-husband?

He bent down to retrieve the painting. 'Listen, I—'

'I said don't move!' She lunged forwards at the same time he held up his hands. He watched in horror as the knife sliced through the arm of his T-shirt and imbedded itself into his right bicep.

As she pulled the knife away, a splatter of red landed on the white tiled flooring.

She screamed.

He wanted to scream himself. The pain was excruciating.

The room began to sway. Flickering lights clouded his vision. He was vaguely aware of a rushing sound in his ears and then he dropped to his knees.

The woman rushed over. 'Oh, God, what have I done?' She looked frantic, torn between wanting to help him and steering well clear. 'I need to call the police.'

'Don't call the cops,' he pleaded, the blood from his arm smearing across the white tiled flooring.

She picked up the *Woman at the Window* and clutched it to her chest. 'You were trying to steal my painting.'

He staggered to his feet. 'I wasn't. I have no interest in that painting.' Which was entirely true … he was after a different painting. 'Please don't call the police.'

She waved the Stanley knife at him. 'Keep your hands where I can see them.'

He lifted his hands, blood running down his right arm.

'I'm really sorry if I frightened you.' He opened his palms. 'But I'm not here to cause trouble.'

She didn't look convinced. Her pale complexion had drained of colour. She began to sway. Was she about to faint, too?

'Are you okay?'

'Funnily enough, no. A man just broke into my gallery, attacked me and tried to steal one of my paintings. I am far from okay.'

Indignation overrode contrition. 'Hey, I didn't attack you. And I didn't break in – the doors were open. And I'm the one who's bleeding.' He pointed at his arm.

'Well ... what did you expect?' She leant against the wall. 'You were trespassing. Now get out, or I will call the police. And you can tell whoever sent you I haven't got it. They're wasting their time.'

He looked puzzled. 'Haven't got what?'

'Don't play dumb.' She tried to sound tough, but her voice shook. 'I won't be intimidated. You hear me? You tell Marcus I'm made of sterner stuff.' Her legs buckled.

'You're in shock. Let me help you—'

'Get away from me.' She batted his hand away. 'If you think I'm—'

'Hey, I was only trying to help.'

'I don't need any help from you, thank you.' She backed over to the stairwell, taking the painting with her. 'And stay ... stay there. You can't be trusted.'

Things were spiralling out of control.

'Look, I don't know why you think I'm after that painting, but I'm not.'

She hugged the painting tighter.

'My name's Oliver Wentworth. I'm here because my sister Louisa Musgrove sent you a painting by mistake.'

She froze. 'Your sister?'

'The collection from Rubha Castle? She sent you our late mother's art collection, but another painting was included that shouldn't have been. I'm here to retrieve it.'

She frowned. 'And why should I believe you? You could be anyone. A con artist. A fraudster. Show me some ID.'

Why hadn't he thought to bring ID? 'I don't have any formal ID, but I'm telling the truth. I was going to explain, but when I got here the place was empty, so—'

'You thought you'd walk in and help yourself?' She looked incredulous.

He shrugged. 'Something like that, yeah.'

'Do you make a habit of just taking things? I mean, is there anything else you'd like while you're here?' Her tone had morphed into sarcasm. 'A lift home, perhaps? A couple of paintings on your way out? A cup of tea?'

'Actually, tea sounds great.' He took a step back when she glared at him. 'Loss of blood. You can't throw me out like this.'

She opened her mouth and then hesitated, as if her mind had changed direction. She looked conflicted. She also looked as cute as hell. But he was smart enough to know mentioning that wouldn't do him any favours.

A beat later, she went over and closed the external doors. 'I can't believe I'm doing this,' she said, heading upstairs.

He followed. 'Is that a yes?'

He took her silence as an affirmative.

The staircase was narrow. When her foot caught on a loose bit of carpet and she stumbled, he reached out to grab her waist. 'Don't faint on me, there's not enough room. And besides—'

'Let me guess?' She swung around to face him. 'You're the one who's bleeding?'

He was about to apologise for the umpteenth time, but then noticed the challenge in her expression. The colour had returned to her cheeks and she no longer looked so shaky.

Maybe he needed a different approach. If he couldn't steal the painting back, maybe he could charm her into giving it to him instead.

He tried for a boyish grin. 'Technically, I'm the victim here. ABH ... use of a lethal weapon.'

Her blue eyes widened. 'It was self-defence.'

He came up a step. 'I'd surrendered.'

'You were trespassing.'

Another step. 'My hands were up.'

'You startled me.'

He was eyelevel now, their bodies separated by the painting. 'You stabbed me.'

After a long-drawn-out pause, where they both stared into each other's eyes, she turned and hurried up the remaining two flights. 'Stay by the doorway. I don't want you bleeding over my carpet.'

Her perfume hung in the air, playing havoc with his ability to think rationally. He had to shake himself out of his trance. Who was playing whom here?

The door at the top of the stairwell opened into a residential dwelling. The space was open-plan and painted soft white with a few period pieces of furniture, including a jukebox. Mark Rothko artwork hung on the walls, providing a splash of colour. It was a mixture of modern and retro, like the owner. A stretch of worktop was decorated with elaborate cupcake stands and boxes of Tupperware.

What he wouldn't do for a sugary snack. He hadn't eaten all day.

The woman came back to the stairwell and shoved a handful of kitchen towels at him. 'Hold that against the wound and sit where I can keep an eye on you.' She pointed to a barstool and then fetched a first-aid kit, stretching up to reach it from the cupboard above.

His eyes were drawn to her shapely legs and he was hit by another wave of dizziness. Christ, how much blood had he lost?

When she turned back, she caught him staring. 'Don't get any funny ideas.'

Before he could reassure her that he wasn't interested in anything other than getting his painting back, their eyes met and something hit him hard in the solar plexus. He immediately squashed the feeling. He was here to save his family. Not flirt with a cute woman.

Seemingly flustered, she busied herself making tea, using a proper teapot. She carried the bone china cup over to him and placed it on the worktop.

He raised an eyebrow at the cherry blossom design that matched her blouse but refrained from comment.

She opened the lid on her first-aid box. 'Roll your sleeve up.'

He flinched when he saw a bottle of witch hazel. 'Will this hurt?'

She tore open an antiseptic swipe. 'For a burglar you're not very brave, are you?'

'I told you, I'm not a burglar.'

'Oh, that's right, you're …?' She snapped her fingers. 'Remind me again?'

'Oliver Wentworth. Louisa Musgrove's brother.'

She laughed. 'Of course you are.'

He might have enjoyed hearing her laugh if she wasn't laughing at him. 'You don't believe me?'

'Let's just say, I have my doubts.'

'Then phone Louisa and ask her.'

'Oh, I intend to. But for now, stop complaining and let me look at your arm.'

He did as asked, making a mental note to phone Louisa and prewarn her. The wound was smeared with blood, but not as ragged as he'd feared. Her face was so close he could see a few freckles on her nose. She smelt nice. Floral.

'It might need stitches,' she said, frowning. 'I'll patch you up temporarily, but you'll need to visit A & E.'

He took a sip of tea. 'Thanks.'

'Don't read anything into it. I'd do the same for anyone.'

She cleaned the wound and covered it with a dressing. Throughout, he sat perfectly still, his eyes switching between her and the Tupperware on the side. He wasn't sure which was more enticing.

Eventually, she reached over and handed him the container. 'Honestly, men and their stomachs.'

He helped himself. 'These are delicious,' he said, trying to charm her with a smile.

'Cake is all that's on offer.' She rolled down his sleeve and turned away. 'Time for you to leave.'

'You're right.' He got off the stool. 'I have another three break-ins scheduled for tonight.'

She swung around so sharply she knocked the first-aid kit off the counter.

He bent down to retrieve the box. 'It was a joke.'

She glared at him. 'Funny guy.'

He placed the first-aid kit on the side. 'I really am sorry for frightening you. Despite appearances, I'm a very trustworthy person.'

She raised an eyebrow. 'Pillar of the community, I'm sure.' She walked over to the stairwell and held the door open. 'Just out of interest, what painting was sent here by mistake?'

He avoided eye contact. 'Nothing special. Just a random painting of an old bloke.'

'Right. So not valuable, then?'

'Worthless.'

She nodded. 'I wonder why you took the trouble to come all this way to retrieve it then. Surely it would've been easier simply to phone me and ask for it to be returned.'

He closed his eyes. He was an idiot.

Without another word, she headed downstairs. It didn't take a genius to work out she'd already discovered the painting.

He followed her down.

'Not to worry,' she said, reaching the bottom. 'I'm heading up to Rubha Castle in the next few days to evaluate the rest of the family's collection. I'll happily take the painting with me and return it to the family, if that's what they wish.' She held the rear door open for him.

Well, that was something.

'Thank you,' he said, holding out his hand in an attempt to repair the damage he'd inflicted on both his reputation and her gallery. 'I appreciate that.'

She ignored his offer of a truce. 'No problem.'

'And thanks for the tea and cake.' He rubbed his arm. 'And not calling the pol—'

The door slammed shut in his face.

So much for trying to 'charm her'. Far from retrieving the painting without arising any suspicion, he'd managed to cast even more doubt over the honesty of his family. And got stabbed in the process. Good one.

To top it all, he was now stranded in Windsor without a place to stay.

Sighing, he collected his rucksack from behind the bins and mulled over his options. His arm was throbbing, he looked a bloody mess and he couldn't imagine he'd be welcomed at the prestigious Castle Hotel in the high street. And then he remembered the advert in the tattoo parlour's window. He'd try there. Plus, it meant he could keep an eye on the gallery and ensure the owner did as promised and took *The Cursed Man* back up to Scotland.

It wasn't a great plan, but it was the best he could come up with tonight.

He backtracked to the front of the building. Tainted Love Tattoos had closed for the night, but the lights were still on inside. He cupped his hand and peered through the glass. A woman was sitting at a table. When he tapped on the glass, she looked up. He pointed to the sign hanging in the window.

She stood up. He could see she was wearing a tight black skirt with matching corset, fishnet stockings and a pair of black patent shoes. The heels alone looked capable of causing serious damage. Around her neck she wore a black choker with tiny rubies hanging from one side that looked like drop-lets of blood from a puncture wound.

Bloody hell. Talk about intimidating.

She walked towards him, her onyx eyes blinking from beneath her *Pulp Fiction* hairdo. She released the bolts on the door and opened it. For a good few seconds she just looked at him, not saying a word.

Unable to take the silence any longer, he said, 'I was wondering about a room for the night?'

She didn't respond.

He pointed to the sign. 'It says you have a room to let.'

She leant against the doorframe. 'I know what it says.'

'Right.' He rubbed his arm. 'Do you have a vacancy?'

She eyed him cautiously. 'You on the run?'

He shook his head.

'What's with the arm?'

He followed her gaze. The dressing was already soaked with blood. 'I fell off my bike.'

Her expression indicated she didn't believe him. 'No drugs.'

He frowned. 'Excuse me?'

She sighed. 'As in, I don't want anyone shooting up on my premises. *Comprendo?*'

He tilted his head to one side. 'You remind me of someone.'

'Fascinating. You want a room, or not? Forty quid a night, two fifty per week, seven hundred for the month. Cash. No tenancy agreement. No refunds. Payment upfront.' She narrowed her gaze. 'Food not included. Phone off limits. Touch my stuff and you'll die a slow and painful death.'

He visibly swallowed. 'Good to know.'

'We got a deal?'

He scratched his head and then shrugged. 'Deal.' He held out his hand.

She ignored him and stepped back to allow him inside. She locked the door behind him. Should he be worried?

'Sit,' she said, pointing to a black leather chair that wouldn't look out of place in a dentist's surgery.

'Excuse me ...?'

Placing her hands on her hips, she stared at him. 'You're contaminating my sterile working environment. I don't appreciate threats to the safety of my clients' well-being.' She narrowed her eyes. 'I'm a softie like that.'

He raised his eyebrows. 'Yeah, I can tell.' He sat down, fearful of what might happen if he didn't.

She pulled out a first-aid kit. He was struck by a sense of déjà vu.

'HIV positive?'

He blinked up at her. 'I'm sorry?'

She sighed and then repeated very slowly, 'Are you HIV positive?'

'Oh, right. Err ... no.'

'Hepatitis B?'

He shook his head.

'Any other diseases I should know about?'

'Not to my knowledge.' He tried not to stare at the tattoo on her left breast, a dagger piercing a heart. 'Shouldn't we get to know each other a little first?'

She snapped on a pair of latex gloves. 'I'm not one for small talk.'

'I've noticed.' He watched her peel away the bloodied dressing applied by his previous first aider. 'You know what you're doing?'

She dropped it into a sanitised disposal unit. 'My job dictates I draw blood. Occupational hazard.'

'I imagine you're very good at it.'

She almost smiled. 'Funny guy.'

The way she'd said 'funny guy' gave him another strong sense of déjà vu. There was something oddly familiar about this woman. But if they'd met before, he'd definitely remember. She wasn't the kind of woman a man forgot.

He looked around the parlour. In contrast to the white gallery next door, this place was jet black. There was a sign on the wall that read: THINK BEFORE YOU INK. It was hung next to the image of a naked woman with a creeping vine entwined around her torso.

'Your designs are exquisite.'

She rubbed something over his cut that stung. 'I know.'

Modest, too. He winced when she pulled the edges of the cut together and taped it.

Unlike the woman who'd tended to him a few minutes earlier, this nurse wasn't offering cups of tea or homemade cakes. Still, if it enabled him to get his painting back, he didn't care.

He looked up at her. 'I may need the room for a couple of nights, if that's okay?'

She tightened the strapping. 'Money upfront.'

He tried to breathe through the pain. 'No problem. Just the room, you understand?'

She snapped off the latex gloves and placed her hands either side of his head. 'I unnerve you, don't I?'

Instinctively, he pushed back against the chair. 'Hell, yeah.'

'Relax, sweetie.' She patted the side of his face. 'You're not my type.' She straightened and held out her hand. 'Money.'

'Money, right.' He got out of the chair and removed his wallet. 'Thanks for the first aid.' He handed her the cash.

She took the money and tucked it into her corset. 'Keep the wound covered. Bleed over my equipment and you'll—'

'... die a slow and painful death. Yeah, I remember.' He pocketed his wallet.

A faint smile played on her lips. She turned and walked away, the sway in her hips disturbingly hypnotic. 'Follow me.'

He did as he was told. He suspected his landlady wasn't quite as scary as she made out. But then, he'd never been smart where women were concerned.

Chapter 5

Lexi jolted when the train braked suddenly. Not that she'd been asleep. She rarely slept these days. Even if she hadn't been lying in a cramped bunk inside a tiny cabin, she'd still be wide awake staring up at the ceiling. Or in this instance, the empty bunk above.

She pushed back the covers and eased herself out of the bunk bed, ducking her head so she didn't bang it on the bed above. Talk about poky. She edged sideways past the ladder to reach the narrow door and escape into the corridor, which wasn't much wider.

Maybe she should have put a jumper on; she felt somewhat exposed walking down a public corridor dressed only in a nightshirt. Not that there was anyone about. It was four a.m. Everyone else was fast asleep. Lucky them.

She used to sleep just fine, but everything had changed that fateful night eighteen months ago when her life had been upended. In hindsight, she should have seen it coming. The signs were all there. The secrecy. The excuses. The elaborate stories that didn't quite ring true. Not to mention her sister's concerns about Marcus's erratic behaviour. Nonetheless, it had still come as a shock.

Marcus had been restless all evening, refusing to come to bed, claiming he was dealing with 'important business stuff'.

She should have realised he was up to something when he closed his laptop so she couldn't see what he was typing. Instead, she'd shrugged it off and gone to bed, only to be woken in the early hours when a door slammed below.

Realising Marcus wasn't in bed, she'd headed downstairs to find the house empty. And that's when she'd found his note, propped against the coffee jar. A sense of foreboding had enveloped her. Tears had blurred her vision as she'd read about his affair with Cindy ... the business going into receivership ... the investigation by HMRC for tax avoidance.

There'd been no heartfelt apology for dropping her in it, or promises to make everything right, just a load of half-hearted excuses for his behaviour. There'd certainly been no mention of his gambling addiction, or emptying of their bank account. That information had only come to light in the days that followed.

Sleep had eluded her ever since.

She shook the memory away and continued down the corridor. A door slammed behind her. She turned sharply, falling against the window as the train rocked from side to side. But there was no one there – not that she could see without her lenses in. Just an empty corridor.

Her paranoia was increasing. Ever since her encounter with the blue-eyed thief, she'd sensed she was being followed. It was crazy, of course. Her imagination was working overtime. But thanks to Marcus, she could no longer trust her instincts.

She used the facilities and returned to her cabin, ignoring the sensation of someone peering out from behind a cabin door. She really needed to dial down her stress levels. It was probably another passenger waiting to use the facilities.

When she was safely back in her cabin, she bolted the door

and checked the painting was still tucked under the sink. It was. See? No one was after her.

Shivering, she climbed into bed and pulled the blanket over her.

Feeling jittery was only to be expected. She was travelling with a potentially valuable Renaissance painting. Although whether it was genuine or not remained unknown.

After her encounter with the blue-eyed thief, she'd phoned Eleanor Wentworth's daughter, who'd confirmed that she did have a brother called Oliver and yes, she'd like the painting returned. Louisa had apologised for any inconvenience caused and claimed she hadn't realised the painting wasn't one of her mother's. However, she'd also sounded extremely confused and unsure as to why there was an issue, so it didn't take a genius to work out the brother was up to something.

Tempting as it was to enlighten Louisa, she'd decided a better approach would be to wait until she was in Scotland. She didn't want to badmouth the brother or ruin her chances of evaluating the rest of the family's art collection. Plus, there was a reason why the brother didn't want her looking too closely at the painting. Once she was in Scotland and away from the stresses of her life, she might be able to discover what that was.

Thinking about the blue-eyed thief made her agitated.

She rolled over, whacking her elbow on the ladder.

She still wasn't entirely sure what had happened the other night. One minute she was in the storeroom cataloguing a new arrival, the next she was witnessing a man stealing the *Woman at the Window*. Or so she'd thought. Her assumption that Marcus had sent one of his idiot cronies to harass her into returning his money had been incorrect. Unfortunately, she hadn't realised this before stabbing the man with a Stanley knife. Unintentionally, of course. Mortifying, nonetheless.

Just thinking about it made her shudder. She could have killed him. Well, maybe not killed, but seriously injured him. He could have reported her for ABH. In fact, why hadn't he? If he was genuinely there on behalf of the family to collect one of their paintings and the gallery owner had randomly attacked him, why wouldn't he have reported her to the police?

At the very least he'd have withdrawn the offer for her to evaluate the rest of the collection. She hadn't exactly acted professionally. The fact that he hadn't only added to her suspicions that something dodgy was going on.

And she'd had her fill of dodgy men. She wasn't about to get involved with another one. No matter how blue those eyes were ...

She rolled over, more awake than ever.

In among the panic she'd felt at seeing an unauthorised man in her basement, she'd also felt a frisson of heat, which wasn't welcome.

She reasoned that it was her hormones having a laugh at her expense, throwing a tall, cute guy in her direction to mess with her instincts. But instead of making him trustworthy and decent, recompense for having been scammed by a cheating liar in the past, the gods had made him a carbon copy of her ex. A good-looking charmer, after whatever he could get, and doing whatever was necessary to 'close the deal'.

Well, she hadn't fallen for it. She'd confronted him. Challenged his motives. Resisted his attempts to charm her ... and then stabbed him.

Oh, God. She buried her head under the pillow.

She'd been so mortified by her actions she hadn't even told Tasha what had happened. By the time her sister had arrived home the blood had been mopped up, the *Woman at the Window* had been returned to the showroom and she was in bed pretending to be asleep. If she'd told Tasha, then her sister would have wanted to know why she hadn't called the police. More significantly, why she'd gone on to invite the blue-eyed thief into their flat and fed him cake. As she didn't know the answer herself, it'd seemed better to keep quiet.

Her alarm buzzed. It was six thirty a.m. and she hadn't slept a wink. She sighed and blinked as the faint Scottish sunlight seeped through the small cabin window, obscured by a thick pleated curtain. She climbed out of bed and spent the next thirty minutes attempting to wash and dress in the cramped space.

A guard knocked on the door. He handed her a breakfast parcel and recommended she head to the lounge car to enjoy the views.

After thanking him, she locked the cabin door behind her and made her way down the corridor. Her eyes were gritty from lack of sleep. A sensible person would have opted for glasses today instead of lenses, but they were packed at the bottom of her suitcase and she hadn't fancied unearthing everything.

As she entered the lounge car, the sight that greeted her more than made up for a sleepless night. They were travelling through the Cairngorms.

She found a seat on a couch and took a moment to absorb the wash of purple heather speeding by. The early morning mist hadn't quite lifted and in the distance she could see snow-capped mountains, at odds with the onset of summer.

She opened her breakfast parcel, delighting at the smell of hot porridge. The tightness in her chest momentarily eased. This was an adventure. She needed to stop focusing on life's stresses and enjoy the experience. After all, where else could you look out of a window and see a stag standing proud just a few feet away, his antlers backlit in the morning sunlight. It was breathtaking.

Her elation briefly dipped when she sensed someone watching her. She turned to see a man disappearing into the corridor. Had he been watching her? She caught herself. It was much more likely he was returning to his cabin to fetch something. Yes, that was more plausible.

She resumed eating her porridge, followed by a banana and a hot cup of tea. She pocketed the mini shortbreads for later and settled in for the remainder of the journey.

The rocking train helped to relax her stiff muscles. She slid lower on the couch and rested her head against the window, admiring the views as they sped past. Green fields filled with sheep, cows and deer. The horizon dominated by huge mountains, the ground covered in dense yellow gorse and clusters of trees. Beautiful.

The train passed through numerous stations without stopping. She caught glimpses of signs in both Gaelic and English, the old station buildings built from grey slate. They travelled over the Glenfinnan Viaduct, the location for Harry Potter and his flying car. Her tummy flipped as the train climbed higher and the landscape disappeared below, almost as if they were airborne.

She was so mesmerised that she startled when the guard announced they were pulling into Inverness. She had to run back to her cabin to collect her things.

A few minutes later, she was ready to disembark. Lifting her suitcase onto the platform while trying not to drop the wrapped nineteen-inch painting tucked under arm proved harder than anticipated. She could have used a courier to return the painting to its rightful owners, but the cost of insuring a potentially valuable Renaissance painting would have been astronomical. Plus, there was no guarantee a courier would take proper care of it. It was safer this way.

Thankfully, she wasn't trying to contend with heels. She'd opted for her 1940s blue-spotted sailor jumper, three-quarter-length jeans and red ballet pumps in an effort to appear 'casual'. But she was still making a meal out of trying to unload her luggage. A friendly guard came to her rescue and wheeled her suitcase towards the exit.

Something made her glance back. Once again, she had the sensation of being followed, but there was no one there. She focused on finding the car hire place, which was situated inside the adjacent shopping precinct.

Having filled in the paperwork, she sent Tasha a quick 'I've arrived' message and made her way down to the car park.

When she spotted her 'budget' vehicle in the allotted space, she wasn't sure whether to laugh or cry. It was a mint green Fiat 500. Would her luggage even fit inside? It was going to be a squeeze.

Her suitcase took up all the boot space, so the painting had to be tucked behind the driver's seat. At least it was secured in a wooden case.

Fifteen minutes later, with her satnav programmed for Shieldaig, she was ready to head off.

Getting out of the car park was the first complication. She inadvertently took a wrong turn and had to double back on herself. Maybe if she hadn't turned off the roundabout too soon she'd never have noticed the red car behind, but when the car did a U-turn so it could pull in behind, her suspicions grew. Another coincidence?

She put her foot down, using the busy dual carriageway to gain some distance from the car behind, driving more erratically than she would normally. It did the trick. As she headed away from Inverness, the red car was nowhere in sight. Good.

She settled back, put the radio on and concentrated on following the satnav's directions. The first part of her journey took her through the city, but the landscape changed as she ventured further into the Highlands. It was hard to focus on driving when the sight of huge mountains and tranquil lochs kept diverting her attention. After an hour's driving, she saw a sign for a photo spot by Glen Docherty and decided to stop.

She pulled into the gravel turn-off and got out. The first thing that struck her was the force of the wind. It whipped her hair around her face, tickling her nose. She breathed in. The air was cool and fresh and smelt of ... nothing. Just air. Bliss.

The view ahead was stunning. A deep valley cut through the hills, their banks covered in grasses and heathers, the foliage bending in the breeze. The colours ranged from bright green to muted browns and coal greys. The sky looked alive, the clouds moving at such speed they cast shadows across the landscape, changing the colour palette.

She wanted to capture the moment in paint. Not that she could do it justice. She settled for taking a few photos, eager to send them to her sister.

Her equilibrium was interrupted by the sound of a car.

She glanced over. The red car from earlier was pulling into the car park.

Anger overrode any fear for her safety and she marched over, noticing the taxi licence displayed in the window. 'Why are you following me?' she yelled, shaking her fist at the driver, who was hidden behind tinted windows.

The car reversed at speed, skidded and turned back onto the road.

'That's right, run away!' she shouted, secretly glad they hadn't been up for a confrontation. 'Coward!'

Shivering, she got back in the Fiat. It was official – she was being followed.

By whom? Had Marcus got wind of her trip to Scotland? Even if he had, he wouldn't know her final destination. A detour was needed. She checked her map. The direct route to Shieldaig took her along the coastal road, but if she used the mountain road it might give her the opportunity to shake whoever it was off.

She reprogrammed the satnav and headed off, constantly checking her mirrors.

The road ahead narrowed and soon became a single lane. Thankfully, there weren't many other cars on the road. There wasn't enough room for two and she had to pull into the passing bays to allow any approaching vehicles past. What with that and checking she wasn't being followed, it didn't allow any time for sightseeing.

Consequently, she hadn't realised the terrain had changed until she'd turned off the main road and began snaking her way up the mountain track. A series of twists and turns followed, the surface precarious and bumpy.

By the time she'd passed the road signs warning 'Not for

Learner Drivers', 'No Wide Vehicles' and 'No Caravans Past this Point', it was too late to turn around. The lane was too narrow. Plus, there was a sheer drop to her right. Where the hell were the protective barriers?

A sign stating 'You have Reached 3000 Feet' didn't help. Neither did the sight of a wreath perched against a tight bend. Had someone driven off? Oh, crumbs.

She slowed to a crawl. The early morning mist had morphed into thick damp fog, obscuring her view. She could barely see past the bonnet. And then a van appeared ahead. She squealed and braked. The van driver seemed unperturbed by the conditions and pulled into the layby so she could pass.

Thank God she was on the left – no way would she want to swerve to the right. Not with that sheer drop.

She edged past as slowly as she could, almost too afraid to look. The van sped off.

Far from feeling relieved, she had a hairpin bend to negotiate and visibility was even worse. Why had she taken the mountain road? What an idiot.

She blinked hard, trying to bring her surroundings into focus. Had her contact lens moved? She rubbed her eye. It made her vision worse ... and then it dawned on her. She'd torn another lens. Blast it. And her glasses were squashed in the bottom of her suitcase. Could things get any worse?

Apparently so.

Headlights appeared behind. The red taxi. Oh, hell.

As much as she wanted to drive off, she couldn't see clearly enough. She looked in her rear-view mirror and saw the blurred image of a man exiting the passenger side.

It wouldn't have been a shock to see her ex-husband walking towards the Fiat. Or one of his hired goons. But the combination of thick fog and one contact lens meant it wasn't until he'd reached the driver's door that she realised it wasn't Marcus. It was the blue-eyed thief.

She groaned and dropped her head against the steering wheel. Why him?

He tapped on the glass. 'Everything okay? Why have you stopped?'

She lifted her head. 'Go away!'

'Open the door.' He tried the handle. 'I'm here to help.'

'Like hell you are.' She revved the engine. No way was she letting him in. She checked the doors were locked. 'You're probably going to throw me over the edge.'

He looked startled. 'Why would I do that?'

'So you can steal the painting.'

Her breath smeared the glass. She rubbed it so she could keep an eye on him, in case he did anything dodgy.

He was dressed in a black T-shirt and faded blue jeans, the colour a match for his eyes. His wavy honey-coloured hair danced about in the wind.

'Why would I steal it?' he said, rubbing his hands.

He was clearly chilly. Good. He deserved to suffer.

'I told you, it's worthless. And besides, you're taking it back to Rubha Castle. I don't need to steal it.'

Did he think she was stupid? 'That's assuming you're who you say you are.'

'I told you. I'm Louisa's brother, Olly. You phoned her, didn't you?'

She switched off the engine. It was hard work shouting over the noise. 'It doesn't mean it's you, though. You could be an imposter.'

He went to say something ... swore and then kicked the

73

ground in annoyance, scuffing his Nike trainers. Why was *he* annoyed? He was the one who was up to no good.

And then he unearthed his phone and held it against the window, showing her a photo of him sandwiched between two women. She covered her left eye so she could focus on the image. A pretty, dark-haired woman was smiling up at him adoringly. The stunning blonde looked pissed off, her eyes cast away from the camera.

'My sisters,' he yelled, gesturing to the photo.

He came from an impressive gene pool, she'd give him that.

He pointed to the dark-haired woman. 'That's Louisa.'

She shrugged. 'It could be anyone. One of your girlfriends.'

He mouthed an expletive, gave her an exasperated look and then searched through his phone again. He held up a WhatsApp message. The name Louisa Musgrove matched the name on the paperwork that had arrived with the Wentworth shipment.

She uncovered her eye. 'So why didn't you show me that the other night when I asked for ID?'

He gave her an incredulous look. 'I was too preoccupied trying not to bleed to death.'

Drama queen. 'It wasn't that bad.'

He lifted the sleeve of his T-shirt, revealing a large dressing. 'I needed eight stitches.'

'Oh.'

'And a tetanus jab.'

'Oh.'

The taxi behind honked its horn. The blue-eyed thief signalled for the taxi driver to wait.

Lexi rubbed her eye, the broken lens was making it sore. 'You haven't answered my question. Why are you following me?'

He was shivering. 'Can you lower the window? It's hard shouting through glass.'

She unwound the window, but only an inch. 'If you're not a thief and you're who you say you are then why are you following me?'

His eyes darted upwards and to the left. A sure sign he was about to lie. 'I wanted to check you arrived at Rubha Castle safely.'

Utter rubbish. 'Why?'

He hesitated. 'Because I'm a nice guy?'

She pinned him with what she hoped was an intimidating glare. 'Do I look like I was born yesterday?'

'This is tricky terrain. People have died up here.' His effort to sound dramatic failed.

'How did you know I'd take this road? It was a detour.'

That got him. He blinked and then swallowed, confirming her suspicion that he was lying. 'The coastal road is temporarily closed. This is the only alternative route to Shieldaig.'

Lying toerag. She knew exactly what he was after. 'You expect me to believe that? This is about you trying to steal the painting.'

'I told you, I wasn't trying to steal—' The taxi behind honked again. He glanced back, looking frustrated. 'Look, the taxi driver's getting worried. The weather's closing in. We need to get off the mountain road.'

He had a point.

'Can you answer my original question and tell me why you've stopped?'

There was no point lying. 'My contact lens broke. I can't see where I'm going.'

His eyebrows shot up. 'Then you need my help.'

'No, I don't.' She wasn't that desperate.

He rested his hands on the car. 'Think of it as me trying to make amends for the other night.'

She met his gaze. 'I'd be happy if you just stopped breaking into my gallery and stealing my paintings.'

'I didn't steal any of your paintings.'

'Only because I interrupted you.'

'Stabbed me, to be precise.'

She was about to assure him he was lucky that was all she'd done, when he said, 'But if you don't want my help, then fine. You have two options. Stay stuck up here, or walk down the mountain.'

Neither sounded appealing.

'Or you could accept that you need help and let me drive you—'

'No way am I letting you drive!'

'Fine.' He held up his hands. 'See you at Rubha Castle.' He walked off.

Good.

And then logic kicked in.

She threw open the driver's door and stumbled out of the car. 'Wait!'

He stopped walking but kept his back to her.

She could unearth her glasses from her suitcase, but there were broken pieces of contact lens in her eye, obscuring her vision. Added to the fact that she wasn't familiar with the terrain and she was exhausted from no sleep, it was probably sensible to accept his offer.

'Okay then.'

He turned to face her. 'Okay then ... what?'

She glared at him. 'I need your help.'

He cupped his ear. 'Sorry, what was that?'

She balled her fists. 'I said ... I need your help!'

Grinning, he ran over to speak to the taxi driver.

She turned and marched back to the car, more stressed than she'd been before arriving in bloody Scotland. So much for a restful break away from everything. She climbed into the passenger side, mumbling expletives. She wasn't happy about accepting help from the blue-eyed thief. She was an independent, resourceful woman. She didn't need a man to bail her out. Especially not a smart-talking, blue-eyed *thief*. Because whatever crap he tried to bamboozle her with, no one would follow someone all the way from Windsor up to the Highlands of Scotland without an ulterior motive. And that motive certainly wasn't a 'valueless' painting.

The driver's door opened and he climbed in, his knees almost pressed against his chest. 'Christ, you have short legs,' he said, adjusting the seat.

'There's nothing wrong with my legs.'

'Finally, something we agree on.' He flashed her a smile.

Her cheeks grew warm. 'Quit with the charm, I'm not interested.' She dug out the packet of shortbread.

His smile widened when he saw the biscuits. His eyes darted from the shortbread to her mouth, an expression of pure longing. 'You know, I missed breakfast this morning.'

She sighed and offered him a biscuit. Jesus. 'Are you going to tell me why you were following me?'

'I told you, I'm making amends for the other night.'

He devoured the biscuit in one mouthful. What was he, a wolf?

'I know what you said, I'm just having a little trouble believing you.' She nibbled on the shortbread, wanting to make hers last. It was buttery and delicious. 'What's your angle?'

He shrugged. 'No angle.'

'Men always have an angle. They never do anything unless there's something to be gained. Money. Sex. Power.'

He raised an eyebrow. 'Could you be any more judgemental?'

'Doesn't mean I'm not right.'

'Have you always been this cynical?'

'Have you always robbed people for a living?'

He sighed. 'How many times? I'm not a thief.' He pinned her with a mischievous grin. 'I'm actually very trustworthy.'

'Trustworthy, my arse. Just drive, will you.'

He started the engine and pulled away, swerving to miss an oncoming truck.

Heaven help her.

She closed her eyes. If they were going to plunge off the mountain, she didn't want to witness it.

Chapter 6

A few minutes later ...

Olly had driven across the mountain road countless times over the years. He was used to the treacherous terrain and challenging hairpin bends. The sheer drop or narrow winding lanes didn't faze him. But trying to negotiate the tricky mountain road in thick fog when his passenger kept squealing and grabbing his thigh was a complication he could do without. The fact that his passenger was hot as hell only increased the likelihood of him swerving off the cliff. And that wouldn't be in either of their best interests.

A distraction was needed.

He glanced across to see her visibly shaking. 'Did you know the circular drive from Applecross to Shieldaig is called The Bealach na Ba. It means Pass of the Cattle. It's considered one of the finest drives in Europe.'

She ducked when an oncoming car swerved past, the grip on his thigh tightening.

'The road rises to two thousand three hundred feet above sea level. It's Britain's highest mountain pass. On a good day you can enjoy spectacular views over the Minch and the Isle of Skye.'

'Hands on wheel!'

He flinched. 'Christ! You want us to end up down there?'

She shook her head. 'No!'

'Then don't shout.' He softened his voice. 'Just relax, will you?'

'Relax?' Her blue eyes widened. One was slightly bloodshot – a match for her red lipstick. 'How can I relax? Look at that drop.'

He glanced to his right. The drop was hidden by thick fog. He didn't think pointing this out would help. 'I've driven this route loads of times and I've never once driven off. Can you please stop panicking? You're making me nervous.'

'How many times?'

'Excuse me?'

'How many times have you driven this route?'

He sighed. 'I grew up here.' Well, mostly, when he hadn't been packed off to boarding school or sent to stay with his cousin in Brighton for the summer. 'As a teenager I used to ride around here on my scooter. If you think being in a car is scary you should try it on a Vespa.'

His attempt to lighten the mood failed. Her face radiated pure terror, and then she realised she was gripping his thigh and removed her hand.

'Oh, God. Sorry.'

He grinned. 'No need to move it on my account.'

She edged closer to the window. 'Don't get any ideas.'

'Wouldn't dream of it.' He flicked on the windscreen wipers, trying to disperse the moisture. 'Feeling more relaxed?'

'No.'

'Want to play I spy?'

She glared at him. 'With one eye?'

'I forgot you were visually impaired. Where are your glasses?'

Her expression turned suspicious. 'How do you know I wear glasses?'

He figured admitting he'd been watching her for the past three days wouldn't make him seem more trustworthy. 'Logic. If you wear lenses, chances are you also wear glasses.'

She didn't look convinced. 'I've had this strange sensation of being followed over the last few days.'

'That's not good. Paranoia can lead to all kinds of mental health issues.'

'My mental health is just fine, thank you. Well, it was until I met you.' She shifted in her seat. 'Admit it, you started tailing me long before we boarded the train in London.'

'Tailing you? Have you been watching too many cop dramas?' He pointed ahead, grateful for an opportunity to change topic. 'Look at the view.'

'Don't lie to me ...' And then her voice trailed off. 'Oh, wow.'

'Impressive, huh?'

The mist had started to clear now they were descending the mountain. The thick grey fog had thinned into pale white, unveiling the sight below. An expanse of green mottled with grey rocks, peppered with narrow streams that snaked down the slopes. Even he was in awe and he'd seen it a thousand times.

In the distance, Rubha Castle came into view. The sight was enough to render his passenger speechless. Good. He hadn't wanted a further interrogation.

He looked at the place he'd grown up in but would never call home, trying to imagine seeing it through a stranger's eyes. It was certainly an impressive sight. From a distance it looked like a doll's house, lost in the middle of the vast loch. But as they neared, its grandeur became more apparent.

And then his phone rang. There was no signal on the mountain road, but as they descended into Shieldaig, contact with the outside world improved. He had three missed calls from Sophie. A couple of text messages also popped up: one from Louisa, asking when he'd be back, followed by a series of heart emojis, the other from Sophie, typed in capitals, her language a lot more explicit than her sister's.

He inserted his earbud so he could answer hands-free. 'Hey there, Sis.'

'Don't *hey there* me. Where the hell are you? Are you still in Windsor?'

'I'm—'

'Louisa's convinced you've run off to South America.'

'Well, I haven't, I'm—'

'You know, I actually stuck up for you when you ran out on her the other day. He must have a reason, I said. Underneath his bullshit exterior, our brother's not a total loser, I said. Maybe I was wrong.'

'No, you weren't, I—'

'First, you lose the plot when you realise a painting was mistakenly sent to the gallery in Windsor, then you disappear for three days, then you phone Louisa wanting her to *lie* to the gallery owner about needing to get the painting back. If you're trying to scam the family, Olly—' She was interrupted.

Good. A vexed Sophie was scary.

He glanced at Lexi, hoping she hadn't heard what Sophie had said.

'Popular, aren't you?' she said, one eyebrow raised.

'My sister,' he mouthed. 'She's highly strung.'

'With you as a brother, I'm not surprised.'

Sophie came back on the line. 'Shit! That was Louisa. She's in labour!'

'What? She can't be. The baby's not due yet.'

'Tell that to the baby.'

He gripped the steering wheel. 'Is Harry with her?'

'He's at work, dipshit. Some people have careers.'

He ignored the slight. 'Has she called an ambulance?'

'Yes, but it could be an hour before they get to her. There's been a road traffic accident.'

'Okay, I'm nearly there. I'll take her to the hospital.'

'You're in Scotland? Why didn't you tell me?'

'You never gave me the chance.' He put his foot down. 'I'm on my way.' He ended the call.

Lexi gripped the seat as they accelerated down the lane. 'Your sister's in labour?'

'I need to get her to hospital.'

'Of course.'

'Can I borrow your car?'

'What? No way.' She looked panicked. 'It's not mine. It's a hire car. You're not insured.'

He shot her a look. 'I'm driving it now, aren't I?'

'Only because this is an emergency.'

'And so is this. You want me to take her on the back of my scooter?'

'Well, no, but—'

'I wouldn't ask if there was another option.'

'I appreciate that, but how do I know I can trust you? This could be another ruse. A plan to steal my car, not to mention the painting.'

Annoyance kicked in. 'You know, I've just rescued you from the bloody mountain. You could show a little gratitude and trust me.'

'Trust you?' She sounded outraged.

'Is that so much to ask?'

'Yes!' She shuffled in her seat, her bouncy blonde hair swinging about her face. 'I'm grateful for your help, but that doesn't mean—'

'Do you trust anyone?'

She looked startled. 'Well, of course I do.'

He shot her a look. 'Really?'

'Yes, really. It's just ...'

'What?'

She bit her lower lip, which was oddly distracting. 'It takes a while for me to trust someone new, that's all.'

'You don't say.'

She glared at him. 'There's no need to be sarcastic.'

'Sorry, but I'm worried about my sister. I swear on my life I'm not scamming you. I just need to borrow your car.' He gave her what he hoped was a pleading look. 'Please?'

She frowned. 'If you double-cross me, I swear to God, you'll—'

'Die a slow and painful death. Yeah, I get it.' Why had he said that?

'Why did you say that?'

What was she, a mind-reader?

'Err ... I don't know. I think you remind me of someone.'

An image of his landlady back in Windsor popped into his head dressed in black PVC. Why she reminded him of the woman from the tattoo parlour, he wasn't sure. They were polar opposites.

He shook the thought away. 'Anyway, if I did run off you wouldn't be the only one after my blood. My sister would beat the crap out of me.'

'Sophie?'

'The one and only.'

She almost smiled. 'I like the sound of her.'

'I'm sure you do.' He had enough women gunning for his blood; he didn't need anyone else joining the lynch mob.

He turned into the village and drove past Nanny's café. The bay was lined with fishing boats, fresh from returning with their catches.

Lexi strained to see, fascinated. And then her mouth dropped open as they crossed the bridge linking the mainland with the castle. He might have enjoyed seeing her reaction if his focus wasn't diverted by the sight of Gilly pushing Louisa in her wheelchair down the great walkway.

He slammed on the brakes, sending the wheels into a spin and grit flying. After throwing open the driver's door, he ran over.

'Are you okay?'

Louisa's pale face was etched in pain. 'I thought you weren't coming back.'

Guilt nudged him in the ribs. 'Of course I was. I told you I would.'

Gilly unhooked an overnight bag from the wheelchair. 'Poor lass has been throwing up all day.'

'Is that normal?'

Gilly sighed. 'Labour isn't fun.'

Louisa wailed and clutched her stomach.

Oh, hell. He patted her head. 'We need to get her to the hospital.'

Lexi appeared next to him. 'Can I help?'

'Put this in the boot, will you?' He handed her the overnight bag. 'I'll get Louisa into the car.'

Lexi unloaded her suitcase from the boot and replaced it with Louisa's bag while he helped Gilly to lift his sister out of the wheelchair.

'I'm so sorry,' she said, hiccupping through tears. 'I'm causing so much trouble.'

'Don't be daft. It's not your fault.' He kissed his sister's tear-stained cheek.

She clutched hold of him. 'Don't leave me.'

'I won't.'

'Promise?'

'Louisa, I'm not going anywhere. Let's get you to hospital.' He fastened her seatbelt and ran around to the driver's side.

He was about to get in, when Lexi shouted, 'Wait!' She shoved him out the way and removed the painting from behind the seat. 'Just in case,' she said, holding it to her chest.

'Seriously?' Not that he could blame her. But he had bigger things to worry about. 'Gilly'll look after you. Make yourself at home.'

'Don't worry about me, I'll be fine.' She waved at Louisa through the window. 'Good luck. I hope everything goes okay.'

But Louisa was too preoccupied to answer, overcome by another wave of pain.

He jumped in the car and drove off at speed, once again feeling totally inadequate when it came to dealing with family emergencies. He wasn't cut out to play the hero. He'd only let everyone down. But like it or not, there was no one else on hand to help. It was up to him. He tried not to panic.

He reached over and squeezed her hand. 'You okay?'

She shook her head. 'I don't want to do this anymore.'

'Do what? Have the baby?' He laughed. 'It's a bit late for that.'

She turned her face away. 'It's not what I thought it would be like.'

Before he could ask why, she doubled over, overcome by another contraction.

Shit! He put his foot down. The sooner they got to the hospital the better. 'Hang in there, Louisa. Not long now.'

What followed was the longest hour of his life. He was just grateful the roads were relatively clear and he could get a move on. The speedometer registered ninety as he hurtled down the A896. He wondered if the Fiat had ever been driven this fast. Would it cope? He hoped so.

Next to him, Louisa groaned and clutched her stomach. At one point, she yelled for him to pull over. For one dreadful moment, he thought she was going to give birth at the side of the road, but instead she threw up. He'd never felt so helpless in his life. All he could do was rub her back and offer her the bottle of water he'd found in the glove compartment.

They were soon back on the road, ignoring speed cameras and repeated calls from Sophie who wanted an update. She'd have to wait.

Louisa only answered her phone when she saw it was Harry calling. Through muffled cries she told him what was happening. The sound of his voice seemed to calm her, particularly when he assured her he would be with her soon. She followed his instructions when he told her to breathe slowly.

It was a blessing when they finally saw signs for the A87.

They entered the hospital grounds twenty minutes later. He screeched to a halt outside the main entrance and almost fell out of the car. He ran to the passenger side and then changed his mind and ran into reception, figuring he needed help. The cavalry arrived in the shape of two orderlies and a nurse. They helped Louisa into a wheelchair.

Unlike him, they appeared unflustered as they wheeled her towards the maternity unit.

'And how's Dad holding up?' the nurse asked as they reached reception.

'No idea.' When the nurse looked confused, he added, 'I'm her brother.'

'Oh, right. Well, if you'd like to wait here, we'll get Louisa settled and come and find you.'

'Don't leave!' Louisa yelled, reaching for his hand. 'Promise you won't leave.'

'I'm not going anywhere. I'll be right here. Okay?'

The doors swung shut behind them. As the noise drifted into silence, he felt the adrenaline drain out of him. He was shattered and he wasn't the one having a baby. And then he remembered he had to move the car.

He ran outside and moved the Fiat to the visitors' car park. When he returned, he went in search of a vending machine. In the absence of coffee, he opted for a can of Coke. He hadn't slept much last night on the sleeper train, and coupled with stressing over the missing Spinelli and a morning spent driving in poor weather, he was spent.

Sipping the Coke, he ambled over to the window. The maternity ward overlooked a small garden. A woman in a dressing gown was slowly pacing up and down. The man with her was rubbing her back, looking as miserable as she did.

He wondered whether he'd ever find himself in the same situation. His feelings surrounding the issue of 'family' were conflicted. As a teenager, he'd been so angry and resentful that leaving home had seemed like the only solution. But it hadn't cured him of his demons – it had only added to his sense of detachment. He still felt lost, untethered, lacking any real commitment to anyone or anything.

The woman in the garden sat down, her face tensing with

another contraction. Her partner began massaging her shoulders. She reached up and squeezed his hand.

Olly let his forehead rest against the glass. Love was a strange emotion. He might not have loved his parents' draconian attitudes towards parenting, but the love he felt for his siblings was unquestionable. It was why he was trying so hard to make amends.

He'd promised Louisa he wasn't going anywhere and he wasn't about to break that promise. With no parents left to support her and her husband often taken away with work, she'd made it clear she was relying on her siblings to help her through the pregnancy. He guessed it had something to do with a fear of abandonment. Louisa had suffered the most at the hands of their cold parents, craving affection and never getting it. No wonder she felt insecure.

Their childhood had been peppered with painful memories and incidents, even before the painting scandal of 2007. One such incident had occurred during the winter of 2001, when they'd been snowed in following a heavy storm. It was the day after Louisa's eleventh birthday and she'd returned from the local shop with an abandoned dog she'd found wandering through the village. The dog was house-trained and well behaved but malnourished and with a torn left ear. Louisa had wanted to keep him, or at least nurse him back to health and shelter him for the winter, but their parents had refused permission and insisted she let the dog go. A distraught Louisa had begged them to reconsider, but her pleading had fallen on deaf ears.

Olly had been torn between obeying their parents and wanting to help the dog. Unable to stand seeing Louisa upset, he'd promised to help her and subsequently hid the dog in the stables. They'd made up a bed for Vincent Van Dog – as Louisa had named him – and for a week took it in turns to feed and care for him.

But one morning their father discovered the dog. He was livid. Louisa was grounded for a month and Olly was made to sleep with the animals for a whole weekend. It was a harsh punishment, especially in the depths of winter. But it was a small price to pay for saving the dog. Or so he'd thought.

The real punishment was yet to come. Their father appeared with a loaded hunting rifle and dragged the dog into the inner courtyard. A hysterical Louisa had thrown herself at their father, clinging hold of his legs, trying to prevent him from hurting the dog. Far from succumbing to the sight of his daughter in such turmoil, his father had coldly announced that she'd 'brought it on herself' by disobeying. The sound of Louisa's screams when the gun fired would haunt Olly for years to come.

So if supporting Louisa through the birth of her first child was what she needed, then that was what she was going to get. It was the least he could do to make up for not having been a part of her life for the last eleven years.

He walked back to the waiting area, wondering how far away Harry was. He knew his brother-in-law would be distressed to miss the birth of his first child. Especially after all the difficulties they'd experienced conceiving. A couple of years of IVF had been hard by all accounts. Emotionally and physically. Yet another thing Olly had missed.

Still, he was here now. And if needed, he'd support her through the birth.

Christ, he really hoped he wouldn't have to.

Where was Harry?

It felt like forever before a doctor appeared with an update. At least she was smiling, that was something.

'Olly, isn't it?' she held out her hand. 'Dr Haslam.'

'How is she? Has she had the baby?'

'Goodness, no.' She shook her head. 'False alarm. Louisa's not in labour.'

'She's not? I mean, how come?'

'We think she has a stomach upset. Her temperature's up and she's dehydrated. We've put her on a saline drip and given her something for the nausea.'

'Is the baby okay?'

'Baby is fine. But Louisa's blood pressure is a little high, so we're going to keep her in overnight to monitor her progress. Everything else appears fine, so there's nothing to worry about.'

'Right.' He wasn't sure what else he could say.

At that moment, the swing doors burst open and Harry came running in looking fraught. He was wearing a business suit, his tie at half-mast.

'Where is she? Has she had the baby? Can I see her?'

The doctor explained what was happening and led Harry through to see his wife.

Olly sat down. After all, he'd promised Louisa he wouldn't leave.

His phone rang. It was his older sister.

'Hi, Sophie—'

'What's happening? Where's Louisa? Is the baby okay? Are you with her? Where's Harry?'

He closed his eyes. It was going to be a long night.

Chapter 7

L exi woke the next morning with a start. The fact that she'd woken at all was remarkable. Waking up meant she'd been asleep, which was more of a shock than her surroundings. It took a moment for her brain to register she was in Scotland and not at her flat in Windsor. A faint crack of morning light seeped through the gap between the long, heavy drapes, confirming it was daylight outside.

She reached for her glasses on the walnut sidetable, which was so far away she nearly tumbled out of the huge four-poster bed. She wriggled into a sitting position, bolstered by the array of cushions behind her, and checked her phone. It was gone nine a.m. Bloody hell. She couldn't remember the last time she'd slept past five a.m., let alone nine a.m.

She climbed out of the gigantic bed, using one of the wooden posts to aid her, and padded over to the window. The stone flooring beneath was cold against her bare feet. She pulled open the heavy tartan drapes, momentarily blinded by bright sunshine.

As her eyesight cleared, she gasped. The view across the loch was jaw-dropping. She had to pinch herself. Was this real? She was staying in a castle in the middle of a loch surrounded by mountains. It felt like a dream.

Smiling, she went into the adjacent dressing room, which

had been updated to include an en suite. Talk about luxury. Not many medieval castles had such modern facilities.

She showered and dressed, opting for retro wide-leg navy trousers and a fitted white sweater, teaming it with flat pumps. She needed to appear not only presentable and professional, but also appropriately dressed for the practicalities of working in rustic surroundings. The grand bedchamber might have an en suite, but from what she could tell there didn't appear to be any central heating, only an open fire or wood-burning stove in each room.

With her hair and make-up done, and new contact lenses inserted, she was ready to face the day.

A knock on the door preceded the sight of Gilly Jennings entering with a tea tray. The woman looked to be in her late sixties, with a cuddly frame and a jovial smile.

'Good morning, lassie. Sleep well?'

'Very well, thanks. It's a comfy bed.'

'I should hope so. It was a gift from the late master to his wife.' She nodded to a portrait on the wall. 'A fine-looking woman, wouldn't you say?'

Lexi glanced over. 'She's beautiful.' The painting depicted an elegant woman with long fair hair and piercing blue eyes, but there was an air of disapproval in her expression. She didn't voice this. It wouldn't be appropriate. 'Any news on Louisa's baby?'

'False alarm, lassie. We'll have to wait a while longer before the new bairn arrives.' She placed the tray on the dressing table. 'Now, you must be hungry.'

'It's kind of you to bring me breakfast, Mrs Jennings. But the family are employing my services, it doesn't seem right to be waited on.'

'Nonsense. You're a guest and you need to eat. You cannae

work on an empty stomach.' She handed her a napkin. 'And call me Gilly. We don't stand on ceremony here.' She gestured to the chair. 'Don't let it go cold.'

Lexi dutifully sat down.

'I'll be in the kitchen if you need anything. Leave the bed, I'll make it later.'

'Thank you, Mrs Jenn ... err, Gilly. This looks delicious.'

'My pleasure, lassie.' She closed the door behind her.

Lexi couldn't remember the last time she'd had scrambled eggs. They were heavenly. Creamy and light, served on thick white toast. By the time she'd finished off the huge mug of tea she was feeling quite serene. Tasha had been right. Coming here was good for the soul.

But then thoughts of cheating ex-husbands, investigating officers and stolen money flooded her brain, and her equilibrium faded. Not to mention the blue-eyed thief, who'd absconded with her hire car. That alone was enough to reignite her agitation.

She shook away the thought. No good would come from stressing.

She made the bed, unwilling to leave it rumpled, and went in search of the kitchen so she could return the tea tray. She didn't want to be seen taking advantage. And besides, she was curious to explore. She hadn't seen much of the place yesterday. By the time she'd been shown to the grand bedchamber, unpacked and eaten homemade Scotch broth, it was late afternoon. Exhausted from her long day, lack of sleep and a nerve-wracking mountain journey, she'd collapsed into bed. Where astonishingly she'd slept. She still couldn't get over that.

She headed downwards, trying to locate the kitchen. The

stone corridors were narrow. The spiral steps even tighter. Her elbows touched the walls as she carried the tea tray down.

She liked the eccentricity of the castle with its intriguing little niches and narrow wooden doorways, but she still couldn't find the blessed kitchen. She ended up in the inner courtyard, gazing around feeling slightly overwhelmed. And then she heard someone calling her name.

She looked up to see Gilly waving from a window and pointing to a door below. Following her instructions, Lexi headed through a door labelled The Keep.

She was met by a panting Gilly, who took the tray from her. 'You dinnae have to do that.'

'It was the least I could do. Breakfast was amazing. Thank you.'

'Och, you're very welcome.'

If the way to a man's heart was through his stomach, then it seemed the way to win over a housekeeper was by complimenting her cooking. The woman was positively beaming.

'Can I look around?'

'Of course, lassie.' Gilly returned to her chores.

'Is it unusual for the kitchen to be away from the main building?'

'Not in a medieval castle. The kitchen would be separate in case of fire.'

'Oh, right.'

The kitchen had been updated, probably in the 1930s judging by the décor. It had a large iron range, above which a selection of copper pots and pans hung. The flooring was wooden, as was the centre table and chairs. There was a coal fire and a dumbwaiter by the door. But the best bit was the scullery. Rows of shelving lined with bottles of pickled onions, cabbage and beetroot with labels dating back to the Thirties. She didn't fancy consuming any of them, but they made for a fascinating feature. She spotted a deep ceramic sink next to a tall larder.

'Is there electricity?'

'Aye, the family had a generator installed back in the 1920s.'

The kitchen was quirky. A mixture of past and present. Lexi loved it.

Gilly was kneading bread dough. 'Do you cook?'

'I'm more of a baker. I have a terrible sweet tooth.'

Gilly laughed. 'You'll get on well with his lordship, then.'

'His lordship?' That was a surprise. She'd assumed he'd died. 'Does he live here?'

'At the moment.' Gilly tutted, pummelling the dough. 'Who knows when he'll be off again?' She sounded disapproving.

Intriguing. 'Well, thanks for letting me look around. I'd better start work. Can you direct me to the south-west wing? I believe that's where all the records are kept.'

Gilly wiped her flour-covered hands on her apron. 'Head down to the inner courtyard and turn left past the gatehouse. You cannae miss it. And feel free to use the kitchen while you're here, lassie. You'll find plenty of baking produce in the larder. I always keep it well stocked.'

'Thanks, Gilly. That's really kind of you.'

Lexi headed outside. Away from the protection of the inner walls, the wind whipped around her, ruining her blow-dry. It was a struggle to walk against the force. She climbed up a set of steps onto the outer wall.

Below was a mass of passageways leading to different levels. It was an interesting array of shapes, circular turrets, square courtyards and curved pathways. To her left she could see the bridge leading to the mainland. It was quite a sight.

Shielding her eyes from the sun, she searched for signs of her car being returned. She had no doubt the need to borrow her car had been genuine, but as to whether her car would be returned safely remained unknown. The jury was still out as to whether Olly was a 'trustworthy guy' as he claimed or a 'charming rogue' as she suspected.

She peered over the walkway, admiring the loch below.

As appealing as Olly was, she had to stay strong. If she was to achieve her goal of a drama-free life with no visits from enforcement officers or threats to her business, then she needed to resist her natural instincts and stay single. That or choose a nice ordinary, unexciting man who might not give her goose bumps, but who wouldn't steal her life savings, either.

Excellent plan.

With renewed determination, she headed down the steps into the south-west wing, resolved to stop thinking about the blue-eyed thief. She was here to work.

It was an impressive room, built entirely of stone with a curved ceiling. The central focus was a fireplace, which wasn't lit. In the middle of the room was a circular Chippendale table with matching antique dining chairs. The walls were bare apart from a set of duelling pistols mounted above the fireplace. Either side were two tall inlets crammed full of boxes.

She went over. It was a struggle to lift the top box without pulling the whole lot on top of her. She felt like Spiderman's inept younger sister as she tried to climb up, her fingers slipping off the cardboard containers. Eventually, she managed to free one of the boxes and carried it over to the table. It was covered in dust, making her nose itch as she blew away the cobwebs. The label said Prelim Sketches in loopy handwriting. Perfect. Just what she needed.

It was a fascinating process scrutinising an artist's early sketches. Usually one of two things happened: either the quality of the artist was confirmed, upholding her decision to consider exhibiting the work, or the preliminary drawings highlighted the artist's weaknesses, in which case she'd politely decline representation. Mostly, she just listened to her gut. A painting either spoke to her, or it didn't. It was as simple as that.

Throughout her studies she'd shown a natural talent for restoration, but running her own gallery had always been the dream. And she was bloody good at it. Her clients trusted her and her artists valued her judgement, which was why she'd been so determined not to let Marcus ruin it for her. His actions had dented her professional reputation, caused financial difficulty and lost her numerous clients. Was it any wonder she'd lost her ability to trust?

The sound of her phone ringing made her jump. The noise bounced off the stone walls, amplifying the sound. It was her sister.

'Hey, Tash. How are things in Windsor?'

Her sister's reply was indecipherable.

'Hang on.' Lexi headed outside, hoping for a better signal. 'Can you hear me now?'

'Where are you, in a dungeon?'

'Kind of. The castle walls are incredibly thick. And the views! God, Tash, this place is amazing. I wish you could see it. Did you get my photos?'

'I did. I'm glad you're having fun.' Tasha sounded sombre. 'Is something wrong?'

'Why do you say that?'

'You sound flat. You might as well tell me, I'll only keep asking.'

Tasha sighed. 'You've had a letter from the official receiver's office. It's a final demand. Unless the debt is paid within twenty-eight days, it'll be passed to the High Court enforcement team.' Pause. 'In other words, the bailiffs are coming.'

'Oh, crumbs. That's not good.' She rubbed her forehead. 'Does it say anything about them investigating Marcus for forging my signature?'

'Nope. Just that if you wish to contest liability for the debt you should seek specialist legal advice.'

'Which I can't afford.' She switched ears, holding her hair away from her face as the wind blew. 'So, in short, I'm stuffed.'

'Unless you happen to have twenty-seven grand lying about.'

Lexi flinched. 'As if.' Her left eye immediately started twitching.

'The way I see it you have four options. Find a way of raising the money, borrow the money, or let me physically extract the money coin by coin from your lying, cheating scumbag of an ex-husband.'

It was certainly tempting. 'As much as I'd love Marcus to get his comeuppance, this is my mess, Tasha. Not yours. It's not fair to drag you into it.'

'You're my sister. I'm in whether you like it or not. And let's face it, when it comes to exacting revenge, I have a much better track record.'

This was true. Nobody messed with Tasha.

Lexi sat down on the stone steps. 'I can't borrow the money – my credit rating hasn't recovered. And I don't own anything of any real value to sell ...' That was a big, fat lie. But now wasn't the time to mention the *Woman at the Window*. 'Anyway, you said four options. What's the fourth?'

'Your last option is to persuade the Wentworths to let you authenticate the Spinelli so you can charge an obscene amount of commission on the sale.'

'Slight snag.'

'Which is?'

'Something happened the other night I didn't tell you about.'

'Go on.'

She sucked in a breath. 'A man snuck into the gallery and tried to take the Spinelli painting.'

It was a second before Tasha exploded. '*What*!?'

'It's okay. I stabbed him before he could take anything.'

Deathly silence followed.

In an odd way, she quite enjoyed shocking her sister. It was usually the other way around.

Tasha found her voice. 'You *stabbed* him?'

'It sounds worse than it is. I mean, I know he broke in, but he looked kind of vulnerable, with the most startling blue eyes and gorgeous smile ...' She trailed off when she realised how it sounded. 'In a mean, brutish kind of way, of course. He was a real hooligan.' Who was she trying to convince?

'And did this vulnerable blue-eyed hooligan help himself to anything else while he was there?'

Her cheeks grew hot. 'Just cake.'

'Cake?'

Lexi stood up, holding on to the iron railing for support. 'The point is, he said he was a member of the Wentworth family and that a painting had been sent to the gallery by mistake and they needed it back.'

'I hope you told him where to go.'

'I did. But it turns out he was telling the truth. The family don't want it evaluated.'

'Then you need to change their minds. Where's the painting now?'

'I brought it with me. Don't worry, I won't hand it over to the blue-eyed thief. I'll wait until Louisa returns from hospital and give it to her.'

Another weighted pause.

'The blue-eyed thief's in Scotland?'

'He … err … followed me up here.'

'What?'

'It's okay. He said he wanted to make amends for scaring me the other night. He rescued me off the mountain road when my contact lens broke.'

'Jesus! And I thought a trip to Scotland might do you good.'

'Anyway, the problem is, he clearly doesn't want me looking into the Spinelli.'

'So don't involve him. Target the sister. And in the meantime, I'll try to hunt down Marcus. That man and I need to have words.'

Lexi almost felt sorry for Marcus. 'Be careful, Tasha. Marcus can be devious.'

'So can I.'

This was true. 'I'll call you tomorrow.'

'Okay, but stay away from the blue-eyed hooligan. He sounds like trouble.'

Like she didn't know. 'Of course I will. I'm not stupid.'

She pocketed her phone and went back inside the south-west wing, Tasha's words ringing in her ears.

At some point, she was going to have to come clean about

101

the *Woman at the Window*. Maybe it would be simpler to admit defeat, sell the painting and pay off the official receiver. But, why should she? She hadn't taken out the insurance policy, or cashed it in. She was innocent.

Except she wasn't, was she? She might have thought the money was from the sale of her Franz Gerste collection, but it wasn't. Now she knew the truth there was no getting away from it.

It was time to face reality. Marcus was never going to pay up, so it was up to her to sort this mess out. As soon as she returned to Windsor she'd arrange to sell the *Woman at the Window* and pay off the official receiver. It was the right thing to do. It was also the only way of avoiding High Court action and stopping the bailiffs. Plus, it would make telling Tasha about her crime a little easier. And she would tell Tasha. Just not yet. She needed to find the right time to confess.

Still, there was nothing she could do while she was in Scotland. She needed to focus on the job in hand and put her money worries to one side.

She eased off the tape sealing the first cardboard box and removed the lid. She was hit by the musty smell of charcoal and dried paint. She lifted out one of the drawings and studied the work, surprised by what she saw.

Far from the sketchings of an early family portrait, this was a copy of Rossetti's *Reverie*. It was partially painted using traditional oils, mostly in reds and greys, capturing the essence of Rossetti's distinctive style. The picture was signed Dazed & Confused, 2007.

For a moment, all she could do was stare. The image was almost as captivating as Rossetti's original, the colours angry and harsh, the light hitting just the right accents, bringing the image to life. The inspiration for this picture had come from a dark place, the artist capturing something new and violent about the image. It was disturbing, and yet it was painted with exquisite beauty and finesse.

She had no idea who the artist was, but she was sure Eleanor Wentworth hadn't painted it. Different style, different technique. Perhaps a shared talent for depicting raw human emotion, but other than that, no other similarity.

She unearthed a few more paintings along with chalk and pencil sketchings of works by Chagall, Vermeer and Cézanne. They were all beautifully crafted. There was no question, when she spoke to Louisa about her mother's collection, she'd be quizzing her about this second unknown artist.

Because whoever Dazed & Confused were, they were someone she'd definitely like to meet.

Chapter 8

Olly unloaded the paintings he'd acquired from a local junk shop and carried them through the portcullis. The bright June sunshine disappeared behind him like a candle being snuffed out. The grandeur of the thick stone walls and ancient architecture evoked awe from visitors, but for him it was a reminder of all the years he'd spent in a cold, soulless dwelling trying to earn the love of his parents and failing miserably.

Spending the last three days by Louisa's hospital bedside had given him time to reflect. She'd spent most of the time drifting in and out of sleep, so when he hadn't been playing cards with Harry or fending off calls from Sophie, he'd used the time to evaluate his life.

He didn't need a therapist to tell him to stop dwelling on the past and focus on his future. The trouble was, he'd spent so long running from his demons that he had no idea what to do with himself now he no longer had to run. He was twenty-nine years old and he'd never had a proper career. Which was sad, embarrassing and infuriating in equal measure. The only thing he'd ever been passionate about was art. But, thanks to his parents' fraudulent actions eleven years ago, his plan to pursue an art degree had been scuppered.

But maybe it was time to test the water and discover whether or not he still had any desire to paint. More significantly, whether or not he still had any talent.

Returning to Rubha Castle had proved useful, though. Not only because it enabled him to build bridges with his sisters, but the array of historic artwork on display had also reignited his desire to be creative.

He nudged open the door to the old library, which had been converted into an art studio for his mother. Apart from boarding school, it was the place where he'd spent most of his youth, watching his mother and learning from her techniques. At the time, he'd assumed she used to make him replicate famous paintings because of her love of the classics. She'd make him repeat the work until she was satisfied it was an exact copy, showing mild pleasure with him when he got it right, and severe displeasure when he went 'rogue' and gave Mona Lisa a tattoo.

Of course, now he knew why.

He'd never been close to his mother. She wasn't affectionate or loving and she'd lacked the ability to laugh at herself. He'd rarely seen her smile and she'd never played games or did anything daft. But he'd admired her. She was a talented artist.

She was also a stickler for the rules. A staunch disciplinarian who'd instilled in her children the difference between right and wrong. He'd been so desperate for her approval that he'd spend ages perfecting a replica Botticelli or Caravaggio in the hope it would make her happy. It rarely did. It was only when he was alone in his bedroom that he'd experiment with his sketches and let his imagination wander.

But everything had changed the night he'd discovered his parents had sold one of his sketches and falsified documents. Knowing they'd deliberately defrauded someone had killed any interest in painting. Even when his father had issued an ultimatum – '*Help the family, or leave home*' – he hadn't been able to override his objections to their dishonesty. Was it any wonder his love of art had abruptly ended?

But his sudden departure from their lives at eighteen had not only quashed his own desire to paint, but also his mother's. By all accounts, she'd drifted into a state of mourning, resolutely refusing all attempts to be drawn out of her depression. Did he feel responsible for her grief? No. She'd made her bed. Did he feel guilty for running away and hurting his sisters? Hell, yes. How he was supposed to reconcile that, he didn't know.

A cough from the doorway startled him. He turned to see Lexi standing there. She was pissed off. He knew this because she was scowling. Her hands were on her hips and she looked primed for battle. She also looked as hot as hell. Her blonde hair was loosely tied up and she was wearing a vintage navy pinafore dress with a blue-and-white striped top underneath.

'Morning,' he said, trying to win her over with a smile. 'How are you settling in?'

'Where's my car?' She clearly wasn't in the mood for pleasantries.

'Parked outside.'

Her gaze narrowed. 'Is it damaged?'

'Of course not. I promised to take care of it and I did.' He dug out the keys from his jeans pocket. 'Thanks for letting me use it. I'm really grateful. Louisa is, too. We got back late last night.'

'I know.' She walked over and snatched the keys from him. 'It's bad enough that you took my car, but you were gone for three days.'

'Sorry about that, but they kept Louisa in for monitoring.

I couldn't leave her.' He tried for an apologetic smile. 'I should've asked Gilly to let you know so you wouldn't worry.' He decided to chance his luck. 'I would've let you know myself, but I didn't have your number. You know, maybe we should exchange numbers—'

'I understand why you didn't want to leave your sister, but that doesn't explain why you took my car again this morning.'

'Ah, so you do believe she's my sister?'

Her cheeks turned pink. 'Stop changing the subject. I want to know why you took my car without permission.'

'I had good reason.'

'I'm sure you did. No doubt you were tailing someone else.'

'I wasn't tailing anyone.'

'But you did run off with my car.'

'So I could get it cleaned.'

That shut her up. 'Cleaned?'

'I've been sleeping in it for the last three nights. It was a bit whiffy.'

Her cute nose turned up in disdain. 'Delightful.'

'Trust me, it wasn't. I had it washed and valeted this morning. And I filled it up with fuel. I also got you this as a thank you.' He handed her a small ribbon-tied box. 'Homemade chocolates from Nanny's café. I know you like sweet things.'

There was a drawn-out moment where he could sense she was torn between rejecting his offering and scoffing the lot in one go. Eventually, she took the box.

'Thank you.'

'No, thank *you*.' He was rewarded by a sarcastic glare. 'How are you settling in?'

'Fine, thanks. Mrs Jennings has been looking after me. I'm very impressed with the quality of the artwork on display.'

Her eyes flickered down to the box. He tugged on the ribbon and untied the bow. 'Talking of artwork, where's the painting you brought back with you?'

'You mean the Spinelli?'

He could tell by her expression she was testing him. He forced a laugh. 'Spinelli? If only, eh? Are you going to try the chocolates?'

Her eyes didn't leave his. 'You know who Albrico Spinelli is?'

'Sure. He was a Renaissance artist. I know nothing about art myself, but my mother was a fan. She liked to collect copies of the greats.' He shrugged, hoping she couldn't sense he was bluffing.

'And you think this particular painting is a copy?'

He swallowed. 'I *know* it is. I remember my mother talking about it. It's not valuable.'

'And yet you travelled all the way to Windsor to retrieve it when it was sent to my gallery by mistake.' It was an innocent enough remark, aided by her wide blue eyes and pink lips. But he wasn't daft. She knew exactly what she was doing. 'I'm still trying to understand why you did that.'

She wasn't the only one. 'It was my mother's favourite painting,' he lied. 'Since she died the painting has become more meaningful. Especially for Louisa. She'd be devastated if it disappeared.'

'But she's the one who sent it to me.'

Good point. 'Yeah, but not knowingly. It's a pregnancy thing. She gets forgetful.' He moved closer to the doorway. 'I figured I'd be a decent brother and fetch it for her before she realised it was missing. You know, to save her any unnecessary suffering.'

She didn't look convinced. 'Then why did she sound so confused when I phoned her? She didn't even know what painting I was talking about.'

'Like I said, pregnancy brain.' He gestured to the door. 'So, if you could go and get it, that'd be great.'

'I'd prefer to give it to Louisa in person. Especially as it holds such sentimental value for her.'

Damn. 'Right. Yeah, sure.' He swallowed, his brain trying to come up with a contingency plan. He didn't want Louisa involved. She might get suspicious.

'Anything else I can help you with?'

She lifted the lid off the chocolates and popped one in her mouth. He watched her expression switch to pure bliss.

'There is, actually. Who's Dazed & Confused?'

He went from staring at her mouth to jolting. He hadn't heard that phrase for over eleven years. His hands suddenly felt clammy. It took all of his willpower not to react. 'Why do you want to know?'

'I found a box of preliminary drawings in the billeting room. I'd very much like to talk to the artist about their work. Chocolate?'

'No, thanks.' He was too rattled to eat. 'Why? They're not worth anything.'

She frowned. 'Why do you say that?'

'They're crap.'

She licked chocolate from her fingers. 'For someone with no knowledge of art you seem very quick to make assumptions. The work isn't *crap*, it's astonishingly good. But you're right in that it has no value.'

'Because it's crap.'

'Because they're only preliminary works.' She ate another

chocolate. 'Goodness, these are delicious. Are you sure you don't want one?'

He shook his head. 'If they have no value, what does it matter who the artist is?'

'Because I'd like to know if there are any finished pieces. If they exist, they could be highly valuable. Assuming they're of the same quality.'

It wasn't often he found himself dumbstruck. Now was one of those occasions. She liked his work? Was she serious?

She licked her lips, sending him into a trance. 'So, who do the sketches belong to?' Her pink lipstick was speckled with icing sugar. 'I'm assuming it's not your mother. Is it another family member?'

He was mesmerised by her mouth. 'Sorry ... what?'

'The name of the artist. What's their name?'

He willed his brain to come up with an answer. Any answer. Just so long as it wasn't the truth. His gaze settled on a framed family photo on the mantlepiece. 'Err ... Tom.'

'Tom?'

'My cousin.'

'Can I have his contact details?'

'No.'

'Why not?'

'Because ... because he's a recluse. He's not good with people,' he added, like she wouldn't know what recluse meant. 'He definitely wouldn't want his work exhibited or sold.'

She sighed. 'That's a shame. I'd like to approach him anyway. He's a most extraordinary talent. I've rarely seen copies so unique yet accessible. They'll appeal to both purist collectors and those looking for a fresh take on the classics.'

She thought he was that good? No one had ever thought

110

he was that good, especially not his mother. But then she'd never been interested in his style of painting. She was a traditionalist. Her son's 'insane' sketches weren't to her taste. More to the point, they were unlikely to make them any money. Or so she'd thought.

'Perhaps you could pass on my details and ask if he'd contact me. I'd really like to talk to him.'

Gilly appeared in the doorway. 'Och, here you are. Lunch is ready in the kitchen.' She looked disapprovingly at the box of chocolates. 'I see you've met his lordship.'

Lexi looked confused. 'Lordship?'

Gilly nodded. 'Master Oliver.'

A beat passed before realisation dawned.

'You're kidding me? *Him?*'

Gilly's eyes grew wide. 'Is there a problem?'

'Of course not, Gilly.' He smiled at his housekeeper. 'Ms Ryan has a few trust issues, that's all. I did try to tell her who I was, but for some reason she wouldn't believe me.' He opened his arms in a 'can you believe it' way.

Gilly's expression confirmed that she could. Traitor.

Lexi glared at him. 'You never said you were a ... I don't even know what you are.'

'Earl,' Gilly added unhelpfully. 'Although I've called him a few other names over the years.'

'An *earl*?' Lexi shook her head in disbelief. 'Heaven help the aristocracy.'

He frowned. He wasn't that bad. 'Maybe now you'll stop questioning my motives and accept that I'm an honest and trustworthy guy.'

Gilly snorted but stopped laughing when he glared at her. 'Apologies, your *lordship*,' Gilly said. 'May I suggest Ms

Ryan joins me in the kitchen for luncheon before it gets cold.'

'Good idea.' He tried not to sound grumpy.

'Will your lordship be joining us?' Gilly stifled a laugh.

He wanted to throttle his housekeeper. 'Funnily enough, no. Enjoy your *luncheon*,' he said, glaring daggers at Gilly. What with Gilly's teasing and Lexi looking at him like he were the devil incarnate, he wanted them both gone.

Thankfully, they took the hint and left, shutting the door behind them.

He returned to the paintings he'd acquired and yanked off the remaining section of frame, taking his annoyance out on the splintered wood. He still didn't have the Spinelli. And now he'd complicated matters by telling Lexi his cousin was Dazed & Confused. Why had he done that? He should have said the sketches were the work of an unknown artist. Instead, he'd piqued her curiosity and that was the last thing he needed.

He carried a canvas over to the easel. Maybe if he'd been thinking clearer he wouldn't have panicked and blurted out another lie. But he'd been distracted by her questions about the Spinelli. The woman was too damned nosey. Now, he had to deal with her suspicions about Dazed & Confused as well as the fake Spinelli. Supposing she researched Spinelli's history and discovered the sale of his preliminary sketch back in 2007? She might put two and two together and realise it was the same artist. His lies were in danger of unravelling.

He was about to clean the canvas, when he heard a thump from the corridor.

Now what?

He went over to find Louisa reversing towards him in her

wheelchair. He reached out to stop her. 'What are you doing? You'll tip.'

She swivelled to face him. 'I was trying to reverse through the door. I didn't want to disturb you.' She strained to see past him into the room. 'Are you painting again?' Her face broke into a smile when she saw the second-hand canvases. 'Oh, my God, you are. Can I see?'

Three decades spent trying to deter his sister from prying into his business had taught him not to bother. He might not have been home for eleven years, but that hadn't stopped her insisting on monthly FaceTime sessions. Her determination to keep in touch had been relentless. In hindsight, he was grateful. He probably wouldn't have come home otherwise.

Resigning himself to a grilling, he wheeled her in. 'There's nothing to see yet.'

'But this is a start, right? You're actually going to paint again?' She looked up at him, hope in her tired expression.

'Maybe.'

'Can I watch? I don't want to put you off, but I need a distraction.'

He wheeled her over to the window. 'Is something wrong?'

'Not really.' She wouldn't make eye contact.

'Is it your leg? You're not feeling sick again, are you?'

'I'm fine, it's just ...' She paused before answering. 'I'm tired and bored of being pregnant.' She grabbed his hand. 'Please don't tell Harry.'

'Of course I won't. But why don't you want him to know?'

She sighed. 'Because I should be grateful. Having a baby is all I ever wanted and if it weren't for the IVF I still wouldn't be having one. So I shouldn't complain, right? I should be joyous and glowing, instead of cranky and miserable. Tell me I'm awful?'

He crouched down to look at her face. 'Louisa, you're not awful.'

'Then why do I feel so low? I don't understand why I'm not happy.'

Her miserable expression broke his heart. Louisa was normally the happiest soul he knew, which was a miracle in itself. They'd all reacted differently to their cold upbringing. Sophie had become self-sufficient, never relying on others and never outwardly showing any pain or weakness. Whereas Louisa had never stopped trying to win their parents' approval. She'd craved the closeness of family, only to be wounded anew with each rejection.

In Harry, she'd found the happiness and love she deserved. He was a true gent, who'd given her a fairy-tale wedding and the promise of lifelong love. Even their mother had approved of the match, until she'd discovered her daughter had a problem conceiving and then her criticisms had returned. But thanks to the miracles of science, Louisa's happy ending was in sight.

He squeezed her hand. 'You're probably feeling low because of everything that's happened recently. Mother dying, problems with probate, arguing with Sophie, breaking your leg. And then I show up and cause more grief. That's a lot to deal with.'

'But I'm glad you're home.'

'I am, too, but it's still ruffled feathers.' He watched her rub her bump. 'I don't know much about pregnancy, but I'm guessing your hormones are all over the place. Being grumpy and tearful is probably normal. I think it's nature's way of letting you know it's time for the little blighter to make an entrance.'

She smiled. 'When did you get so wise?'

'No idea.' He got up and went over to the easel. 'I still think you should tell Harry how you feel. He'll understand.'

She shook her head. 'I can't. He's so excited. It'll ruin it for him.'

He lifted his grandfather's portrait off the wall and propped it next to the easel. 'It won't ruin it, but it might stop him worrying so much. He's not stupid. He knows something's wrong. He asked me about it when we were playing cards at the hospital.'

'He did?' She looked mortified. 'What did you say?'

'I said you were probably fed up of arguing with Sophie over the future of Rubha Castle.'

'Did he believe you?'

'Why wouldn't he? It's the truth.'

'I am fed up of arguing.'

'But it's not the whole story, is it?' He soaked a cloth in white spirit. 'Anyway, you don't need to worry about Sophie. She's promised to quit hassling you until after the baby's born.'

'Big of her.'

'She's worried about you.' He squeezed out the excess fluid.

'If she was that worried she wouldn't be badgering me to sell my home.' She went quiet for a moment, lost in her thoughts.

He returned to cleaning the canvas.

A moment later, she said, 'Is that what you're going to paint? It's not your normal style.'

'I don't have a style. I haven't painted for years.'

'I mean the stuff you used to paint when you were younger, the deranged copies.'

He poured white spirit into an empty jam jar. 'That was

kids' stuff.' He rubbed at a few greasy marks on the canvas. 'I thought I'd try being a grown up for once. Isn't that what everyone keeps telling me? Stop wandering the planet and settle down.'

'I've never said that.' She sounded hurt. 'And those paintings were far from kids' stuff. They were highly disturbing.'

He laughed. 'A glowing endorsement. Thank you.'

'They were also unique, inventive and highly evocative.'

He looked over and raised an eyebrow. 'Is that right?'

'Yes.' She stuck out her chin, daring him to contradict her. 'They were the exact words Mother used to describe your work. And whatever else she lacked, knowledge of art wasn't one of them.'

He was surprised to hear his mother had said that. She'd certainly never praised him to his face. Finding fault and criticising seemed to be her favoured method of communication.

'It was just a shame she didn't praise your other qualities. Maybe if she had, you wouldn't have run off.' She angled herself so she could look out of the window.

He went over to help turn the wheelchair. 'According to Sophie, I don't have any other qualities.'

'Rubbish. You're no saint, but deep down we both know we can trust you.'

He flinched. He'd been deceiving them for eleven years.

'Even as a kid you always owned up to everything. It's why you ended up in so much trouble.' She rolled her head to look at him. 'Do you remember the time you set fire to the garden?'

He did remember. He also remembered the hiding he'd received afterwards.

'You screamed the place down because you thought Roger Rabbit was about to get barbequed.'

'Those flames were perilously close to the pet enclosure.' Even now she looked traumatised by the memory. 'Father was given a roasting by the fire officer and told to install better discipline in his kids. Sophie almost got the blame because she'd burnt her hand trying to put out the flames. But you went running in there yelling it was you, refusing to let her take responsibility.'

But his sister didn't know the whole story. She wouldn't be laughing if she did. And maybe if he'd known the horror of being made to scrub bird droppings from the north tower he might not have been so willing to own up. 'That just means I don't like people taking the crap for my mistakes.'

'Everyone always thought you were the black sheep of the family, but you were no worse than us two. You just used to admit to everything. We didn't. Did you know I spilt a whole bottle of Mother's perfume over her bed and let Mrs Jennings take the blame?'

He looked at his angelic sister. 'You rebel.'

'I know. But you never tried to hide it. I once heard Mother say to Aunty Carolyn, only ever ask Oliver his opinion if you're prepared to hear the truth. I don't think she meant it as a compliment.'

He went back to the painting. 'I don't think she did, either.'

'She was really proud of you, you know.'

He mixed up a basecoat and began stabbing the brush into the canvas. 'Now who's fibbing.'

'She was, honestly. I'm not dumb, Olly. I know something happened all those years ago to make you run away. Don't worry, I won't ask what it was. You would've told me by now if you'd wanted me to know.'

He couldn't look at her. It was better she didn't know. Better no one knew, which was why he went to such an effort to keep his parents' secret.

'I know Mother felt rotten about it. She might've been angry and bitter, but she knew she was in the wrong. I asked her about it once, what had happened to make you leave. Do you know what she said?'

He kept his focus on the brush, forcing it across the canvas. He wasn't sure he wanted to hear the answer.

'She said, the trouble with Oliver is that he's essentially honest. It's why he's such an extraordinary artist. When he paints, only the truth emerges.'

His hand froze mid-stroke, clumping the paint.

'I had no idea what she was on about, but you do, don't you, Olly?' She waited for him to look at her. 'You know exactly what she meant.' She succumbed to a huge yawn.

Balancing the brush on the jar, he went over and draped a discarded throw over her. 'Try to get some rest.'

She glanced up at him. 'You're not going to disappear on me again, are you?'

Guilt knocked him sideways, as it always did when reminded of running out on his siblings. He kissed her cheek. 'And miss getting to be an uncle? No way.'

She rubbed her tummy. 'If it's a boy, we're calling him Oliver.'

He hadn't seen that coming. He knew he should probably say something, but for the life of him he had no idea what.

She yawned again. 'Wake me up when Harry gets home.'

He returned to the canvas. The brown mottled background

118

floated in front of him. Is that why he'd stopped painting? Because he was scared of what it might reveal?

He stared down at the brush in his hand covered in paint, like a murder weapon dripping with the blood of his crime. Perhaps his mother had understood him a hell of a lot more than he'd given her credit for.

It was a highly disturbing thought.

Chapter 9

Thursday 7th June

Lexi needed a break from concentrating. She got up from the Chippendale gaming table and walked around the room, taking a moment to savour her surroundings. For the past three days, she'd been cataloguing archive boxes in the billeting room, but today she'd decided to switch to studying the artwork displayed in the grand banqueting hall. It was nice to have a change of scenery.

The room was stunning. Lights from the chandelier merged with pockets of sunlight bleeding through the stained-glass windows, making the whole room glow. The ceiling and panelling were carved from thick wood, designed in baronial gothic style, and the floor was covered in a large tapestry rug. As with the billeting room, the central focus was a carved stone fireplace, depicting a hunting scene and a coat of arms.

But the artwork was the real star of the show. Huge portraits hugged the walls, encased in gilt-gold frames. Family members sat alongside works by Henry Raeburn and James Guthrie. She wasn't an expert on Scottish painters, so it had been fun to research their work. In among the portraits were landscapes by Horatio McCulloch and William McTaggart and a beautiful still life by Anne Redpath. It was quite a compilation. Not only valuable, but also impressive, showing the family had an astute eye when it came to adding to their collection.

She stopped by the portrait of a grand fellow wearing a kilt. He was dressed in the full regalia: sporran, garters, sash and stockings. He had a proud look about him, despite balancing his weight on a walking stick. The plaque below said: Henry Charles Wentworth 1947–2015, Earl of Horsley.

'Except you're not, are you?' She studied his superior expression. 'Your son is.'

She shook her head, still reeling from the news that the blue-eyed art thief was a flipping earl. He didn't look like an earl. He wore scruffy jeans and T-shirts. His hair was a mess of honey-blond waves and he rode a Vespa.

However she imagined an earl might look, he wasn't it. But it was more than that. There was nothing stuffy about Olly. He certainly looked nothing like his father. He'd inherited his mother's good looks, just as his sisters had. Not that outward appearances were what made a person attractive. It was what lay hidden beneath that mattered. And Oliver Wentworth's character was highly questionable.

Louisa appeared in the doorway, struggling to manoeuvre her wheelchair through the gap. 'Am I interrupting?'

'Not at all. I was just admiring your father's portrait.' She went over to help.

'Grumpy sod, wasn't he?'

Lexi laughed. 'Distinguished might be a better description.'

'I guess he was that, too.'

Lexi held the door open so Louisa could wheel into the room. 'I notice there's no signature. Did your mother paint it?'

'Not that one. She'd stopped painting long before he had that one commissioned.'

That might explain why she couldn't find any Eleanor Wentworth paintings post 2007. 'What made her stop painting?'

Louisa paused before answering. 'She had her heart broken.'

It was an odd answer. The father hadn't died until 2015. Maybe he'd had an affair? Or a long-term illness? The art historian in her wanted to delve deeper, but she could tell from Louisa's body language that further questioning wouldn't be welcomed.

'Your mother's collection isn't extensive, but it's impressive.'

Louisa sighed. 'She certainly had a talent for painting.'

Lexi sensed there was more to that remark, but it wasn't her place to pry.

'How are you getting on with the cataloguing?'

'Good, thanks. It's a fascinating place. It must be quite an experience living here?'

'Tell me about it.' Louisa rolled her eyes. 'Medieval castles weren't designed for wheelchair access. I'm confined to the main rooms for the next few weeks. Until I can get rid of this damned thing.' She pointed downwards.

Was she referring to the baby or the orthopaedic boot? She'd broken her leg falling over a Shetland pony, apparently. Not surreal at all.

As if realising what she'd said, Louisa flinched. 'I'm excited about the baby, of course.' Somehow her tone didn't match her words.

Lexi decided to change topic. 'I know we spoke about displaying your mother's collection at the gallery in Windsor, but I can't help feeling Rubha Castle would be a better setting.'

'Here?' Louisa seemed surprised.

'It would make a stunning backdrop for the pieces. Especially as they all appear to have been painted in the castle or grounds.' She gestured to the other esteemed paintings lining the walls. 'And with such an impressive collection, I think an exhibition here would drum up a lot of interest.'

Louisa considered this. 'I guess that makes sense. But we're very remote up here. Would enough people come?'

'I'd hope so. Especially as the castle isn't normally open to the public. But I take your point. Maybe we could do both? Use the exhibition to create local interest and then display any unsold paintings at the gallery in Windsor.'

'When were you thinking? I'm not exactly in a fit state to play host at the moment.'

'You wouldn't have to do anything,' Lexi assured her. 'I'd oversee the event. I'm going to be up here for a few weeks, so it makes sense to have the exhibition during my stay. It'll reduce costs, for one thing.'

Louisa nodded. 'I'm sure Mrs Jennings would provide refreshments and I could ask Olly to help, too? My brother's a born salesman. He could charm anyone into buying anything.' She laughed.

Lexi kept her thoughts to herself on that topic. 'I'll draw up a plan for your approval.'

'I'll talk to Sophie and Olly and make sure they're okay with it. I'm sure they will be.' She hesitated. 'You know, perhaps we could sell off a few other paintings, too. Not the Scottish masters, of course – Mother would turn in her grave – but maybe some of the other works. It would be good to generate some extra income.'

She sounded embarrassed, as though voicing the issue of money was terribly scandalous. It was the opening Lexi had been waiting for. 'Well, now you come to mention it, there is a painting that might be worth selling.'

Louisa's expression grew hopeful.

'It's the painting that was sent to my gallery by mistake.'

Louisa's face fell. 'Oh.'

Undeterred, Lexi went over to the table and unclipped the wooden case housing the Spinelli. She'd kept the painting hidden in her room, waiting until Olly wasn't around. He'd disappeared early this morning on his Vespa, so she knew it was safe to test out her theory. A theory that had taken a surprising twist when she'd researched sale records for Albrico Spinelli and discovered the seller of its sister painting was sold at auction in 2007 by Henry Wentworth. A coincidence? No flipping way.

She carried the painting over and balanced it on a chair. She turned to Louisa, waiting for her to look at the painting. It was time to find out whether Olly was the honest trustworthy guy he claimed to be, or whether he was the no-good, lying art thief she suspected him to be.

Louisa looked at the painting. 'Is that it?'

'You don't recognise it?'

Louisa shook her head. 'Should I?'

According to Olly, yes, she should. All that rubbish he'd spouted about the painting being his mother's favourite and it having 'sentimental value' was a load of bull. Louisa had never seen the painting before.

It was official. Oliver Wentworth, the Earl of Horsley, his *lordship*, was a big, fat, cheating, no-good liar.

Lexi kept her expression neutral. 'Do you know why your brother was so keen to get it back?'

Louisa's cheeks coloured. 'Not exactly, but I know it isn't one of Mother's. It shouldn't have been sent to you. I'm sorry for any inconvenience we've caused.'

'Believe me, it's not an inconvenience.'

Louisa frowned. 'I don't understand.'

It was time to enlighten her. 'Have you ever heard of the Renaissance artist Albrico Spinelli?'

She shook her head. 'Art isn't really my thing.'

'Well, his paintings are very valuable.' She perched on the edge of the desk. 'Rumour has it two of his paintings vanished from the Vatican in the early 1700s. Their whereabouts remained a mystery until 2007, when *The Sacrificial Woman* was sold at auction for nearly two million pounds. Its sister painting, *The Cursed Man*, has never materialised.' She paused for dramatic effect. 'Until now.'

Louisa's eyes grew wide. 'You mean?' She pointed at the painting.

Lexi nodded. 'It could be a copy, but my gut tells me it's the original painting.'

'Oh, my goodness. But … but how? I don't understand.'

'Neither do I at the moment. I'd need to research the provenance to know how it ended up here. But here it is.' She smiled. 'Quite something, huh?'

Louisa looked stunned. 'If it's genuine, how much would it be worth? As much as the first painting?'

'If not more.'

'Oh, goodness.' Her hands went to her cheeks. 'We wouldn't have to sell the castle.' And then she realised what she'd said. 'Sorry, I didn't mean to say that aloud.'

'It's okay, I won't breathe a word. Discretion is part of my job.'

It didn't take a genius to work out money was an issue. Lexi had carried out enough valuations in her time to know that people rarely sold off family heirlooms unless they had to. She couldn't imagine it was cheap to run a castle.

Louisa's expression switched from embarrassment to confusion. 'I wonder why my brother didn't tell me the painting might be valuable? He made it sound like it was worthless. And he knows how much we need the money.'

Lexi chose her response carefully. It wouldn't be professional of her to badmouth the brother. However much she suspected he was up to no good. She was already playing a dangerous game by going behind his back. 'Maybe he didn't want to get your hopes up. He told me he doesn't think the painting's genuine. He believes it to be a fake.'

Her face fell. 'Oh, well, he'd know better than anyone.'

Why was that? she wondered. Oliver Wentworth claimed to know nothing about art. But perhaps he was lying about that, too? Either way, she'd rather distrust Olly and allow Louisa to improve the family's fortunes than let his lordship pull off a scam. 'Can I make a suggestion?'

'Please do.'

'Why don't I send the painting to a colleague of mine who specialises in works by Albrico Spinelli? That way, we'll know what we're dealing with. If it turns out to be fake, then no harm's been done and no one needs to know. But if it proves to be genuine, then you'll have the pleasure of surprising your brother with the good news.'

Her face brightened. 'Oh, I like that idea. I'd hate for my brother to think I'm doubting him. This way he doesn't need to know.'

'Exactly.' And then her phone rang. 'Excuse me, Louisa. It's my sister.'

'I'll give you some privacy.'

'Please don't leave on my account. The signal isn't great down here. I'll take it outside.'

She went through the main entrance and into the inner

126

courtyard, greeted by a gust of wind that immediately messed up her hair. Holding her hair away from her face, she answered the call.

'Hey, Tash. How's it going?'

'Not great.'

'No luck persuading Marcus to pay off the official receiver?'

'Worse.'

How could it be worse?

'Didn't you manage to track him down?' Not that she was surprised. Marcus had been at the gallery when the investigator had shown up. He would have gone to ground by now. He was probably back in Spain with Cindy.

'Worse than that.'

'Don't leave me hanging. What's happened?'

'Scumbag Marcus has been inside the gallery.'

'What?' Lexi slumped against the iron railings. 'How do you know?'

'He left a note.'

Her stomach dipped. 'A note?'

'I was lying in bed last night when I heard a noise downstairs. The bastard must've heard me, but by the time I got down he'd gone. There were no signs of a break-in, but then I saw his note on the counter.'

'What did it say?'

'Now we're even.'

Oh, hell. She swallowed. 'Was anything taken?'

'Nothing of value, not that I could see.'

Well, that was something.

'Just your copy of the *Woman at the Window*.'

Shit! Her legs went from under her and she slid to the ground.

'Why on earth he took that, I don't know. It's a copy, right? A good copy, but you have far more valuable paintings on display. He's probably messing with your head. The bastard knows you love that painting and that's why he took it.'

Tasha didn't know the half of it.

'And what does he mean by, now we're even?'

She couldn't answer. Her throat had constricted.

'Lexi ...? Are you there?'

'I'm here,' she managed, forcing her mouth to work.

'Don't worry, okay? I've arranged for the locks to be changed first thing tomorrow. Sod the expense. I'm paying for it. It's my fault he got in.'

'It's not your fault, Tasha.'

'Yes, it is. I'm the one who persuaded you to go to Scotland. I said I'd look after the place and I didn't. But you don't need to worry, he's not getting in again.'

It didn't matter. It was too late. The only thing of value she owned had been nicked. How the hell was she going to pay off the official receiver now? Marcus obviously hadn't believed her when she'd told him it was a copy. Somehow, he'd still known it was the original. Damn him.

What the hell was she going to do? 'I'd better come home.'

'Why? There's nothing you can do here. Stay in Scotland and leave this to me. I'll track down Marcus if it's the last thing I do. He's not getting away with this. He's the one who should be paying off the insurance debt, not you. You haven't done anything wrong.'

But she had.

'I've a good mind to call the cops—'

'No police!'

'But we could have him charged with unauthorised entry.'

128

'He has keys, Tasha.'

'So we tell them about him forging your signature on the insurance claim. And what about him stealing the money from the Franz Gerste sale? Theft is a serious criminal offence.'

Like she didn't know.

'That bastard needs to pay for what he's done.'

What about what *she'd* done?

'Please stay in Scotland, Lexi. There's nothing you can do here. I'll sort this, I promise. Okay?'

Tasha was right, there was nothing she could do. 'Okay.'

'What's happening with the Spinelli? Have you spoken to the sister?'

On that subject, at least, she had news. 'Louisa's agreed to let me send the painting off for authentication.'

'Thank God for that. You need that sale commission. Now more than ever.'

Understatement of the century.

'She's also agreed we can hold the exhibition here at the castle.'

'Good. Focus on your work, try not to stress and under no circumstances get involved with the blue-eyed hooligan, you hear me?'

'Thief.'

'Whatever. He sounds like trouble.'

She couldn't agree more. 'I can handle Olly.'

'You sure about that? Nobody tails someone all the way from Windsor to Scotland without an ulterior motive. And I'm guessing you're it.'

'Beg your pardon?'

'For a smart woman, you can be very dim sometimes. Whatever he was after when he broke in, I'm guessing the shopping list changed the moment he saw you. As your twin, I'm aware this is going to sound vain, but men forget their own names when you're around. Trust me, he's after something.'

'Well, he's not going to get it.'

'Good. And if he does try anything, I'll chop off his nuts with a carving knife and blend them into a blue-eyed hooligan smoothie.'

Ouch! Lexi never thought she'd end up feeling sorry for Olly.

'You need to steer well clear of shady men, Lexi.'

A life lesson, if ever there was one.

Chapter 10

When Olly was satisfied that Louisa was asleep, he tucked the duvet around her and crept from her bedroom. Closing the door quietly behind him, he then headed down the corridor, stopping to glare at the portrait of his parents hanging at the bottom of the stairwell.

'Boy, you've got a lot to answer for,' he said, resisting the urge to punch the canvas.

Growing up in an environment where love and approval were both limited and conditional had severely impaired his sister's self-confidence. Why else would she be too afraid to tell Harry she was struggling? Pretending to be happy when she wasn't must be exhausting. And it wasn't like Harry didn't suspect something was up. Louisa had virtually thrown him out this morning, insisting he visit his elderly grandmother as planned and assuring him she was fine. It was only after he'd driven off that the tears had surfaced. Unsure what to do, Olly had stroked her back and let her cry herself to sleep.

He headed across the inner courtyard. It wasn't the first time he'd felt inadequate as a brother. He should be doing more. But he was clueless when it came to playing 'happy families'. Should he tell Harry, or keep quiet? Maybe Louisa needed to see her GP? Perhaps he should confide in Sophie? Not that his older sister was the touchy-feely type, but she cared a lot about

Louisa. She'd want to know if her younger sister was unhappy. There were too many questions and not enough answers. It was too much for his brain to cope with.

He skipped up the stairs to the kitchen, surprised to find Lexi standing at the ceramic sink washing-up. The sleeves of her retro pink top were rolled up and her hair was loose and wavy. Mrs Jennings, she wasn't.

'What are you doing?' he said, trying not to focus on the way her narrow jeans hugged her backside. 'You don't have to do that.'

She rinsed the plates. 'It's no bother. Mrs Jennings wasn't around. I felt bad about leaving my breakfast things on the side.'

'She's visiting her sister in Edinburgh. She'll be back tomorrow night.'

'Even more reason not to leave dirty plates lying around. How's Louisa? She looked tired last night.'

His sister wasn't the only one. There was something off about Lexi today. She looked troubled. Her expression lacked its usual spark.

He opened the fridge door. 'She's okay. Nothing a chocolate brownie won't fix. I'm hoping Gilly made some before she left, they're Louisa's favourite.' He searched the containers in the fridge. Soup. Casserole. Lasagne. Ready-made sandwiches but no brownies.

'Find anything?'

'Nope.' He looked in the larder. Banana bread and scones, but still no brownies. 'I'll head into the village later and see if I can get some from Nanny's.'

She dried the plates. 'You obviously care a lot about your sister.'

132

He went over and took the plates from her. 'No need to sound so surprised. I'm not the villain you think I am.' He nodded to his arm. 'Unlike some people I know, I've never stabbed anyone.'

He was expecting a feisty comeback. Instead, she grimaced. 'How is it?'

'Better now I've had the stitches removed.'

Guilt clouded her face. 'I'm really sorry. I feel awful.'

'Don't worry about it. I deserved it.' He put the plates away. Something was definitely wrong. Perhaps she needed provoking? 'You could make it up to me, you know.'

Her guilty expression switched to one of suspicion. 'How?'

'By handing over the painting. I know you haven't given it to Louisa yet.'

'You're right, I haven't. She asked me to hold on to it until after the baby's born.'

He frowned. 'Why?'

'In case she forgets where she put it. Like you said, baby brain.'

She broke eye contact but her left eye had started twitching. There was more to this than she was letting on.

'Have you been in touch with Tom yet? I'm keen to speak to him.'

It was his turn to bluff. 'Not yet. He's ... abroad, travelling.'

'A recluse who travels?'

'Yeah ... he's an enigma like that.'

She frowned. 'Surely he's contactable?'

'Unfortunately not. He's in a remote area of ...' He looked around the kitchen and spotted a jar of garam masala. 'India. No phone signal. Or email.'

She frowned. 'Then how do you know where he is?'

Crap. 'He sent a postcard.'

She raised an eyebrow. Clearly, she didn't believe him.

He couldn't blame her. It was time to change topic. Provoking her was proving dangerous. 'What have you got planned for today?'

She leant against the sink. 'Well, as it's the weekend, I thought I'd take some time off. It seems criminal to come all this way and not explore.'

'I agree. Well, have fun.' But then he was struck by an idea. It wasn't like he had plans today. And Louisa was asleep, so she didn't need him yet. He turned to Lexi. 'Actually, would you like the guided tour?'

Her surprised expression switched to confusion, quickly followed by suspicion. He was sure she was about to refuse him, when she surprised him by saying, 'Okay.'

'Okay?'

'You know this place better than anyone.'

As much as anyone who'd been absent for eleven years. 'Come on, then.'

She followed him down the steps into the courtyard. 'Where do we start?'

'The west guard tower.'

'Will I need a jacket?'

He pointed skywards. 'The sun's shining.'

'But there are dark clouds looming.'

'It's Scotland. There are always dark clouds looming. Live dangerously.'

She rolled her eyes. 'Words no woman ever wants to hear.'

He laughed.

They entered the tower room and he led her over to the glass cabinet fixed to the wall. 'See that small piece of tartan?

It's believed to have been worn by Bonnie Prince Charlie when he led the last Jacobite uprising in 1745.'

She peered into the glass, her eyes travelling over the various ancient weapons and memorabilia. 'That's quite a collection.'

'Impressive, huh?' He beckoned her over. 'This way.'

She followed him down the narrow staircase leading to the sea gate.

'The tower used to be a jail,' he said, pointing to the iron restraints attached to the wall. He stepped onto the ledge and pointed down. 'Prisoners were pushed from this point into the loch. If they survived and swam to shore they were shown mercy and allowed to escape.'

She peered over, gripping hold of the rail. 'Harsh.'

He opened the gate.

'Don't even think of pushing me in.'

'As if.' He grinned. 'This way.'

They descended the steps and he took her past the field guns on display outside the castle.

She squinted up at the coat of arms attached to the wall. 'Is that the Wentworth crest?'

He nodded. 'It's inscribed with the family motto, *candide secure*.'

'I'm rubbish at Latin. What does it mean?'

'Honesty is the best policy.'

A beat passed before she burst out laughing. 'Seriously? Your family motto is honesty is the best policy?' She doubled over, resting her hands on her knees.

He might have enjoyed watching her laugh if he wasn't the cause of her mirth.

She wiped tears from her eyes. 'Oh, the irony.'

He folded his arms. 'Are you done?'

'That's the best laugh I've had in ages.'

'Glad I amuse you.'

She was still giggling as they headed away from the castle. At least her spark was back.

Her laughter only died when they approached the wooden outbuildings. A frown crept over her face as the farmyard smells permeated the air. She stopped walking. 'Animals?'

He nodded.

She looked wary. 'What kind?'

'All sorts.' He gestured to a stable door. 'Want me to let them out?'

'No way.' She stepped back.

He opened the top half of the door. 'I promise they don't bite.'

She edged closer.

'Although the llama does spit,' he added, just as she stuck her head through the doorway.

She retreated so fast she almost fell over.

'Don't worry, these are alpacas.'

She glared at him and then tentatively peered inside the shed. Her nose wrinkled at the smell, but she was smiling. 'They look like they're wearing furry trousers. What are their names?'

'Buddy and Holly.' When she raised an eyebrow, he shrugged. 'My sister's mind is a varied and fascinating place.' He moved on to the next shed. 'This is the llama. He's the one who spits, but only when he's nervous, so try not to look threatening.'

'Is it okay if I look scared?'

'Scared is fine.' He opened the door. 'Meet Dalai.'

She was laughing before she even saw the animal. 'The Dalai llama?'

He motioned for her to step closer. 'You'll be okay. He looks calm today.' The llama was standing at the back of the shed, eating from a bucket attached to the wall. 'He might look tough, but he's a big softy, really.'

'A softy that spits.'

'Only when he's threatened.' He turned to look at her. 'He reminds me of someone.'

'I won't dignify that with a response.' She raised her chin and walked over to the next door. 'What's in here?'

He opened the shed housing the lambs and piglets. The animals started squealing the moment they came into view. He reached into a pen and picked up a piglet. 'Would you like a cuddle?'

'No, thanks.' She watched him cradle the piglet. 'Do they have names, too?'

He nodded. 'I can't for the life of me remember them all. I know one's called Butty.'

She looked alarmed. 'As in ...?' When he nodded, she said, 'That's sick.'

'We never eat any of our animals, Louisa's rules. They're just pets.'

'Glad to hear it.'

He lifted the piglet to eyelevel. 'Not a very cost-effective way to run a farm though, is it, Butty? Or whoever you are.' He placed the piglet back in the pen. 'Would you like to see the deer?'

She visibly swallowed. 'Oh, my God. You have deer?'

'This way.' He crooked his finger. 'We need transportation.'

'You're not going to make me ride a horse, are you?'

He laughed. 'Not today.'

Her eyes grew wide when she realised they were headed for a tractor. 'Do you have a step ladder?'

'No need.' Before she could protest, he put his hands on her waist and lifted her up, depositing her on the seat. It was worth it to see the look on her face.

'Thank you,' she said, swinging her legs around. 'I think.'

He climbed in beside her. 'Hold on.'

She startled at the engine noise, gripping the seat as they pulled away.

The ground was muddy and uneven, making progress slow, but once they were on flatter grassland the wheels gripped and the tractor steadied. He took the scenic route, zigzagging his way around the edge of the island so she could see the loch at its best.

She adjusted to the rhythm and relaxed a little, fascinated by the views, craning her head one way and then the other, trying to see everything.

'The grounds are bigger than I imagined!' she shouted over the engine noise.

When they reached the top end of the island, he nudged her. 'Look.'

She followed to where he was pointing.

He knew it was an impressive sight, but it was nice to see the look on her face just the same. That first glimpse of the deer huddled together, their red coats glowing in the sunshine, was a sight to behold. He eased the tractor to a halt.

When the engine noise died, she said, 'Isn't it safe to go any closer?'

'It's better to let them come to us. The noise can startle them. They know the drill. The tractor indicates food. It won't take them long to spot us.'

The herd began to wander over.

She leant forwards in the cab. 'Look at the size of their

antlers! They're so beautiful.' Her face was animated and excited. He found himself watching her rather than the deer, only snapping out of his trance when she said, 'That one looks like Bambi.'

He dragged his attention back to the deer. 'That's an axis.'

She glanced at him. 'What's an axis?'

'One of the breeds. There are four types. Red deer, fallow, sika and axis. Most of these are red deer, you can tell by their colouring, plus they're bigger than the others.'

'There're so many of them.'

'This is only about half. The fallow deer tend to stick to the lower ground this time of day.'

The deer reached the tractor. They piled closer, no fear, only a desire for feed. Lexi had a look of pure wonder on her face as they jostled for position.

He jumped from the tractor and climbed into the trailer behind.

She twisted in her seat, watching as he scooped up handfuls of feed. 'Won't they bite?'

'Not intentionally. They don't have very sharp teeth. It doesn't hurt even if they do accidentally nip. Would you like to help?'

'No, thanks. I'd rather just watch you.'

I'd rather just watch you too, he almost said, before his brain reminded his mouth that would be a bad idea. 'It's okay to touch them,' he assured her. 'Their coat's really soft.'

She reached out and cautiously touched one of the does. 'He's so soft.'

'She.'

'Oh.' She looked at the herd. 'Are the males the ones with antlers?'

'Not always, it varies from species to species.' He nodded to the stag nuzzling his hand. 'This big fella here's the new alpha male.'

She stared at his large antlers. 'What happened to the old one?'

'Roy challenged him for the position and won.' He grabbed another handful of feed and threw it some distance, giving the calves an opportunity to feed. 'Louisa was in bits. Westley had been the alpha for years. She adored him. It was very violent, by all accounts.'

'You didn't see it?'

'It was before I came back.'

'Came back? Where had you been?'

It was an innocent enough question, but he flinched just the same. He'd forgotten she didn't know about his extended absence. Why would she? 'I moved away for a while.' He reached out to touch the antlers. 'You wouldn't believe it to touch them, they feel so soft, but they can do a lot of damage.'

She shuffled back in her seat. 'I thought you said they didn't bite?'

'They don't, but they do rut. There's only one alpha in a pack, so occasionally you get a challenge for the leadership. That's when things get nasty. Most of the year you can mingle with them and stroke them, they're as placid as anything. It's only during October when the stags' antlers are fully developed that you don't want to get in their way.'

She looked alarmed. 'Thank goodness it's only June.'

He picked up a smaller bag of feed and jumped off the back of the trailer, coming around to climb in next to her.

'What are you doing?' she said when he nudged her towards the edge of the seat.

He filled her hands with feed. 'This is something you should experience.'

'What, being impaled by antlers? Or getting my fingers bitten off?'

'I told you, they don't bite. Keep your palms flat and tuck your thumb in. That's it, now hold your hand out slowly.'

She squealed when two deer began nuzzling from her hand.

He grinned at her. 'That wasn't so bad, was it?'

She shook her head.

For the next half-hour or so, Lexi fed the deer. It was highly entertaining. She was part excited, part terrified and part mesmerised by them. Her confidence grew and she allowed them closer. Her earlier sadness had lifted, replaced by laughter and smiles. He was glad. It was oddly bewitching.

Her good humour only faded when it was time to head off and the tractor wouldn't start.

'Slight problem,' he said, scratching his head. 'We've run out of fuel.'

She didn't look overly perturbed. 'We can walk back. It's not far, is it?'

'Not too far, no.' He helped her down from the cab. 'It might be a bit muddy underfoot.' Her pink plimsolls weren't exactly fit for hiking. 'We'll take the short route through the woods.'

They ambled towards the trees. She seemed in no hurry. Nor was he. The grass was damp from last night's downpour, but it was relatively dry otherwise.

The pathway through the trees was overgrown. They had to climb over various bushes and foliage. He spotted a grass snake disappearing into the undergrowth but decided not to mention it.

'Don't you ever get lost out here?' She trailed her hands

through the long grass, looking like something from a Flake advert. 'I can't even see the path anymore.'

He snapped a twig from an overhanging tree. 'I used to camp out here as a kid. I know my way around.'

She smiled. 'How very Bear Grylls of you.'

'It's romantic camping under the stars.' He stopped walking. 'You should try it sometime.'

'Yeah, right.' She almost bumped into him. 'Why have we stopped?'

'Listen.'

She strained to hear. 'What am I listening for?'

'Rain.'

She looked up. The sky was rapidly darkening, barely visible through the thicket of trees. A spot of rain bounced off her face and trickled down her cheek. He watched, utterly transfixed as she closed her eyes, letting the rain drizzle onto her face. The rainfall became heavier and incessant, almost musical, like a thousand drums beating out a hypnotic rhythm. When she opened her eyes, blinking through wet eyelashes, she caught him staring at her.

He grabbed her hand. 'Come on. We'll make a run for it.'

She giggled as they ran. Her laughter increasing as she attempted to hurdle various branches, and squealing when a bush sprang back and slapped her in the face.

'Come under here,' he said, leading her under an overhang.

The tree shielded them like a giant umbrella. The air smelt of damp grass. Steam evaporated from their bodies as they silently waited for the rain to stop.

He let go of her hand and shook out his hair. She did the same and squeezed out her top. He watched as she reached out to touch the gnarled branches of the tree they were sheltering under. 'This is old,' she said, running her fingers over the bark.

'Very old.'

He showed her where the trunk was split in two. Each side was as wide as the other, jutting out from the ground at a weird slant. Through the gap, three gravestones were visible, each one covered in moss and leaning at an angle. A large stone angel guarded over the sunken crypt.

'This is the site of the original castle. It dates back to King Alexander the Second. He built it as a defence against the Norwegian invasions. It survived until the 1600s. This is all that remains.'

'It's amazing,' she said, crouching to read the inscriptions on the gravestones. 'There's so much history in this place. And you grew up here, surrounded by all this?'

'Mostly, yeah.' He offered her his hand and pulled her up. 'You're soaking.'

She nodded to his T-shirt. 'So are you.'

A few raindrops fought their way through the mass of leafage and trickled down his face. He ran his hand through his wet hair. The movement lifted his T-shirt and he saw her eyes dip to his stomach. The atmosphere suddenly seemed to grow thick and humid.

She stepped away. 'You said you mostly grew up here. Where else did you live?'

'Boarding school.'

She looked at him quizzically. 'You didn't like it?'

His expression must have given him away. 'You could say that.'

'How old were you when you went there?'

'Five.'

143

'Jesus, that's young. Did your parents know you didn't like it?'

He laughed. 'Oh, they knew.' He rubbed the back of his neck. 'There was no point fighting it. Wentworths are sent away, educated, toughened up and brought back to start the whole hideous cycle again with another generation.' He shrugged. 'I was too much of a mummy's boy.'

She raised an eyebrow. 'I find that hard to believe.'

'Yeah, well, it was soon knocked out of me.' Wasn't that the truth? He walked over to the edge of the tree. 'Come on,' he said. 'The rain's eased.'

They splashed their way onto the pathway, although it had long since resembled anything other than a parting in the bushes. As they negotiated a steep crevice, they were greeted by the sound of running water.

'Damn.'

She caught up with him. 'Problem?'

'I forgot it's high tide.' He nodded towards the stream. 'We'll have to head further downstream to where the level's lower.'

'Can't we jump it? It's not that wide.'

He turned to look at her.

'What? We're already wet, what's the worst that can happen?' Her hands went to her hips. 'Don't tell me you're chicken?'

He grinned. 'It's not me I'm worried about.'

She looked indignant. 'Stand back, I need a run-up.'

He caught her by the shoulder. 'No, you don't. You'll end up in the mud. Get on my back, I'll carry you across.'

'You must be kidding. You can't carry me, you'll sink.'

He indicated for her to climb on. 'I'm trying to be chivalrous. Shut up and get on.'

'You're mad,' she said, putting her arms around his neck.

'You're the one who wants to cross it,' he said, hoisting her up.

Ignoring the feel of her thighs wrapped around his middle, he focused on not dropping her as he edged down to the stream. He could feel the heat of her body seeping through his wet T-shirt. God, she smelt good.

But the moment he stepped into the water, all chivalry disappeared. The ground sank beneath him and it wasn't long before he was knee-high in mud, unable to move.

'I can't lift my leg,' he said, sinking further.

She was laughing. 'Is that it, then? Are we stuck here forever?'

'Looks that way.' He clutched at her legs, trying to keep his balance. 'I could throw you across to the other side?'

'No, thanks, I'll go back to my original plan and jump.' She slid off his back and squelched over to the side. 'Can you move now I'm off you?'

'I think so.' He sucked his foot from the mud. 'Shit, my trainer.' He shoved his hand into the water and felt around. 'I've lost my trainer.'

She stood on the bank, watching him squelch through the mud, her nose wrinkled. 'That looks disgusting.'

He grinned. 'Actually, it's quite nice.' He waded further across the stream. 'Take your shoes off and try it.'

'No way. My shoes are staying on.'

He reached the other side and dragged himself from the water. He was soaking, his legs covered in mud and minus a trainer. He held out his arms. 'See, hardly a mark. Jump, then.'

'You don't think I can do this, do you?'

'I have no idea, but I'm really looking forward to seeing you try.'

'Smart-arse.' She ignored his laughter. 'Don't put me off, I have to concentrate.'

He watched her take a run-up. She slipped before she even took off. Her feet wedged into the mud and she slapped straight into the stream. The only reason he didn't immediately dive in and rescue her was because he was laughing so hard.

She emerged from the water, gasping for air. Her blonde hair was flat over her face and she was covered in mud.

He waded into the stream, splashing water everywhere. 'You should see your face.'

She plucked a hand from the soggy, stench-ridden sod and wiped the hair from her eyes. 'It's not funny.'

'You're right, it's not,' he said, reaching her.

'Then why are you laughing?'

'Because you look so indignant.' He bent down so he was eyelevel and tapped her on the shoulder. 'Lexi ...?'

'What?' she said, spitting mud from her mouth.

'While you're down there, you couldn't look for my trainer, could you?'

She picked up a handful of mud and threw it at him.

There was no doubt about it. Lexi Ryan was very entertaining company.

Chapter 11

L exi was out of breath. She'd always considered herself to be fairly fit, but her weekly exercise classes hadn't prepared her for hiking in the Highlands. She'd woken early, disturbed from another bad dream in which Marcus had smashed into her gallery dressed as the Terminator and stolen all of her paintings.

The bad dreams had started when she'd discovered Marcus had taken the *Woman at the Window*. Unsurprising, really. She wasn't sure which was worse. Not sleeping at all, or being jolted awake several times a night in a state of panic.

Unable to settle again, she'd decided to get up early and see what Shieldaig had to offer. Louisa had lent her a rucksack, walking boots and a waterproof jacket, so she felt quite the explorer as she headed across the bridge to the mainland. She followed the nature trail signs and soon found herself off-road and enjoying her Sunday morning amble, which turned into more of a slog as the incline increased.

Puffing hard, she climbed onto a grassy mound and collapsed onto a bench seat overlooking Loch Torridon. The view was gorgeous, a contrast of dimensions, from tiny flowers underfoot to the expanse of the sky above. It was windy but warm. More significantly, it wasn't raining.

Thoughts of rain dragged her mind back to the events of yesterday. She'd had to shower twice to remove all the mud and slime stuck to her hair and clothes. It was disgusting. And cold. And annoyingly amusing.

Nonetheless, she'd crossed a line. There were rules when it came to fulfilling a work contract. She was expected to regulate her conduct, show respect and keep a professional tone to the working relationship. Not partake in mud wrestling in a stream.

Of course, it wasn't only her. His *lordship* had behaved equally badly, ducking her under the water, challenging her to a mud fight, and then picking her up in a fireman's lift and dumping her on the bank, where they both lay laughing, legs entwined, until the cold forced them to concede defeat.

It wasn't until she'd seen the look on Louisa's face when they'd returned to the castle that she'd registered a problem. Olly's sister hadn't look disapproving. Far from it – she was smiling in that 'knowing' kind of way where a person thinks they've cottoned on to something you've been trying to keep secret. And that's when the panic had set in. It wasn't like that, she'd wanted to assure her, they'd just been having a laugh, messing around. But she knew there was no point protesting, Louisa would never believe her. She wasn't sure she believed it herself.

So much for avoiding shady men.

Thoughts of shady men evoked an image of Marcus. He'd phoned last night, no doubt worn down by the numerous messages she'd left on his phone. He'd been his usual charming self, faking confusion at her claims that he'd 'stolen her painting' and expressing concern that it had gone missing. Lying rat. His denials had been both pathetic and unconvincing. He'd called her 'babe' a lot, which she now realised was a definite sign he was lying. It was just a shame she hadn't spotted his 'tell' years earlier. She could have saved herself a lot of heartache.

Despite Marcus's assurances that he wasn't 'in hiding', Tasha hadn't been able to track him down. She'd visited his old haunts, contacted family members and friends, but no one was talking. Not exactly the behaviour of an innocent man, was it?

But there was nothing she could do about it today. Stressing wouldn't help. She needed to stay calm, enjoy her beautiful surroundings and hope a solution presented itself soon. What else could she do?

She looked around. The view in front led down to the loch. Behind her, the pathway was covered in dense gorse. Pink and yellow wild flowers provided a pop of colour against the muted greens, greys and browns. Purple heather peppered the rolling hills. Not for the first time, she wished she were a good enough artist to capture the moment.

She resumed walking, one minute fighting against the wind, the next fascinated by how still it was. It was quite invigorating. Not to mention warm. She removed her jacket and tied it around her middle.

Her legs ached as she climbed the incline. It felt good to be out of breath. A purge for her guilt.

When she reached the top, she shielded her eyes from the sun. The main pathway continued around the mountain, but there was an offshoot that led down to the loch.

She headed for the smaller path, slipping on the loose stones, using her hands to steady herself. It took a while to descend, but it was worth the effort. She was greeted by still blue-green water, no wind, and absolute peace and quiet.

She climbed over a large stack of grey boulders and found

a tiny section of pebbled beach hidden the other side. Shrugging off her rucksack, she walked to the water's edge. Beneath the clear surface she could see fish, coral and more grey boulders. The only sound she could hear was lapping water. It was pure bliss.

Unearthing her water bottle, she found a smooth section of rock on which to sit. She crossed her legs and sipped her water, absorbing the moment. No traffic. No electronic devices. No signs of modern life. Just nature at its finest.

Her eyelids became heavy. Using the rucksack as a pillow, she lay down and closed her eyes. She could feel the sun on her face, the breeze tickling her nose and lifting her hair. The lapping water soothed her, along with a bird chirping nearby. All was tranquil ... until she heard the faint sound of a boat engine.

Opening her eyes, she rolled her head to one side, but the loch was empty. The noise gradually increased, but it was a minute or so before the boat came into view.

As the vessel turned into the cove, she could see a man on board reeling in a basket from the sea. A tall, good-looking man with honey-coloured hair.

She sat up. 'You've got to be kidding me?'

It was too late to run and hide – he'd spotted her. He waved and then stilled as if he was as surprised as she was. Yeah, right. Did he think she was born yesterday?

He steered the boat towards her, cutting the engine so it floated across the water. 'What are you doing out here?' he shouted, cupping his hands around his mouth.

'Trying to have some privacy,' she shouted back, annoyed that her equilibrium had been disturbed. 'I should report you for stalking.'

He looked confused. 'You think I'm following you?'

'It's one hell of a coincidence if you're not.'

'You really need to get that paranoia under control.' He moved to the side of the boat. He was wearing faded ripped jeans and a white T-shirt with a beer logo on the front. His hair was blowing in the breeze and he looked tanned and relaxed. 'I've been out since seven this morning. How would I know where you'd be?'

He had a point. 'I still think it's odd.'

'Maybe you're following me,' he grinned. 'Can't say I blame you.' He opened his arms in an 'aren't I irresistible' pose but then lost his balance and nearly fell in the water.

She laughed. Served him right.

'I'm still finding flakes of mud from yesterday,' he shouted, regaining his balance. 'I don't want to end up wet again.'

She got to her feet, brushing loose stones from her backside. 'Have you been fishing?'

He rested his arms on the side. 'Your powers of observation are exceptional.'

Sarcastic sod.

'Want to join me?'

Her brain's response was an immediate 'no way'. But her heart betrayed her by leaping up and down in excitement. What was that all about?

Okay, so he was a hot guy, her attraction was understandable, but that didn't mean she needed to risk spending time with him. She was employed by the family. Maintaining a professional relationship was in both their best interests. Except she'd blown any chance of appearing professional when she'd stabbed him and indulged in a bout of mud wrestling. It was hard to come back from that.

She picked up her rucksack. There was no harm in joining him for an innocent jaunt around the loch, was there? As long as she kept her wits about her. 'How am I going to get on board?'

He pointed to a ledge jutting out from the rock face. 'Climb up there. I'll bring the boat to you.'

She hopped onto the rock and waited for him to pull alongside.

As the boat neared, he held out his hand. 'Jump across.'

'Last time I tried that I ended up in the water.'

He grinned. 'A sight I'll never forget. You'll be okay, just don't look down.'

Great advice.

She shuffled closer and reached for his hand. Before she could doubt herself, she launched herself from the rock and landed safely in the boat, knocking him backwards with her momentum.

'You have the grace of a gazelle,' he said, rubbing his bruised shin.

'You're the one who told me to jump.' She spotted the fishing basket on the floor. 'What have you caught?'

He lifted the lid, tilting the basket so she could see. 'A couple of crabs and an eel. I've never caught a red eel before.'

She peered closer. 'It's glowing. Is it electric?'

He laughed. 'I hope not.' He tipped the contents over the side.

'You don't keep them?'

'I just like the tranquillity of being out on the water.' He attached the basket to a large reel hanging over the side.

He had an affinity with wildlife, she decided. She'd witnessed that yesterday. It didn't mean he was trustworthy, though. He was still a shady liar. But maybe he wasn't all bad.

She watched the basket disappear underwater. 'Quaint.'

'There's no other way of doing it. Commercial fishing's not allowed in these parts.' He beckoned her towards the front of the boat. 'Come on, I'll take you around the loch.'

When they pulled away, she had to hold on. They weren't going that fast, but it was a bumpy ride. 'What are those?' she asked, pointing to several large cages in the water.

'Salmon farms. The eggs are hatched on land in freshwater tanks, but they're transferred to the floating pens when they're about twelve months old.'

She was impressed by his local knowledge. But then, he grew up around here. Well, apart from attending boarding school and leaving home for a bit. He'd been quite mysterious about that yesterday. Perhaps he'd been in prison? Oh, hell. Is that why he'd been so cagey?

He pointed to a group of islands, distracting her from her thoughts. 'See the herons?'

She shook away the image of him dressed in prison attire and looked to where he was pointing. Several lanky white birds were dotted about the island. 'Impressive.'

'Hopefully we'll see some seals.'

He searched the coastline, his enthusiasm evident. Not that she was swayed by it. He could still be an ex-con.

'Over there,' he said, pointing.

She looked over. Sure enough, a seal was lying on the bank, basking in the sun. They were so close she could see its whiskers twitching. 'Oh, wow.'

There was so much to see. Everywhere she turned she saw something new. She decided to focus on the beauty around her rather than allowing her mind to run riot.

He circled the islands so she could see a group of seals

congregated on the beach. They were almost camouflaged against the grey pebbles.

'Look!' He pointed skywards towards the mountains. 'A sea eagle.'

'An eagle?' It was a while before she saw the tiny speck of a bird swooping in and out of the trees. 'I've never seen so much wildlife before.'

'Seriously?'

'I haven't travelled much.'

Holidaying in Spain didn't count. Despite owning a house there, they hadn't explored much. Marcus had preferred hanging out in the ex-pat bars. But in a way, she had travelled. Studying art had allowed her to be transported to all kinds of far-off places. She was a time traveller, moving through the centuries, sampling life and cultures. On canvas, anyway.

'Didn't you holiday with your ex-husband?'

'How did you know I was married?'

'You mentioned it the night we met.'

'Broke in, you mean.'

He shot her a look. They'd exited the loch now and were in open sea, sailing parallel to the shoreline. 'You thought your ex-husband had sent me to steal the painting of a woman looking out of a window.'

She'd forgotten about that.

'I'm guessing your ex wasn't a nice man.'

Understatement of the century. 'You could say that.'

It still smarted that she'd fallen for a complete rotter with few redeeming qualities. But she'd been blinded by Marcus's charm. It'd never occurred to her she was being played. His attentiveness and generosity had seemed genuine, and maybe when lady luck was on his side it was. But when his winning streak had ended and the debts started piling up, his true character had been exposed. Unlike her, Tasha hadn't been surprised when it all went tits-up. She'd suspected it was an act from the start but, as for herself, she hadn't seen it coming. How had she been so easily fooled?

She sighed. 'At the time, I wanted to believe that he was a good man who resorted to doing bad things when his used-car business got into trouble. But it turns out he was shady from the start and I didn't want to see it.'

'Is that why you find it hard to trust people?'

'Can you blame me?'

'One bad experience shouldn't stop you from trusting everyone.'

'By everyone, you mean you?' She rolled her eyes.

He shrugged. 'Not just me.' The boat bounced over the waves. 'What did he do that was so bad? Your ex, I mean.'

She deliberated how much to say. He might as well know the truth. Well, some of it. 'He committed fraud. He ran off with his PA and he nearly gambled away my gallery.'

'Wow, he *is* a dick. You're well rid of him.'

She didn't need him to tell her that. Still, it was nice that he did. 'Thank you.'

'And the painting of the woman looking out the window?'

Trust him to come back to that. 'Marcus broke in the other night and took it.'

'Did you call the police?'

She ducked when water sprayed over the front of the boat. 'No proof. Plus, he has keys. He says it wasn't him, but I know he's lying.'

'Is the painting valuable?'

There was no point denying it. He wasn't to know she'd

nicked the money to buy it. 'Yes, but it's more about the sentimental value. I lost almost everything when Marcus was made bankrupt. Including my dignity. Watching bailiffs remove your personal belongings while the neighbours look on isn't a pleasant experience.'

It had been utterly humiliating. She didn't know which was worse, seeing her possessions being loaded up, or watching the bailiffs walk around her house with a clipboard pricing everything up, like her whole existence was being valued.

She shook the memory away. 'The *Woman at the Window* was all I had left. All the other paintings are owned by the gallery. Marcus stole it as revenge. A deliberate act meant to hurt me. He knows I love it and I'm desperate to get it back. And that means he has leverage over me. That's what I don't like.' Why was she divulging so much? It must be the sea air, lowering her inhibitions.

'What are you going to do?'

'No idea.'

They fell into silence.

She turned her head so he couldn't see the tears threatening to undo her. Without the painting, she couldn't repay the official receiver. Which meant bailiffs would be calling again and everything she'd fought so hard to save would be taken away.

The motion of the boat sent water spraying up, masking her tears. She was grateful. Crying in front of Olly wasn't any less professional than mud wrestling.

They sailed along the coastline for some distance. It enabled her to regain control of her emotions. When she glanced over, she realised they were approaching a secluded cove.

'This okay for lunch?' He nodded to the empty stretch of white sandy beach.

Was he kidding? 'This looks amazing.'

'I wasn't expecting company, so you'll have to share my petrol station sandwich.'

'That's okay, I brought a packed lunch.'

He moored the boat by the rocks. They removed their shoes and rolled up their trousers so they could wade through the water to reach the beach.

She was dumbstruck by how breathtaking it was. It was like something from the Mediterranean. The sun sparkled off the water like dancing diamonds. Either side were rocks, sheltering them from the wind. It was perfect.

Ignoring the warning voice in her head telling her it was also very romantic, she unpacked her rucksack and placed a rug on the sand before sitting down and unwrapping her bag of goodies: two egg mayonnaise rolls, a banana and a fruit smoothie. Nothing romantic about that.

Olly appeared carrying his sandwich and bottle of water. 'Blimey, you came prepared. Are you going to eat all of that?'

She handed him a roll. She was getting accustomed to his appetite.

'Thanks. This looks way better than my limp sandwich.'

When she unearthed a small Tupperware containing two freshly baked chocolate brownies, she thought he might combust.

His eyes grew wide. 'Are they ...?'

'I baked them this morning. You said they were Louisa's favourite, so I thought I'd make some for her. She seemed happy when I gave them to her.'

'I'll bet she did.' He sat down next to her. 'That was incredibly kind of you, Lexi.' He looked at her with such sincerity she had to look away.

She opened the container and offered him one. 'Want one?'

'Hell, yes.'

They sat side by side on the blanket watching the sea, eating their picnic in companionable silence.

His lordship was quite a conundrum, she decided. One minute he was trying to scam his sister, the next he was caring for her. He loved animals, didn't eat the fish he caught, and he was generous and fun. It was just as well he was a liar, or she might have fallen for him. And what a disaster that would be.

She finished her roll and wiped her fingers. 'Tell me about your sisters.'

He gave her a quizzical look. 'Why?'

She drank a mouthful of smoothie. 'I'm still trying to work you out. I figured it might help if I knew about your family.'

He shrugged. 'What can I say? They're both outgoing and sociable, they're loyal and they're smart. They were good at sports when they were young and they both still enjoy horse-riding. More than anything, they're both incredibly resilient.'

She unpeeled her banana. 'In what way?'

He seemed to consider this. 'Growing up in a remote castle isn't the fairy tale some might imagine. It can be brutal. Especially in winter.'

When nothing more was forthcoming, she asked, 'What do they do? For a living, I mean.'

'Louisa runs Rubha Castle. She also works for an animal charity. She heads up their fundraising activities. It involves a lot of people interaction, which she's very good at, and public speaking, which she excels at. She's very adept at persuading rich people to part with their money.'

'A handy trait to have.'

He finished his brownie, eyeing up hers surreptitiously.

She moved it out of reach. 'Don't even think about it.'

'Worth a try.' He smiled. 'Sophie's equally clever, although she uses her skills to different effect. She writes a weekly blog for various fashion and lifestyle magazines. She also coerces people into doing what she wants, but instead of extracting money, it's gossip she's after. I don't know how she does it. She's been socialising with the same crowd for so long you'd think they'd have wised up by now. But once the champagne starts flowing and she lays on the charm, they spill.'

'Sounds like you're very proud of them.'

He took a swig of water. 'They've overcome a lot.'

She nibbled on her brownie. 'You're obviously close.'

He turned to look at her. 'Why do you say that?'

'The way you all bicker. It reminds me of my sister and me. We argue, disagree, annoy the hell out of each other, but there isn't anyone I trust more.'

'You have chocolate on your lip.'

She licked her lip. 'Gone?'

His eyes lingered a little too long on her mouth.

She cleared her throat. 'What about your parents? I'm sensing from what you said yesterday there was a falling out of some kind.'

'You could say that.'

'What happened? If you don't mind me asking.'

He took another mouthful of water before answering. 'The short version is that I left home at eighteen and didn't return for eleven years.'

Wow. 'And the long version?'

He sighed. 'It's complicated. Let's just say, it spawned from years of disagreements and not being the dutiful son they

159

wanted me to be. How I saw my life panning out didn't match the life they had planned for me. They refused to see things from my perspective and I couldn't agree to their demands. In the end, my father gave me an ultimatum. Back down or leave. So I left. After that, my parents disowned me. I never saw them again.'

There was such agony in his expression it broke her heart. She offered him the last bite of brownie, but he shook his head. 'What about your sisters? How did they feel about you leaving?'

'Louisa came to visit me a few times. Tried to persuade me to come home, but I always refused.'

'Why?'

He shrugged. 'Stubbornness, I guess. Shame, too.'

For a moment, she couldn't speak. The anguish on his face was hard to watch. 'That's such a sad story.' She reached over and squeezed his hand. 'I'm sorry.'

It was an impulse reaction to reach out and touch him. And if her guard hadn't been lowered by his heart-breaking confession, her sensible inner self would have alerted her to the danger of touching him. But it was too late. It was probably the relief of discovering he wasn't an ex-con.

His eyes remained fixed on the sea, but his fingers slid between hers and he held her hand so tightly she could feel the pulse in his wrist. She ignored the rise in her own pulse and returned to staring at the sea – it was safer than looking at the troubled man next to her.

Chapter 12

Later that day ...

It was gone seven by the time they left the beach at Red Point. Even then it had been with some reluctance. There was something magical about watching the sky fade from pale blue to orange, to mauve, while listening to the rhythmical sound of the waves caressing the sand. Lexi had fallen asleep next to him, lulled into slumber by the tranquillity of the secluded beach.

He'd been content to lie next to her, absorbed by his own thoughts, switching from enjoying the views around him to enjoying the one next to him. There was no escaping his attraction. Lexi wasn't his usual type. Did he even have a type? He'd never stayed in one place long enough to find out. He'd resisted forming any attachments – long-term relationships weren't conducive to travelling – but perhaps it was like his mother had said. If he let his guard down the truth would emerge. And there was no way he could risk that.

When Lexi stirred, she was shocked to discover she'd been asleep for over two hours. She blushed, straightened her clothes and smoothed down her hair, suddenly self-conscious.

He understood that. There was something intimate about sleeping in front of another person. The ultimate lowering of a protective barrier. He could have teased her about the cute noises she'd made while sleeping, or how she'd cradled her hands close to her chest, but he didn't want to embarrass her further.

Instead, they packed up and headed to the boat. The temperature had dropped, so he dug out a blanket for her to wrap herself in while they sailed along the blustery coastline.

The sea was choppy, sending up sprays of water, making it hard to keep the boat steady. Thankfully, it wasn't a long journey.

'This isn't Shieldaig,' she said when they pulled into Port Henderson.

'It's Gairloch,' he said, jumping onto the jetty and dragging the boat closer to its mooring. 'The boat belongs to a friend. I borrowed it for the day.'

She looked concerned. 'How will we get back to Shieldaig?'

He helped her off the boat. 'My Vespa.'

Her eyes grew wide. 'And I thought the tractor ride was risky.'

'I'll call you a taxi if you want.' He secured the tarpaulin flaps and joined her on the walkway.

She seemed to consider this. 'That's okay. I'm learning to live dangerously.'

He smiled. 'Hungry?'

'Starving.'

'There's a great pub up the road, but I need to drop the boat keys back first.' He showed her where the pub was and promised to join her when he'd finished dealing with the boat.

He arrived at The Badachro Inn fifteen minutes later. Lexi had found a table by the open fire and was drinking a glass of ale. 'You're on the beer?'

Her cheeks were rosy from the fire and she'd unbuttoned her retro pink top, revealing a white vest top underneath. 'I ordered prosecco, but the barmaid persuaded me to try this. No idea how you pronounce it.' She pointed to the label. 'I ordered you one, too.'

'It's called An Teallach. It's brewed locally. Do you like it?'

She nodded. 'But I'll need to eat soon or you'll be carrying me home unconscious.'

He laughed. 'That'll make the journey interesting.' He picked up his ale and clinked glasses with her. 'Cheers.'

'Cheers. Thanks for a lovely day.'

'My pleasure.' He sipped his ale. 'It's not over yet.'

She rolled her eyes. 'Ah, yes. The excitement of riding pillion on a Vespa.'

'Ever ridden a motorbike before?'

'God, no.' She studied the menu. 'This trip is opening me up to a whole new world of transportation.'

The barmaid came over and took their orders. He opted for pan-fried scallops. Lexi ordered the tarka dhal.

When the barmaid disappeared, she relaxed against the padded bench seat. 'I'm curious,' she said, studying him like he was an interesting art subject. 'You said you left home at eighteen and went travelling for eleven years.'

'That's right.'

'How did you finance the trip? If you don't mind me asking.'

He took a swig of ale. 'I did some bar work, fruit picking, a few temp jobs. But mainly I used my inheritance. My grandfather left us a lump sum in his will. I don't think he envisaged me using it to run off. I know my parents didn't approve of me squandering it by "wandering the planet", as they called it, but I don't regret it. I've lived in some amazing places and met some wonderful people.'

And it wasn't like he'd had a choice. Staying in the UK hadn't been an option.

She sipped her ale. 'Where did you travel to?'

'I started off in America, bought a beaten-up 1975 Chevrolet

163

Camaro and worked my way along the East Coast from Boston to Miami. I stopped off for a few months in New York, but when my visa expired, I headed to South America.'

She looked wistful. 'I've always wanted to visit South America. What's it like?'

He knocked back a mouthful of ale. 'Depends where you go. Like anywhere, it has its beauty, but it also has areas of severe deprivation. I spent a year in Colombia. Bogotá's a modern city, cosmopolitan and business-focused. Cartagena's a historic walled city steeped in tradition and culture. And then there's Magdalena, areas of which have poor sanitation, low school attendance and high child mortality rates.' He took another swig of ale, remembering some of the horrors he'd witnessed. 'I worked in a school there.'

The barmaid arrived with their food. Lexi waited until they were alone again. 'What did you do in the school?'

'Taught English mainly. That and removed snakes from the classroom each morning.'

She flinched. 'Did you ever get bitten?'

'Not by a snake. I did get stung by a scorpion in Botswana.'

'You've been to Africa?' Her expression was a mixture of wonderment and envy. 'You've certainly seen more of the world than I have.'

'It's never too late.'

Her expression turned regretful. He wondered what her story was. He knew she was a successful businesswoman, but her private life didn't sound overly happy. Did that make her a kindred spirit? Or an emotional car crash best avoided? He wasn't sure.

She ate some of her dhal. Her expression switched to one of pure bliss. She certainly liked her food. A definite plus in her favour.

'Good?'

'Delicious.' She tucked in, smiling as she ate.

It was nice to have company. He'd never divulge all his shameful secrets, but it was good to relax. Something he couldn't do with Sophie or Louisa. Not completely, anyway.

They chatted while they ate their food. She asked more about his travels, genuinely interested, so he told her about teaching in Vietnam, fruit picking in Australia and working on a commune in Goa. He told her about visiting Angel Falls in Venezuela and getting stranded for three days in the rainforest. All the while, she listened intently, seemingly fascinated.

When they'd finished eating, the barmaid removed their empty plates.

'There's one thing that puzzles me,' she said, settling back to enjoy the open fire. 'The way you talk about your travels makes it sounds like the opportunity of a lifetime.'

He knew what was coming next.

'And yet, it wasn't enough, was it?'

He tilted his head to one side. 'Why do you say that?'

She chewed her lower lip. 'Well, you didn't leave through choice, did you? So although you've made the best of it, there's a sadness behind the story that you cover with humour. You talk about being free and the joys of travelling the world, but when no one's watching you look troubled.'

She was astute, he'd give her that. 'Been watching me, have you?'

She raised an eyebrow. 'Which just proves my point.'

'What can I say? No one said life was easy. Whether you're travelling the world, or stuck in an office all day. Shit happens.' It was time to change topic before she delved any deeper. He didn't want to lie to her. Well, any more than he had to. 'Ready for another adventure?'

She sighed. 'As I'll ever be.'

It was dusk outside but not fully dark. That was the beauty of living so far north. They walked down the lane to where his Vespa was parked. He unlocked the security chain and handed her his open-faced helmet.

'What are you going to wear?'

'There isn't much traffic this time of night. I'll be fine.'

'But it's illegal.' She looked horrified.

He grinned. 'Haven't you ever broken the law?'

'Of course not.' Her left eye started twitching.

He laughed and lifted the seat. 'Put your rucksack inside, little Miss Innocence.'

'I don't know what you mean?'

He helped her on with the helmet. 'I mean, never play poker. You'll lose badly.'

Her cheeks coloured.

He secured the strap and lowered the visor. She looked cute with her hair squashed inside the helmet. 'Ready?'

'Not really.'

He switched on the ignition and kicked the start lever. 'Climb on,' he said, straddling the Vespa.

She lifted her leg over. 'Don't drive too fast.'

'It's a scooter, not a superbike.' He turned to smile at her. 'Hold tight and lean into the bends, okay?'

'I'll try.'

Her arms tightened around him so tightly he could barely breathe. He considered asking her to loosen her grip but decided he quite liked being hugged, which spoke volumes about his lack of female company of late.

She squealed when he pulled away. They were barely doing ten miles an hour.

They headed away from Gairloch. He kept the speed below forty. Partly because of his nervous passenger, but also because he wasn't wearing a helmet.

The first couple of times he braked, she head-butted him, which hurt more than he let on. The lanes were quiet, winding and narrow. He was grateful for the lack of traffic. Especially as it was so dark. There were no streetlights in these parts.

By the time they rode through Kinlochewe, her grip had relaxed and he could breathe again. It was another forty minutes before they reached Rubha Castle. He didn't mind. He enjoyed the ride. It was a clear night, so the stars were visible. Scotland might not feel like home, but he loved this place more than any other he'd visited on the planet.

As they approached the bridge leading from the mainland to the castle, he slowed and parked up. He switched off the engine and flicked the stand down.

She lifted the visor. 'Why have we stopped?'

'It's your turn,' he said, getting off.

She did a comedy double-take. 'What? No way. I'll crash.'

'No, you won't. Move forwards on the seat. It's lesson time.'

She opened her mouth as if to protest but then sighed. 'Don't come crying to me if I kill us both.'

He placed her hands on the front levers. 'Your right hand controls the throttle and front brake. Use your left hand to change gear. Squeeze the clutch lever and twist the handle to engage first gear. As you release the clutch, slowly rotate the accelerator clockwise.'

'Which way is clockwise?'

'Seriously?'

She grinned.

'You had me worried there.' He started the engine and climbed on behind her. It was nice to hold her for a change. 'The rear brake pedal is on the floor by your right foot. Don't pull the front brake too hard or we'll go over the handlebars.'

'I can't believe I'm doing this.' She twisted to look at him. 'Suppose I crash into the loch?'

'Then we'll get wet again. You'll be okay. You don't have to negotiate any turns. Just ease the bike forwards and aim for the portcullis.' He kicked up the stand. 'Ready when you are.'

She was tentative at first, holding on to the clutch too long and not revving enough. The engine whined in protest, sounding like a strangulated wasp. When she realised her mistake, she twisted the accelerator and let go of the clutch. Consequently, the bike shot forwards. She squealed as she tried to control the bike.

'Less accelerator,' he shouted as they swerved, nearly hitting the wall.

She was laughing and shrieking, trying to control the bike.

'You're doing really well,' he lied.

'Look at me!' she yelled excitedly. 'Valentino Rossi!'

He didn't like to point out they were driving so slowly he could get off and overtake her on foot.

'You're a natural,' he shouted as the portcullis came into view. 'Now gently squeeze the brake.'

'Which one's the brake?'

Oh, hell. 'The lever on your right.'

She squeezed the accelerator. The wall loomed ahead.

'The right! Use the floor pedal!'

She yanked on both brakes, sending the bike into a skid.

He closed one eye and braced himself. Gravel sprayed up as they lurched forwards, the wheels spinning. With any luck, they'd end up in the loch rather than crashing into the wall. Either way, it was going to hurt. But she swerved at the last minute and the bike skidded to a stop. The Vespa's front wheel was an inch away from the portcullis.

There was a moment's silence before she said, 'Close enough?'

He burst out laughing. 'Christ, you've taken ten years off me,' he said, dismounting and helping her off.

She was smiling. She was also shaking. 'That was so much fun.' She lifted the visor. 'At least, I think it was.' The combination of nerves and adrenaline were clearly confusing her.

'Glad you enjoyed it.' He eased the bike onto its stand and removed her rucksack from under the seat.

'Thank you,' she said, trying to undo the helmet strap with shaking hands. 'That can't have been an easy ride for you.'

'Oh, I don't know.' He released the strap and carefully removed the helmet. 'Strangely, it was fun.'

He looked down at her glowing face. Her eyes were wide and her mouth was partially open. Something inside him dropped like a dead weight. She seemed to register the moment, too, and stilled. Silence hung in the air. The next thing he knew he was kissing her, fumbling her backwards into the south-west wing.

He dropped the rucksack at the bottom of the stairs, trying not to lose his mind as she clung to him. 'You liked riding the bike, then?' Engaging his brain in conversation might distract him from thinking about what he was doing. What *they* were doing – she was definitely joining in.

'I did,' she said, coming up for air. 'It was exhilarating.'

'Uh-huh.' He lifted her higher, manoeuvring her up the steps. 'Want to do it again?'

'God, yes.' Her teeth dragged across his earlobe. 'Frequently.'

He stumbled and fell against the steps.

'Who knew there was a biker chick waiting to be unleashed ... Oh, God, that's nice ... Maybe I'll join the Hell's Angels.'

He pulled back to look at her. 'Seriously?'

'No.' She slid her hands into his hair. 'Don't stop.'

He couldn't if he'd wanted to. Except the steps were rock hard and he didn't want to put his back out. 'We need a bed,' he said, pulling her upright. 'My room's closest.'

Somehow he managed to locate the door and bundle her through it.

'Part of me enjoys bending the rules,' she said.

'You don't say.'

'Is that bad?' She was driving him crazy with her tongue. 'Tell me I'm bad.'

'You're bad.' He kissed her, occupying her mouth in an effort to distract her.

'But what can I do?' She raked her nails down his back.

Christ! A few things sprung to mind.

'I should fight it.' She unhooked his belt, ripping it from his jeans in one lightning-quick motion. 'But not tonight.'

'No, not tonight.'

Definitely not tonight.

The sensation of her hands running over his chest drained the blood from his brain. 'I've wanted to do this ever since I stabbed you.'

He sucked in his breath. 'That could be the first time anyone's ever used that line to another human being.'

'You smell nice.' She kissed him again. 'I want you.'

He kicked off his trainers. 'I want you, too.'

He bounced her onto the bed. They rolled one way, then the other, their feet tangling in the bedding.

She twisted him onto his back, her eyes drugged with lust, her strength surprising as she pinned his hands above his head.

His kind of woman.

'But can I trust you?' She covered his mouth with hers before he could offer a suitable response.

To give his brain credit, it did its best to compute that last question, but it was hard to focus when a hot woman was kissing her way down his stomach, her hands deftly unbuttoning the fly on his jeans.

He tipped her off him, rolling over until she was under him. 'I told you, I'm a trustworthy guy.'

He was at the point of lowering her vest top, when something hard hit him across the shoulder blades. He jerked forwards, bumping heads with her. 'Shit! What was that?'

'*That's* for molesting my sister.' Another hit, across his bum this time. 'Get off her!'

He rolled over to see a woman wearing a sleeveless black PVC catsuit climbing onto the bed. Her expression turned from rage to full-blown fury. '*You* ...?' And then she grabbed the antique wooden shoehorn hanging above his bed and hit him across his stab wound with it.

Pain shot down his arm.

'Tasha, stop it!' Lexi wriggled out from under where he'd landed on top of her.

He grabbed the shoehorn, his brain registering that the woman beating the crap out of him was his landlady from the tattoo parlour. What the hell was she doing here?

'Don't think I don't know who you are, matey.' She wrestled control of the shoehorn. 'I know all about you.' A hard tug on the shoehorn sent her bouncing onto the mattress next to Lexi. 'You're the blue-eyed hooligan.' She kicked him in the leg with her stiletto-heeled boot.

Ouch! ... He was who?

'Tasha, please, it's not what you think.' Lexi grabbed the shoehorn. All three of them were now wrestling over it. 'He wasn't taking advantage of me. It was consensual.'

This was ridiculous. He'd fantasised many times over the idea of a three-way, but romping about the bed trying not to get impaled by a dominatrix brandishing an eighteenth-century antique hadn't ever featured in his desired role-play. Funny that.

When a knee narrowly missed connecting with his manhood, he'd had enough of playing it nice. Using the advantage of his weight, he pinned the woman to the bed, yanking the shoehorn from her hand. 'I don't know what the hell this has got to do with you, but ...'

He stilled.

He stared at her face before switching to look at Lexi. *No way.* He stared harder. Different hair colour. Different fashion sense. But ... He sat back on his haunches.

'Are you two ...?' He pointed from one to the other.

Lexi sighed and then nodded.

Crap! He jumped off the bed and landed on something soft.

A woman yelped and pushed him off her foot.

He spun around. *Jesus.* Was someone selling tickets?

Sophie stood in the doorway, looking daggers. 'What the fuck's going on?' She was wearing an overcoat and outdoor boots. She'd clearly just arrived. She pointed at the two women currently embroiled in a wrestling match on his bed. 'Who the hell are they?'

Great. He was most likely going to get thumped by his sister now.

But Lexi was too focused on her own sister to worry about his. 'Just for once, it would be nice if I could enjoy a bit of privacy without my sibling interfering.' She scrabbled off the bed, looking flustered, dishevelled and cute as hell. 'What are you even doing here?'

'Saving you from the likes of him.' Lexi's sister glared at him. 'My taxi pulled up just as you and the hooligan here were getting it on. I followed you inside. And just as well I did.'

Next to each other, the similarities were obvious. How the hell hadn't he spotted it before? But *twin* ...? 'I can't get my head around the fact that she's your *sister*?'

Tasha climbed off the bed, towering above her barefoot twin in killer heels. 'Not the sharpest tool in the shed, is he?'

Sophie stepped forwards. '*Oi*! No one slags off my brother except me.'

Lexi was about to respond, when she suddenly swung around to face him.

'Hang on a sec. How the hell do you two know each other?'

Tasha picked up the shoehorn from the floor. 'He was my lodger. He stayed with me for a couple nights last month.'

'Lodger?' Lexi turned to him, her anger switching target. 'So you *were* following me?'

Before he could defend himself, Tasha interrupted. 'Of course, if I'd known he was the blue-eyed hooligan who broke into the gallery and attacked you, I'd have chopped his balls off in his sleep.'

Olly covered his crotch.

Sophie rounded on him. 'You attacked her?'

He ignored Sophie and spoke to Lexi. 'Okay, for the record.' He pointed at Tasha. 'First, I had no idea you and Morticia Addams here were related—'

Tasha scoffed. 'Figures. Blind as well as stupid.'

Sophie stormed over. 'I'm warning you! Quit with the comments.'

Olly caught Sophie's arm, dragging her away before Round Two kicked off. 'And secondly, I didn't attack anyone.' He switched his glare to Lexi. 'I'm the one who got stabbed.' The words were out before he could stop them.

Sophie spun around to glare at Lexi. 'You stabbed my brother? You're a dead woman.'

Tasha blocked Sophie's path. 'Touch my sister and you'll die a—'

'... slow and painful death,' Olly cut in. 'Yeah, we get it. You're scary.' He rolled his eyes, but everyone was far too mad to take notice.

Sophie and Tasha were almost nose to nose. They were staring at each other like a pair of primed boxers about to step into the ring. Lexi tugged on her twin's arm. He did the same with Sophie. He'd experienced some strange things in his life. The last ten minutes were right up there.

And then Harry rushed into the room and said, 'Louisa's having the baby!'

Everyone stopped yelling.

All eyes turned to look at Harry, who was standing in the doorway holding a wet towel. 'Her waters have broken.'

Oh, hell.

Chapter 13

L exi woke with a jolt from another bad dream. Or rather, a horrific nightmare. She'd dreamt that her sister had shown up at Rubha Castle and attacked Olly with a shoehorn. Except it wasn't a dream, was it? Her sister really had done that.

Groaning, she rolled out of the four-poster bed and dragged herself into the shower. Maybe drowning herself would help to eradicate the humiliation of being sprung while 'getting it on' with his lordship. Talk about embarrassing.

The events of last night were still a blur. One minute everyone was arguing, the next Olly and Sophie were running from the room, reacting to the news that Louisa was having her baby. Mrs Jennings had arrived shortly after and offered to make up a room for Tasha, but her sister had declined and stormed out, leaving Lexi utterly confused and wondering how on earth things had deteriorated so quickly.

To say she was out of sorts this morning was an under-statement.

Needing to regain control, she chose her blue 1940s linen suit and matched it with her polka-dot shirt in an effort to feel more 'businesslike' and less like the kind of woman who'd seduce the man she was working for. She tied her hair up and sent Tasha a WhatsApp message suggesting they meet for breakfast at Nanny's café. Her sister was staying at the Tigh an Eilean Hotel in the village, so it was only a short walk.

Cataloguing the Wentworth art collection would have to wait. She wouldn't be able to concentrate until she knew why her sister was in Scotland. And there was no way she was having that conversation at the castle.

When she opened the bedroom door, Mrs Jennings almost fell into the room. Had she been eavesdropping?

The woman covered her guilt by straightening a picture on the wall. 'Morning, lassie. I hope you slept well. Quite a commotion last night, wasn't there? Will you be wanting breakfast?'

'No, thank you. I'm meeting my sister in the village.'

Mentioning Tasha piqued the housekeeper's curiosity. 'You should've warned me she was coming. I could've made up the guest room for her. But maybe you dinnae know she was visiting.' There was a questioning look in her eye, which Lexi ignored. She wasn't in the mood to fuel gossip. 'Not very alike, are you?'

There was little point enlightening her. Sometimes the truth was too far-fetched to believe. She left the bedroom and closed the door. 'Any news on Louisa?'

'She's had a wee boy. Five thirty this morning. His lordship sent me a text. "The alien has landed", he wrote. Cheeky blighter.'

Lexi smiled. 'I'm delighted for them.'

'They're calling the baby Oliver. A bonnie name, aye?'

Lexi forced a smile. 'Lovely. Now, if you'll excuse me, Gilly, I'd best be getting on.'

Gilly followed her down the corridor. 'Nothing as important as family, I always say. Perhaps you'd like a bairn of your own one day?'

So much for preventing gossip. News of her dalliance with

his lordship had already spread through the castle. 'My gallery's my main focus for now,' she said, speeding down the steps. 'See you later, Gilly.'

If she didn't need fresh air before, she did now. What had she been thinking kissing his lordship? Everyone knew, including the staff!

She walked across the bridge to the mainland, replaying the events of yesterday. There was no denying it had been a fun day. Picnicking on the beach had been both relaxing and enlightening. His lordship might be a charming rogue, but he had depth, too. Underneath the bluster and banter was a sensitive soul.

He was well-travelled, he had a social conscience and he liked to help others. He was bruised too, fragile even. She sensed there was an honest heart tucked away inside that lying, cheating chest of his ... But that was probably her hormones again, clouding her judgement.

More likely, she was a mug who'd been seduced by his 'woe-is-me' sob story, and was an idiot for trusting him to do anything other than break her heart and leave her penniless. After all, she'd trusted Marcus and look where that had got her?

As she walked alongside the rows of SUVs and caravans parked outside the holiday cottages, she watched two fish-ermen unloading their haul onto the jetty. A sign was propped against the boat. 'Today's Catch – Squat Lobster and Langoustine'. The smell of fresh fish filled the air, tickling her nose. And then she became aware of the sound of bagpipes in the distance. It was faint at first, but as she neared Nanny's she could see a piper standing outside the café dressed in the full kilted regalia. A crowd had gathered to watch.

She perched on a bench seat so she could listen, waiting

for Tasha to arrive. The music proved a good distraction – it was haunting and poetic.

Her sister showed up a few minutes later. Tasha's presence caused quite a stir. She was wearing a black top with a skull-and-crossbones design on the front, black trousers covered in zips and her stiletto buckled boots. A huge pair of black sunglasses masked her eyes. The sight was so intimidating that the piper lost composure and hit a bum note.

Tasha lowered her glasses and glared at him.

His bagpipes made a whining noise as they deflated.

Tasha often had that effect on men. Pushing her glasses back up her nose, she continued walking.

Lexi stood up. 'Morning, Tash. Sleep well?'

Her sister strode past and went into Nanny's. 'I need caffeine.'

Well, that answered that question.

Lexi followed. Why she felt guilty, she didn't know. It wasn't like she'd been expecting Tasha to show up last night. But she knew it had more to do with hooking up with unsuitable men.

Nanny's café was quaint and sunny. Wooden tables and red chairs were dotted about, creating a 'shabby-chic' look. A vase of bluebells decorated each table and the counter was filled with an array of baked goods, which looked amazing.

The café's popularity was evidenced by the packed tables, which was great for local trade but not so good when trying to keep a low profile. The patrons descended into silence when Tasha entered. Unsurprising, really. Her sister made quite an impact. She wasn't exactly dressed for a walking holiday.

All eyes watched them order breakfast.

Lexi felt the need to smile at everyone and wish them a

'good morning' as she and her sister searched for a table at the back of the café.

It was only when they were seated that Tasha removed her sunglasses. A waft of Valentino's Rock n' Rose Couture filled the air, mingling with the smells of baking. 'You've been avoiding me,' she said, resting her arms on the table. 'I tried calling you several times yesterday. You never picked up. Where were you?'

It was pointless to lie about what she'd been doing. 'I was fishing.'

'*Fishing?*' Anyone would think she'd said she'd been 'bludgeoning seals'. 'Why were you fishing? Actually, forget that. Who were you *fishing* with?'

'I think you know the answer to that.' She avoided eye contact. 'I went for a picnic, I bumped into Olly and he asked me if I'd like to join him. And I wasn't avoiding you, I didn't take my phone with me.' She shrugged. 'Not a lot more to add, really.'

Tasha looked incredulous. 'No, of course not, silly *moi*. Only the minor detail of how you went from *fishing* to hooking up with the blue-eyed hooligan. What were you thinking?'

'Well, I—'

'I don't know what I'm madder about. The fact that you're risking the commission on this job by messing about with your client, or that you got sucked in by another lying scumbag.'

Lexi flinched. 'I haven't been sucked in by anyone. And do you know how judgemental you sound? You don't even know Olly.'

'And you do?'

The waitress arrived with their breakfasts. Lexi and Tasha

179

simultaneously sat back in their chairs and faked a smile. The waitress looked warily between them before handing Tasha her bacon roll and Lexi her Scottish pancakes. 'I'll be back with your drinks.'

Lexi nodded. 'Thank you.'

Tasha squirted tomato ketchup on her roll. 'I'm not done arguing about this.'

Lexi squirted heather honey over her pancakes. 'I didn't think for a moment you would be.'

They glared at each other.

The waitress arrived with their drinks. 'How's your food?'

'Delicious,' they both said in unison.

The waitress looked mildly alarmed as she placed their drinks down, keeping her distance from Tasha. 'Let me know if you need anything.'

Lexi watched her go, realising that half the people in the café were also watching them. She subjected them to a beaming smile, waiting until they'd turned away before taking a mouthful of tea and hoping no one had heard their argument. It was a small village. Everyone was bound to know the Wentworths.

When it became clear showtime was over, the other patrons returned to enjoying their food. Relieved, Lexi devoured her breakfast, which was mouth-wateringly good.

They ate in silence. Not exactly companionable, but she wasn't in the mood for one of Tasha's interrogations. She was confused enough as it was. She hadn't meant to kiss Olly. It had just happened. Her guard had been lowered. Impeded by good food, homemade ale and hearing about his sad upbringing. Was it any wonder she'd been seduced?

She couldn't even blame Olly. Even before the scooter ride

she'd wanted to kiss him. Her resolve had disappeared when she'd nearly crashed his Vespa. Instead of being angry, he'd laughed. All restraint had melted away and she'd practically thrown herself at him.

Tasha was frowning. 'What's wrong?'

Lexi looked up, surprised. 'Nothing's wrong.'

'Why did you groan?'

She'd groaned? 'No reason.' She finished her pancakes. 'Are you going to tell me why you're in Scotland?'

Tasha took a swig of black coffee and then wiped a smudge of purple lipstick from the rim. 'I told you why. I couldn't get hold of you yesterday. I was worried.'

'So you came all the way to Scotland just to check I was okay? You expect me to believe that?'

Tasha shrugged. 'I needed to speak to you about Marcus.'

'What about him?'

'I haven't been able to track him down.'

'I already knew that.'

'Or the painting.'

'I knew that, too.'

Tasha folded her arms. 'I've had the locks changed on the gallery.'

'For which I'm very grateful, but again, something I already knew. It still doesn't explain why you've travelled all this way.' She reached across for her sister's hand. 'What aren't you telling me?'

Tasha looked away. 'You're going to hate me.'

'Not possible. You're my sister. I love you.'

'I've done something bad.'

Oh, hell. It must be awful if Tasha thought it was bad. 'How bad?'

'*Really* bad.'

'Tasha, you're scaring me. What have you done?'

There was a pause before she answered. 'It was me who reported Marcus to HMRC.'

For a moment, everything around Lexi stilled. All sound disappeared. And then a burst of laughter filled the air, breaking the moment. A group of hikers had entered the café, chatting animatedly.

Lexi pulled her hand away. 'What do you mean, it was you?'

Tasha fiddled with her chunky onyx ring. 'I was scared for you. I could see Marcus was up to no good, but you didn't want to see it.'

'And you think that justifies reporting him?'

Tasha shook her head, making her black bob sway. 'No, but every time he did something shady you found a reason to justify his behaviour. He'd stay out all night and you'd believe his lies about working late. He'd disappear for weekends and feed you a load of bullshit about trying to find investors for the business and you'd shrug it off. Lie after lie. Everyone at the garage knew he was cheating on you with Cindy, but you refused to believe it.'

Lexi couldn't believe what she was hearing.

Tasha twisted her ring as if trying to unscrew her finger. 'I tried talking to you about it, but you weren't ready to accept the truth. I waited, hoping you'd finally realise what he was doing. But even when your car was towed away you assumed there was a legitimate business reason, even though debt collectors were turning up at your home.'

There was a smidgeon of truth in what Tasha was saying. She hadn't wanted to believe Marcus was scamming her. No wife wants to believe that about their husband. 'That still doesn't justify you reporting him.'

'And then he stole the money from the sale of your Franz Gerste collection. That's when I knew I had to do something to get him out of your life.'

'But that was my decision to make, Tasha. Not yours.' She yanked her hand away when Tasha tried to take it.

'But he was using you, Lexi. He *stole* from you. He was dragging you down with him. I couldn't stand back and let that happen.'

'So you did something that jeopardised my entire livelihood.'

Tasha's expression switched to anguish. 'That's the bit I regret. I swear to God, Lexi, I had no idea the business wasn't limited and you'd be jointly liable for the debts. I never would've reported him if I'd known.'

'Is that supposed to make it okay?'

'It's not enough, I know.'

'You're damned right, it's not.' She banged the table, making her sister flinch. A few patrons glanced over, but she was too angry to stop. 'I don't care about the house and possessions, that's just stuff. But I nearly lost my gallery, Tasha. Our grandmother's legacy.'

Tears pooled in her sister's eyes. 'I know.'

'That gallery means everything to me.'

'I know.' Tasha wiped her eyes, smudging her black eyeliner. 'I'm so sorry, Lexi. But I saw how much he hurt you and I wanted to hurt him. I wanted to make him pay.'

Lexi rubbed her hands; they were clammy and shaking. 'Is that why you've been so hell-bent on tracking Marcus down? Because of a guilty conscience.'

Tasha stared at the table. 'I was desperate to make up for what I'd done. I thought if I got your painting back it might help.'

'You think that makes up for lying to me? Betraying me?'

Tasha flinched.

'All this time you've watched me suffer and the whole time it was you who sparked the investigation.'

Black watery tears ran down Tasha's cheeks. 'I hate what I've done. But I couldn't keep lying, I had to tell you.' Her thick lashes were wet with tears.

It was obvious Tasha was mortified. And Lexi knew she should assure her sister that everything would be okay and they'd get past this, but the words wouldn't come.

She was a hypocrite, she knew that. She was furious with Tasha for lying, but she'd lied, too. She'd never told Tasha about taking the twenty-seven grand. Her sister had no idea the *Woman at the Window* was the original and not a copy. She should confess to what she'd done. But she was too angry. Too hurt by her sister's confession.

But the main reason she didn't want to confess was because admitting she'd also lied would ease her sister's guilt. The tables would turn and Tasha would be as disappointed in her as she was with her sister. And she wasn't ready to let go of her anger. Not yet.

She got up. 'I need to be alone.'

'Lexi, please—'

She walked out of Nanny's, leaving her sister in tears.

Lexi's vision started to blur. Her chest felt tight and she felt sick. It was the same feeling she'd experienced the night she'd discovered Marcus's letter telling her what he'd done.

It was the feeling of betrayal.

Chapter 14

Thursday 14th June

Olly shifted his weight, his leg numb from being squashed in the window seat for so long. He'd officially been left 'holding the baby' while Louisa and Harry had their much-needed heart-to-heart. The last three days had been stressful. Everyone's emotions had been heightened, his included. And now, with a new addition to the family, the dynamics had changed again and they were all trying to adjust.

None of them had slept much since returning from the hospital on Tuesday evening, which was par for the course where a new baby was concerned. Although he hadn't realised it would affect him quite so much. He was just the uncle.

It had started Sunday evening. One moment he'd been rolling about on his bed undressing Lexi, the next he'd been physically attacked by her sister and verbally attacked by his. He'd then found himself hurtling towards the Broadford Hospital on his Vespa, where he'd spent the next ten hours pacing corridors, waiting and stressing.

Having been admitted to the delivery suite, Louisa had requested a range of homeopathic remedies all designed to ease the pain of labour. When nothing had worked, she'd resorted to hard drugs and screaming at her husband. *This is your fault*,' she'd bellowed at Harry. '*You're never touching me again!*'

Olly had exchanged a horrified look with his sister Sophie,

relieved to be waiting in the corridor and not inside the delivery suite.

Finally, at five twenty-seven a.m. the following morning, they were ushered inside to meet the latest member of the Wentworth family. Louisa's screaming had been replaced by the sound of collective crying. First Harry, stroking his wife's forehead and telling her how amazing she was. Then Louisa, blubbing that she was finally 'a mummy'. Even the normally stoic Sophie was wiping her face and trying her best to rein it in.

He'd been the only one holding it together. Until the midwife had held up the tiny bundle. At which point he'd joined in the crying, too.

The midwife had placed a writhing Oliver junior on Louisa's chest. His sister's tears were mixed with laughter as she'd apologised to Harry for all the abusive names she'd called him. Harry hadn't seemed to mind.

But since arriving home, Louisa's fragile mental state had been exposed and she was no longer able to hide the truth from her husband. The guilt she'd felt at not enjoying pregnancy had been replaced by utter joy at finally having a baby. Thankfully, she was totally smitten with her son. It was Harry's turn to feel guilty. He hadn't realised the extent of his wife's unhappiness. So this morning he'd insisted on treating Louisa to chocolate brownies at Nanny's so they could clear the air without being interrupted by their screaming son.

Olly had been assigned the role of babysitter. A job that hadn't been high on his agenda when he'd returned to Rubha Castle, but Louisa had had other ideas.

'It's a skill you might need yourself one day,' she'd said when he'd queried the need to perfect the art of nappy changing.

He felt this was unlikely, seeing as the only woman he'd ever come close to feeling serious about was currently avoiding him.

Baby Olly made a noise, indicating he needed more space. Grown-up Olly knew the feeling and shuffled out of the window seat.

Adjusting his nephew in his arms, he wandered around the art room. It was one of the few rooms in the castle he felt comfortable in, despite its painful connotations. The second-hand canvases he'd picked up from the junk shop were propped against the easel, partly covered in his efforts to paint his grandfather's portrait and hidden beneath a dustsheet.

Having lied about knowing nothing about art, he didn't want Lexi to see them and realise he'd told yet another fib. His brushes were soaking in jars and the faint smell of turpentine hung in the air, but there was nothing he could do about that. And besides, it was a comforting smell. A reminder of how important art was to him. He'd missed painting.

This realisation had enabled him to reach a decision about his future. He could either stay angry with his parents and never paint again, or let go of his resentment and build a new life for himself. It hadn't been a difficult choice.

Baby Olly fidgeted in his arms. His nephew was a demanding little bugger. But big Olly was grateful. If nothing else, his namesake was providing a much-needed diversion from thinking about the events of the last few days. Particularly, what had happened with Lexi.

He paced the room, trying to pacify the little guy squirming in his arms.

The same question kept playing on his mind. What would have happened if they hadn't been interrupted and Louisa hadn't gone into labour? Would they have spent the night together? Would their casual hook-up have developed into something more? Or would she have regretted letting things escalate? One thing was certain: things couldn't be anymore awkward than they currently were.

Footsteps in the hallway alerted him to the arrival of company. The ancient door swung open and Sophie marched in. Oh, good. Just what he needed. Another bollocking.

She looked her usual styled self, wearing a floaty wrap-around dress. Her blonde hair was loose and shone like something from a shampoo advert. Only Sophie could weather the effects of three days with little sleep and still look like she'd stepped out of *Vogue* magazine.

'He's due for a feed,' she said, walking across the room, her jewelled flip-flops slapping against the wooden flooring. 'I've warmed it as per Louisa's instructions.' She handed him a bottle of expressed milk and then moved away, clearly unwilling to be lumbered with the task.

'I don't think he's hungry,' he said, trying out the soft teat against the baby's lips. Like a Venus flytrap, his nephew's mouth was around the rubber and suckling before he'd even tilted the bottle. 'Okay, what do I know?'

Sophie lifted the dustsheet and looked at the canvases he'd been working on. 'You're painting again?' There was a hint of accusation in her tone.

He angled the bottle higher. His nephew had inherited his ability to down a pint in seconds. 'Is there a problem?'

Sophie glanced over. 'Of course there's a problem.'

'Why's that?' He kept his focus on his nephew.

'Because it pisses me off.' She dropped the dustsheet and turned to face him. 'You disappear for eleven years leaving us to deal with our parents, and when the conflict's over, you swan back in like the prodigal son and pick up where you left off like nothing's happened. You have no idea the shit Louisa and I had to endure while you were exploring the world.'

She was right, he didn't. But if she thought he'd had an easy time of it, then she was mistaken. Except, he couldn't tell her that, could he?

She walked over. 'It was easier when you weren't here. I could hate you without feeling conflicted.'

He flinched. 'Sorry.'

'So you keep saying. I've yet to see any evidence you mean it.'

Her comment stung. 'I'm trying, Soph. But nothing I do is good enough. Tell me what you want me to do.'

She folded her arms. 'Not messing around with the woman paid to value our art collection would be a start.'

He had no defence there.

'And what was that nonsense about you breaking into her gallery and getting stabbed?'

He focused on feeding the baby. 'A misunderstanding.'

'Bollocks. More likely another example of us trying to deal with the family's estate and you messing it up. Do you have any idea what a tabloid would make of this? We'd be a laughing stock. Can you imagine the headline? The Earl of Horsley caught with his pants down.'

He hadn't thought of that. He'd been too focused on preventing the Spinelli scandal hitting the papers to worry about his own behaviour.

Sophie stood over him, unnervingly like his mother used to do, wearing an equally disappointed expression. 'You say you want to make amends, but all I see are more examples of your selfish, destructive behaviour.'

He glanced up. 'Do you want me to leave?' The idea of leaving filled him with dread. But if he was making things worse by staying then he had no choice. 'I'll go, if that's what you want.'

She let out a long breath. 'Like I'd do that to Louisa. She's been through enough.'

He wished Sophie wanted him to stay for her own sake, but she wasn't ready to forgive him. Could he blame her? Still, it was up to him to change her opinion of him. He couldn't change the past, but he could make the future better. For all of them.

She perched on the arm of the battered Edwardian sofa. 'Why is her sister here?'

'Tasha?' He shrugged. 'No idea.'

She crossed her legs. 'What do you know about her?'

'Not a lot. Other than she runs a tattoo parlour in Windsor.' And could do a lot of damage with a shoehorn.

'Windsor?' Sophie stood so quickly she knocked his arm, jerking the bottle from Baby Olly's mouth.

His nephew protested at having his tea interrupted.

'Jesus, calm down. You're hardly likely to bump into her, are you? I imagine you socialise in very different circles.'

Sophie paced the room, deep in thought. Her hair swung behind her like a river. It didn't surprise him that she'd been voted one of the country's fifty most eligible women a few years back. But if any man had won her heart, Olly had yet to know about it. Whoever they were, they'd need a strong constitution.

He resumed feeding his nephew. 'Have you thought anymore about which property we should sell?'

'There is no *we*,' she snapped. 'This is between Louisa and me. You gave up your right to have a say when you buggered off.'

She went over to the window and gazed out, her posture rigid and closed, like she was fighting to keep control. Not for the first time, he wondered what she was hiding.

As siblings, they were very different, but the one commonality they shared was the ability to pretend. He knew deep down Sophie's anger wasn't only about him. There was more going on. But what? A lack of love? Depression? Work issues? Whatever it was, it was eating away at her, just as keeping his parents' secret was eating away at him.

She rested her head against the glass. 'There's nothing to think about. Selling Rubha Castle is the logical decision. It costs ten times more than the Windsor townhouse to maintain. Not to mention the difference in resale value. We could live off the proceeds of this place for the rest of our lives. Selling the Windsor property would barely cover his upbringing.' She pointed at her nephew.

'But it's not that straightforward, is it?' Olly realised the bottle was empty. 'There's also our heritage to consider.' He eased his nephew onto his shoulder and rubbed his back.

Sophie looked incredulous. 'Don't you dare throw that in my face. You have no right to talk about our heritage.'

He stopped patting. 'Maybe not, but Louisa does.'

'You're taking Louisa's side?'

'Only because she's not up to taking you on right now.'

Baby Olly burped, reminding big Olly to continue rubbing.

Sophie snatched a paintbrush and pointed it at him. 'Are you accusing me of being a bully?'

Heaven forbid. 'You're quite a formidable opponent.'

She tapped the brush against her palm like a riding crop. 'Like I've ever managed to persuade Louisa to do something she doesn't want to do. I'm not the only stubborn one in this family.' She marched over and smacked his thigh with the brush. 'And while we're on the subject of money, when are you going to get a job? We're not bankrolling you for the rest of our lives, Olly.'

'I don't expect you to.' Although what the hell he was going to do, he didn't know. His CV wasn't exactly impressive. 'But this isn't about me, it's about you two. If funds weren't an issue, which property would you sell?'

'Neither.'

'But if you had to sell one?'

She threw her arms in the air. 'There's no point wasting time thinking about it, because money *is* an issue. And the sooner you both accept that, the better.'

He stopped rubbing his nephew's back. 'You're not going to mention this to Louisa, are you? Not while she's still fragile.'

Sophie glared at him. 'No, Olly, I'm not. Because unlike you, I know how to honour a promise.'

He flinched. She had him there.

The door swung open. Lexi's sister stood in the doorway, looking at odds with her medieval surroundings. She was wearing a black velour top and purple miniskirt covered with leather straps. Spiderweb earrings hung below her asymmetric bob and her long, toned legs were visible beneath fishnet tights. Her buckled stiletto boots brought back memories of Sunday night and nearly being impaled by one. He felt his manhood recoil.

Never one to be intimidated, Sophie drew herself up to her full height. 'Can we help you?'

Tasha walked into the room. 'I'm looking for my sister. Your housekeeper said to try in here.'

Sophie glided over. 'As you can see, she isn't here.'

'Do you know where she is?'

'No.'

Tasha switched focus to Olly. 'Do you know where Lexi is?'

Sophie stepped in front of her. 'No, he doesn't.'

Tasha raised an eyebrow. 'Can't he answer for himself?'

'I'm answering for him.' Sophie nodded at the door. 'That's your cue to leave.'

Tasha held her ground. 'Not very friendly, are you?'

'Not towards everyone, no.'

'I don't know what your problem is, but it was your brother who broke into my sister's gallery.'

'And it was your sister who stabbed him.'

Tasha took a step closer. 'Maybe he deserved it.'

Sophie also took a step closer. 'And maybe we should reconsider our choice of gallery for dealing with the family's estate.'

Olly wasn't sure what would have happened if Lexi hadn't appeared in the doorway. She looked startled when she saw Tasha and Sophie nose-to-nose. 'Tasha? What are you doing?' She raced over and tugged on her sister's arm. 'Stop that.'

Tasha's eyes remained locked on Sophie's. 'I was looking for you.'

Sophie wasn't backing down, either. 'And now you've found her.'

Lexi glanced over, looking for an ally.

Olly smiled, offering his support. In truth, he couldn't help smiling. She was wearing a cherry-patterned summer dress with red ballet pumps. She looked adorable.

Her eyes dipped to the bundle in his arms and she half-smiled before seeming to shake herself free from the sight of a man cradling a baby.

'I'm sorry,' she said, reverting to business mode. 'I had no idea my sister was here.' She pushed Tasha towards the doorway. 'We won't disturb you any further.'

Tasha turned back when she reached the door. 'It was a pleasure chatting to you,' she said, her tone dripping with sarcasm.

Sophie's hands went to her hips. 'Oh, the pleasure was all mine.'

Olly wanted to laugh, until he glanced down and realised he had sick all over his T-shirt. He stared at his nephew. 'You know, it's just as well I like you.'

Chapter 15

Monday 18th June

Lexi buttoned up her navy cardigan, shivering in her denim pedal pushers and red ballet pumps. It was cold in the banqueting hall. The mist had rolled down from the mountaintops and was hovering above the loch like a mass of cobwebs. The view from the castle, normally so bright and beautiful, looked miserable and spooky this morning. No less impressive but imposing for a different reason.

The morose weather matched her mood. She was feeling unsettled from arguing with Tasha. It had been a week since they'd fallen out. Tasha had spent the first three days trying to apologise, turning up at the castle every morning only for Lexi to turn her away repeatedly.

But when Tasha hadn't shown up last Friday, Lexi realised she'd been too hard on her sister. It was her own guilt she had a problem with, not Tasha's. So she'd headed into the village, intending to confess about taking the twenty-seven grand – only to discover Tasha had checked out of her hotel and returned to Windsor.

Lexi had left numerous messages asking Tasha to contact her, but it was radio silence. She'd called Mel in desperation. Her assistant had assured her the gallery was fine and so was Tasha. Which should have made her feel better but didn't. They'd never gone this long without talking. No matter what

195

had happened in their lives, they'd always stuck together. She felt sick at the thought of not having Tasha in her life.

She removed her glasses and wiped away tears. Her eyes were scratchy from a lack of sleep. So much for thinking her insomnia was cured.

She lifted the lid on the Tupperware container and removed a homemade Chelsea bun. She was almost done cataloguing the Wentworth art collection. The exhibition was scheduled for this Friday. This time next week she'd be back in Windsor, where she could hopefully make up with Tasha, sort her life out and work out how the hell she was going to pay off the official receiver.

She rubbed her chest, hit by a sudden pang. She'd be sad to leave Scotland. Olly, too. However much she distrusted him, she couldn't help liking him. It wasn't logical, or sensible. And maybe Tasha was right. Perhaps she did have a weakness for unsuitable men. But that didn't make walking away from him any easier. He'd brought some much-needed laughter to her life and stopped her stressing over the future of her gallery. And for that, she would be eternally grateful.

She continued updating her spreadsheet, when an email popped into her inbox advertising an auction at Sotheby's in Edinburgh next week: Renaissance Masters – Copies of the Greats. She was about to close it, when she noticed one of the listings. The unattributed *Woman at the Window*. The seller was Mr M. Aldridge.

Lexi stared at the screen. He wouldn't?

She clicked on the details. It was her painting. Bloody Marcus! He hadn't hung around, had he?

Trying to stem the panic coursing through her, she got up and began pacing, her ballet pumps slipping off the tartan rug. He was selling her precious painting? *Bastard*. Like he

196

hadn't hurt her enough? She wanted to scream. She wanted to do more than scream, but losing the plot wouldn't help. She needed to think.

God, she wished Tasha was here.

Two Chelsea buns later, she arrived at the conclusion that there were only two viable options: go to the police with the paperwork proving she was the rightful owner, or get the painting back before the auction.

If she went to the police, she'd have to explain why she'd never reported it stolen. Which might lead to questions about where she'd got the money to pay for it. The painting would be confiscated, she'd be charged with theft and her professional reputation would be ruined. But at least the official receiver would get his money. Marcus would be punished for his crimes and this whole sorry mess would be over.

A bang made her jump.

She turned to see Louisa wheeling into the room, her broken leg still in an orthopaedic boot. She was wearing a padded body warmer with a blanket draped over her knees, Baby Olly asleep in her lap.

'Need a hand?' Louisa asked.

Lexi helped her through the doorway. 'There's not much more to do. I'm sending the catalogue details to the printers today and I need to finalise the buffet details with Gilly, but other than that we're good to go.'

'It's freezing in here. Don't you want the fire on?'

'I'm okay,' she lied, not wanting to put Louisa out. 'How's motherhood?'

'Exhausting,' she said, beaming. Her hair was freshly styled and her cheeks were glowing. Motherhood suited her. 'I've barely slept and my boobs hurt.'

Lexi laughed. 'Sounds idyllic.'

'He's worth it.' Louisa stared down at her sleeping son, her face a picture of love. 'I'll be glad to get out of this chair. It's driving me crazy. Are you sure there's nothing I can do to help?'

'I don't think so.' She picked up her to-do list from the table. 'Oh, there is one thing. Your cousin, Tom.'

Louisa frowned. 'Tom? What about him?'

'I wondered if he'd been located yet.'

Louisa lifted an eyebrow. 'I didn't know he was missing.'

'Oh, he's not. At least, I hope not. It's just that Olly said he was uncontactable right now. There's no phone or internet connection where he is.'

Louisa looked confused. 'What, in Brighton?'

'Isn't he in India?'

'India?' Louisa looked startled.

It was as she'd thought. Olly was up to something. She decided to dig a little deeper. 'I was hoping to persuade him to exhibit his work along with your mother's this Friday. I appreciate your cousin's a recluse, but I really feel taking the opportunity to show samples of his work will attract considerable interest. If you do manage to get hold of him, maybe you could ask him to contact me. I truly believe he has a promising career ahead of him. He's extremely talented.'

Louisa shook her head. 'I'm sorry, you've lost me.'

'I spoke to Olly about it. Didn't he mention it?'

'He didn't say a word.'

'Oh ... Well, I found a box of preliminary works in the billeting room. Copies of the masters but with a contemporary twist. I'd like permission to display them. Olly said he'd speak to Tom and try to persuade him.'

Louisa's confusion hadn't lifted. 'What's it got to do with Tom?'

'He's the artist. I need his permission to exhibit the work.'

Louisa laughed. 'Tom doesn't paint.' And then she frowned. 'At least, not to my knowledge.'

'So who painted the sketches? They're clearly not the work of your mother.'

'They probably belong to ...' Louisa stilled. There was a long-drawn-out moment where she blinked, rubbed her forehead and then cleared her throat. 'Can I have a look at one of the sketches?'

Lexi scrolled through her phone. 'I took a couple of photos.' She handed Louisa her phone.

Louisa was quiet for a good few seconds. 'And Olly told you Tom painted these?'

Lexi nodded.

Another pause.

'Now I come to think of it ...' She cleared her throat. 'I do remember we found a box of old sketches when we cleared out the art room after Mother's death.' She handed the phone back to Lexi, not making eye contact. 'But ... *Tom* made it clear he wasn't interested in keeping them. The reason I didn't remember was because he doesn't paint anymore. In fact, it's been years. It's a sore subject in our family.' She glanced away, making a point of adjusting Baby Olly's blanket.

'That's such a shame. He's astonishingly talented.'

'I couldn't agree more.' Louisa looked up, her expression turning ponderous. 'You know, perhaps displaying his work will finally convince him he has a true gift.' She tapped her fingers on the arm of the wheelchair as if deciding something.

'Let's do it. You have my permission to exhibit my *cousin's* work at the exhibition.'

Lexi wasn't sure what was going on, but she was delighted nonetheless. 'Oh, thank you. We'll apply the same commission rate to any sales, obviously.'

Louisa rubbed her forehead. 'I hope I don't live to regret it.'

'Are you worried about going behind Olly's back again?'

She gave a rueful smile. 'Something like that.'

'I don't want to cause any friction.'

'Don't worry, I can handle Olly.' Louisa wheeled over to the door. 'But maybe just keep it between us, okay?'

Lexi nodded. 'Sure, whatever you say.'

When Louisa had left, Lexi finished updating the spread-sheet. Deceiving Olly wasn't a good feeling, but she really felt the paintings deserved to be shown. Plus, she needed all the commission she could get. Especially if she couldn't get the *Woman at the Window* back. She needed another way of paying off the official receiver.

She'd just searched for the Insolvency Service website, when the door opened again. God, she hoped it wasn't Sophie. The woman scared the life out of her.

She turned to find Tasha standing in the doorway, looking sheepish. Well, for her, anyway. She had on a black PVC jacket, a beret and black skinny jeans.

Lexi ran over and hugged her. 'You came back?'

Tasha stiffened in her arms. 'I couldn't stay away knowing you were pissed off with me.'

'I'm so glad you're here.'

'You're not still mad at me?'

'Hell, yes.' Lexi hugged her tighter, overcome with love and the scent of Rock n' Rose Couture. 'But I understand why you did it. I love you.'

'I love you, too. But unless you let go of me, you're not going to have a sister to fight with. I can't breathe.'

'Sorry.' Lexi let go and looked up her sister. 'You have no idea how glad I am to see you.'

'I'm really sorry—'

'Don't.' She stepped away. 'There's something I need to tell you and it'll be worse if I let you apologise again.'

Tasha removed her wet jacket. 'Does it have something to do with the *Woman at the Window*?'

Lexi frowned. 'How did you know?'

'Educated guess.' Tasha slung her jacket over a chair. 'First, I'm your twin. You think I can't tell when something's bothering you? Secondly, you've been twitchy ever since you bought that painting. Thirdly, Marcus wouldn't have taken it if it wasn't valuable.' She sat in the wingback chair and crossed her legs. 'Finally, I'm no dummy. You think I can't tell a genuine Renaissance painting from a copy?'

'You knew? Why didn't you say something?'

Tasha shrugged. 'I figured you must have had a good reason for lying.' She rested her hands in her lap. 'I'm guessing I'm about to find out what that is.'

It was time to confess. No more prevaricating. 'You remember when I had to get a solicitor to gain access to the house before the enforced sale?'

Tasha nodded.

'Well, I found a bag containing a lot of money.'

'How much money?'

'Twenty-seven thousand pounds.'

Tasha raised an eyebrow.

'It was stuffed inside a holdall in the airing cupboard. I thought it was the money Marcus received for selling my Franz Gerste collection.'

'A fair assumption.'

'So I took it. I know I should've declared it, but I didn't. Six months went by and still no one asked about it, so I bought the *Woman at the Window* as an investment.' Lexi braced herself for the fallout.

'Good for you. I'd have done the same.'

She wasn't expecting that. 'You would?'

'Marcus stole from you. Repeatedly. For two years. He owed you.'

Lexi adjusted her glasses. 'Well, yes, that's what I figured. But it was still wrong of me.'

'Legally, yes. Morally, no.' Tasha tilted her head. 'Why are you looking at me like that?'

'It's not the response I was expecting. I thought you'd be mad at me. Ashamed that I stole something that didn't belong to me.'

'Do you think Marcus obtained that money legally?'

'I know he didn't. It's the proceeds from the life insurance policy.'

'An insurance policy he fraudulently took out in your name.' Tasha stood up. 'So let me ask you this? What do you think would've happened if you hadn't taken the money?'

'Marcus would've taken it.'

'Exactly. He would've taken the money and run back to that tart, Cindy, in Spain and you wouldn't have seen a penny of it.'

'That doesn't make what I did right.'

'But it doesn't change the outcome, either.' Tasha walked

over. 'If you didn't take the money, would it have stopped the official receiver coming after you?'

'No.'

She shrugged. 'So either way the debt is still owing.'

'There's one big difference.'

'Which is?'

'When I had the painting, I had a means of paying off the debt. Now I don't. I should've sold the painting as soon as I knew about the insurance policy. I didn't. So it's my own stupid fault that I'm in this mess.'

Tasha's hands went to her hips. 'Are you for real? Marcus "Scumbag" Aldridge is the reason you're in this mess. No other reason. If it weren't for him you wouldn't have been made bankrupt. You wouldn't have lost your home. And you'd still have the money from the sale of your Franz Gerste collection.'

Her sister had a point. 'There's something else.'

Tasha rolled her eyes. 'Why am I not surprised?'

'Marcus has listed the *Woman at the Window* for auction next Monday.'

'Good.'

Another reaction she hadn't expected. 'How is that good?'

'Because we know where the painting will be on Monday. Which means we have an opportunity to get it back.'

'That was my first thought, too. You really are my twin.'

'Don't ever forget it.' Tasha kissed her cheek. 'What's the phone signal like down here?'

'Terrible.'

'I need to tell Mel I'll be staying longer than planned. Don't do anything illegal while I'm gone.' Tasha headed for the door.

'Tash?' When her sister turned back, she smiled. 'Thank you.'

203

'What for?'

'For not punishing me for my mistake. Like I did with you.'

'Your mistake was justified. Mine wasn't.' She paused. 'Well, not entirely,' she said, disappearing outside.

Lexi slumped onto a chair and removed her glasses. She let her head drop to the table, her mind a whirl. There was so much going on it was hard to focus. At least she wasn't alone. Tasha was on her side.

And then a man's voice said, 'Alone at last.'

Her head jerked up.

Olly was standing in the doorway. The sight of him leaning against the doorframe in a V-neck T-shirt and worn jeans was enough to make her breath hitch.

She tried to contain her relief at seeing him and went for a glare instead, putting her glasses back on. He wasn't getting off that easily. 'Go away. I'm busy.'

His cocky demeanour didn't falter. 'You know, you really need to start locking doors if you don't want to be disturbed.'

She turned to face her laptop, trying to hide a smile. 'Locked doors have never stopped you in the past.'

He grinned. 'This is true. Miss me?'

'No.' *Liar*.

He came over and pinched one of her Chelsea buns. 'You've been baking again?'

She moved the container out of reach. 'I bake when I'm stressed. And Mrs Jennings said I can use the kitchen whenever I like.'

'Why are you stressed?' He took a bite of the bun. 'Christ, these are nice.' He perched on the table. 'What's wrong?'

She gave him a reproachful look. 'Have you forgotten what happened last Sunday night?'

'God, no. I've been replaying it in my mind several times a day. Well, up until the moment when your sister smacked me with a shoehorn. How is Morticia?'

'Don't call her that. Underneath the scary exterior is a pussycat.'

He choked on his bun. 'A pussycat with nine-inch nails.'

'Your sister isn't exactly Tinkerbell.' She handed him a bottle of water.

'True,' he said and took a swig of water. 'So, what's bothering you?'

She leant back in the chair. 'Where do I begin? How about discovering that you lodged with my sister in Windsor last month?'

He flinched. 'Yeah, about that.'

'Let me guess, it had nothing to do with getting your painting back. You didn't follow me up to Scotland and turning up on the mountain road was a complete coincidence.' She folded her arms so she wasn't tempted to do something crazy, like jump him. The memory of his hands caressing her still made her skin tingle.

He grinned, which did strange things to her insides. 'Exactly.'

She rolled her eyes and turned back to her laptop, trying to break the effect he was having on her. 'Why am I even surprised. Now, go away. I have bigger problems to deal with.'

But instead of leaving, he stood behind her and began massaging her shoulders. 'Is it your ex? What's he done now?'

God, he had lovely hands ... 'He's listed my painting for auction.'

'The one he stole?'

She angled the laptop so he could see the Sotheby's email. 'Yep.'

'Have you called the police?'

'I told you before, I have no proof he stole it. He'll say I gave it to him.'

'But if you're the registered owner then he can't sell it without your permission.' He stopped massaging. 'Unless there's something you're not telling me?'

She twisted to look at him. 'Have *you* told me absolutely everything about your life?' Her words evoked a flinch. Just as she thought.

He continued massaging. 'If you can't report him, what are you going to do?'

'Go to the auction house and try to get the painting back before the sale.' Her shoulders creaked. His fingers worked deeper and she could feel the muscles starting to relax. It was heavenly.

'And how are you going to do that?'

'No idea, but I'm sure we'll think of something.'

'We?'

'Tasha's back.'

His hands stilled. 'Oh, good. I've missed her warmth.'

'Quit having a go at my sister. *She's* never let me down.' Well, apart from reporting Marcus to HMRC. But she was over that. Mostly.

'And nor have I.'

'Are you kidding?' She shuffled around to face him, ready to contradict him, but then realised he was right. Sort of. He'd rescued her off the mountain road, carried her over a stream and taught her how to ride a Vespa. If it wasn't for the whole *lying* thing, he might be a man she could trust. It was quite a disturbing thought. 'It's not the same thing. Ours is a temporary arrangement. My sister's a permanent fixture in my life.'

He was quiet for a few seconds. 'Do you have the owner-ship papers with you?'

'No, but I can get them. Why?'

'If you show them to the auction house they might hand over the painting. If nothing else, it'll delay the sale. They can't continue if there's a question mark over ownership.'

'Maybe. But questions would still be asked.' Like how someone who was made bankrupt a year ago could afford to buy a Renaissance masterpiece.

He looked ponderous. 'I might have an idea.'

She stood up. 'If it's illegal, I don't want to know.'

He moved forwards, trapping her against the table. 'When are you going to believe that I'm a trustworthy guy?' He kissed the side of her neck.

Well, he could stop that for a start … Just not right away. 'Is this idea of yours totally legit?'

'One hundred per cent.' He continued to kiss her – light, feathery kisses that made her insides melt.

'It doesn't involve breaking the law in any way?'

'It's perfectly legal.' He blew softly against her ear, sending shivers up her spine. 'All you have to do is ask nicely.' He lifted her onto the table and nudged between her legs.

Subtle. 'Is that all?'

His arms slid around her. 'That's all.'

He pulled her close and she moaned as their lips met. His hands slid inside her cardigan, breaking down her resolve. She'd promised herself this wouldn't happen again. It wasn't professional, or sensible. But boy, it was certainly enjoyable.

And then a woman barked, 'Not again!'

Their heads knocked together as they jumped apart.

Tasha stood in the doorway, hands on hips. 'Seriously?'

If that wasn't enough, Sophie appeared in the opposite doorway, adopting the same stance. 'Is this your idea of being professional? Seducing my brother in the banqueting hall?'

Oh, hell. Lexi struggled to climb off the table.

Tasha strode into the room. 'Don't blame her. It's your brother who needs a leash.'

Sophie met her halfway. 'I don't see her fighting him off.'

'And I don't see him keeping it in his pants!'

'How dare you—'

Olly ran over and caught Sophie's arm. 'Sophie, pack it in!' He turned back to Lexi. 'You deal with your sister. I'll deal with mine.'

Lexi straightened her cardigan. 'No, problem.'

It wasn't like her day could get any worse.

Chapter 16

Olly had spent the last three days locked inside the castle. He felt like one of those Jacobite prisoners from a bygone era, trapped in the dungeons with no means of escape. Only his imprisonment was self-inflicted – not to mention necessary if he was to prevent Lexi from finding out he could paint. Or that he was the artist known as Dazed & Confused. And especially not that he was the artist responsible for replicating the *Woman at the Window* – his master plan for getting her painting back.

His reasons for lying hadn't changed – he was still trying to keep his family's secret. Bizarrely, though, Lexi had stopped asking about the Spinelli. When he'd asked Louisa whether the painting had been returned, she'd confirmed that it had and that it was currently being stored somewhere 'safe'. Whatever that meant.

Did that mean Lexi had accepted it was a copy? She'd been so convinced it was genuine he'd expected her to research the painting's provenance, which would have made life extremely awkward. Especially if she'd discovered his family had sold the other supposed Spinelli eleven years ago along with one of his sketches. Instead, the topic hadn't been raised since. And he couldn't work out whether that was a good thing, or a bad omen.

He shook the thought away and continued painting his latest

commission. Far from replicating a Renaissance masterpiece, he was currently painting a speckled toad sitting on top of a bright red toadstool. Louisa had asked him to design a mural for the nursery. It should have been the easier of the two tasks, but he had to resist the urge to paint demons instead of sprites and wolves instead of mice. He didn't want to give his nephew nightmares. But at least Louisa was in better spirits.

Having finished work on the *Woman at the Window* yesterday, he'd then had to 'bake' it in the Aga before beating the crap out of the canvas to make it look authentically old. Forging the painting had been harder than anticipated. He hadn't been able to match the right shade of blue and realised an overnight courier was required.

L. Cornelissen & Son were one of the few remaining stockists of lapis lazuli blue, a pigment made from the lapis rock, more valuable in weight than gold. He'd also purchased a quantity of phenol-formaldehyde resin to harden the paint, necessary if he stood any chance of passing even the most basic of forensic tests. The instructions had warned him the resin became toxic, corrosive and highly flammable when heated, but he hadn't realised what an understatement that was. He'd been left with burnt fingers, a bitch of a headache and a newfound respect for the lengths art forgers went to in order to dupe the experts.

So, having completed one project, he was now halfway through another.

A knock on the door interrupted him mid-stroke. He didn't think Lexi knew where the nursery was, but he couldn't take any chances. If she walked in and found him painting an intricate mural, his lie about knowing nothing about art would be exposed. Hence the need for a locked door.

The door handle rattled. 'Olly ...? Are you in there?'

Sophie. He stepped over the roller trays and unlocked the door.

She frowned. 'Why's the door locked?'

'So people don't walk in and knock over paint,' he lied, even though it was a valid enough reason.

Sophie didn't look convinced and barged past. No doubt she suspected he was secretly harvesting a cannabis farm. Her expression changed when she saw the mural covering the walls. 'Oh! you weren't lying.'

Why did everyone accuse him of lying all the time?

And then he remembered why.

'It's beautiful,' she said, turning to take in the woodland scene.

Coming from Sophie, that was quite a compliment.

'Louisa wanted to bring the outside in, but with a fairy-tale twist.'

She went over and studied the far wall. He'd mirrored the view from the panoramic window, making the colours more vibrant and the foliage more cartoonlike.

'I love this.' She pointed to the otters playing in the loch. 'Is that an eagle?'

'Yep.' His thoughts had drifted to his fishing trip with Lexi and the next thing he'd known he'd painted the eagle mid-flight.

'Can I help?'

He laughed.

'I'm being serious.' She scowled at him. 'Believe it or not, I love my nephew, too.'

'I don't doubt it. But you hate painting.'

'Do you want help, or not?' Her hands went to her hips.

It was a sight he'd seen many times, but there was a hint of insecurity about Sophie today. But perhaps his radar was off, skewed by the phenol-formaldehyde. He handed her a large brush. 'I wasn't going to do much more tonight. The light's fading. But the back wall needs a base coat of pale green, if you're okay to do that?'

'I think I can manage to paint a wall, Olly.'

'Need overalls?'

Anyone would think he'd suggested she shave her hair off. But then she glanced down at her designer jeans and snatched the plastic jumpsuit from him. 'Fine.'

'I think the word you're looking for is thank you.'

'Don't push it,' she said, climbing into the overalls.

He wouldn't dare. Except, it had been a long few days and he was tired of being used as her punchbag. 'Can I ask you something?' He returned to his forest design. He wanted to add little wooden doors to the tree trunks to make it look like animals lived inside. 'Why are you so angry?'

She zipped up the jumpsuit. 'Are you for real?'

'I get that you're pissed off with me,' he said, not sure whether turning his back on his sister was such a smart idea. 'But at some point, you're going to have to let it go.'

'Why? You deserve it.'

'I've been home for months. I've apologised on numerous occasions. I've promised to stay in the UK and I've offered to help with the estate. I know I've messed up, but cut me some slack, Sophie. What more can I do?'

'If you think I'm about to forgive you, think again.'

His brushstrokes slowed. 'I'm not talking about forgiveness. But it feels like there's something else going on.'

'Like what?'

'I don't know. That's why I'm bringing it up.' He turned to look at her. 'I'm asking if you're okay.'

She wouldn't look at him. 'I'm fine.'

'Are you unhappy in your job?'

'My job's fine.'

'Is your health okay?'

'Jesus, Olly.' She turned to glare at him. 'Everything's fine, okay? My job, my health, my life. All is good.'

'Is it a man? Has someone done the dirty on you?'

She threw the paintbrush down. 'Not everything revolves around men!'

'I only meant—'

She stormed over. 'Just because I don't advertise my relationships, it doesn't mean something's wrong.'

'I realise that.'

'And I don't need a man to validate my worth.'

'Of course not.'

'Or complete me as a person. I'm a confident, self-sufficient woman.'

'I know.'

'I have good friends, a great job. I travel. I party. I work hard. There's nothing a man can offer me that I can't provide for myself.'

'Whoa, Sophie.' He held up his hands. 'I hear you, okay?'

'Good.' Her cheeks were red from yelling.

Christ, he'd really struck a nerve. 'But if your life's so wonderful, then why aren't you happy?'

She baulked. 'Who says I'm not happy?'

'No one can be this angry and say they're happy.'

She folded her arms. 'Well, I am.'

'You can talk to me, you know.'

'Yeah, because you've made such a success of your life.'

'Maybe that makes me the perfect person to talk to. I'm not going to judge you, whatever you say.'

'Big of you.' She kicked at the plastic sheeting covering the floor. 'Like you'd understand.'

So there was something wrong. 'Try me.'

She shook her head. 'Some things are better kept hidden.'

He could certainly relate to that. He touched her arm. 'If you change your mind, I'm here for you, okay?'

She stepped away. 'Yeah, right. Like you have been for the past eleven years.' She removed the overalls and dumped them on the floor. 'This was a mistake.' She was out of the room and slamming the door behind her before he could stop her.

What the hell was that all about?

He turned back to the wall, but the shadows were making it hard to see. It was time to pack up for the night.

By the time he'd cleared up, his stomach was rumbling. He had a quick shower and headed to the kitchen. Gilly would have finished for the night, which meant he could raid the fridge without being scolded like a naughty schoolboy.

He could hear music before he reached the top of the steps. The radio was on. He stopped by the door and glanced in.

Lexi was singing along to a Supremes song and frantically beating the life out of a bowl of cake mixture. '*Where did our love go?*' she sang, her hips swaying from side to side.

He watched her for a moment, enjoying the way she moved. She seemed less stressed, less troubled than when they'd talked on Monday. No wonder baking was so important to her.

And then she spotted him and her hips stopped wiggling. 'Don't creep up on me like that.'

'Don't stop on my account. What are you making?' He went over.

'Pancakes for Tasha. She's staying for dinner and I didn't want to put Mrs Jennings out.' She spotted the burns on his hands. 'How did you get those?'

'Hot oven.' She had a burn on her arm, too. 'You ...?'

'Hot oven.'

He laughed. 'What a pair, eh?'

She half-smiled. 'Want some?'

'God, yes.'

He stepped closer with the intention of kissing her, but she backed away, laughing. 'I meant, do you want some pancakes?'

'Can I have both?' He was about to try kissing her again, when he was struck by an idea. 'Hold that thought,' he said, racing from the room. 'Don't go anywhere, I'll be back.'

He heard her sigh and resume singing. '*Ooh, don't you want me?*'

God, yes.

It only took a couple of minutes to fetch the *Woman at the Window* from his room.

His motivation for replicating the painting had arisen from wanting to help Lexi get her prized possession back. He could argue it was because he was still trying to make amends for his numerous shortcomings, but if he were honest, it stemmed more from trying to win her over. He'd fallen for her. He hadn't meant to, but he had. And seeing her stressed over the loss of her painting was hard to watch. He wanted to make it better for her.

Plus, it'd been fun to test out his skills and see if he still had an eye for copying the masters. It was only when he'd finished painting the damned thing that he'd wondered whether or not

215

he was being an idiot. So far he'd managed to hide the fact that his parents had fraudulently sold one of his sketches back in 2007. But if Lexi knew he'd painted this latest work there was no way a smart, art-educated woman like her wouldn't suss that he was Dazed & Confused, or that he'd been lying about his reasons for wanting to get *The Cursed Man* back.

Therefore, another lie was required. No way could she find out he was the artist responsible for copying the *Woman at the Window*. He needed to keep his wits about him.

After checking the painting was dry, he wrapped it in a cloth and returned to the kitchen.

She glanced up when he entered. 'What have you got there?'

He unwrapped the painting and lifted it up. The first test. How long would it take her to spot it was a copy? A couple of seconds? A couple of minutes?

She let go of the whisk. It clattered to the floor, spraying pancake mixture across the kitchen. 'What the ...?' Placing the bowl on the worktop, she raced over, wiping her hands on the front of Gilly's floral apron. 'You got it back? But how? I don't understand.' She took the painting from him.

He was sure this was the moment she'd realise it was a forgery. He knew he couldn't fool the smart gallery owner for long. But with low-key lighting, tiredness and desperation for a solution, the longer it took her to cotton on the better.

He watched her face, waiting for the penny to drop.

'I can't believe it,' she said, her eyes welling as she took in the sight of the demure Italian. 'But ... how ... when? I don't understand.' She balanced the painting on the worktop. 'Actually, you know what, I don't care. I'm just so happy you got it back for me.' She wrapped her arms around his neck. 'Thank you.'

Okay, so her response was better than he could have dreamed of. Not only because his copy was good enough to fool her, but because she was back in his arms, dragging his mind back to when they'd almost got naked.

But as nice as she felt pressing against him, he needed to break the bad news. 'It's a copy,' he said, hating the way her body immediately stiffened.

She drew back. 'What?'

'Sorry. I didn't mean to give you false hope. The good news is, if you're fooled by it, chances are your ex will be, too.'

Her face radiated disbelief and then disappointment followed by annoyance. 'A copy?' She grabbed the *Woman at the Window* and examined it closer. 'That's impossible.' She assessed the canvas, her keen eye finally accepting the truth as she studied the brushwork and smell of phenol-formalde-hyde. 'Who the hell painted this?'

'A mate.'

She spun around to look at him. 'A mate ...?'

He shrugged. 'What can I say, I have accomplished friends.'

'This isn't an amateur copy, Olly. This is the work of a trained artist.' Her gaze was now that of an art expert, not an ex-wife grieving for a lost possession. 'I'm not joking, Olly. This painting's exquisite. I'm going to ask you again, who painted it?'

He took the painting from her. 'Look, it doesn't matter who painted it. All you need to know is, it's someone you can trust.'

'Rubbish. Anyone who paints like that is either a working artist or running a scam.'

Not necessarily, he mused, placing the painting on the worktop. Although, technically he *was* suggesting they run a scam, so perhaps she was right.

She wasn't done quizzing. 'A copy of this quality would sell for a small fortune. No one in their right mind would give it away.'

A small fortune, huh? 'No one outside of this room knows this painting exists.'

'Except the artist.'

She had him there. 'Except the artist, of course.' He gestured for her to take a seat. 'Okay, so here's how I think we should play this—'

'It's not stolen, is it?' She jumped up from the table. 'Where did you get it, a private collector? A museum? Where? Tell me!'

He let out an exasperated sigh. 'It's not stolen. Could you please just trust me?'

Her demeanour switched to fury. 'Are you kidding me? You show up here with a remarkable Renaissance copy with no explanation and you expect me to accept it and not ask questions?'

He pinned her with a glare. 'Yes, that's exactly what I expect you to do.' He overrode her attempt to interrupt. 'In case you hadn't noticed, I'm trying to help. I'm doing this to try to get your flaming painting back. You think I want to piss off your ex-husband?'

She folded her arms. 'Which begs the question, why the hell *are* you doing this?'

He closed the gap between them, clasped her face in his hands and kissed her. It was the only way to shut her up. When her lips softened, his body betrayed him, responding to the urgency of her mouth, relinquishing any control he might have had. He needed to get a grip. Who was fooling whom here?

As he pulled away, she stumbled into his chest, reluctant to end the kiss. 'Oh. That's why?'

'Got it in one.' He should feel bad for duping her, but he needed to stop the incessant questioning.

She smiled. 'Explain it to me again.'

He laughed, happy to oblige, until Tasha walked into the kitchen and said, 'Oh, for God's sake, you two, get a grip.'

Lexi glared at her sister. 'Play nice, Tasha. Olly has a plan to get my painting back.'

Tasha raised an eyebrow. 'This I have to hear.' She sat down next to Lexi at the table.

Two identical faces gazed at him expectantly. He was still struggling to get his head around that. 'Okay, here's the plan. As you can see, I've managed to obtain a copy of the *Woman at the Window*.' He gestured to the canvas. 'On Monday, we go to the auction house in Edinburgh and try to swap it for the original.'

If he'd expected a round of applause, it didn't come.

'Is that it?' Tasha didn't look impressed. 'We'd worked that much out for ourselves. Why should we involve you? Your track record isn't exactly impressive when it comes to unlawful behaviour.'

Lexi elbowed her sister. 'Pack it in, Tasha.'

'Why? You remind him of his inadequacies all the time.'

'I'm allowed.' She frowned at her twin. 'You're not. And it's a good copy – it fooled me.'

'Fine. Keep your hair on.'

Olly continued. 'The point is, we need to create an opportunity to swap the painting.'

Lexi looked puzzled. 'And how do we do that?'

'By sweet-talking the auction house into letting you see the

219

painting before the sale. Tasha then needs to cause a distraction. Something I'm sure she'll find extremely easy to do.'

His words evoked an eye-roll from Tasha.

'At which point, we initiate the swap. No one's any the wiser.' He went over to Lexi. 'You're an expert in the Renaissance period and yet you didn't notice straight away this was a copy. I'm guessing Marcus won't, either.'

Lexi frowned. 'But what about the potential buyer of the copy? I don't want to defraud anyone.'

'You won't be. The *Woman at the Window* is listed as a copy. No law will be broken.'

'Oh, my God, you're right.' She paused. 'Does that mean Marcus doesn't realise it's the original painting?'

Tasha grunted. 'Either that, or he's so desperate for money he's prepared to sell a genuine painting for a fraction of its true value.'

'Which is more likely.' Lexi sighed. 'We'll just have to hope the auction house don't realise it's the original.'

'Why would they?' Olly tilted his head. 'There's no need for them to authenticate copies, and it's not like they'll be expecting the original. I doubt they'll even glance twice at it.'

Lexi looked ponderous. 'You know, your plan might work.'

Tasha shook her head. 'Or we could do the intelligent thing and shop Marcus to the cops. That way my sister gets her painting back and her scumbag ex gets what's coming to him.'

Olly shrugged. 'Or we could do that.'

Lexi gave her sister an exasperated look. 'I don't want to involve the police.'

Tasha threw her hands in the air. 'Put yourself first for once, will you. Your business is on the line. Everything you've ever worked for.' She banged the table. 'Haven't you learnt anything from your dealings with that dickwit ex of yours? He's an arsehole. He can't be trusted. The minute he discovers you've played him he'll come after you.'

The room descended into silence.

Olly wanted to ask why Lexi's business was on the line, but he figured this wasn't the appropriate time. Instead, he squeezed Lexi's shoulder. 'Your sister has a point.'

'Thank you,' snapped Tasha, sounding less than appeased.

'You need to think of yourself here.' He smiled at Lexi. 'It's your choice. If you don't want to use the copy, that's fine. If you do, I'm happy to help.'

Guilt nudged him in the ribs. However he dressed it up, he was lying to her. Just like her ex. He might have a bloody good reason for doing so, but once she knew the truth, he'd be added to the list of men who'd betrayed her. It was a depressing thought.

Lexi shook her head. 'I know you're right, both of you. But I don't want Marcus arrested unless there's no other choice.' She looked at Olly. 'Or you.'

A warm ripple of something he didn't quite recognise wrapped itself around his guilt. Christ, he was a fraud. 'So, are we agreed we have a plan?'

Lexi nodded. 'I'm in.'

He turned to her sister. 'Tasha?'

'Fine. But this has disaster written all over it.'

He couldn't argue with her there.

Chapter 17

Friday 22nd June

Lexi looked around the banqueting hall and mentally hugged herself. She couldn't believe how beautiful everything looked. All her hard work had paid off. Which was just as well. She was exhausted. She'd been up half the night ensuring everything was ready for the exhibition today. Mrs Jennings had organised a fantastic spread of food and although there'd been no need for her to get involved, Lexi hadn't been able to resist baking a few sweet treats. As her sister had pointed out, she baked when she was stressed. And boy, was she stressed.

She draped the newly acquired tartan tablecloth over the Thomas Sheraton table and placed the spray of white orchids interspersed with purple heather in the centre.

Perfect ... unlike her life. Because however she looked at it, she owed twenty-seven grand to the official receiver, her ex-husband had stolen her only valuable possession and on Monday she was going to attempt to 'swap' it back.

She shuddered at the thought. What the hell was she thinking? It was crazy even to contemplate pulling off such a daring heist. She wasn't cut out for a life of misdemeanour. Or prison, for that matter. Her ex might be comfortable duping the authorities, but she wasn't.

She straightened the vase, trying to calm her nerves.

Did it count as breaking the law if the item already belonged to her? Or was she simply trying to justify her actions? Either way, she needed to focus on today and not let her mind torture her with endless questions. Like how the hell Olly had obtained a copy of the *Woman at the Window* so good it had fooled her into believing it was the original. She was still smarting over that.

She picked up the bowl of whisky dip to go with the seared Scottish salmon and took it into the billeting room where the buffet was laid out. She wanted to believe there was a perfectly simple explanation as to how he'd come by the painting. But a more likely scenario was that his *lordship* was as crooked as her ex and once again she'd fallen for a dishonest rogue. Which depressed her a lot more than it should.

A pair of hands squeezed her waist.

She squealed. 'If you make me drop this dip I won't be happy.'

Olly's arms circled her waist. 'You know what would make *me* happy?' he said, kissing the side of her neck.

The man had a skilful mouth. 'I can only guess.'

'When can I get you alone?'

She turned in his arms, sliding the dip onto the table, fully intending to end their flirtations once and for all, because despite her attraction, Olly wasn't a man she could trust. But her protestations died on her lips when she saw his neatly combed hair. He was wearing a soft blue shirt and smart jeans, and she couldn't help smiling. She'd asked him to make an effort and he had. He also smelt divine, a woody scent that could easily seduce a woman into removing her underwear. Damn.

'Tonight, after the exhibition,' she said, resigned to her fate. There was no point fighting it. After all, come Monday it would all be over. This could be her last chance to have some fun. 'Think you can last until then?'

His response was to lift her onto the table. 'Sure. Can you?'

Christ, he could kiss. She felt the pull deep in her stomach. For a moment, all of her stresses melted away and she kissed him back, loving the feel of him in her arms, holding her, touching her ... and then sanity kicked in and she pulled away, breathless and dishevelled. A reporter from *The Scotsman* was due any moment and this wasn't the photo she wanted appearing in next week's paper.

'Behave. We have work to do.'

'Spoilsport.' He helped her off the table. 'What needs doing?'

She pointed upstairs.

He raised an eyebrow. 'Don't get me wrong, I'm game if you are, but is there time?'

She couldn't help laughing. 'I meant, go upstairs and help Mrs Jennings bring down the rest of the food.'

'Oh, right.' He gave her a quick kiss. 'Can't blame a guy for trying.'

She smiled. 'Today needs to be a success.' Not just because his family's finances were on the line, but the future of her gallery was hanging in the balance, too. 'Quit with the flirting. I need to behave like a professional.'

'You're a woman in control, I get it. It's one of the things I love about you.'

They both stilled.

Had he just said, 'love'?

Olly looked as surprised as she felt. There was a long-drawn-out moment where they stared at each other. And then his blue eyes widened and his cheeks coloured. 'Err ... I'd better go,' he said, bolting out of the door and knocking into a chair.

Life with Olly around was never dull. But love? Surely not?

Slightly thrown, she went over to the ornate mirror hanging in the alcove and dug out her lipstick. Her hand shook as she tried to reapply the colour, which Olly had removed with his attentive lips. For a woman supposedly in control, she sure felt wobbly.

He couldn't be in love with her. It wasn't logical. And she certainly wasn't in love with him. At least, she was pretty sure she wasn't. It was just physical attraction making her feel giddy and whimsical. And as nice as that was, she had to be cautious. After Marcus, she'd promised never to let lust lead her astray again. Overactive pheromones clouded the brain and made a woman say crazy things like 'I do'. She couldn't let that happen again.

Olly was a good-looking charmer. He was sexy, fun and had a big heart. But was he trustworthy? All she really knew was that he was the type of guy who could make a woman forget her own name and that was a recipe for disaster.

Analysing the situation would have to wait. She had more important things to focus on. She smoothed down the front of her turquoise Bettie Page dress, checked she didn't have lipstick on her teeth and fluffed up her hair. It was game time.

Voices from next door alerted her to visitors arriving. Louisa and Harry were in the banqueting hall discussing the display. Lexi joined them. She waited by the doorway, eager to see their reaction to the ornate statues and candelabras she'd found hidden away in the Chippendale cabinet. The room glowed even more than normal. The soft gold lighting showed off the paintings at their best.

Louisa was in her wheelchair, Baby Oliver asleep in her lap. She wore a navy velour dress with a tartan sash. Despite her injury, she looked elegant and serene.

'It's so beautiful,' she said, clutching her husband's hand. 'I never expected this.'

Harry smiled down at her. 'Looks great, doesn't it?'

Lexi let out a breath. They liked it. She walked into the room. 'The paintings depict everyday life of the aristocracy set against a backdrop of a stately home. I wanted something to compliment your mother's vision and inspiration for the work.'

Louisa dabbed her eyes. 'She would've loved this. Thank you.'

Lexi smiled. 'My pleasure.'

Harry squeezed his wife's shoulder. 'Do you need anything before I head off to work?'

Louisa shook her head. 'I'm fine. Have a good day. Love you.'

Harry bent down and kissed her. 'Love you too, honey. Hope the exhibition goes well.' He kissed his son and left.

Lexi turned away. More declarations of love. Was there something in the air? But it was nice to see a couple happy and in love, a reminder that not all relationships ended with a visit from the bailiffs. Maybe one day she'd meet a man who looked at her the way Harry looked at Louisa. But then she realised she already had.

Tasha appeared in the room, changing the dynamic.

Sophie appeared in the opposite doorway. Were they somehow linked by an outside force? They looked like opposing chess queens. Sophie was wearing an elegant white maxidress, her blonde hair tied up, showing off her long neck and dangly earrings. In contrast, Tasha was wearing her black PVC Matrix coatdress and heeled boots, ready for her role as 'security' for the event.

They both stilled when they spotted each other, their postures straightening as they considered their next strategic move.

Lexi wasn't about to give them the opportunity to cause a scene. 'Has the piper arrived?' she asked her sister.

Tasha's eyes remained locked on Sophie's. 'He's setting up outside.'

'Excellent.' Lexi turned to Sophie. 'It would be great if you could greet the guests as they arrive and direct them to the banqueting hall. Would that be okay?'

Sophie didn't so much as blink. 'I said I'd help, didn't I?'

'You did, and I'm very grateful.' Lexi turned to Louisa. 'Are you happy staying in here and chatting to the guests? I'm sure they'll want to discuss your mother's work and meet members of the Wentworth family.'

Louisa nodded. 'Yes, of course—'

'Is my brother helping?' Sophie interrupted. 'Or is he lazing about somewhere letting everyone else do the hard work?'

Lexi felt a frisson of annoyance on Olly's behalf. The man was far from lazy. He spent his days helping with the farm animals, running around after Louisa, babysitting his nephew and running chores for Mrs Jennings. Not to mention coming up with ideas to get her painting back. And although she wasn't about to air her feelings on the subject, she felt Sophie was being too hard on her brother.

'Olly's helping Mrs Jennings bring down the buffet food. He's going to help Tasha with security and ensure guests don't venture into the private quarters.'

Sophie didn't look impressed. 'How long have we got?'

Lexi checked her watch. 'Not long. The reporter from *The Scotsman* will be here soon. Can everyone take up their positions, please.'

Tasha and Sophie didn't budge.

Lexi sighed and forcibly pushed her sister towards the door. Honestly. Talk about unsubtle. 'Time to go.'

Tasha eyeballed Sophie as she was marched out. 'What *is* that woman's problem?'

'I think you are.'

Tasha frowned. 'Me? What have I done?'

'You don't know?'

Tasha shrugged. 'Not a clue.'

'And I always thought you were the smart one.' Lexi pointed towards the inner courtyard. 'I've got my phone on me. Call if there are any problems.'

'I need the loo first.'

'Fine, but hurry up. The reporter'll be here soon.'

Lexi returned to the billeting room. She had one last task before the guests started arriving. She removed the box containing the Dazed & Confused sketches from the alcove and carried it over to the table. Lifting the lid, she carefully removed them.

As she arranged them, the faint sound of bagpipes filtered through the narrow slit windows. The weather was good, thank goodness. A wet and windy day would discourage visitors. But the sun was out and it was already warm.

The melodic music helped to stem her nerves as she secured the sketches to the display boards. God, she hoped today would go without a hitch.

When she'd finished, she stood back to admire the display. Her first impressions had proved correct. These works might be unfinished and primitive, but they were nonetheless exquisite pieces of art. She wasn't losing her touch. After the fiasco last night and not spotting the *Woman at the Window* was a fake, it was a comforting thought.

Thinking about the *Woman at the Window* made her peer closer at the sketches. There was a familiarity in the way the lines glided across the paper, a confident use of tone and colour. If she were a betting woman, she'd say the same artist was responsible for both sets of work. But that was impossible. Tom was in India travelling. Or at home in Brighton, depending on who you believed.

She was so absorbed in thought that she didn't hear anyone approach. So it was something of a shock to turn and find her ex-husband standing in front of her. 'Marcus! What the hell are you doing here?'

'I saw the event listed on your website. I thought I'd stop by and say hi.' He stepped closer. 'Miss me?'

'No.' Was he for real? 'Where's my painting?'

'What painting?'

'You know damn well what painting.' She considered admitting she knew it was listed for auction next week, but figured that might jeopardise her chances of getting it back. If he knew she was on to him, he'd be on his guard and less likely to fall for a scam. 'Why are you in Scotland?'

'I think you know why.' He pulled her close, a strong waft of Paco Rabanne rooting her to the spot. Unlike Olly's enticing kiss, Marcus's effort was harsh, like he was trying to claim something that was no longer his.

She twisted away from his mouth. 'Let go of me.'

His hand slipped around the back of her neck, preventing her from moving. 'Time apart has made me re-evaluate what

I want. I need you in my life, Lexi. I meant what I said before. I want you back.'

She pushed him away. 'You think I'd trust you again, after everything you've done?'

He sighed. 'I've made mistakes, I get that. But I've changed. You can trust me now.'

Was he serious? She took in his deep suntan, designer jacket and expensive haircut. For someone supposedly bankrupt he looked decidedly well groomed.

Outrage fuelled her anger. 'Marcus, you hid a gambling problem from me. You stole the sale money from my Franz Gerste collection and you forged my signature on a bogus insurance policy, not to mention emptying our bank account and running off to Spain with your PA.' Her hands went to her hips. 'Trusting you is something I won't be doing.'

'What insurance policy?'

God, he was a good liar. Anyone watching their exchange would assume it was her who was being unreasonable.

'I've no idea what you're talking about.'

But gone were the days when she'd doubt her own sanity. She could see Marcus for what he was now. A conman. A player. A man willing to sacrifice the woman he loves to protect his own interests. 'Don't play dumb, Marcus. You know exactly what insurance policy. And just so you know, I reported you to the official receiver for forging my signature.'

'I never—'

'Yes, you did. And you know what? I hope they catch you. I can't believe I spent so long protecting you. I've had enough. Now get out. Or I'm calling the police and reporting you for theft as well as fraud.'

He had the audacity to laugh. 'You threatened to call the

cops before, but you didn't do it, did you? Which means you must still love me.' He reached for her.

Was he for real? She stepped away. 'No, Marcus, it simply means I'm not a lowlife rat like you are. And there's still time to involve the police. Now leave, or I'll be forced to add harassing your ex-wife to your growing list of misdemeanours.'

Marcus wasn't fazed. 'I don't think you have the nerve.'

She stood her ground. 'Maybe not. But I do have the nerve to call Tasha. She's here, you know. At the castle. Only a phone call away.'

He looked wary. 'You're bluffing.'

She pulled her shoulders back. 'Try me.'

They were interrupted by a man's voice. 'Are you Ms Ryan?'

She swung around to see a young guy wearing thick-rimmed glasses and carrying a leather satchel. He held up a notepad. *Damn*. The reporter. How long had he been standing there? She swallowed and darted over. 'Hi, you must be ...?'

'Eddie Newell.' He shook her hand. '*The Scotsman*.'

'Good to meet you. Do come through to the exhibition. It's being held in the banqueting hall.' She steered him towards the doorway, glancing back to glare at Marcus, who blew her a kiss. Bloody man.

She turned away, torn between not wanting to leave him alone and wanting to get as far away as possible.

'Here we are,' she said as they entered the banqueting hall. 'The paintings along the left-hand wall are from the Eleanor Wentworth collection. The others are selected pieces being offered for sale.'

'Nice,' he said, looking around.

She glanced at the door, unnerved at leaving Marcus to his own devices. It was no good, she had to get rid of him. 'Would

231

you excuse me a moment? There's an urgent matter that needs my attention.'

He dug out his camera. 'Okay if I take some shots?'

'Please do.' She left him and ran over to Louisa, who was chatting with Mrs Jennings. 'The guy over there's from *The Scotsman*,' she whispered. 'Can you keep him occupied? There's something I need to do.'

Louisa looked alarmed. 'Is everything okay?'

'Absolutely peachy,' she lied, forcing a smile. 'Get him a drink, or something.'

Leaving them to entertain the reporter, she ran back to the billeting room. The guests had started to arrive. A group were heading through the doorway. Where was Marcus? Had he left? Somehow, she doubted it.

She searched the corridor. No sign of him. She turned sharply and bumped into Olly.

He reached out to steady her. 'Hey, what's the emergency?'

'My ex-husband,' she said, wringing her hands together. 'He's here.'

'Marcus?'

She nodded. 'And now the reporter from *The Scotsman* is here, too.'

'Why's your ex-husband here?' And then he spotted something over her shoulder. His expression changed from confusion to pure horror and the colour drained from his face.

She turned to see what had spooked him. 'Olly, what's wrong?'

He nodded to the display. 'Those godawful pictures,' he said, sounding annoyed. 'Why the hell have you displayed them? Take them down. They're ruining the integrity of the show.'

What was he on about? 'The Dazed & Confused sketches? Don't be ridiculous. They're astonishingly good. They deserve to be on show. No way am I taking them down.'

'But I told you Tom wouldn't want them displayed. You had no right.'

She'd never seen Olly angry before. 'Louisa gave her permission.'

He swore under his breath. 'Well ... Tom didn't.' His agitation increased. 'He's likely to sue. He's a bloody barrister, for crying out loud.' He rubbed his forehead.

'A barrister? I thought he was an artist?'

'What?' He looked rattled, and then he groaned and chastised himself. 'Right, yeah. Painting's a hobby. He's a barrister by day.'

She frowned. 'Who's currently travelling around India?'

'That's right.'

'And is a recluse?'

Olly searched for another lie. She knew this, because his eyes flitted upwards and to the left. 'That's why he's taken extended leave ... to deal with his issues.'

Rubbish. Something wasn't adding up. Her hands went to her hips. 'Well, tough. Louisa's given her permission, so they're staying. If you've got a problem, talk to her. But for now, I need to stop my ex-husband ruining this exhibition. So do something constructive and keep the journalist occupied while I try to find him.'

She turned to go, but Olly caught her arm. 'Sorry, I didn't mean to snap. It's just—'

'Just what, Olly?'

She waited, hoping he'd tell her what was going on, but he shook his head, and said, 'It doesn't matter.'

Typical. She was sick of everyone lying to her. 'I need to go.'

She marched into the banqueting hall and found Marcus embroiled in a conversation with Louisa and the reporter. Oh, hell. Panic nearly wiped her legs from under her. She wanted to run over but realised she needed help. Specifically, her sister.

She sent Tasha a message: *Banqueting hall. NOW!*

Marcus glanced over. His smile was charming, open and totally sincere, which just showed what a practised liar he was. He knew she couldn't make a scene with witnesses, which only added to the glee radiating off him. He really was a piece of work.

She went over, wondering how on earth she was going to extract the reporter from Marcus's clutches. Help came in the form of Olly, who raced past, took Eddie by the elbow and steered him towards two paintings of his aunty Clementine.

'These will interest you,' he said. 'They're of Lady Beit, owner of Russborough House. It's an interesting story, way back in 1756 ...'

Lexi was grateful. Olly might be up to something dodgy, but he was also saving her bacon. She turned her attentions to her ex. 'I thought you were leaving?'

'Not at all,' he said, unleashing his charm on Louisa. 'Louisa was telling me about her mother's collection. Such a fascinating story.'

Louisa adjusted Baby Olly in her arms. 'Mr Aldridge is buying the painting of Father in the study.' She looked excited. 'He was about to write a cheque.'

A cheque? Oh, no. Lexi wasn't about to let Marcus con the Wentworth family. She faked a smile. 'Cash only, I'm afraid, Mr Aldridge.'

He patted his pockets. 'I seem to have forgotten my wallet.'

Convenient. 'Oh, that's a shame. Next time, perhaps. Let me show you out.'

'It's no problem,' Louisa said, her need for money clouding her judgement. 'A cheque is fine.'

Marcus looked like he'd won the lottery. 'You're too kind.'

Lexi kept her smile in place. 'And as soon as it clears, we'd be delighted to arrange delivery.'

'And incur unnecessary delivery fees? I can't ask you to do that,' he said as if doing them a favour. 'Taking it away today would make more sense.' He lifted the painting off the stand. 'It's no bother.'

Lexi grabbed the frame. 'I can't allow that, Mr Aldridge.'

He pulled the painting towards him. 'But the lovely Louisa has no objections. And it is her painting, after all.'

Lexi pulled the painting towards her. 'But the exhibition is being run by Ryan Fine Arts and gallery rules state payment in full prior to delivery.'

Marcus wasn't relenting. 'You can make an exception for your husband—'

'*Ex*-husband,' Lexi corrected, tugging on the painting. 'And no exceptions, I'm afraid.' Especially not for lying, cheating scumbags who specialised in bouncing cheques.

A flash startled her. She turned to see Eddie, the reporter, snapping away, no doubt eager to capture the scoop.

Olly was trying to deter him, but young Eddie had sniffed out a story and wasn't to be diverted. 'Can you look this way?' he said to Lexi. 'You too, sir.'

But before Eddie could take another photo, Sophie appeared out of nowhere and jerked his arm, sending his camera clattering to the floor. 'Oh, I'm so sorry,' she said, dazzling him with a wide-eyed looked of mortification. 'How clumsy of me.' She bent down to retrieve the camera, ensuring he got an eyeful of her cleavage as she did so.

And then Marcus yelped.

Lexi turned to see her sister standing next to Marcus. There was nothing obvious happening, but when Lexi glanced down she realised Tasha's stiletto heel was digging into Marcus's foot. God, she loved her sister.

Marcus's grip on the painting relented. Lexi placed it back on the stand.

There was a brief silence before Olly said, 'How about a family photo? In front of the fireplace?' When the reporter hesitated, he added, 'With both of my sisters.' It was enough to persuade Eddie to switch interests and resume gawping at Sophie. 'The coat of arms is worth a photo alone. This way.' He led Eddie away from the fracas.

When they were out of earshot, Lexi turned to Tasha. 'Get him out of here.'

'My pleasure,' she said, twisting Marcus's arm behind his back.

Marcus looked pleadingly at Lexi. 'Is that any way to treat your husband?'

'Ex-husband,' Tasha and Lexi said in unison.

'Move before I stamp on something else,' Tasha added. 'And I don't mean your foot.'

Marcus flinched. 'You're sick, you know that?'

Tasha smiled. 'And don't you forget it.'

Lexi watched Tasha drag Marcus from the room. Any remaining animosity towards her sister faded. Tasha had been right to report Marcus to HMRC. He wasn't a nice man. She'd just been too weak to see it. Or too in love. Whatever the reason, she was over him. And she wouldn't be making the same mistake again.

The next three hours whizzed by. Thankfully, drama-free. She mingled with the guests, chatted about the merits of the artwork on display, and tried not to dwell on the damage her ex-husband could have caused if Sophie, Tasha and Olly hadn't come to her rescue. She'd thank them later. For now, she needed to concentrate on being a professional art dealer.

As she eased her way through the crowd, she was pleased to note that no one looked in any hurry to leave. The Drambuie, Edinburgh Gin and Highland Elderflower Wine was flowing, the buffet was being enjoyed, and Eddie, the reporter, had left with his story ready to print. She just hoped it was a glowing report on the success of the exhibition and not an exposé about her spat with her ex-husband.

By the end of the day, they'd secured several sales. With the refreshments running low and the bagpiper blasting out his final tune, numbers had started to dwindle. Her feet hurt from standing in heels all day, so she made her way into the billeting room to sit down.

She hesitated when she realised Sophie was also in the room. She was standing by the Dazed & Confused display, her head tilted to one side.

Lexi kicked off her shoes and sat down. 'Talented, isn't he?'

Sophie glanced over. 'Oh, it's you.' She turned back to the display. 'Annoyingly, yes.'

Lexi rubbed her feet. 'Annoyingly? Don't you get on?'

'Observant, aren't you?'

What an odd remark. 'Being observant has nothing to do with it. I've never met your cousin. How would I know whether you get on or not?'

Sophie turned to look at her. 'My cousin?'

'Tom. The artist, Dazed & Confused?'

Sophie laughed. 'You think Tom painted these?'

Lexi frowned. 'Didn't he?'

'My cousin doesn't have an artistic bone in his body.'

Lexi was confused. 'Are you saying Tom isn't the artist?'

'That's exactly what I'm saying.'

A sense of dread settled in her stomach. 'And I'm guessing he's not currently travelling around India?'

'Why on earth would you think that? He's a barrister, not a flipping hippy.'

Lexi almost didn't want to ask the next question. 'So, if Tom isn't Dazed & Confused, who is?'

Olly pushed Louisa's wheelchair into the room. 'That's the last of the guests gone,' he said, smiling. 'I think the exhibition was a success. Don't you?' And then he spotted Lexi's expression and his smile disappeared. 'What?'

Sophie folded her arms. 'Lexi, I'd like you to meet Dazed & Confused.'

The air left her lungs with a whoosh. Even though she'd suspected Olly of lying, this was a blow she hadn't seen coming. Or perhaps subconsciously she had. The lights around her seemed to dip and she feared she might faint.

'I can explain,' he said, moving towards her.

But she wasn't interested in more lies. 'I don't want to hear it,' she said, rage replacing any desire to pass out. 'It's too late.'

All this time she'd been fooling herself that maybe he was trustworthy. Maybe he was an honest and decent human being, and maybe this time she wouldn't fall in love with a no-good, lying, cheating crook. But he was no better than Marcus. And she was a fool for thinking otherwise.

She marched over to him in her bare feet. 'I have one question, Olly.' She held his gaze, her hunch from earlier rearing its ugly head again. 'Are you also responsible for copying the *Woman at the Window?*'

When he closed his eyes, she had her answer.

Chapter 18

Saturday 23rd June

Olly woke early the next morning. Not that he'd slept much. His mind had been on permanent overdrive, replaying the events of yesterday. Lying in bed dwelling hadn't helped, so he'd dressed and left the castle. Ignoring the low mist hanging mournfully over the mountains, he'd busied himself mucking out the animals and feeding the deer.

As dawn broke, the sky cleared and the light changed from grey to mauve to turquoise in the space of a few hours. The loch mirrored the sky, the purpley-blue merging into the green foliage behind, making it look almost like tartan.

But even the glasslike water reflecting the sunlight wasn't enough to erase the pain gripping his chest.

'You lied to me,' Lexi had yelled, pointing to his sketches. 'You played me for a fool. You're a liar and no better than Marcus!'

Her words had stung. He'd wanted to believe he was better than her ex. But when he'd tried to reason with her, she wasn't interested in hearing him out.

'*I never want to see you again*!' she'd screamed, shoving him in the chest.

Her parting words had tortured him all morning. To say he was gutted by her reaction to the discovery that he was Dazed & Confused would be an understatement. Although, not entirely unexpected. How did he think she'd react?

240

He jumped from the tractor and emptied the rest of the feed into the troughs. The deer nestled closer, vying for position as he fed them. He stroked their velvety coats, remembering how enchanted Lexi had been when she'd met them.

He could cope with her being angry with him for lying to her, but it was the hurt on her face that'd done him in. She felt betrayed and he felt like a prize arse.

He walked back to the tractor, rubbing his chest. He had an ache that wouldn't shift. She hadn't been gone a day and he missed her already.

It was eerily quiet when he got back to the castle. Lexi's mint-green hire car was conspicuously absent from the parking area. His Vespa sat alone in the vast space, looking as small and as insignificant as he felt.

Why had he thought lying was a good idea? The truth was bound to come out. He'd justified lying to her because he didn't want her asking awkward questions or looking too closely at the family's association with the two Spinelli paintings. But Lexi had stopped asking about *The Cursed Man* weeks ago. His family's secret was safe. The painting was stored away in the castle, out of harm's way. Job done.

So why did he feel so crap?

Because the cost of protecting his family had been losing Lexi.

He washed his hands using the outside tap, glad of the cold water biting his skin. It felt good to be punished. He deserved it.

Wiping his hands on his jeans, he headed inside the main keep. There was nothing he could do about Lexi leaving, but there was something he could do to protect his family from future exposure. As long as *The Cursed Man* existed, there was an evidence trail back to his parents. It was like an unexploded bomb, ticking away beneath them, counting down until it destroyed the entire family and four hundred years of history.

Well, no more.

The only reason he hadn't acted before was because of his love of art. *The Cursed Man* was an exquisite painting. But it was also incriminating evidence. It was time to detonate the bomb.

He found Louisa in the banqueting hall. She was nursing Baby Olly and chatting to Gilly, who was picking up discarded exhibition flyers from the floor. They stopped talking when he entered. It didn't take a genius to work out he'd been the topic of conversation.

Gilly's smile brightened, but it was a little forced. 'Will you be wanting breakfast this morning, your lordship?' There was no hint of sarcasm in the housekeeper's address today. She could tell he wasn't in the mood to be provoked. Or perhaps it was because he was standing there dirty and dishevelled, smelling of animal feed and barely holding it together.

'No thanks, Gilly.' He walked over. 'Would you excuse us a moment. I need to speak with my sister.'

Gilly looked torn between relishing the prospect of gossip and knowing it wasn't her place. 'I'll be in the kitchen if anyone needs me.' She glanced at Louisa before reluctantly leaving.

Louisa frowned up at him. She looked tired. She obviously hadn't had the best night's sleep, either. 'You were up early this morning. Everything okay?'

He waited until he was certain Gilly had disappeared. 'Not really.'

Louisa kissed her son. 'Are you going to tell me why you pretended Tom painted your sketches?'

And there it was. He'd anticipated the question. He had a rehearsed answer at the ready. 'Insecurity, I guess. I didn't think they were any good. I didn't want to draw attention to myself. You said it yourself, I'm exposed when I paint and I'm not comfortable with that.'

Guilt nudged him in the chest. Constantly lying was exhausting. Necessary but exhausting.

Louisa looked unconvinced. He couldn't blame her.

'Anyway, it's irrelevant now,' he said, admiring the flowers Lexi had arranged for the exhibition. 'Lexi's gone. But there's something else I need to talk to you about.' He knelt next to her wheelchair.

'And what's that?'

Her eyes were cast downwards. If he didn't know better, he'd say she knew he was about to lie. His guilt levels increased. But it also confirmed what he had to do next. 'Where have you stored the painting we sent to the gallery? I wouldn't ask if it wasn't important.'

She held his gaze. 'You mean the Spinelli?'

That startled him. He swallowed awkwardly. 'How did you know it was a Spinelli?'

'Lexi told me.'

She'd gone behind his back? He tried not to feel aggrieved. 'When?'

'When she told me it was potentially valuable and asked for permission to send it off for authentication.'

The room began to spin. He felt the air stick in his lungs. 'Please tell me you said no.'

She didn't answer.

Oh, crap. 'Has it gone?'

She nodded.

He bit back an expletive. There was no point yelling. 'When?'

'A couple of weeks ago.'

'Why didn't you tell me? You should've talked to me first.'

His sister's expression switched from mildly remorseful to incensed. 'Why? So you could lie to me again?'

There was a challenge in her expression that made him flinch. His sister's normally affable demeanour was absent this morning.

'The painting may or may not be genuine, Olly. But please don't insult my intelligence by pretending the reason you were so desperate to get it back was because it was rubbish.'

His lies were unravelling.

Her green eyes pinned him with a glare. 'You knew it was potentially valuable. The question is, why did you keep it a secret? We're struggling financially. Sophie and I are at logger-heads over which property to sell and yet you kept hidden the fact that we might own a painting that could resolve all of our problems. Why?'

He didn't answer. He had no defence. Not one he could admit to.

'I've always stuck up for you, Olly. When Sophie doubted your integrity, I defended you. I never believed for one second that you'd ever do anything to hurt us.'

'I wouldn't.'

'So you weren't planning to run off with the painting and sell it to fund your travels?'

He jumped to his feet. Is that what she thought? 'Of course not.'

'Sure about that?' The sound of Sophie's voice made him turn. She was leaning against the doorframe, wearing a striped monochrome jumpsuit. 'Because it looks like you were trying to scam us, Olly.'

Panic enveloped him. 'No way. I'd never do that.'

She walked into the room, the same height as him in heels. 'Let's say we believe you. Which means there's another reason why you kept the truth hidden.' She was holding a book. 'Recognise this, Olly? It's the catalogue raisonné for Albrico Spinelli. It lists every piece of artwork ever attributed to him. Louisa told me all about the painting.' She opened the book to a page with a Post-it Note attached. 'Would it surprise you to learn there's a nineteen-inch oil canvas listed in here that matches the description of the painting we mistakenly sent to the gallery in Windsor.'

The blood drained from his head. He was in danger of blacking out.

'Would it also surprise you to learn that its sister painting was sold at auction in 2007 by our beloved parents for nearly two million quid?'

Oh, hell. He had no idea what to do.

Sophie snapped the book shut, making him flinch. 'Louisa and I were up half the night wondering why we never knew this. And then we realised something.'

He waited.

'2007 was the year you ran off. Could this be the reason you fell out with our parents, we wondered.' She obviously already knew the answer. 'So that just leaves one unresolved puzzle. If you weren't planning to run off and sell the second painting behind our backs, why didn't you want us to know about it?'

His mouth wouldn't work. He'd stopped breathing. Pain gripped his chest.

'I have a theory,' she said, leaning against the table. 'Lexi asked Louisa if she could send the painting to an expert. Which means there's a question mark over its authenticity. And this made me think. What if the other Spinelli wasn't an original, either?'

His heart rate was so accelerated he thought he might pass out. His hands were clammy and he could feel beads of sweat running down his forehead.

'And then I thought, surely I'm not the only person to think this?' She pushed away from the table. 'You needed to retrieve *The Cursed Man* from the gallery because you think it's a forgery, don't you? And if that's the case, then it's likely the first painting was a forgery, too. Am I right?'

He'd been sprung. He tried to focus, but the room was a blur. He rested his hands on his knees, trying to breathe. Christ, was he having a panic attack?

Louisa wheeled herself over. 'Is that why you fell out with our parents, Olly?' There was no accusation left in her voice, it was soothing and calm. She gently rubbed his back. 'It's okay. We understand. You don't have to pretend anymore.'

There was no point continuing to lie. 'I ... I'm sorry.'

Silence descended, broken only by the sound of his ragged breathing.

Sophie came over. 'Did our parents know it was a forgery?'

Again, there was no point lying. His sisters were too smart to be outwitted. 'I tried to persuade them not to do it, but they wouldn't listen. I didn't want you to find out. I knew you'd be devastated. I'm so sorry.'

A beat passed before Sophie said, 'What are you not telling us?'

He was about to deny it, when he realised they might as well know the whole truth. He was sick of lying. 'I found out they sold one of my replica sketches ahead of the auction. A preliminary drawing of *The Sacrificial Woman*. They created false provenance for it so it appeared to be the work of Albrico Spinelli.'

Louisa gasped.

Sophie's eyes widened. 'Our parents falsified documents?'

He nodded. 'They also created fake provenance for the main painting. That's how they managed to pass it off as an original.'

Sophie swore. 'I'm not sure whether I'm impressed, or horrified.'

Louisa burst out crying. 'Oh, Olly!' She tried to hug him, but Baby Olly was in the way. Her son protested when he got squashed between them. 'You poor, poor thing. What an awful burden to carry. No wonder you stayed away.'

Her words had an odd effect on him. It was like someone had cracked open his chest with a tyre iron. A mixture of pain and relief flooded him.

For a long while, no one spoke. He suspected they were all too stunned. He knew he was.

Eventually, Sophie broke the silence. 'You know you've been a right bloody idiot, don't you?'

'I was trying to protect my family. What else could I do?'

'Don't get me wrong, I understand your reasoning, but if you'd come to me we could've sorted this. We wouldn't be in this mess.'

She had a point. He rubbed his wet eyes. 'It's done now. The truth's bound to come out. I'm just hoping it doesn't result in the buyer of *The Sacrificial Woman* suing us. Our finances couldn't cope with that.'

Louisa squeezed his arm. 'Hey, don't give up. We just need a better plan.'

He raised an eyebrow. 'We do?'

She nodded. 'You're not on your own anymore, Olly. We're in this together. Isn't that right, Sophie?'

Sophie pulled a face. 'Yeah, one big happy family.' But her sarcasm was preferable to anger. She moved around the room looking ponderous. 'Okay, so here's what we do.' She turned to face him. 'Lexi's already sent off the painting for authentication, so there's nothing we can do about that.'

He frowned. 'But she'll discover it's a fake.'

'So what? It's not like she'll alert the press or authorities, is it? I mean, she's mad at you, who wouldn't be? But she's a professional art dealer. She must've come across loads of works that don't turn out to be the real deal. Why should this be any different?'

He pointed to the art catalogue. 'Because the minute she discovers our family sold the other Spinelli she'll suspect a scam. Especially now she knows I've been lying to her.'

Sophie looked nonplussed. 'Maybe, but she wouldn't deliberately hurt you, would she? Or us, for that matter. Especially if she's feeling particularly *loved-up*.'

Loved-up? 'Are you serious? She hates me. She never wants to see me again.'

'And with good reason. But she wouldn't be this angry if she didn't have feelings for you.'

He frowned. 'She wouldn't?'

Sophie gave him an incredulous look. 'Men can be so dumb.' She perched on the arm of the wingback chair. 'The painting you were working on last week? Was that for her?'

He nodded. 'Her ex-husband stole the original painting from her gallery. He's listed it for auction at Sotheby's in Edinburgh this coming Monday. I painted a copy and suggested she use it to try to get the original back.'

Louisa lifted Baby Olly onto her shoulder. 'How?'

'By swapping it for the original before the auction.'

Sophie tapped her forehead. 'So that's what they were talking about last night.'

He frowned. 'Who?'

'Lexi and Tasha. I went after them when they stormed off. I wanted to check they didn't torch the place after your little spat.' She glared at him. 'I overheard Lexi telling her sister she didn't want to go through with the swap anymore. She just wanted to return home to Windsor. I had no idea what they were on about at the time.'

'You mean, she's not going to try to get her painting back?'

'Doesn't sound like it.'

He couldn't believe it. 'But why? She loves that painting. She told me it means the world to her. Why would she back out now?'

Sophie rolled her eyes. 'Oh, I don't know, Olly. Maybe because she's had enough of men stealing from her and *lying* to her.' She walked over and whacked his arm with the catalogue. 'That last accusation is aimed at you, by the way.'

'That much I'd gathered.' He rubbed his scar. 'But that's why I need to make amends. She deserves better. I have to do something.'

Sophie's hand settled on her hip. 'Suppose I helped you get it back for her?'

He blinked. 'Why would you do that?'

She rolled her eyes. 'Well, for a start, if we get her painting back she's less likely to report us to the authorities when she finds out *The Cursed Man* is a fake.'

He shook his head. 'That's not why I'm doing this. This is about making amends. There's no ulterior motive.' He needed to prove to Lexi that he was more than just a lying scumbag.

Sophie shrugged. 'Fair enough.'

He frowned at her. 'You're still prepared to help me? Why?'

She threw her hands in the air. 'Why do you think, numbnuts? Because you're my *brother*. Believe it or not, I care about you.'

'We both do,' Louisa said, patting her son's back. 'And we'd do anything to help you. Especially if it means winning Lexi back.' Her face broke into a huge smile. 'It's so *romantic*! And it's about time Lexi got what she deserved. A faithful, loving, loyal man who'd risk life and ruin to rescue her.' She looked at him expectantly. 'That's you, by the way.'

He startled. 'Me?'

Louisa nodded. 'You love her, don't you? You want her to forgive you and live happily ever after?'

He looked from one sister to the other, both with expectant expressions. It suddenly dawned on him. 'Yeah, I do.'

'Damn straight you do.' Sophie tucked the catalogue under her arm and headed for the door. 'So let's get her painting back. Go and pack a bag. We're leaving for Edinburgh this afternoon and if we're going to pull this thing off, we need one hell of a plan.'

She wasn't wrong there.

Baby Olly let out a massive burp.

Louisa smiled down at her son. 'See? Even Baby Olly approves.'

Big Olly closed his eyes.

Heaven help them all.

Chapter 19

Lexi had never been so nervous in her life. Her hands shook as she tried to lift the cup of tea to her lips. She wasn't hungry, but Tasha had insisted she have breakfast before they headed over to Sotheby's.

Even thinking about what they were about to do made her nauseous. How on earth was she going to hold it together?

She glanced around her. The Lime café in Thistle Street was busy. It reminded her of Nanny's with its quaint tables and home-cooked food. If her stomach wasn't tied in knots she might enjoy the steaming bowl of porridge topped with cinnamon and maple syrup. But it was as much as she could do to drink her tea.

Thoughts of Nanny's reminded her of Shieldaig, which led to thoughts of Rubha Castle and inevitably to thinking about Olly. The memory of Friday night was still raw. Burnt onto her brain. One moment she'd been basking in the success of the exhibition, the next she'd been reeling from discovering that Olly was the artist, Dazed & Confused. He'd lied to her. Not just lied. He'd played her for a fool. Just as Marcus had done.

The waitress removed her cold porridge, concerned that there was something wrong with it. Lexi reassured her it was delicious and feigned an upset stomach before returning to staring at the checked tablecloth and forcing down another mouthful of tea.

She was angry with herself. Angry that she hadn't learnt from her mistakes with Marcus. She'd vowed never to let a man swindle her again. But he had. And she'd let it happen. Instead of trusting her instincts and seeing Olly for what he was, a practised liar, she'd been seduced by his open smile and mischievous blue eyes. She'd ignored the warning signs, the inconsistencies and fabricated stories, and believed him to be a decent man with a sad childhood. *Never play poker*, he'd said, *you'll lose badly*. Well, boy had she lost.

She wiped away tears and checked the carry case containing the *Woman at the Window* copy was still safely tucked under the table.

The bell above the door tinkled and her sister appeared in the doorway, causing heads to turn. Tasha strode across the café in her usual confident manner, looking stylish in a black Victorian-styled jacket and knee-length skirt. Her biker boots had been replaced with plain courts and she was carrying a suitcase.

Despite her misery, Lexi almost smiled. 'Is this your idea of inconspicuous?'

Tasha sat down and removed her sunglasses. 'I thought I'd done quite well,' she said, holding out her hands. 'No nail polish. No skull rings. And no tattoos on show.'

'Apart from the one on your chest.'

Tasha adjusted her jacket, covering the dagger entwined in a rose. 'Better?'

Lexi nodded. 'It's me who's the problem.'

Tasha frowned. 'You're wearing exactly what I told you to. You look classy, businesslike and unremarkable. Although you need to stop crying. It's not a good look.' She crossed her legs. 'He's so not worth it,' she said, sounding like a bad L'Oréal advert.

Lexi blew her nose, feeling far from professional in her

navy trouser suit and white shirt. 'It's not just about Olly. It's everything that's happened over the past two years. Marcus's betrayal. Nearly losing the gallery. The fraudulent insurance policy. I think it's all catching up with me.'

Tasha leant across and squeezed her hand. 'I know, sweetie. But you need to get a grip. We're not going to pull this off if you're a quivering mess.'

'That's my point. I can't do this. I shouldn't have let you change my mind.'

'Nonsense. You're just nervous.'

Lexi shook her head, making her earrings sway. 'You were right when you said I should leave it to the authorities to sort out. It was crazy even to think we could pull this off.'

Tasha sighed. 'No, you were right when you said we needed to retrieve the painting ourselves.'

'Only because I wasn't thinking straight.' Lexi removed her jacket, suddenly hot. She'd allowed Olly to get into her brain and scramble her thoughts. She'd been seduced by his talents – not to mention his other attributes – and had gone along with his crazy plan. But that was before she'd realised he couldn't be trusted. 'It's safer if I present the ownership papers to Sotheby's and let them deal with it.'

Tasha didn't look convinced. 'And risk the painting getting confiscated? They're not going to hand it over, Lexi. There'll be a long-drawn-out investigation, arguments over ownership, and you'll be tied up in red tape for months.'

'But at least I won't be breaking the law.'

'And how are you going to deal with questions about how you paid for the painting? The date of the purchase was within the bankruptcy period, so it'll be classed as an asset. An asset you should've declared.'

Her sister had a point.

'The painting will be sold and the proceeds will be offset against the original debt. *Marcus's* debt. And you'll still be left owing the official receiver twenty-seven grand. Not to mention a potential investigation for fraud.'

'I hadn't thought of that.'

'Well, lucky for you, I did.' Tasha sat back in her chair. 'I'll admit not straight away. But since you told me about taking the money from the house, I've been doing some research. The only way out of this is for us to get that painting back and transfer ownership to me. That way, I can legitimately sell it and give you the money. Then you can pay off the official receiver saying your sister gave you the money, which would be the truth.'

'There'd still be a paper trail back to me.'

'Not necessarily. You paid for the painting in cash, right?'

Lexi nodded.

'Right. So we say I gave you the money to buy the painting on my behalf. No one can prove otherwise. It's a business transaction. And as you've already proved in court, the gallery is excluded from the bankruptcy.'

Lexi rubbed her forehead. 'More lies.'

Tasha reached across and took her hand. 'Time's running out. We have a plan, Lexi. We need to stick to it.'

Lexi nodded. 'Okay.'

'Now, come on.' She checked her watch. 'We need to time our arrival perfectly. Arriving too early will allow the auction house the opportunity to involve Marcus. Arriving too late might see the painting sold before we've had the chance to put our plan into action.'

'Did you check the schedule?'

'Yes. The *Woman at the Window* is listed as Lot one hundred and twenty-three. It has a reserve price of five grand. I reckon that gives us about an hour before bidding begins. Just enough time to recover the wretched thing.'

Lexi's mouth had gone dry. She took a last swig of tea. Her precious painting valued at a fraction of its worth. Talk about depressing.

Tasha stood up. 'In an hour this will all be over and we can go home.'

God, Lexi hoped so.

Chapter 20

Monday 25th June

When Olly and Sophie had left Rubha Castle late Saturday afternoon, he'd already known his Vespa wasn't the fastest mode of transportation in the world. With Sophie riding pillion, they might as well have driven a mobility scooter to Inverness – eighty miles had never seemed so long. At one point, he'd felt it would be a miracle if they reached Sotheby's by the end of the month, let alone by Monday.

Their saving grace had been the empty Highland lanes, enabling them to get a move on. Well, as much as the Vespa would allow. Failing to stop at three traffic lights had also helped. He'd worry about that when the tickets arrived. If their plan stood any chance of working, they needed enough time to put everything into place.

Having stored his scooter in the long-stay car park at the station, he'd incurred Sophie's wrath when they'd discovered they'd missed the last train. After an uncomfortable night in a B & B, they'd eventually boarded the train for Edinburgh early Sunday morning.

It was now Monday morning and they were seated in Café Marlayne on Thistle Street. He'd have preferred the smaller Lime café further down the road, but Sophie had insisted on French cuisine. Recompense for being forced to ride his scooter.

'And you're certain Lexi hasn't changed her mind and they're not at the auction house?' He pushed his eggs around the plate. A fear of failure had killed any desire to eat.

Sophie tucked into her French toast, not suffering from the same affliction. 'I'm positive. I looked everywhere, even the toilets. Trust me, they're not there.'

'How can we be certain?'

Sophie lowered her fork. 'If you'd had the foresight to get their phone numbers, we could've called them to check. But you didn't, did you?' She glared at him and resumed eating.

'It's not like I didn't try.' Lexi hadn't trusted him enough to share her details. Something that had felt unfair at the time and now felt entirely justified.

'Stop stressing,' Sophie said, reaching for her iced tea. 'We won't do anything until we're satisfied they're not at the auction house. Okay?'

He nodded.

The waiter appeared and topped up his coffee.

It had seemed like such a simple plan when Sophie had suggested it. But now they were about to put the plan into action he was getting cold feet.

'Supposing we get caught?' he said when the waiter disappeared. 'The scandal could ruin us.'

'Caught doing what? We're not stealing the painting, Olly. We have a logical and perfectly reasonable explanation worked out. Nothing will go wrong.'

'But what if it does? Have you forgotten, we've already got another scandal hanging over our heads?' He checked no one was listening before whispering, '*The Cursed Man*.'

But nobody was paying any attention. The café was bustling

with patrons, laughing and chatting over good food and the ambient surroundings.

Sophie dabbed at her mouth with a napkin. 'And have *you* forgotten that today is about stopping that scandal from happening?' She wiped her hands. 'Not to mention helping you win back Lexi.'

The idea of winning Lexi back seemed even more impossible than getting her painting back. 'I never had her in the first place.'

'Well, now's your chance. Eat up.'

'I'm not hungry.'

She sighed. 'You're being defeatist.'

'It's easy for you to say. You're not the one who was caught lying. For weeks, I've been begging her to trust me. Telling her I'm a decent bloke. Trying to prove myself. But I'm a fraud. Why should she trust me? I've pretended to be someone I'm not.'

Sophie didn't immediately respond. She took a sip of water. 'But with good reason.'

'Is there ever a good reason to lie? Lying is all I've done for the past eleven years. Look where it's got me.'

Sophie pushed her plate away. 'You lied to protect your family.'

'You've changed your tune. You didn't feel that way a few days ago.'

'Because now I know the reason.'

'And you think that makes it okay? I don't think so. Not anymore.' He rubbed the back of his neck. He had a headache to rival the ache in his chest.

She frowned. 'So you wish you'd come clean? All those years ago.'

'Honestly? I don't know.' He slumped back in his chair. 'All I know is, I'm nearly thirty years old and I've spent my entire adult life running from the truth. Existing in a perpetual state of panic. Scared of anyone finding out. Hiding from those I love.'

It was a while before she spoke.

'I guess that must be hard,' she said, sounding sad and very unlike Sophie.

'You have no idea. Maybe it would've been better if I'd spoken up at the time and forced our parents to face the music. Because let's face it, they weren't happy either, were they? You and Louisa certainly weren't.'

The waiter came over and cleared their plates. He dug out his wallet to pay, but Sophie stopped him.

'I'll get this.' She turned to the waiter and dazzled him with a smile. '*L'addition, s'il vous plaît.*'

The waiter bowed his head. '*Bien sûr, madame.*'

Olly sighed. Another man struck by his sister's charms.

Sophie settled the bill and slipped on her grey jacket. She was dressed in business attire, aiming for an air of authority. 'We'd better get going,' she said, picking up her briefcase. 'The auction is about to start.'

Resigned to his fate, he joined her by the door. 'Christ, I hope we pull this off.'

'So do I.' She hooked her arm through his. 'And just so you know, I do understand why you lied. Sometimes it's necessary to protect those we love.'

'I doubt you've ever lied,' he said. His sister was scarily honest. Brutal, at times.

'Actually, I have.' She turned to him. 'I've been lying even longer than you have.'

He frowned. 'What about?'

She waited for a pause in the traffic.

'I'm gay,' she said, crossing the street and leaving him standing on the pavement with his mouth hanging open.

Chapter 21

A few minutes earlier ...

Lexi followed Tasha through the ornate olive green door into Sotheby's auction house. It was an impressive building. Smaller than the London setting but spectacular in its own right. The grand foyer was a vast space with a high ceiling. A huge chandelier cast the room in bright, soft lighting. In the centre, a series of partitions sectioned off the room. Paintings were displayed on the makeshift walls, each one lit and secured with heavy brass chains.

Lexi walked around the displays with the other patrons, admiring the work. She'd normally relish an opportunity like this, if it weren't for the shake in her hands and the knot in her stomach. If she was in any doubt before today about her ability to cheat people, she was now certain a life of deceit wasn't for her. When this was over she was going to lead a very uneventful and boring life. No lying. No illegal scams. And definitely no hooking up with blue-eyed thieves.

Thoughts of Olly threatened to derail her. She shook away the image of kissing him and reminded herself she was better off without him. Chances are, she'd never see him again anyway. Which depressed her a lot more than it should.

A bell rang in the foyer, causing a ripple of excitement among those gathered. The auction was about to get under way.

Tasha appeared by her side. 'I've spoken to the deputy

director, Nadia Anderson, and I've arranged a private viewing of the painting ahead of the sale. A couple of other people have also requested a viewing, so that's good.'

'How so?'

'Because it means our request isn't unusual. It shouldn't invite suspicion. Plus, it'll be easier to cause a distraction with more people in the room.' Tasha glanced around the masses of people making their way into the auction room. 'Have you seen Scumbag yet?'

'No, thank goodness. I'm not sure my nerves could cope with seeing Marcus.'

'It's better he doesn't know we're here.' Tasha led her across the room. 'He'll know we're up to something. Stop shaking.'

'I can't help it.'

'Try harder.' Tasha stopped by a side door. 'Now remember, once we're in the room you need to open the carry case like I showed you. When you're given the painting, remove the frame and clip it to the front section of the case. Tell them you need total darkness to use the black light wand. When the lights go out, turn the case around. The copy is clipped to the reverse.'

Her sister made it sound so easy. 'Surely someone will notice me doing it?'

'Not if I create enough of a disturbance to allow you time to rotate the case.'

'What are you going to do?'

'I'm not sure yet. Fall over. Faint. Pretend to see a spider, or something. It depends on the layout of the room and who's in there. When the lights are back on and the switch has been made, finish the examination so it doesn't look suspicious.'

Lexi wasn't convinced. 'This isn't going to work.'

'Sure it will.' Tasha opened the door. 'Trust me.'

Lexi tried to do as her sister asked, but it was hard when her heart was thumping so hard she could feel it in her teeth.

She walked into the room, which wasn't big. There were no windows. The room was lit by artificial lighting. And then she spotted the *Woman at the Window* displayed on a small stand in the middle of the table. Her chest tightened. Her beautiful painting. She almost wanted to run over and hug the demure Italian. She didn't, of course. That really would look suspicious.

A security guard stood by the door. He asked to see her ID proving she was a legitimate dealer. Her hand shook as she removed her Association of Women Art Dealers membership card. A second female staff member was standing across the room talking to a middle-aged couple.

Lexi walked into the room, clutching hold of the carry case.

Tasha leant closer. 'Only two staff members, that's good.'

Lexi nodded, on autopilot.

'And the frame has already been removed. Even better,' Tasha added.

Again, Lexi nodded. If the auction house knew it was the original painting they'd probably have better security in place. She wanted to turn and run, but it was too late.

Tasha was moving around the room, adding a sway to her walk. It was enough to invite an interested look from the security guard. His eyes dipped to her backside, distracting him from his duties.

Tasha had spotted this and her sway switched to a full-blown sashay.

There was another potential buyer in the room. An Asian man. Lexi waited for him to complete his analysis of the painting before approaching the table. She glanced over her shoulder. The couple were still occupying the female staff member. The security guard was still watching Tasha.

It was now or never.

She lifted the carry case onto the table and opened it. She picked up the *Woman at the Window* and glanced over at the security guard, waiting until he'd nodded his approval that it was okay for her to move the painting before sliding it into the carry case and securing it firmly.

She picked up her jeweller's loupe and made a show of examining the painting. This was something she'd done many times. It was perfectly reasonable as an art dealer to assess a piece of work. But far from feeling confident in her abilities, she felt as tense as a guy rope lashed to a tent in a gale-force wind. She half expected sirens to go off.

She lowered the loupe and picked up her black light wand. She wanted to look at Tasha, hoping it would calm her nerves, but she knew it would look suspicious. Instead, she took a breath and cleared her throat. 'Any chance we could turn off the lights, please?'

The female staff member looked over. 'Is that necessary?'

Lexi nodded, or tried to. Her neck felt so stiff she could barely move it. 'I need it for the next stage of my assessment.'

The woman didn't look happy but excused herself from talking to the couple. 'Be quick, please,' she said, nodding at the security guard, who cut the lights.

Time was critical. Especially as it wasn't completely dark. Her movements were still visible. The second she heard Tasha scream, she flipped the carry case. She had no idea what Tasha had done, but she heard a loud thud, followed by a crash.

'Turn the lights on!' yelled the female staff member.

When the lights came on, Lexi realised the replica painting was upside down. She tried not to panic.

Thankfully, all eyes were on Tasha, who was lying on the floor next to an upturned chair clutching her ankle.

'I'm so sorry,' her sister said, playing the damsel in distress. 'How clumsy of me.'

Lexi glanced around the room. When she was certain no one was watching, she turned the painting the right way around.

The security guard helped Tasha up. 'Do you need a medic?'

'No, I'm fine, thank you. I'm not used to walking in heels,' she said, holding on to his arm. 'I'll pop to the ladies and put a cold compress on it.'

The female staff member turned to Lexi. 'Have you finished your examination?'

'I have, yes. Thank you.'

'Good.'

The woman came over and placed Olly's copy back on the stand. Lexi held her breath, waiting to see if she'd noticed it was a different painting. She didn't.

'The auction is under way. We need to clear this room,' the woman said, indicating the door.

Lexi almost couldn't believe it. It had worked. She had the *Woman at the Window* back. Trying to contain her relief, she clipped the carry case shut and lifted it off the table.

She'd just reached the door, when the woman stopped her. 'One moment, please.' She lifted a walkie-talkie to her ear. 'Yes, Nadia? Yep ... Okay ... understood.' She finished her call. 'Apologies, but there's been a security incident. You'll need to wait here a moment.'

Lexi and Tasha exchanged a look.

265

'I hope we won't miss the auction.' Lexi's voice wavered slightly.

The woman smiled. 'I'm sure whatever it is, it won't take long.'

Lexi hoped so, too. Because until they were far away from the auction house, there was still a chance their plan could implode.

Chapter 22

Twenty minutes earlier ...

'You're gay?' Olly ran after his sister, who'd left him standing speechless on the pavement. 'Seriously?'

Sophie kept walking, forcing him to speed up to keep up with her. 'What, because I don't dress like a man and have a short haircut, I couldn't possibly be a lesbian? Is that it?'

'Of course not. It's just ...' He caught her arm. 'I never knew.'

She stopped walking. 'No one did.'

'But, I don't understand. Why haven't you ever told anyone?'

She pinned him with a glare. 'Why do you think, Olly? Mother nearly disowned Louisa when she thought she couldn't reproduce. How do you think she'd have reacted if she'd discovered her eldest child was gay?'

She had a point. But still. 'So all that partying with eligible men and rumours about who you were dating?'

She shrugged. 'All engineered to keep up appearances. As long as Mother thought I was playing the field in search of the perfect blue-blood beau, she was happy.'

The look on his sister's face was heartbreaking. It suddenly all made sense. The anger, the resentment. No wonder she'd barricaded herself away.

He took her hand. 'But *you* weren't happy, were you?'

She stared down at her feet. 'Sometimes we do things to protect others. You of all people should know that.'

And he knew how crap it felt. 'I'm so sorry, Sophie.'

'What have you got to be sorry about? It's not your problem.' But her wounded expression didn't match her aggressive tone. She was struggling to remain composed. 'I only told you because I wanted you to know I understand what it's like to keep a secret. It's exhausting. And unfair. It hangs over you like a guillotine waiting to drop.'

She tried to move away, but he held on to her. 'Sophie—'

'There's no time.' She tugged her hand free and opened the green door leading into the auction house. 'We have a painting to retrieve.'

There were so many things he wanted to say. So many questions. But she was right, now wasn't the time. And knowing Sophie, she'd probably timed her confession deliberately so he couldn't question her. Her barrier was back up.

He followed her into the auction house.

They were greeted by a man wearing a smart burgundy uniform. 'Ladies and gentlemen. Welcome to Sotheby's.' He opened the double doors leading to the auction room. 'If you'd like to make your way through, bidding will commence in five minutes.'

The reception area began to empty. People filed into the auction room, eager to spend their cash. Or maybe simply watch others spend theirs, who knew? Olly searched the faces, looking for Lexi, but he couldn't see her.

His eyes scanned the rows of plush seating and phone tables set up at the side, each with a member of staff logging onto a computer in preparation for the sale. Still no sign of Lexi. Good. Hopefully that meant she was back in Windsor.

Standing on a small stage at the front was a man wearing a black suit and bow tie. He tested the microphone, tapping the end to check the connection.

Olly hadn't realised Sophie wasn't with him until he turned and saw her making her way through the throng of people.

'I've checked the register,' she said, keeping her voice low. 'Looks like Nadia Anderson's the person to talk to. She's the deputy director.'

'Lexi definitely isn't in the auction room. Have you checked everywhere else?'

'Yes, no sign of her. Looks like she got cold feet.'

'I guess so.'

He'd be happier knowing for certain. But there was no way of checking and time was running out. It was now or never.

'Okay, let's do this.' He signalled a young woman with a clipboard. 'I'd like to speak to Nadia Anderson as a matter of urgency. I believe one of the paintings registered for today's sale is stolen.'

The woman looked startled. 'I'll fetch Ms Anderson right away. Please wait here.'

While they waited, Olly watched as the first painting for sale was carried out and placed on the easel next to the stage.

The auctioneer approached the microphone and the chatter in the room quietened. Welcoming the bidders, sellers and guests to the sale, he briefly detailed appropriate etiquette for bidding before banging down his gavel. 'Lot number one. Hieronymus Bosch. Estimated value nine thousand pounds.' The screen next to him sprung into life, showing an image of the painting. 'I'm starting the bidding at five thousand.'

A woman in a green scarf waved her hand.

The auctioneer pointed at her with his hammer. 'Madam, can I see your paddle?'

The woman lifted what looked like a numbered table tennis bat.

'Thank you. Any advance on five thousand?'

A few people joined in the bidding. The sale price went up in increments of five hundred pounds until only Scarf Woman was left with her paddle aloft.

'Fair warning,' the auctioneer said, lifting his hand. 'I'm selling in the room at seven thousand.' He banged down his hammer. 'Sold. Paddle number one hundred and forty-five.'

Olly looked on in mild fascination. Despite his mother's profession, he'd never been to one of these events before. The bidding was frenetic. Blink and you'd missed your chance.

'Lot two,' the auctioneer announced. 'Rembrandt's *Christ Crucified between Two Thieves, The Three Crosses*. Estimated value two hundred and fifty thousand. Who will start the bidding?'

Olly wondered if he'd heard correctly. And these were copies?

The young woman with the clipboard reappeared. 'Would you care to follow me? Ms Anderson is waiting for you in her office.'

Olly and Sophie were led into the deputy director's office. A woman stood up to greet them. 'Nadia Anderson,' she said, her sharp gaze sizing them up, assessing how much trouble they were about to inflict. 'This is my assistant, John Moreton.' She nodded towards an older bespectacled man. 'I understand you have information regarding one of the paintings on auction today?'

'That's right. The *Woman at the Window*.' Olly stepped

forwards. 'It's not a copy being auctioned off but the original work.'

The two Sotheby's employees exchanged a look.

'It was stolen from a gallery in Windsor,' he added.

'And you are?' Nadia Anderson gave him a questioning look.

'A representative of the gallery owner, Lexi Ryan. This is my associate, Ms ... Huntworth,' he said, giving Sophie a fake name. He wasn't sure why. Other than if this went tits-up he didn't want her to suffer any bad publicity. He motioned to where Sophie was standing. 'I'd like the painting removed from the sale and returned immediately.'

Nadia frowned. 'May I ask why you haven't contacted the police and instructed them to deal with the matter?'

Bloody good question. Luckily, he'd anticipated it. 'The owner only became aware of the theft this morning. The painting was taken without her knowledge. I have it on good authority the perpetrator of the crime is planning to auction off the original this afternoon. She didn't have time to contact the authorities. As her representative in Scotland, she asked me to come straight here and alert you.'

The deputy director rubbed her forehead. 'And you're certain the painting listed in today's auction isn't a copy?'

He nodded. 'I'm positive.'

'Well, to say I'm shocked would be an understatement. I've heard of copies being masqueraded as originals, but never the other way around.' She picked up the phone on her desk and pushed a button. 'Jenny? It's Nadia. Instruct Arthur to remove Lot number ...' she flicked through the sales catalogue, 'one hundred and twenty-three from the auction listing. Have it brought to my office immediately. And alert security, would you? Don't let anyone leave the building. We have a potential Code four.' She replaced receiver. 'Obviously, we'll need to contact the gallery owner, but I see no merit in involving her until we've established the painting isn't a copy.' She moved around to the front of the desk. 'Please, take a seat.'

Olly and Sophie sat down.

'Excuse me a moment, would you?' Nadia walked over to the door. 'My assistant will keep you company until I return.' She looked over at her colleague. 'You can use Doug's office, John. I'll be as quick as I can.'

As she left, John Moreton unearthed a bunch of keys from his suit pocket and unlocked an internal door. He disappeared through it, closing it behind him. So much for keeping them company.

The room descended into silence, broken only by the loud tick of the ornate grandfather clock.

Olly glanced at his sister. 'So, gay, huh?'

Her head rested against the wall behind. 'Is it so hard to believe?'

'Kind of, yeah.'

'It's the twenty-first century, Olly. It's okay to be gay.' She sounded angry.

'So why keep it quiet?'

She didn't answer straight away. 'I told you why.'

'Oh, right. Our parents.' He looked around the room. It was a typical office. Beige carpet, cream walls, potted plants on the floor. Hardly the appropriate setting for a heart-to-heart. 'Are you sure there isn't more to it?'

'Like what?'

He shrugged. 'I don't know. Maybe not telling our parents was an excuse.'

She rolled her head to stare at him. 'What's that supposed to mean?'

'Do your friends know you're gay?'

She hesitated. 'I doubt it.'

'What about work colleagues?'

She glowered at him. 'Which part of *I kept it a secret* is hard for you to understand?'

'So you never told anyone?'

'No,' she snapped. 'I didn't. Your point?'

'Are you ashamed of being gay?'

Anger flashed across her face. 'That's so judgemental.'

He held up his hands in defence. 'I don't mean to be, but this is a new situation for me. I'm trying to understand. Our parents are both gone, so I'm wondering why you're still pretending to be someone you're not?'

She didn't answer. It would be easier to shut up, but Sophie wouldn't have told him if she wasn't ready for a confrontation. Painful as it was, he needed to persevere. 'Are you going to tell Louisa?'

She folded her arms, like she were trying to fold herself into the tiniest space. 'I suspect she already knows.'

'So I'm the first person you've told?' He patted her knee, not sure what else to do. 'That was incredibly brave of you, Sophie.'

She batted his hand away. 'Don't patronise me.'

'I didn't mean to. I'm just saying, you no longer need to pretend. Keeping quiet hasn't made you happy. So maybe it's time to embrace who you are.'

'Like it's that simple.'

'No, but unless you admit who you are and love who you are, how can you expect anyone else to?'

She turned to yell at him, but it was like the words had got lodged in her throat. Instead, she thumped his damaged arm.

He didn't mind. Whatever helped her to let go of the pain she was carrying.

The office door opened and Nadia reappeared carrying the *Woman at the Window*, accompanied by two security officers.

'If you'd care to follow me.' She marched through to the adjacent office where her colleague had set up a wall-mounted light box. She placed the painting on the ledge. 'Over to you, John.'

The man picked up a magnifying glass and began examining the painting.

Olly tried to calm his agitation. There was nothing to be edgy about. It was the original painting. He glanced at Sophie, but her expression gave nothing away. It seemed to take forever. The man wasn't exactly speedy.

Finally, he turned to his waiting audience. 'I can categorically state that this work of art is not a sixteenth-century Renaissance painting but a copy.'

Olly wondered if he'd heard correctly. 'Excuse me?'

'It's a fake,' he said slowly as if speaking to a particularly dim child. 'A good fake, but not the original painting.'

'But it can't be.'

Olly looked at Sophie. She appeared as puzzled as he was.

The man aimed a remote control at the light switch. The room dimmed. 'Look.' He pointed to the painting with a narrow wand. 'There's another image hidden beneath the top painting. It looks mid 1800s, possibly. There's absolutely no way the top painting is five hundred years old. Judging by the application of paint, I'd be very surprised if it was five *months* old.' He snickered, obviously pleased with his little joke.

Olly felt his insides twist. It was the copy he'd painted. What the hell was going on? It should be the bloody original. Did that mean Lexi had already swapped it? Oh, hell.

The lights came back on.

'Return the painting to the auction room, would you, John. Apologise to Arthur for the inconvenience.' Nadia Anderson turned to Olly. 'I assume this was an elaborate ruse designed to walk out of here with a semi-valuable painting?'

It took him a moment to cotton on to the allegation being thrown his way. 'No, of course not. I was led to believe the painting listed for auction today was the original.'

The deputy director looked nonplussed. 'Either way, I don't appreciate having my time wasted. The police can deal with this. I have an auction to oversee.' She strode for the door.

'Now, hang on a minute.' Sophie tried to follow, but one of the security guards blocked her path. 'We were clearly given the wrong information. There's no need to involve the police. No harm's been done.'

'On the contrary, Ms Huntworth.' Nadia Anderson opened the door. 'Your misplaced allegations could've damaged Sotheby's reputation and involved them in unnecessary scandal. We don't take kindly to such slander. And besides, this way you'll get to report the theft of your painting, if that's truthfully what happened.'

She disappeared, followed by John Moreton and the two security officers, who were instructed to stay the other side of the door. The distinctive sound of a lock being turned followed their departure.

Sophie strode over and tried the handle. 'I can't believe this. How did this happen?' She turned to look at Olly.

He shrugged. 'Don't look at me. I've got no idea.'

And now the police were on their way.

This was not how this was supposed to play out.

Chapter 23

Later that day ...

Shortly after being detained, a bespectacled man appeared and removed the *Woman at the Window* from the room. It was another fifteen minutes before the door opened again – during which time Lexi had wanted to shout, scream and pace the room, her panic levels threatening to spill over. Only Tasha's calming voice telling her to '*get a grip*' prevented her from causing a commotion. 'Try not to look so guilty,' her sister had whispered, which was easier said than done, considering she *was* guilty.

When the door finally opened, a security guard appeared followed by a woman who introduced herself as Nadia Anderson, the deputy director of Sotheby's. She was cordial in manner and professional in appearance, and didn't seem to be accusing them of anything untoward. So when she politely asked them to accompany her to her office to help 'clear something up', it was hard to refuse and would have made them look even more suspicious if they had. Which was how they found themselves being led through the busy auction area packed with art collectors eagerly bidding on the works being displayed.

Lexi scanned the rows of heads, trying to spot Marcus. The auctioneer was in full flow, holding the attention of the eager crowd as he pointed to someone on the phone.

'Selling on the telephone at thirty-seven five hundred.'

Despite feeling extremely conspicuous at being 'escorted' through the room, no one seemed to notice them as they edged past. All eyes were fixed ahead, focused on the bidding.

The auctioneer pointed to the phone man again. 'The room came in first. I'm sorry, sir. I'll take thirty-nine if you like?'

And then Lexi spotted her ex-husband sitting in the front row. His striking looks and tanned features sent a wave of panic rushing through her. Oh, cripes. She must have faltered, because Tasha bumped into the back of her.

Her sister reached out to steady her. 'You okay?'

She shook her head, trying to curtail the urge to bolt. 'Marcus,' she whispered, nodding to where her ex-husband was sitting watching the bidding.

Tasha gently pushed her forwards. 'Head down, keep walking.'

Easy for her to say. Her legs hadn't turned to jelly.

Why hadn't she refused the deputy director's request? Calling the woman's bluff was a bold move. But as Olly had pointed out, she didn't have the attributes for poker. Her left eye started twitching manically, as if proving a point.

'Forty-one thousand clears my books,' the auctioneer said, raising his hammer. 'Sold to the commissioned bidder.' He smacked down his hammer, making Lexi jump. 'Next up, Lot eighty-two, Matisse's *Blue Nude*. I have a reserve price of ten thousand. Shall we start the bidding at ten thousand five hundred?' He motioned to the tables running along the side. 'We have an early bid from cyberspace. Eleven thousand, thank you, sir.'

They reached a doorway. The security guard opened the door and ushered them inside. Lexi felt like a naughty child being sent to the headmistress for stealing sweets.

'I'm looking for twelve thousand,' the auctioneer said behind them. 'Eleven thousand seven fifty? I'll accept your bid, as you're clearly a woman on a budget. Can I introduce you to my wife?'

The room rippled with laughter. The noise faded when the door closed behind them. The security guard positioned himself by the door, cutting off any means of escape. Ominous.

There were two other people already in the room. It took a while for Lexi to realise it was Olly and Sophie. What the hell were they doing here?

They stood when Lexi and Tasha entered, their expressions a mixture of surprise and supressed panic. Not unlike her own.

Emotion bubbled inside her. Was it relief? Or anger? She couldn't tell. Whatever it was, the urge to yell at them for scuppering her getaway was curtailed by Tasha tugging on the bottom of her suit jacket and hissing, '*Get a grip*,' jolting her out of her shock. She smiled and smoothed back her hair, trying to hide her reaction, so she didn't blow their cover. Questions would have to wait.

Nadia Anderson positioned herself in front of the large office desk. Her dark eyes darted from one person to the next, as if waiting to see who would crack first.

The *Woman at the Window* was balanced on the chair next to her, watching events unfold, an amused expression on the sultry Italian's face. It was like she knew she was causing trouble and was relishing the scandal.

'I'm hoping you can clarify something,' Nadia said, gesturing to the painting. 'And prevent the need for us to contact the police.'

Police? Lexi tried to keep her expression neutral, which was hard when her left eye was twitching like an exposed nerve. 'I'll do my best.'

'This gentleman claims to be an associate of yours?' Nadia left the question hanging, waiting for a response.

Lexi glanced at Olly. If he was nervous, he was hiding it well. He was wearing dark jeans and a black shirt, emphasising his deep blue eyes and honey-coloured hair. The sight of him made her traitorous heart speed up. But she couldn't afford to lose her composure. Not now.

She studied his expression, looking for clues, noticing a note of pleading in his eyes. 'That's correct,' she said, hoping that was the right answer.

The relief on Olly's face indicated it was. Phew.

'I understand a painting was stolen from your gallery?' Another loaded question from Nadia.

Lexi figured the truth was probably safest. 'That's right. The *Woman at the Window*.'

Nadia gestured to the painting. 'This painting?'

Lexi could feel the tension reverberating off Tasha next to her. 'Yes, that's correct.'

Nadia tilted her head as if waiting for more. Oh, hell. What was she supposed to say?

Thankfully, Olly came to her aid. 'As I explained to Ms Anderson, the painting was stolen from your gallery in Windsor. As your Scottish representative, you sent me here to alert the auction house to the theft and prevent a fraudulent sale.'

So that was his plan? She wasn't sure whether to hug him for attempting to rescue her painting, or punch his lights out for jeopardising their carefully masterminded heist.

Judging by the pained expression on her sister's face, she guessed Tasha was in favour of the latter.

'The original painting? Not a copy?' Nadia said, watching Lexi closely.

Lexi glanced at Olly. He gave a slight nod.

'Yes, the original painting,' she said before realising she should be reacting to its safe return. 'I'm so glad you got here in time,' she said to Olly, feigning relief. 'Thank you for responding so promptly to my request for help.'

Nadia didn't look convinced. Lexi couldn't blame her. 'And you're sure this is the painting that was taken from your gallery?'

Lexi realised Nadia didn't know a second painting existed. Lexi wasn't supposed to know, either. Crikey, things were getting complicated. She studied the painting on display, choosing her response carefully. 'It certainly looks like my painting, but without a proper examination I couldn't be certain.'

Nadia nodded slowly. 'My colleague has already examined the painting.'

Oh, hell. The twitch in her left eye increased. 'And his conclusion?'

'It's not the original painting.'

There was a delay before Lexi gasped. Even to her own ears it sounded fake. 'It's ... not?' Her hand went to her chest in mock horror, but she lowered it when Sophie raised an eyebrow, indicating her reaction was overkill.

'I was as surprised as you are, Ms Ryan,' Olly said, his acting a lot better than hers. 'We were led to believe this was the original painting.'

Lexi nodded. 'As was I, which is why we rushed up here.

Our intel must've been poor,' she said, regretting her choice of words when Tasha cringed. 'What I mean is, our information was incorrect. I'm sorry for the confusion and for wasting your valuable time.'

Nadia wasn't buying it. 'You asked for a private viewing prior to the auction. Correct?'

Lexi's heart was thudding so hard she was surprised everyone else couldn't hear it. 'That's right. We didn't want to cause a fuss until we knew it was the right painting.'

Nadia's expression turned quizzical. 'And what conclusion did you arrive at?'

Oh, cripes. 'Err ...'

'We didn't get the chance to finish our assessment,' Tasha said, coming to her rescue. 'The painting was removed from the room before we'd formed a judgement.'

God, Lexi loved her sister.

Nadia's expression didn't give much away. 'How convenient.'

There was another weighted pause, during which Nadia viewed them all suspiciously.

Their collective efforts to look innocent varied from Tasha feigning assertiveness to Sophie looking bored and Olly looking mildly alarmed. Lexi was envious of their ability to remain calm and composed. She was the only one struggling not to crack. This was a poker game of high stakes and she was in danger of revealing her hand.

Someone knocked on the door. The bespectacled man from earlier appeared in the doorway. 'Apologies for interrupting, Ms Anderson. I've tracked down the seller, Mr Aldridge. I have him outside if you'd like to speak to him?'

Lexi held her breath. Marcus? Oh, hell. *Please say no ... Please say no ...*

'Ask him to join us, would you?'

Damn it!

The dynamic in the room changed the moment Marcus entered. He was complaining in a loud voice, telling anyone who'd listen that his treatment was 'outrageous'.

'What's this about?' he demanded, looking stylish in an expensive grey suit teamed with a pale pink shirt, playing the part of a wealthy art seller to perfection. And then he spotted Lexi. 'Lexi?'

Nadia Anderson looked mildly surprised. 'Do you two know each other?'

'This is my ex-husband,' Lexi said, striking first while Marcus was still wrong-footed. 'The man I believe stole the painting from my gallery.'

Marcus reacted with outrage. 'That painting was bought with *my* money,' he yelled. 'I only took what I was owed.'

Finally, an admission!

'But as we've already established, this isn't the original painting,' Nadia pointed out, cutting short Lexi's joy.

Marcus swung around to face Nadia. 'What are you on about?'

'My colleague has examined the work and confirmed it's a copy.'

'A copy?' Marcus looked dumbstruck. 'But ... that's impossible.'

Nadia's eyes narrowed. 'Are you saying the painting you submitted was the original, Mr Aldridge?'

'I know it was.'

'Then may I enquire as to why you listed it as a copy?'

That got him.

Marcus fumbled around for an answer. 'Well ... what does

it matter?' he blustered. 'It's my painting, I can do what I like with it.' He switched to attack mode. 'But if that's not the painting I submitted, then where's mine?' His eyes travelled down to the carry case by Lexi's feet. 'She must have swapped it. Ask her what's in there.'

Lexi's insides flipped. Her world was about to come crashing down.

But Olly intervened. 'Even if the original painting is inside the carry case, it makes no difference. Ms Ryan is the registered legal owner.'

'Exactly,' Tasha said, stepping towards Marcus, intimidating in her black suit. 'It's your word against hers. Can you prove she bought the painting with your money?'

Her sister was playing a dangerous game mentioning the money, but Marcus stood to lose as much as she did if the authorities got involved. Tasha knew that, which was probably why she was calling his bluff.

Sophie inspected her nails in a nonchalant fashion. 'Even if you do have a valid money claim against Ms Ryan, you'll need to present your argument in court and let a judge decide about ownership. Until then, possession remains with the purchaser.' She subjected Marcus to a patronising smile. 'My cousin's a barrister. I could call him, if you like?'

Marcus looked furious. His fists were bunched and the veins in his neck pulsed.

Nadia turned to Lexi. 'Do you have proof of ownership?'

Lexi removed the ownership papers from the front of the carry case and handed them over, trying to hide the shake in her hands. 'You'll find they're all in order.'

Nadia read through them. 'The registered owner is Miss Natasha Ryan,' she said, turning the page. 'Purchased from

Ms Alexia Ryan ...' She raised an eyebrow. 'This morning?' She looked between Lexi and Tasha. 'That's rather convenient.'

'Not really.' Tasha lifted her chin. 'My sister purchased the painting on my behalf. We've only recently got around to amending the paperwork and transferring funds.' She shot Marcus a warning look. 'I'm afraid any ownership claim will be against me,' she said, folding her arms. 'Not my sister.'

Marcus looked close to combusting. 'It's a scam! They're in it together.'

'That's as maybe,' Nadia said, handing the papers back to Lexi. 'But the paperwork appears to be legitimate. I won't be pursuing the matter further. You've wasted enough of my time as it is.'

Marcus adopted an air of outrage. 'I'm not listening to this rubbish any longer.' He strode for the door. 'I'm returning to the auction, where I expect *that* painting,' he pointed at the *Woman at the Window*, 'to be sold as listed. I've been inconvenienced enough.'

'One moment, please.' Nadia instructed the security guard to stop him leaving.

'What now? You said it yourself, that painting's a copy. It doesn't belong to *her*,' he said, pointing at Lexi. 'So why can't I sell it?'

'Because I've yet to see proof that it belongs to you, Mr Aldridge.' Nadia looked annoyed. 'You've admitted this isn't the painting you submitted for sale. If you're asking me to reinstate it, I need to ascertain that you're legally allowed to sell it. Can you provide such evidence?'

Marcus faltered.

Nadia checked her watch. 'I'm waiting, Mr Aldridge.'

'He's not the registered owner,' Olly said, glancing at Lexi. 'I am.'

Nadia's agitation switched to annoyance. 'And you're only mentioning this now because?'

Olly shrugged. 'Because you've only just asked the question about ownership,' he said, totally unfazed. 'I sent the painting to Ms Ryan in the hope she might offer me representation. I can only assume whoever broke into the gallery stole the wrong painting. Or both. Who knows?'

Nadia frowned. 'Are you saying that you're the artist?'

'If you remove the frame you'll see my signature on the reverse of the canvas.'

Nadia sighed. 'Fine. But if this is more time-wasting, I *will* be calling the police. I've had enough of this nonsense.' She nodded at the bespectacled man, who removed the frame and held up the canvas.

True enough, signed on the back were the words Dazed & Confused, June 2018.

'I'm Dazed & Confused,' Olly said.

'Right now, so am I,' Nadia said, shaking her head.

'He's telling the truth.' Lexi felt it was necessary to back him up, even though she was still angry with him. 'I've seen preliminary drawings of his other work.'

Nadia turned to Olly. 'Do you want the police contacted?'

Olly glanced at Lexi, indicating it was her call. When she shook her head, ignoring her sister next to her who was frantically nodding, he said, 'No, I don't.'

'Would you like the painting returned?' Nadia asked.

'You might as well include it in the sale as it's been listed.'

Nadia sighed. 'Fine. Now, if you'll excuse me, I have an

auction to get back to. John, please escort these people from the premises and ensure they leave.'

Lexi wasn't about to argue. She was happy to get out of there.

They were ushered out of the office by the security guard, who led them through the auction room, which was still buzzing with activity. They'd reached Lot one hundred and one, which meant the *Woman at the Window* would be up soon. Lexi was curious to know how much it would sell for. But her desire to escape was greater.

The five of them were unceremoniously removed from the building and ended up on Thistle Street. Lexi didn't care. Their plan had worked ... of sorts. She had her precious painting back.

Marcus turned to her. 'You think you're so clever, don't you? Well, this isn't over. I want my money.'

Tasha went for him. 'Why you—'

Lexi grabbed her sister's arm. 'It's okay, Tash. I've got this.' It was time to have it out with her ex-husband once and for all. She was tired of lying. Tired of keeping secrets. This ended now. She turned to her ex-husband, glad of the passing traffic noise and bustle of a busy Edinburgh street. 'What money would that be, Marcus?'

'You know damn well what money. The cash you stole from the house,' he said. 'Admit it.'

He was right. It was time to come clean. 'Okay. I admit it. I took twenty-seven thousand pounds from the house.' There, she'd said it. It was quite liberating to say it aloud.

He looked pleased with himself. 'I knew it!'

'I took the money, Marcus. I didn't tell anyone, or declare

it to the official receiver as I should've done. Instead, I bought the *Woman at the Window*. I lied when I told you it wasn't the original.' There was something cathartic about purging her sins. But to achieve proper closure, he needed to admit his wrongdoing, too. 'A painting that you later stole from my gallery, Marcus.'

'I didn't steal anything—'

'You admitted it in the auction house, Marcus.'

Tasha stepped towards him. 'We all heard it, scumbag.'

'It's not stealing if you're taking back what's owed. You refused to hand over *my* money, so I took the painting.'

'But it wasn't your money, was it, Marcus? It was the proceeds of a life insurance policy you took out and surrendered without my knowledge.'

'Prove it.'

'I don't need to prove it, Marcus. Because I have the painting.' She lifted the carry case. 'You were right. I did switch paintings.'

He tried to grab it, but she moved it out of the way.

'I want my money back!' he yelled. 'You owe me!'

Tasha and Sophie simultaneously blocked his path when he tried to reach Lexi.

He seriously thought she owed him? The man was delusional.

Perhaps it was having the back-up of three other people. Or because she didn't have to hide the truth anymore. Either way, she realised Marcus no longer had a hold over her. It was a liberating thought.

'You've taken everything from me, Marcus. You've cheated on me. Stolen from me. Defrauded me. And nearly lost me my gallery. I don't owe you a damn thing.'

His expression turned indignant. 'You reported me to the tax man.'

'No, I didn't.'

'You cost me my business.' His voice cracked. It was the closest thing she'd seen to genuine emotion. 'Now give me that painting.'

When he lunged for the carry case a second time, the force knocked her off balance and she hit the wall behind, knocking the wind from her lungs.

'That does it!' Tasha punched Marcus, sending him reeling backwards. 'Lexi didn't report you to HMRC. I did.'

He staggered backwards, rubbing his jaw. 'I might've known. You never thought I was good enough for your sister.'

'Well, you're not.' Tasha glared at him. 'Thank you for proving me right.'

Olly helped Lexi up from the pavement. She turned to thank him, but he'd already walked away. Odd.

Marcus took a step towards Tasha. 'You know your problem? Jealousy. You couldn't stand anyone coming between you and your precious twin. Even before my business got into trouble you were trying to split us up. You couldn't stand seeing her happy, could you?'

Lexi wasn't sure what Tasha would have done if Sophie hadn't stepped between them.

'Back off, mate.' Sophie's voice was deathly quiet. 'Or you'll have me to answer to.'

Tasha tried to get past Sophie. 'You're a lying, cheating scumbag, Marcus. You were never good enough for my sister. I'm just glad she's realised it for herself now. Come anywhere near her again and you'll regret it.'

'Is that a threat?'

'You're damned right it is!' Tasha lunged forwards, but Sophie held her back.

Lexi rushed over before her sister annihilated her ex-husband. 'As soon as I get back to Windsor, Marcus, I'm selling the *Woman at the Window* and paying off the official receiver. I could fight it and take legal action to prove I knew nothing about the insurance policy, but I'm not going to do that. You want to know why? Because I want you out of my life once and for all.' She looked him squarely in the eye. 'Consider this my parting gift. You get to return to Cindy in Spain and I get to move on with my life without constantly looking over my shoulder, wondering when the bailiffs will turn up. We're quits, Marcus. I don't owe you anything and you don't owe me. Agreed?'

When he tried to argue, Sophie raised her hand. 'Accept the deal, mate.'

He must have seen the steel in her expression, because he faltered and straightened his grey jacket as if trying to regain his composure. 'Fine, you win. But don't think just because I'm not in your life you'll be happy. As long as *she's* around,' he said, pointing at Tasha, 'you'll never be happy. No man will ever be good enough.'

Sophie took him by the arm. 'Time to leave.'

Tasha took his other arm and they 'escorted' him towards the train station.

Lexi watched them go, thinking what great bouncers Tasha and Sophie would make. Thank God she had them in her life ... Well, Sophie would be in her life soon. With any luck.

Spent adrenaline had zapped her energy. She turned to Olly, hoping for a heartfelt makeup scene like they have in the movies, when they'd run to each other, passionately kiss and vow never to fight again. It'd been the only thing keeping her going.

Even though she was angry with him for lying to her, he'd followed her to Edinburgh to retrieve her painting. Compared to Marcus, he was a saint. A slightly dodgy saint. But underneath the charming rogue exterior was a decent, kind-hearted man, who she'd be a fool to walk away from. He was nothing like Marcus. And she'd been an idiot for thinking otherwise.

But any ideas of a romantic reunion evaporated when she saw the expression on his face. Far from looking like a romantic hero about to sweep her off her feet, his gorgeous face was etched with anger. 'You stole twenty-seven thousand pounds?'

She hadn't expected that. 'Technically, yes. But it wasn't stealing—'

'What was it then?' He rubbed the back of his neck. 'Revenge? Payback? What?'

It was hard to explain. 'Marcus owed me.'

'Right.' He laughed, but it wasn't a humorous sound. 'That's supposed to make it okay, is it?'

Why was he so irate? She was the injured party. 'You don't understand.'

'You're right, Lexi. I don't.' He moved towards her, hurt flashing in his blue eyes. 'All this time you've been questioning my honesty, wondering whether you can trust me, and the whole time you were no better than I was.'

'That's not true—'

'Isn't it? What was it you called me? The blue-eyed *thief*.' His voice cracked. 'Well, turns out I wasn't the only one.'

She moved towards him. 'But I had good reason.'

'Perhaps I had good reason, too. Ever think of that?'

No, she hadn't. But then, why hadn't he told her what it

was? She wasn't a mind-reader. And anyway, his misdemeanours were way worse than hers. 'I wasn't the one who lied about their cousin being Dazed & Confused.'

'No, but you *did* lie.' He looked so wounded she had to take a step backwards. 'You kept going on about how I broke into your gallery. How I couldn't be trusted. And the whole time you were hiding a secret, too.' He pointed a finger at her. 'You know what you are, Lexi?'

She was too afraid to ask. Tears were threatening.

'A hypocrite.'

His words made her flinch.

'A lying, thieving, hypocrite.'

As she watched him walk off, her legs buckled and she slumped onto the cold, hard pavement. She might have her painting back ... but she'd lost Olly in the process.

Chapter 24

Tuesday 3rd July

Olly's back was killing him. Along with every other part of him. He ached from the blisters on his toes to the stretched tendons in his fingers. Even his eyes hurt – although that was mostly from the effort of trying not to blub. He refused to give in. But the effort of not wailing like his namesake, Baby Olly, had constricted his throat, making it difficult to swallow. He didn't care. He was glad to be suffering. And despite having spent the last eleven years hating himself for hurting his sisters, this was a whole new level of self-loathing.

He picked up another hay bale and carried it over to the feeding troughs, wincing when his back went into spasm.

It had been a week since the disastrous events at the auction house. His anger had abated but his remorse hadn't. The image of Lexi's hurt expression haunted him. Sure, he'd been angry, justifiably so. But he shouldn't have been so cruel. He'd behaved like a jerk.

He emptied the hay into the troughs and hastily retreated so he didn't get trampled on by stampeding Shetland ponies. One broken leg in the family was enough.

He swept the area, pushing the discarded hay and manure into a pile. Abusing his body seemed to be the only way of dealing with his shame. He'd barely stopped all week. If he wasn't mucking out the animals, he was running chores for

Louisa, or helping Gilly in the kitchen. He'd spent his evenings working on the mural in Baby Olly's nursery and sketching ideas for future paintings. He'd even started work on replicating Botticelli's *Birth of Venus*. Anything to stop his mind torturing him. He'd fallen into bed each night exhausted, only to wake the next morning still riddled with guilt.

Aside from his emotional misery, it felt strange to be painting again. He'd resisted for so many years, denying his talent by way of punishing his mother. He now realised how shortsighted that had been. He loved painting. He always had. Not painting wasn't an option. And now it seemed like there was money to be made from it.

His copy of the *Woman at the Window* had sold at auction for seven thousand pounds. He was still reeling from the shock. Not a bad return for two days' work. And then he'd been contacted by a wealthy art collector, who'd commissioned him to paint five Renaissance replicas for her properties around the world. He'd never heard of the woman, but Sophie had done some digging and discovered she was a prominent business-woman who'd been at his mother's exhibition. When she'd phoned him to commission the work, she'd waxed lyrical about his preliminary sketches, claiming to have fallen in love with his 'twisted' infamous images and calling him 'refreshingly modern'. He'd only believed it was a genuine offer when ten thousand pounds had landed in his bank account as a down payment. Something he was still trying to get his head around.

He went over to the water pump and attached the hose. It was a warm day, the high sun burning the back of his neck. He sprayed the ponies as they fed and refilled the water butts.

Coupled with the money raised from selling their mother's paintings, it meant they had more time to decide what to do about the future of Rubha Castle. They were no closer to agreeing on which property to sell, but with Sophie back at the Windsor townhouse, the arguments had yet to resume.

Louisa's leg was being X-rayed this morning. With any luck, the orthopaedic boot would come off, and she'd be able to escape the wheelchair and return to managing the estate, something she was keen to do. Things would soon return to normal. For a while, at least.

As for him, his love life might be dead in the water, but at least he'd decided on a career path. Painting replicas was a profitable business. It would enable him to support his family and fulfil his desire to be creative. He had no idea what the future held, but one thing he did know was that he needed to step up and help his sisters deal with whatever was coming down the line. He'd never be a traditional earl like his father, but maybe he'd be a modern, 'twisted' version, like his paintings.

The sound of a woman's yelp startled him. He turned to see Tasha Ryan stepping over piles of horse manure. What the hell was *she* doing here?

She was wearing shiny black leggings that looked like they'd been spray-painted on and a black see-through mesh top, her black bra visible beneath. Hardly country attire.

'God, that stinks,' she said, the disgust on her face evident even behind huge sunglasses. Sunlight glinted off the buckles on her stiletto boots, providing the only respite to the onslaught of black. 'Your sister said I'd find you here.'

He frowned. 'I thought Louisa was still at the hospital with Harry?'

'Elder sister,' she said, stepping onto a dry section of soil. 'Sophie's in Scotland?'

'We bumped into each other on the sleeper train last night.'

'I bet that was fun for the other passengers, watching you two fight un-refereed.' He turned off the water tap. 'Was hair-pulling involved?'

Tasha removed her sunglasses. 'It was a factor, yes.'

Christ. At least they hadn't killed each other, that was something.

He wound up the hosepipe. 'If you've come all this way to bollock me, you're too late. I already know I was a bastard to your sister.'

Her hands went to her hips. 'Damned straight, you were.'

'I shouldn't have stuck the knife in.'

'No, you shouldn't have.'

'She's had a crap time of it and I was a prick for making her feel even worse.' He walked over to the animal sheds.

Tasha followed, her heels puncturing the soil. 'No argument from me.'

'But I'm also angry with her.'

'Understandably.'

'She punished me for lying to her and yet the whole time she was lying, too.' He picked up a pitchfork.

'Agreed.'

'Calling her a hypocrite was justified.' He opened the shed door housing the alpacas.

'It was.'

He dug the fork into the bedding. 'I'm glad we agree.'

She placed her sunglasses on her head. 'So what's the problem?'

He stopped shovelling. 'Excuse me?'

Tasha looked over the top of the stable door. Unlike Lexi's fascination when she'd been introduced to the animals, Tasha eyed Buddy and Holly with pure disdain. 'You've listed perfectly valid reasons as to why you're angry with my sister. So why do you look like a man who's had his heart removed with a blunt spoon?'

'Poetic.' He carried the forkful of hay out of the shed.

'I'm a woman of many talents.' She wafted her hand in front of her face. 'That doesn't answer my question.'

He sighed. 'Why are you here, Tasha?'

'Because I love my sister.' She kicked the stable door shut, preventing him from re-entering. 'And I think you do, too.'

He glared at her, ignoring the twinge in his chest. 'What does it matter? I've blown it. Even if I understand why she lied and forgive her, you think she'll forgive me after what I did? I can't even forgive myself.' He gave up trying to muck out the alpacas and walked over to the lambing sheds.

Tasha followed. 'Your sister said as much last night.'

He glanced over his shoulder. 'Before or after the hair-pulling?'

'Before.' A wry smirk played on her lips. 'Like you, she asked me why I was coming all the way to Scotland to see you. I told her it was because I was undecided as to whether or not you could be trusted.'

'You picked the right person to ask.' He unhooked a bag of feed. 'I'm sure Sophie didn't hold back.'

'She didn't.'

No surprise there.

'Do you know what she said?'

'I can guess.'

'That she'd trust you with her life.'

He'd guessed wrong.

He turned slowly. 'Was she drunk?'

'Not at that point.' Tasha's expression turned rueful. 'Anyway, she told me you were a good man, who had a bloody good reason for lying. She wouldn't tell me what it was, but she defended you with a passion I found quite ... alarming.'

She wasn't the only one. Sophie defending him was a new experience.

He walked along the pens, emptying feed into the troughs.

'It helped me solve a conundrum.' Tasha leant against a pillar, her expression unimpressed when she realised it was covered in animal hair. 'I'm normally a good judge of character and I knew you were full of bullshit the first time I met you.' She brushed dirt from her arm. 'All that crap about falling off your bike? I know a stab wound when I see it. And then I discovered you'd broken into my sister's gallery, followed her to Scotland and wormed your way into her bed.'

Charming. And if only. 'Your point?'

'I assumed you were a lowlife, lying scumbag.' She appeared in front of him. 'And there was no way I was letting another arsehole ruin my sister's life.'

'I hear you, Tasha. I'm a liar. I can't be trusted. I'm just like Marcus. You didn't need to come all this way to warn me off. I get the message, okay?'

'That's not what I'm doing.'

'Then what *are* you doing?' It was strange to stare into such familiar eyes. For two people who shared identical DNA, they couldn't be less alike. God, he missed Lexi.

Tasha folded her arms. 'Despite all the evidence pointing to you being a carbon copy of Marcus, you're not.'

'And how do you figure that?'

'Because Marcus lied to protect himself. You lied to protect others.'

What did it matter? Lexi got hurt either way. 'What are you saying?'

'You were willing to risk your own reputation to rescue my sister's painting. You knew how much it meant to her and even though she was mad with you, you still tried to help her.'

That was before he'd found out she'd stolen twenty-seven thousand pounds. Would it have made a difference if he'd known? He wasn't sure.

Tasha unfolded her arms. 'My opinion of you changed when you came up with that crazy scheme to switch the paintings. There was nothing in it for you and yet you were prepared to help her. I began to ask myself why.'

He'd asked himself the same question. 'And what conclusion did you come to?'

'Well, apart from the obvious.' He was subjected to a steely glare. 'I figured you must be in love with her.'

There was no point denying it. 'So was Marcus.'

'But Marcus would never have paid off the official receiver.'

Olly's stomach dipped. *How the hell …?*

'You're wondering how I know?' She tilted her head to one side, her black hair sliding away like liquid onyx. 'I had a meeting with the Insolvency Service this week to discuss a repayment plan. I was hoping to clear the debt and prevent Lexi from having to sell her precious painting. Imagine my surprise when the investigator told me a repayment plan was already in place.' She stepped closer, unnerving him. 'And that ten grand had been paid off.'

The tattoo on Tasha's chest blurred, making it look like the dagger was about to stab him. He realised he'd stopped breathing and sucked in a breath.

'That's when I knew I'd misjudged you. Sophie defending you last night was the final piece of the puzzle.'

'Which is?'

'You're bent, but you're not untrustworthy.' She held his gaze. 'And despite everything, I've decided that you're good enough for my sister.'

Wow. He hadn't expected that. 'Are you saying I have your approval?'

'You don't need it, but you have it anyway. My sister's free to date whoever she likes.' She glanced into one of the pens, recoiling from the sight of romping piglets. 'Maybe I was wrong to interfere with her and Marcus. But I don't regret it. She deserves a man who'll adore her, risk everything to keep her safe, and who'll love her unconditionally.'

No pressure, then. 'That's a lot to live up to.'

She patted his chest. 'You're up to the challenge.' And then her eyes met his. 'At least, you'd better be.'

He struggled to swallow. 'I'm far from perfect.'

'She doesn't need perfection. She has me for that.'

When she smiled, he couldn't help laughing. Her face changed completely when she wasn't scowling. She looked more like Lexi.

'My sister has an adventurous soul. She's funny, kind and eccentric. She needs a partner who'll share her love of art, who'll travel with her and who'll laugh with her. If you can accept that she's flawed, fantastic and enjoy eating her cakes, you'll probably be idiotically happy together.'

'This is assuming she'll forgive me.'

Tasha shrugged. 'Only one way to find out.'

His head was so full of questions it was hard to formulate a plan.

Tasha sighed dramatically. 'What are you waiting for? *Go!*' She pointed to the door.

He slung the feeding bag into a wheelbarrow and turned to leave, but Tasha caught his arm.

'Just remember, hurt my sister and—'

'I'll die a slow and painful death. Yeah, I get it.' He rolled his eyes. And then he kissed her cheek. 'You're not so tough.'

'Want to bet?' She rubbed her cheek in disgust. 'And take a shower,' she called after him as he ran off. 'You stink!'

When he glanced back, she was smiling.

The next hour whipped by in a blur. It was hard to rush when his body was so battered, but somehow he made it back to the castle. He stumbled into the shower, leaving a pile of dirty clothes behind him. Mrs Jennings wouldn't be happy. He'd make it up to her.

He closed his eyes, letting the water pummel his face. Tasha was right, he didn't need her approval, but he was bloody glad he had it. She wasn't someone you wanted offside.

She was also right when she said Lexi had to be able to trust him. And she wouldn't be able to if he continued to lie to her. It was time to confess about the Spinelli paintings. He needed to explain why he'd lied and hope she understood and didn't report his family for fraud. Honesty was the best policy … according to his ancestors' motto, anyway.

The tightness in his chest eased, like his body had been waiting for him to realise what was happening. He didn't want to walk away from Lexi. He wanted to tell her the truth. About his family, the Spinellis and about the fact that he loved her.

Bloody hell, he was in love?

He slung on a pair of jeans and a T-shirt and packed an overnight bag. The pain in his back no longer seemed quite so sore. Funny that. Love proved to be an effective painkiller.

He ran across the inner courtyard and into the main keep, looking for Sophie. She wasn't in the billeting room or the banqueting hall. He knew she hadn't gone riding; all the horses were still in the stables. Where was she? Not in the kitchen, or the drawing room.

He climbed the stairs to the private bedchambers and rang her phone. He could hear it ringing down the hallway. The door to her bedroom was ajar.

'Sophie? You in there?' He pushed the door open. 'I'm going to see Lexi in Wind—' His words died on his lips.

Lying on the huge four-poster bed was his sister Sophie.

Next to her was Tasha Ryan.

They were kissing.

Chapter 25

Lexi buttoned up her pink cardigan, shivering in her denim pedal pushers and 1960s slingbacks. The heatwave had lulled. The temperature had dropped and it was drizzling with rain, keeping shoppers away. The view from her gallery window was murky and grey. A pretty good description of how she felt about life in general, really. Everything seemed a little dull and overcast at the moment.

Logic dictated she shouldn't be feeling quite so low. The exhibition at Rubha Castle had been a huge success. All of Eleanor Wentworth's works had sold, and after expenses and fees, her commission had totalled nearly eighteen thousand pounds. She'd been able to pay several outstanding bills and planned to give the remaining seventeen thousand to the official receiver. It wouldn't clear all the debt, but hopefully it would delay the removal of goods and allow her time to sell the *Woman at the Window*.

But that was a worry for another day. Today she was wearing her art historian hat, glad of the distraction. Anything to stop her mind torturing her with thoughts of Olly and her time spent in the Highlands.

Ignoring the pang of longing in her chest, she logged on to The Getty Provenance Index Database and scanned the list of paintings corresponding with those detailed in the Albrico

Spinelli catalogue raisonné. She was searching for evidence of a nineteen-inch oil canvas matching the description of *The Cursed Man*. Over the last week, she'd occupied herself by building up a trail of ownership for the work since its creation in 1593, to see whether or not it could be linked to the painting currently sitting upstairs in her flat.

There was no doubt the painting checked out as far as initial examination went. It matched in style, description and fundamental materials. But unless she could build up a decent provenance to support the forensic evidence supplied by The Courtauld Institute of Art, gaining the stamp of approval that it was an original Albrico Spinelli would be a tough ask.

So far, she'd discovered the painting had been bequeathed to the Vatican following the artist's death in 1627, where it remained until 1689. The records became a little sketchy after that. The next confirmed listing was in 1771, when the grandson of a former curator of the Vatican sold two Spinellis to a Russian count. But despite checking various sites and catalogues, there was nothing official listed.

However, she'd discovered numerous references to Renaissance works being on display at the home of Count Vachlav of St Petersburg. *The Cursed Man* wasn't specifically named, but the Nazis had seized the count's entire art collection during the Second World War, so her next task had been to check the war records.

She'd discovered two interesting facts. First, during the Second World War a specific Nazi military unit known as the *Kunstschutz* had been set up to acquire valuable art from those unfortunate souls occupied by the German invasion. Her second discovery was that at the end of the war, the Allies had set up their own team to recover the stolen artefacts and return them to their rightful owners. The Monuments Men had impressively recovered all thirty-three of Count Vachlav's paintings and delivered them to the central collection point in Munich. Even more fascinating was the discovery that Helena Vachlav, whose daughter, Agata, later married Herbert John Wentworth, had claimed several of the paintings.

Her research had uncovered a direct link between the painting's alleged time in Russia and the Wentworth family. She still needed to prove the painting owned by Count Vachlav was *The Cursed Man*, but she was getting closer to a definitive answer.

The missing piece of information lay concealed inside one of two unopened letters lying on the counter next to her. Tempting as it was to rip open the forensic results from The Courtauld Institute as soon as they'd arrived this morning, along with the painting, she'd resisted. The scientific findings might influence her conclusion and lead her to make assumptions about the painting's provenance. She needed to delay opening the letter until she'd formed a preliminary judgement as to the painting's authenticity.

The second letter remained unopened for an entirely different reason. It was from the official receiver. Enough said.

Her phone beeped, reminding her she had several new messages. She leant across and switched it off. Despite her phone ringing incessantly over the last few days, none of the calls had been from Olly. Not that he had her number. Knowing Olly, that wouldn't have stopped him. But the real reason he hadn't contacted her was because he was furious with her. She'd lied to him. He thought she was a hypocrite. And he was right.

No wonder he never wanted to see her again.

Overcome with sadness, she got up from the counter and

went over to the front door. Using the sleeve of her cardigan to rub away condensation, she peered through the glass. The view hadn't improved. The teashop opposite had packed up for the day, the owner battling with the rain as she carried the tables and chairs inside. Even the tourists had given up and returned to their hotels to dry off. Windsor Castle loomed large in the distance, its grey stone walls ominous in the miserable weather. It was an impressive sight. A permanent reminder of her time spent at Rubha Castle.

She was struck by another pang. She'd foolishly assumed she was immune to further heartache. Nothing could be as bad as the trauma of splitting up with Marcus. But she was wrong. And she didn't even have Tasha to comfort her. Her sister was currently in Scotland where, unlike her, Tasha's love life had taken a turn for the better. And good luck to her.

As delighted as she was for Tasha, thoughts of Scotland inevitably led to thinking about Olly and how much she missed him. She was desperate to speak to him. She had so many unanswered questions. Like, why had he tried to rescue her painting from the auction? Why the bloody hell hadn't he told her he could paint? And why, having finally convinced herself that it was safe to love again, he couldn't find it in his heart to forgive her?

But she already knew the answer to that one.

It was ironic that having spent so long mistrusting him, it was her own dishonesty that had ruined things between them. What an idiot she'd been.

She turned the sign to Closed, locked the door and switched off the lights. She'd had enough for today. Picking up her phone and the two unopened letters, she then headed upstairs.

She made tea and ate one of the Florentines she'd baked earlier. Not because she was hungry, but because eating sweet treats reminded her of Olly. How sad was that? She'd made them in the hope he might show up and devour them ... and her. But that was just wishful thinking.

She kicked off her shoes and curled up on the sofa. It had been over a week since the auction – eight days during which she'd been able to gaze lovingly at her precious *Woman at the Window*, who was currently propped next to *The Cursed Man*. They made quite an unusual pairing. One young and beautiful, the other old and wizened, and yet both stunning in their own right. But as she gazed into the Italian's seductive eyes, she felt a wave of sadness consume her. Even if she paid the official receiver seventeen thousand pounds, she'd still owe another ten. There was no other option but to sell her only asset. It was as heartbreaking as it was unavoidable.

With a sigh, she picked up the unopened envelopes and tore open the letter from the official receiver, resigned to further demands on her meagre finances. Time had run out, the twenty-eight days were up. Marcus was never going to do the decent thing and pay up, and she didn't have the energy to fight him anymore. It was up to her to end the torture. On the plus side, her ex-husband was finally out of her life for good. And that's the way she intended it to stay.

But as she read the letter, she was amazed to discover it wasn't a final demand but approval of a repayment plan. What repayment plan? Her confusion deepened when she noticed the receipt for ten thousand pounds stapled to the letter. She hadn't made any payments. What on earth was going on?

Stunned, she opened the second letter from The Courtauld Institute and skimmed over the test results, absorbing Professor

Young's conclusions as to the date of the materials used in the painting. She read it through twice, just to be sure.

She slumped against the cushions. Well, would you believe it?

With her brain fizzing, she emptied her tea down the sink and poured a glass of wine instead. By the time she'd selected a playlist on the jukebox, undressed and run a bath, she was on her second glass and feeling warm for the first time that day.

She lit scented candles, using the posh bath bomb her sister had given her for Christmas last year to enhance the experience, and lowered herself into the water. Bliss.

She rested her head against the bathtub, letting the dulcet tones of Connie Francis wash over her as she sang 'Everybody's Somebody's Fool'. Oh, the irony.

The candle next to her flickered, the flame struggling to stay alight as bubbles splashed over the rim. She took a deep breath and tried to reconcile the juxtaposition of anxiety and delight coursing through her.

Connie was just singing about how she was '*a fool who comes running back for more*', when someone rang the back doorbell.

Lexi's first instinct was to ignore it. It was gone eight o'clock and she wasn't expecting anyone. She wanted to enjoy her soak. Whoever it was, they could go away. But ten minutes later, when the unknown caller refused to be ignored, she reluctantly dragged herself from the bath, cursing and spilling soapy water over the floor.

'This had better be important,' she mumbled, grabbing her satin robe and dripping water on the carpet as she padded barefoot down the back stairs. 'I'm coming,' she yelled when her caller upped the ante by holding down the buzzer.

She trod on a discarded shoe, her annoyance escalating until finally she yanked open the door, only to find Olly leaning against the doorframe.

Shock rooted her to the spot. Or was it lust?

His blue eyes widened at her lack of attire. 'You know, you really need to wear more clothes.'

She was so stunned she couldn't speak.

'Not that I'm complaining, but not everyone has the restraint I do.'

Her hand came up to check her robe hadn't slipped. 'You're ... you're here?'

He held up a carrier bag. 'I come bearing gifts.'

She felt herself blushing. 'Why?'

'I need to make amends.'

His voice was soft and endearing, his hair dishevelled and damp from the rain. It took all her restraint not to launch herself at him.

'At least you didn't break in this time,' she said, trying for humour.

He raised an eyebrow. 'I thought I'd try the traditional approach. Committing a felony didn't work out so well for me last time.'

Her face grew warm. 'Only because I interrupted you.'

'Stabbed me, to be precise.' It was his turn at humour.

Relief flooded her. He wasn't angry anymore.

And then he blew softly against her neck. 'You're covered in bubbles.'

Shivers ran across her skin. 'I was in the bath.'

'So I see.' He pushed away from the doorframe. 'Are you going to let me in?'

Above her, Bobby Vee started up with 'Devil or Angel'. It seemed fitting.

Olly unearthed a bottle of Pinot Grigio. 'I guessed rosé.'

'You guessed right.'

He pulled out a takeaway bag. 'I also brought food. Tasha reliably informed me Thai green curry and tofu peanut satay were the key to winning you over. You haven't eaten, right?'

'I haven't.' Her stomach rumbled. 'You've spoken to Tasha?'

'You could say that.' And then his expression turned tentative. 'Did you know about her and Sophie?'

His bewildered expression made her smile. 'You mean, you didn't?'

'Not a clue.'

And she'd thought it was so obvious. But perhaps that's because she knew her sister so well and could tell when she was smitten. 'You didn't sense the tension when they were fighting?'

'Well, yeah, but I thought it was because they hated each other.'

She laughed. 'Not very astute, are you?'

'In fairness, I was distracted by other things.' His eyes dipped to her mouth. 'Am I coming in?'

She stood back. 'You are.'

He waited until she'd closed the door and followed her upstairs, no doubt checking out her bare legs. At least, she hoped so.

As they headed up, she had a strange sense of déjà vu.

'This is familiar,' he said as if reading her mind. 'You're not going to stab me again, are you?'

310

'Depends what you're here for.'

'I told you, I need to make amends.'

'Why? It's me who's in the wrong.'

'This is true.'

She swung around to face him. 'You're hardly blameless.'

'Never said I was.'

'And you lied first.'

He came up a step. 'I did.'

'More than once.'

Another step. 'Guilty as charged.'

'And I'm still mad at you.'

He was eyelevel now. 'Understandably.'

'I may never forgive you.'

His smile turned flirtatious. 'You already have.'

She suppressed a shudder. It felt exposing standing in the narrow stairwell wearing only a flimsy robe. 'What makes you think I've forgiven you?'

'Same reason I knew you were going to let me in.'

'And what's that?'

He leant closer and whispered in her ear, 'Like I said, never play poker.'

The sensation of his breath on her damp skin sent a wave of shivers running up her spine. She could feel the heat building between them. If she didn't move, something would happen. Was that a bad thing? She'd been longing to kiss him since opening the door. But this was hardly the most romantic setting.

His arm slipped around her waist. Was he going to kiss her?

Her breath hitched. Every nerve ending in her body sprung to life.

He leant forwards, his lips tantalisingly close ... and then he reached past and pushed open the door to her flat. 'Have you been baking?'

Bloody tease.

She covered her reaction and followed him inside. 'I have.'

He looked around the flat, which was bathed in candlelight. The scent of Thai curry mingled with the smell of baked Florentines, creating an oddly seductive ambience. He spotted the two paintings sitting side by side on matching stands and his posture stiffened. 'When did you get the painting back?'

'This morning.' She moved over to him. 'I was enjoying one last look before I returned it to you.'

A beat passed before he turned to look at her. 'There's something I need to tell you about that painting. It's the reason I tried to break in here.'

'You don't need to explain.'

'Yes, I do.' His brow furrowed.

'In that case, we'd better open the wine.'

He dumped the bag on the worktop. 'Where will I find glasses?'

She pointed to a kitchen cabinet. 'I'll put some clothes on.'

'No need to dress for dinner on my account,' he said, flashing her a smile. 'I like the casual look.'

'I'll stick with tradition and put some underwear on, if you don't mind.'

'Underwear is overrated,' he called after her, making her smile.

She went into her bedroom and threw on a pair of leggings and a loose-knit top. She couldn't resist spraying on some perfume and fluffing up her hair before rejoining him in the lounge.

'Do you want to eat before or after my confession?' he said, carrying two glasses over to the Fifties-style dining table. 'I nicked a Florentine, by the way.'

'I'd be disappointed if you didn't.' She sat down. 'Dinner afterwards is fine.'

He uncorked the wine and poured her a generous measure. 'So, you know I told you I had a falling out with my parents when I was eighteen?'

'Yes.'

'I didn't tell you the whole story.' He sat down opposite.

'I figured as much.' She took a sip of wine – something told her she was going to need it. 'Go on.'

He paused, almost as if needing to build up the courage to speak. 'I discovered that my parents were planning to sell a fraudulent painting at auction.'

She almost choked on her wine. She was about to ask what painting, when she realised she already knew the answer. Her research had uncovered as much. '*The Sacrificial Woman*?'

He nodded.

She glanced over at *The Cursed Man*. 'What made you think it was fraudulent?'

'I overheard them talking.'

He sounded so morose, it broke her heart.

'The painting was definitely from that era, but they had no official paperwork to support its origins, so they falsified provenance.'

'And you confronted them?'

Another nod. 'We had a massive row. But they wouldn't back down. And then I discovered they'd sold one of my replica sketches of *The Sacrificial Woman*. I'd used sixteenth-century materials, so it wasn't hard for them to pass it off as an original Albrico Spinelli. It increased the main painting's value and added weight to its authenticity. But the whole thing was a lie, a scam designed to defraud.'

'Goodness.' She took another mouthful of wine, needing the alcohol. 'I can't believe they got away with it.'

'Me neither. They said there was no other way to save Rubha Castle. They said I'd make the whole family destitute if I told anyone.'

'That's an awful burden to place on a teenager.'

'Tell me about it.' He rubbed the back of his neck. 'The hardest bit was keeping it from Louisa and Sophie.'

Lexi lowered her glass. 'They never knew?'

He shook his head. 'I hated lying to them. It felt like I'd committed a crime, too. When the painting sold for nearly two million quid, I knew I had to leave home. Even without my father's ultimatum. My parents weren't even sorry. As long as the Wentworth legacy continued, they didn't care. Hypocrites, the pair of them.'

She flinched at the word hypocrites. But his anger made more sense now. She'd behaved no better than his parents. Shame on her. 'So that's why you left home.'

'It's also why I stopped painting. I couldn't stand the pressure of keeping their secret, or risk anyone finding out the sketch was a fake. The guilt consumed me and stifled any desire to paint.'

No wonder he'd kept quiet about being the artist, Dazed & Confused. She reached across and squeezed his hand. 'Do your sisters know now?'

He nodded. 'They guessed most of it.' He looked over at *The Cursed Man*. 'My reaction to the second Spinelli being sent to you by mistake aroused their suspicion. It didn't take them long to work out why I was so desperate to get it back.'

'So that's why you broke in?' It all made sense now.

He nodded.

'How did they react to finding out?'

'Surprisingly okay. But they were still angry that I'd buggered off for eleven years.' He shook his head. 'All that wasted time spent worrying about what would happen if they found out. I thought they'd be devastated to discover our parents were immoral fraudsters, but they were more upset about me not being around.'

'I can understand that.' She couldn't bear to be apart from Tasha for eleven days, let alone eleven years. 'Thank you for telling me. I appreciate it can't have been easy. But I promise to keep your secret, Olly.'

He raised an eyebrow. 'What, that my family sold fraudulent art?'

She smiled. 'No, that their son is essentially honest.'

'Shocking, huh?' He studied her face for a long while. 'What are you thinking?'

She glanced down at their linked hands, enjoying the way they fitted together. 'I guess I'm trying to get my head around the fact that you're not really crooked.'

He rubbed his thumb over the back of her hand. 'And I guess I'm trying to get my head around the fact that you *are*?'

She laughed, enjoying the teasing note in his voice. 'Perhaps now you've confessed it'll ease the guilt and you'll be able to enjoy painting again. It'd be such a shame to let your talent go to waste.'

He looked sheepish. 'I've already started painting again.'

'You mean, apart from copying the *Woman at the Window*?'

He nodded. 'Did you know it sold for seven grand?'

She smiled. 'I'm not surprised. It's an exquisite work of art.'

His cheeks flushed at the compliment. 'I want you to have the money.' He removed an envelope from his pocket and handed it to her.

She pushed his hand away. 'Don't be daft. You don't have to do that.'

'Yes, I do. Especially as I nearly ruined your carefully planned heist.' He grinned at her. 'Nicely played, by the way.'

'Are you kidding? I was a quivering wreck.' She shivered at the memory. 'I'm never doing anything like that again.'

He laughed. 'I had no idea there was so much money to be made from painting copies.' He tucked the envelope under the candle on the table. 'Don't even think about returning it.'

His insistence made her smile. 'Is that what you want to do? Paint copies?'

'Yeah, but my own versions. I was contacted by this fancy art collector who wants me to paint five Renaissance copies in the style of Dazed & Confused. She's paid me ten grand as a down payment. Can you believe it?'

'Art is a profitable business. Especially when the artist is as talented as you are.'

He looked bemused by the idea of being a successful artist, which only endeared him to her even more.

'I don't care for my family's ancestral heritage the way my siblings do, but I'm going to do my best to support them. I've no idea whether or not we can hang on to Rubha Castle, but this way I can make a decent contribution to the upkeep and maybe delay having to sell.'

Lexi suddenly pulled her hand away, struck by a realisation. 'Did you give the official receiver ten thousand pounds?'

He flinched. 'You weren't supposed to find out about that yet. Are you mad?'

She frowned. 'I should be. I mean, why would you do that? You need the money yourself. Haven't you just been telling me about the problems of financing Rubha Castle?'

'I didn't want you to lose the *Woman at the Window*.'

'That's my problem, not yours.' What was he thinking? 'I'm not comfortable about you paying off my debts.'

'I knew you wouldn't be. So I have a proposal for you.' He rested his arms on the table. 'I was hoping you'd agree to mentor me. That's what you do, isn't it? Help new artists to build a career?' He seemed nervous asking her. 'The ten grand could be a down payment. Your cut for the first commission.'

She shook her head. 'That's a crazy idea. I only charge fifteen per cent.'

'So I won't pay you again until we reach that amount.' He looked determined. 'I won't take no for an answer.' He held out his hand. 'Do we have a deal?'

She looked into his gorgeous blue eyes and could tell he wouldn't be dissuaded. The hold around her heart contracted a little tighter. Coupled with the seventeen grand from her commission, it would clear the debt. She couldn't believe it. She wasn't going to lose her precious painting.

She shook his hand. 'Deal.'

He smiled, but then his humour faded. 'There's something I have to do first.'

'What's that?'

He nodded at the Spinelli. 'Burn that bloody painting.'

She almost fell off her seat. 'What?'

'Don't you get it? If *The Sacrificial Woman* was a fake, then *The Cursed Man* must be, too. That's why I was so desperate

317

to get it back. I was scared you'd realise and contact the authorities. I'm sorry I didn't tell you. And I'm sorry I lied. I was trying to protect my sisters. The best thing for everyone is if I take the blessed thing outside and set fire to it.' He got up and marched over to the painting.

She scrambled out of her seat and ran after him. 'I wouldn't do that if I were you.'

'Why not? It's caused nothing but trouble.'

She placed her hands on his chest, preventing him from moving. 'Because it was valued this morning at approximately eleven million pounds.'

He turned so pale she thought he might faint. 'Wh ... what?'

She held him steady. 'Your parents may or may not have sold a forged Spinelli eleven years ago, but they legitimately owned a sixteenth-century masterpiece.'

'Are you joking?'

'I'm deadly serious. Come over here.' She led him over to the sofa and sat him down. 'I've managed to build up the painting's provenance from its creation to its recovery by the Allies in 1945.' She sat next to him. 'The painting was part of a collection owned by Count Eduard Vachlav of St Petersburg. A painting matching the description of *The Cursed Man* was claimed in 1946 by Helena Aleksandrov-Vachlav and passed down to her daughter, Lady Agata Wentworth, on her death in 1947.'

His eyebrows shot up. 'Grandma Aggie?'

She nodded. 'You have very interesting relatives, by the way.'

'Thank you.'

'I'm guessing you know this, but your grandmother is descended from Russian nobility.' She reached across to pick

318

up a folder lying on the coffee table. 'It's all in here if you'd like to check.'

He shook his head. 'I believe you. And the painting checks out?'

'Forensic tests confirmed what I'd hoped.' She gestured to the painting. 'Our gentleman priest here was painted using sixteenth-century materials. My former professor at The Courtauld Institute very kindly arranged a formal authentication appraisal with a group of experts. Everyone agrees it's an original Albrico Spinelli.'

Olly stared at *The Cursed Man*. 'I can't believe I was about to destroy an eleven-million-pound painting.'

She laughed. 'And who knows, its sister painting might turn out to be genuine, too. Without testing the materials, I couldn't be certain, but the second painting recovered by the Allies matches the description of *The Sacrificial Woman*. There's certainly enough evidence to build a case if anyone challenges its authenticity.'

He looked stunned. 'So my parents went to all that bother to dupe the art world and they didn't have to?'

She shrugged. 'Maybe not. At least you can stop worrying about people finding out now.'

'Not about the main painting, but my forged sketch is still out there.'

She considered this. 'Do you know who bought the sketch?'

'The same French buyer who purchased the main painting. He paid a few thousand quid for it.'

She smiled. 'Then I wouldn't worry. News that *The Cursed Man* is an authenticated Albrico Spinelli will only increase the value of *The Sacrificial Woman*. He's not going to be worried about a few thousand pounds when he owns a painting worth millions. And besides, if the truth does come out then he'll own an original Oliver Wentworth.' She took his hand. 'You have an amazing career ahead of you, Olly. Owning one of your early sketches will be a real asset. I've no doubt it'll end up being worth a lot more than a few thousand pounds.' She squeezed his hand. 'You can relax, okay?'

He let out a laugh. 'I'm still trying to get my head around all this.'

She reached over and kissed his cheek. 'Congratulations. You're a very rich man.'

'We won't have to sell Rubha Castle. Or the Windsor town-house.'

She smiled. 'Looks that way.'

'My sisters won't believe this. I'm not sure *I* believe it.' He looked bewildered. 'Thank you, Lexi.'

'I didn't do anything.'

'Are you kidding me? You're the reason all this happened.'

'Technically, it was Louisa. She's the one who sent me the painting by mistake.'

He rolled his eyes. 'She'll never let me hear the end of it.'

Lexi laughed. 'And thank *you* for helping me to get my painting back. No one's ever done something so nice for me before ... or so crazy.'

He twisted his body nearer to hers. 'I'm sorry I lied to you. Can you forgive me?'

'I understand now why you did it. Can you forgive *me*?'

'Already done.' He stroked her hand.

She held his gaze. 'In case you hadn't realised, you're an extraordinarily good painter.'

'I believe you.'

She laughed. 'That was easy.'

He leant forwards and kissed her left eye. 'Like I said, I always know when you're lying.'

A burst of warmth landed in her belly. 'Which could prove tricky, seeing as we're about to form a professional working partnership.'

He kissed her cheek. 'Not to mention our very *non*-professional partnership.' A wicked glint found its way into his eyes.

'This is also true.' She traced her hands over his chest. 'It's going to be quite hard to build a relationship if you're living in Scotland.'

He kissed her other cheek. 'I've been thinking about that. You know, Windsor is looking very enticing as a base.'

'Really?' Her arms went around his neck. 'But regular trips to Scotland would be good, too. The Highlands are an amazing source of inspiration.'

'Tell me about it.' He looked pleased. 'You like it up there?'

'I do.' When his expression turned soppy, she chanced her luck. 'Perhaps I could come with you?' She missed Rubha Castle with its imposing architecture and rugged landscape. She'd never get tired of visiting.

'I'd love that ... And I love you,' he said, his mouth finding hers.

She sank into him, loving the sensation of his hands in her hair and the feeling of heat building within her. When they came up for air, she whispered, 'I love you, too.'

'I know you do.' He looked at her with such tenderness her insides melted.

She laughed. 'You know, all this lying has made me realise something.'

'What's that?' He kissed her neck, trailing his fingers teasingly over her skin.

'Sometimes in order to live an honest life, you have to do dishonest things.'

He laughed and kissed her again, sliding his hands up her top and making her crazy with his tongue. But then he pulled away, as if struck by an idea. 'You know, that could be the new family motto.'

She laughed. 'I like it. It's a little twisted ... like you.'

'Like us,' he said, yanking on the cushion behind, causing her to bounce back on the sofa as Sandi Sheldon sang, 'You're Gonna Make Me Love You'.

So she did.

Author's Note

This story is set in the beautiful village of Shieldaig, in the Wester Ross area of the Highlands in Scotland. I've tried my best to be as accurate as I can about the area, but with one exception. I've 'borrowed' Eilean Donan castle, renamed it Rubha Castle, and relocated it forty miles north. I think it's called 'poetic licence', but I do hope it doesn't offend anyone!

I've also borrowed the grand auction room at Sotheby's in London and rehoused it in their Edinburgh offices.

Acknowledgements

This book wouldn't have been possible without carrying out extensive research. Firstly, I'd like to thank Gordon and Stella Murray for allowing us to stay at the beautiful Rubha Lodge in Shieldaig. I hope I've done the place justice, but any errors are mine and mine alone. I'd also like to thank Alan Kluckow from Alan Kluckow Fine Arts in Sunningdale for allowing me to quiz him about the art world and running a gallery. His paintings are all originals – I promise!

My family continues to support me in my writing endeavours and I'm hugely grateful. Mum and Dad eagerly await their proof copy and are always proud as punch when the book is published. Seeing their enjoyment never grows old. The rest of my extended family all read my books and encourage their friends to do so too. Thank you! I love you all.

The Avon team are an amazing support. Especially Molly Walker-Sharp, my lovely editor, and Elke Desanghere and Sabah Khan who enthusiastically come up with marketing ideas. Thanks also to my fab agent, Tina Betts at Andrew Mann, for her continued support, belief, and friendship. And all the bloggers, readers and reviewers for giving up their time to read my books and leave reviews on various sites. You'll never know how much I appreciate it.

This book is dedicated to my gorgeous partner, Simon. A man mountain of a guy, with the biggest heart imaginable. I couldn't do it without him, and I wouldn't want to.

Lastly, a big thank you to my lovely friends Debbie and Robin Newell, who we holidayed with in Scotland. Getting stuck on the mountain road, breaking a contact lens, and being lumbered with a mint green Fiat 500 were all genuine things that happened to us! You couldn't make it up, as they say – even though most of the time I do.

Thank you for reading *Secret Things and Highland Flings*. I do hope you enjoyed it. If you'd like to get in touch or follow my blog, please contact me via my website www.tracycorbettauthor.co.uk or via social media.

Twitter: @tracyacorbett
Facebook: tracyacorbettauthor
Instagram: tracyacorbett

Love doesn't always bloom the way you expect …

'Warm, witty and wonderful'
Rosanna Ley

The
Forget-Me-Not
Flower
Shop

Tracy
Corbett

Love Tracy Corbett? Then why not read her first novel.